John Griffith London (born **John Griffith Chaney**; January 12, 1876 – November 22, 1916) was an American novelist, journalist, and social activist. A pioneer in the world of commercial magazine fiction, he was one of the first writers to become a worldwide celebrity and earn a large fortune from writing. He was also an innovator in the genre that would later become known as science fiction. His most famous works include The Call of the Wild and White Fang, both set in the Klondike Gold Rush, as well as the short stories "To Build a Fire", "An Odyssey of the North", and "Love of Life". He also wrote about the South Pacific in stories such as "The Pearls of Parlay" and "The Heathen". London was part of the radical literary group "The Crowd" in San Francisco and a passionate advocate of unionization, socialism, and the rights of workers. He wrote several powerful works dealing with these topics, such as his dystopian novel The Iron Heel, his non-fiction exposé The People of the Abyss, and The War of the Classes. (Source: Wikipedia)

Literary works:
The Cruise of the Dazzler (1902)
A Daughter of the Snows (1902)
The Call of the Wild (1903)
The Kempton-Wace Letters (1903)
The Sea-Wolf (1904)
The Game (1905)
White Fang (1906)
Before Adam (1907)
The Iron Heel (1908)
Martin Eden (1909)
Burning Daylight (1910)
Adventure (1911)
The Scarlet Plague (1912)
A Son of the Sun (1912)
The Abysmal Brute (1913)
The Valley of the Moon (1913)

A DAUGHTER OF THE SNOWS & LOVE OF LIFE AND OTHER STORIES

JACK LONDON

PRINCE CLASSICS

PRINCE CLASSICS

This is a work of fiction. Names, characters, places, and incidents either are the product of the author's imagination or are used fictitiously. Any resemblance to actual persons, living or dead, events, or locales is entirely coincidental.

Copyright © 2020

All rights reserved. No part of this book may be reproduced in any form or by any electronic or mechanical means including information storage and retrieval systems, without permission in writing from the author. The only exception is by a reviewer, who may quote short excerpts in a review.

First Printing: 2020

ISBN 978-93-90262-74-8 (paperback)

ISBN 978-93-90262-75-5 (Hardcover)

Published by Prince Classics

www.princeclassics.com

Contents

A DAUGHTER OF THE SNOWS	**11**
CHAPTER I	13
CHAPTER II	26
CHAPTER III	32
CHAPTER IV	41
CHAPTER V	51
CHAPTER VI	55
CHAPTER VII	65
CHAPTER VIII	71
CHAPTER IX	79
CHAPTER X	87
CHAPTER XI	97
CHAPTER XII	103
CHAPTER XIII	109
CHAPTER XIV	116
CHAPTER XV	124
CHAPTER XVI	131
CHAPTER XVII	143
CHAPTER XVIII	151
CHAPTER XIX	155
CHAPTER XX	166
CHAPTER XXI	181
CHAPTER XXII	188
CHAPTER XXIII	194
CHAPTER XXIV	202
CHAPTER XXV	215
CHAPTER XXVI	232
CHAPTER XXVII	244
CHAPTER XXVIII	250
CHAPTER XXIX	265
CHAPTER XXX	276

LOVE OF LIFE, AND OTHER STORIES	**281**
LOVE OF LIFE	283
A DAY'S LODGING	303
THE WHITE MAN'S WAY	322
THE STORY OF KEESH	335
THE UNEXPECTED	344
BROWN WOLF	366
THE SUN-DOG TRAIL	383
NEGORE, THE COWARD	403
About Author	**417**
NOTABLE WORKS	**439**

A DAUGHTER OF
THE SNOWS
&
LOVE OF LIFE
AND OTHER STORIES

A DAUGHTER OF THE SNOWS

CHAPTER I

"All ready, Miss Welse, though I'm sorry we can't spare one of the steamer's boats."

Frona Welse arose with alacrity and came to the first officer's side.

"We're so busy," he explained, "and gold-rushers are such perishable freight, at least—"

"I understand," she interrupted, "and I, too, am behaving as though I were perishable. And I am sorry for the trouble I am giving you, but—but—" She turned quickly and pointed to the shore. "Do you see that big log-house? Between the clump of pines and the river? I was born there."

"Guess I'd be in a hurry myself," he muttered, sympathetically, as he piloted her along the crowded deck.

Everybody was in everybody else's way; nor was there one who failed to proclaim it at the top of his lungs. A thousand gold-seekers were clamoring for the immediate landing of their outfits. Each hatchway gaped wide open, and from the lower depths the shrieking donkey-engines were hurrying the misassorted outfits skyward. On either side of the steamer, rows of scows received the flying cargo, and on each of these scows a sweating mob of men charged the descending slings and heaved bales and boxes about in frantic search. Men waved shipping receipts and shouted over the steamer-rails to them. Sometimes two and three identified the same article, and war arose. The "two-circle" and the "circle-and-dot" brands caused endless jangling, while every whipsaw discovered a dozen claimants.

"The purser insists that he is going mad," the first officer said, as he helped Frona Welse down the gangway to the landing stage, "and the freight clerks have turned the cargo over to the passengers and quit work. But we're not so unlucky as the Star of Bethlehem," he reassured her, pointing to a steamship at anchor a quarter of a mile away. "Half of her passengers have pack-horses for Skaguay and White Pass, and the other half are bound over the Chilcoot. So they've mutinied and everything's at a standstill."

"Hey, you!" he cried, beckoning to a Whitehall which hovered discreetly on the outer rim of the floating confusion.

A tiny launch, pulling heroically at a huge tow-barge, attempted to pass between; but the boatman shot nervily across her bow, and just as he was clear, unfortunately, caught a crab. This slewed the boat around and brought it to a stop.

"Watch out!" the first officer shouted.

A pair of seventy-foot canoes, loaded with outfits, gold-rushers, and Indians, and under full sail, drove down from the counter direction. One of them veered sharply towards the landing stage, but the other pinched the Whitehall against the barge. The boatman had unshipped his oars in time, but his small craft groaned under the pressure and threatened to collapse. Whereat he came to his feet, and in short, nervous phrases consigned all canoe-men and launch-captains to eternal perdition. A man on the barge leaned over from above and baptized him with crisp and crackling oaths, while the whites and Indians in the canoe laughed derisively.

"Aw, g'wan!" one of them shouted. "Why don't yeh learn to row?"

The boatman's fist landed on the point of his critic's jaw and dropped him stunned upon the heaped merchandise. Not content with this summary act he proceeded to follow his fist into the other craft. The miner nearest him tugged vigorously at a revolver which had jammed in its shiny leather holster, while his brother argonauts, laughing, waited the outcome. But the canoe was under way again, and the Indian helmsman drove the point of his paddle into the boatman's chest and hurled him backward into the bottom of the Whitehall.

When the flood of oaths and blasphemy was at full tide, and violent assault and quick death seemed most imminent, the first officer had stolen a glance at the girl by his side. He had expected to find a shocked and frightened maiden countenance, and was not at all prepared for the flushed and deeply interested face which met his eyes.

"I am sorry," he began.

But she broke in, as though annoyed by the interruption, "No, no; not at all. I am enjoying it every bit. Though I am glad that man's revolver stuck. If it had not—"

"We might have been delayed in getting ashore." The first officer laughed, and therein displayed his tact.

"That man is a robber," he went on, indicating the boatman, who had now shoved his oars into the water and was pulling alongside. "He agreed to charge only twenty dollars for putting you ashore. Said he'd have made it twenty-five had it been a man. He's a pirate, mark me, and he will surely hang some day. Twenty dollars for a half-hour's work! Think of it!"

"Easy, sport! Easy!" cautioned the fellow in question, at the same time making an awkward landing and dropping one of his oars over-side. "You've no call to be flingin' names about," he added, defiantly, wringing out his shirt-sleeve, wet from rescue of the oar.

"You've got good ears, my man," began the first officer.

"And a quick fist," the other snapped in.

"And a ready tongue."

"Need it in my business. No gettin' 'long without it among you sea-sharks. Pirate, am I? And you with a thousand passengers packed like sardines! Charge 'em double first-class passage, feed 'em steerage grub, and bunk 'em worse 'n pigs! Pirate, eh! Me?"

A red-faced man thrust his head over the rail above and began to bellow lustily.

"I want my stock landed! Come up here, Mr. Thurston! Now! Right away! Fifty cayuses of | mine eating their heads off in this dirty kennel of yours, and it'll be a sick time you'll have if you don't hustle them ashore as fast as God'll let you! I'm losing a thousand dollars a day, and I won't stand it! Do you hear? I won't stand it! You've robbed me right and left from the time you cleared dock in Seattle, and by the hinges of hell I won't stand it any more! I'll break this company as sure as my name's Thad Ferguson! D'ye hear my spiel? I'm Thad Ferguson, and you can't come and see me any too quick for your health! D'ye hear?"

"Pirate; eh?" the boatman soliloquized. "Who? Me?"

Mr. Thurston waved his hand appeasingly at the red-faced man, and turned to the girl. "I'd like to go ashore with you, and as far as the store, but you see how busy we are. Good-by, and a lucky trip to you. I'll tell off a couple of men at once and break out your baggage. Have it up at the store to-morrow morning, sharp."

She took his hand lightly and stepped aboard. Her weight gave the leaky boat a sudden lurch, and the water hurtled across the bottom boards to her shoe-tops: but she took it coolly enough, settling herself in the stern-sheets and tucking her feet under her.

"Hold on!" the officer cried. "This will never do, Miss Welse. Come on back, and I'll get one of our boats over as soon as I can."

"I'll see you in—in heaven first," retorted the boatman, shoving off.

"Let go!" he threatened.

Mr. Thurston gripped tight hold of the gunwale, and as reward for his chivalry had his knuckles rapped sharply by the oar-blade. Then he forgot himself, and Miss Welse also, and swore, and swore fervently.

"I dare say our farewell might have been more dignified," she called back to him, her laughter rippling across the water.

"Jove!" he muttered, doffing his cap gallantly. "There is a *woman*!" And a sudden hunger seized him, and a yearning to see himself mirrored always in the gray eyes of Frona Welse. He was not analytical; he did not know why; but he knew that with her he could travel to the end of the earth. He felt a distaste for his profession, and a temptation to throw it all over and strike out for the Klondike whither she was going; then he glanced up the beetling side of the ship, saw the red face of Thad Ferguson, and forgot the dream he had for an instant dreamed.

Splash! A handful of water from his strenuous oar struck her full in the face. "Hope you don't mind it, miss," he apologized. "I'm doin' the best I know how, which ain't much."

"So it seems," she answered, good-naturedly.

"Not that I love the sea," bitterly; "but I've got to turn a few honest dollars somehow, and this seemed the likeliest way. I oughter 'a ben in Klondike by now, if I'd had any luck at all. Tell you how it was. I lost my outfit on Windy Arm, half-way in, after packin' it clean across the Pass—"

Zip! Splash! She shook the water from her eyes, squirming the while as some of it ran down her warm back.

"You'll do," he encouraged her. "You're the right stuff for this country. Goin' all the way in?"

She nodded cheerfully.

"Then you'll do. But as I was sayin', after I lost my outfit I hit back for the coast, bein' broke, to hustle up another one. That's why I'm chargin' high-pressure rates. And I hope you don't feel sore at what I made you pay. I'm no worse than the rest, miss, sure. I had to dig up a hundred for this old tub, which ain't worth ten down in the States. Same kind of prices everywhere. Over on the Skaguay Trail horseshoe nails is just as good as a quarter any day. A man goes up to the bar and calls for a whiskey. Whiskey's half a dollar. Well, he drinks his whiskey, plunks down two horseshoe nails, and it's O.K. No kick comin' on horseshoe nails. They use 'em to make change."

"You must be a brave man to venture into the country again after such an experience. Won't you tell me your name? We may meet on the Inside."

"Who? Me? Oh, I'm Del Bishop, pocket-miner; and if ever we run across each other, remember I'd give you the last shirt—I mean, remember my last bit of grub is yours."

"Thank you," she answered with a sweet smile; for she was a woman who loved the things which rose straight from the heart.

He stopped rowing long enough to fish about in the water around his feet for an old cornbeef can.

"You'd better do some bailin'," he ordered, tossing her the can.

"She's leakin' worse since that squeeze."

Frona smiled mentally, tucked up her skirts, and bent to the work. At every dip, like great billows heaving along the sky-line, the glacier-fretted mountains rose and fell. Sometimes she rested her back and watched the teeming beach towards which they were heading, and again, the land-locked arm of the sea in which a score or so of great steamships lay at anchor. From each of these, to the shore and back again, flowed a steady stream of scows, launches, canoes, and all sorts of smaller craft. Man, the mighty toiler, reacting upon a hostile environment, she thought, going back in memory to the masters whose wisdom she had shared in lecture-room and midnight study. She was a ripened child of the age, and fairly understood the physical world and the workings thereof. And she had a love for the world, and a deep respect.

For some time Del Bishop had only punctuated the silence with splashes from his oars; but a thought struck him.

"You haven't told me your name," he suggested, with complacent delicacy.

"My name is Welse," she answered. "Frona Welse."

A great awe manifested itself in his face, and grew to a greater and greater awe. "You—are—Frona—Welse?" he enunciated slowly. "Jacob Welse ain't your old man, is he?"

"Yes; I am Jacob Welse's daughter, at your service."

He puckered his lips in a long low whistle of understanding and stopped rowing. "Just you climb back into the stern and take your feet out of that water," he commanded. "And gimme holt that can."

"Am I not bailing satisfactorily?" she demanded, indignantly.

"Yep. You're doin' all right; but, but, you are—are—"

"Just what I was before you knew who I was. Now you go on rowing,—that's your share of the work; and I'll take care of mine."

"Oh, you'll do!" he murmured ecstatically, bending afresh to the oars.

"And Jacob Welse is your old man? I oughter 'a known it, sure!"

When they reached the sand-spit, crowded with heterogeneous piles of merchandise and buzzing with men, she stopped long enough to shake hands with her ferryman. And though such a proceeding on the part of his feminine patrons was certainly unusual, Del Bishop squared it easily with the fact that she was Jacob Welse's daughter.

"Remember, my last bit of grub is yours," he reassured her, still holding her hand.

"And your last shirt, too; don't forget."

"Well, you're a—a—a crackerjack!" he exploded with a final squeeze.

"Sure!"

Her short skirt did not block the free movement of her limbs, and she discovered with pleasurable surprise that the quick tripping step of the city pavement had departed from her, and that she was swinging off in the long easy stride which is born of the trail and which comes only after much travail and endeavor. More than one gold-rusher, shooting keen glances at her ankles and gray-gaitered calves, affirmed Del Bishop's judgment. And more than one glanced up at her face, and glanced again; for her gaze was frank, with the frankness of comradeship; and in her eyes there was always a smiling light, just trembling on the verge of dawn; and did the onlooker smile, her eyes smiled also. And the smiling light was protean-mooded,—merry, sympathetic, joyous, quizzical,—the complement of whatsoever kindled it. And sometimes the light spread over all her face, till the smile prefigured by it was realized. But it was always in frank and open comradeship.

And there was much to cause her to smile as she hurried through the crowd, across the sand-spit, and over the flat towards the log-building she had pointed out to Mr. Thurston. Time had rolled back, and locomotion and transportation were once again in the most primitive stages. Men who had never carried more than parcels in all their lives had now become bearers of burdens. They no longer walked upright under the sun, but stooped the body forward and bowed the head to the earth. Every back had become a pack-saddle, and the strap-galls were beginning to form. They staggered beneath the unwonted effort, and legs became drunken with weariness and titubated in divers directions till the sunlight darkened and bearer and burden fell by the way. Other men, exulting secretly, piled their goods on two-wheeled go-carts and pulled out blithely enough, only to stall at the first spot where the great round boulders invaded the trail. Whereat they generalized anew upon the principles of Alaskan travel, discarded the go-cart, or trundled it back to the beach and sold it at fabulous price to the last man landed. Tenderfeet, with ten pounds of Colt's revolvers, cartridges, and hunting-knives belted about them, wandered valiantly up the trail, and crept back softly, shedding revolvers, cartridges, and knives in despairing showers. And so, in gasping and bitter sweat, these sons of Adam suffered for Adam's sin.

Frona felt vaguely disturbed by this great throbbing rush of gold-mad men, and the old scene with its clustering associations seemed blotted out by these toiling aliens. Even the old landmarks appeared strangely unfamiliar. It was the same, yet not the same. Here, on the grassy flat, where she had played as a child and shrunk back at the sound of her voice echoing from glacier to glacier, ten thousand men tramped ceaselessly up and down, grinding the tender herbage into the soil and mocking the stony silence. And just up the trail were ten thousand men who had passed by, and over the Chilcoot were ten thousand more. And behind, all down the island-studded Alaskan coast, even to the Horn, were yet ten thousand more, harnessers of wind and steam, hasteners from the ends of the earth. The Dyea River as of old roared turbulently down to the sea; but its ancient banks were gored by the feet of many men, and these men labored in surging rows at the dripping tow-lines, and the deep-laden boats followed them as they fought their upward way. And the will of man strove with the will of the water, and the men laughed at the old Dyea River and gored its banks deeper for the men who were to follow.

The doorway of the store, through which she had once run out and in, and where she had looked with awe at the unusual sight of a stray trapper or fur-trader, was now packed with a clamorous throng of men. Where of old one letter waiting a claimant was a thing of wonder, she now saw, by peering through the window, the mail heaped up from floor to ceiling. And it was for this mail the men were clamoring so insistently. Before the store, by the scales, was another crowd. An Indian threw his pack upon the scales, the white owner jotted down the weight in a note-book, and another pack was thrown on. Each pack was in the straps, ready for the packer's back and the precarious journey over the Chilcoot. Frona edged in closer. She was interested in freights. She remembered in her day when the solitary prospector or trader had his outfit packed over for six cents,—one hundred and twenty dollars a ton.

The tenderfoot who was weighing up consulted his guide-book. "Eight cents," he said to the Indian. Whereupon the Indians laughed scornfully and chorused, "Forty cents!" A pained expression came into his face, and he looked about him anxiously. The sympathetic light in Frona's eyes caught him, and he regarded her with intent blankness. In reality he was busy reducing a three-ton outfit to terms of cash at forty dollars per hundred-weight. "Twenty-four hundred dollars for thirty miles!" he cried. "What can I do?"

Frona shrugged her shoulders. "You'd better pay them the forty cents," she advised, "else they will take off their straps."

The man thanked her, but instead of taking heed went on with his haggling. One of the Indians stepped up and proceeded to unfasten his pack-straps. The tenderfoot wavered, but just as he was about to give in, the packers jumped the price on him to forty-five cents. He smiled after a sickly fashion, and nodded his head in token of surrender. But another Indian joined the group and began whispering excitedly. A cheer went up, and before the man could realize it they had jerked off their straps and departed, spreading the news as they went that freight to Lake Linderman was fifty cents.

Of a sudden, the crowd before the store was perceptibly agitated. Its members whispered excitedly one to another, and all their eyes were focussed upon three men approaching from up the trail. The trio were ordinary-looking creatures, ill-clad and even ragged. In a more stable community their apprehension by the village constable and arrest for vagrancy would have been immediate. "French Louis," the tenderfeet whispered and passed the word along. "Owns three Eldorado claims in a block," the man next to Frona confided to her. "Worth ten millions at the very least." French Louis, striding a little in advance of his companions, did not look it. He had parted company with his hat somewhere along the route, and a frayed silk kerchief was wrapped carelessly about his head. And for all his ten millions, he carried his own travelling pack on his broad shoulders. "And that one, the one with the beard, that's Swiftwater Bill, another of the Eldorado kings."

"How do you know?" Frona asked, doubtingly.

"Know!" the man exclaimed. "Know! Why his picture has been in all the papers for the last six weeks. See!" He unfolded a newspaper. "And a pretty good likeness, too. I've looked at it so much I'd know his mug among a thousand."

"Then who is the third one?" she queried, tacitly accepting him as a fount of authority.

Her informant lifted himself on his toes to see better. "I don't know," he confessed sorrowfully, then tapped the shoulder of the man next to him. "Who is the lean, smooth-faced one? The one with the blue shirt and the patch on his knee?"

Just then Frona uttered a glad little cry and darted forward. "Matt!" she cried. "Matt McCarthy!"

The man with the patch shook her hand heartily, though he did not know her and distrust was plain in his eyes.

"Oh, you don't remember me!" she chattered. "And don't you dare say you do! If there weren't so many looking, I'd hug you, you old bear!

"And so Big Bear went home to the Little Bears," she recited, solemnly.

"And the Little Bears were very hungry. And Big Bear said, 'Guess what I have got, my children.' And one Little Bear guessed berries, and one Little Bear guessed salmon, and t'other Little Bear guessed porcupine. Then Big Bear laughed 'Whoof! Whoof!' and said, '*A Nice Big Fat Man!*'"

As he listened, recollection avowed itself in his face, and, when she had finished, his eyes wrinkled up and he laughed a peculiar, laughable silent laugh.

"Sure, an' it's well I know ye," he explained; "but for the life iv me I can't put me finger on ye."

She pointed into the store and watched him anxiously.

"Now I have ye!" He drew back and looked her up and down, and his expression changed to disappointment. "It cuddent be. I mistook ye. Ye cud niver a-lived in that shanty," thrusting a thumb in the direction of the store.

Frona nodded her head vigorously.

"Thin it's yer ownself afther all? The little motherless darlin', with the goold hair I combed the knots out iv many's the time? The little witch that run barefoot an' barelegged over all the place?"

"Yes, yes," she corroborated, gleefully.

"The little divil that stole the dog-team an' wint over the Pass in the dead o' winter for to see where the world come to an ind on the ither side, just because old Matt McCarthy was afther tellin' her fairy stories?"

"O Matt, dear old Matt! Remember the time I went swimming with the Siwash girls from the Indian camp?"

"An' I dragged ye out by the hair o' yer head?"

"And lost one of your new rubber boots?"

"Ah, an' sure an' I do. And a most shockin' an' immodest affair it was! An' the boots was worth tin dollars over yer father's counter."

"And then you went away, over the Pass, to the Inside, and we never heard a word of you. Everybody thought you dead."

"Well I recollect the day. An' ye cried in me arms an' wuddent kiss yer old Matt good-by. But ye did in the ind," he exclaimed, triumphantly, "whin ye saw I was goin' to lave ye for sure. What a wee thing ye were!"

"I was only eight."

"An' 'tis twelve year agone. Twelve year I've spint on the Inside, with niver a trip out. Ye must be twenty now?"

"And almost as big as you," Frona affirmed.

"A likely woman ye've grown into, tall, an' shapely, an' all that." He looked her over critically. "But ye cud 'a' stood a bit more flesh, I'm thinkin'."

"No, no," she denied. "Not at twenty, Matt, not at twenty. Feel my arm, you'll see." She doubled that member till the biceps knotted.

"'Tis muscle," he admitted, passing his hand admiringly over the swelling bunch; "just as though ye'd been workin' hard for yer livin'."

"Oh, I can swing clubs, and box, and fence," she cried, successively striking the typical *postures*; "and swim, and make high dives, chin a bar twenty times, and—and walk on my hands. There!"

"Is that what ye've been doin'? I thought ye wint away for book-larnin'," he commented, dryly.

"But they have new ways of teaching, now, Matt, and they don't turn you out with your head crammed—"

"An' yer legs that spindly they can't carry it all! Well, an' I forgive ye yer muscle."

"But how about yourself, Matt?" Frona asked. "How has the world been to you these twelve years?"

"Behold!" He spread his legs apart, threw his head back, and his chest out. "Ye now behold Mister Matthew McCarthy, a king iv the noble Eldorado Dynasty by the strength iv his own right arm. Me possessions is limitless. I have more dust in wan minute than iver I saw in all me life before. Me intintion for makin' this trip to the States is to look up me ancestors. I have a firm belafe that they wance existed. Ye may find nuggets in the Klondike, but niver good whiskey. 'Tis likewise me intintion to have wan drink iv the rate stuff before I die. Afther that 'tis me sworn resolve to return to the superveeshion iv me Klondike properties. Indade, and I'm an Eldorado king; an' if ye'll be wantin' the lind iv a tidy bit, it's meself that'll loan it ye."

"The same old, old Matt, who never grows old," Frona laughed.

"An' it's yerself is the thrue Welse, for all yer prize-fighter's muscles an' yer philosopher's brains. But let's wander inside on the heels of Louis an' Swiftwater. Andy's still tindin' store, I'm told, an' we'll see if I still linger in the pages iv his mimory."

"And I, also." Frona seized him by the hand. It was a bad habit she had of seizing the hands of those she loved. "It's ten years since I went away."

The Irishman forged his way through the crowd like a pile-driver, and Frona followed easily in the lee of his bulk. The tenderfeet watched them reverently, for to them they were as Northland divinities. The buzz of conversation rose again.

"Who's the girl?" somebody asked. And just as Frona passed inside the door she caught the opening of the answer: "Jacob Welse's daughter. Never heard of Jacob Welse? Where have you been keeping yourself?"

CHAPTER II

She came out of the wood of glistening birch, and with the first fires of the sun blazoning her unbound hair raced lightly across the dew-dripping meadow. The earth was fat with excessive moisture and soft to her feet, while the dank vegetation slapped against her knees and cast off flashing sprays of liquid diamonds. The flush of the morning was in her cheek, and its fire in her eyes, and she was aglow with youth and love. For she had nursed at the breast of nature,—in forfeit of a mother,—and she loved the old trees and the creeping green things with a passionate love; and the dim murmur of growing life was a gladness to her ears, and the damp earth-smells were sweet to her nostrils.

Where the upper-reach of the meadow vanished in a dark and narrow forest aisle, amid clean-stemmed dandelions and color-bursting buttercups, she came upon a bunch of great Alaskan violets. Throwing herself at full length, she buried her face in the fragrant coolness, and with her hands drew the purple heads in circling splendor about her own. And she was not ashamed. She had wandered away amid the complexities and smirch and withering heats of the great world, and she had returned, simple, and clean, and wholesome. And she was glad of it, as she lay there, slipping back to the old days, when the universe began and ended at the sky-line, and when she journeyed over the Pass to behold the Abyss.

It was a primitive life, that of her childhood, with few conventions, but such as there were, stern ones. And they might be epitomized, as she had read somewhere in her later years, as "*the faith of food and blanket.*" This faith had her father kept, she thought, remembering that his name sounded well on the lips of men. And this was the faith she had learned,—the faith she had carried with her across the Abyss and into the world, where men had wandered away from the old truths and made themselves selfish dogmas and casuistries of the subtlest kinds; the faith she had brought back with her, still fresh, and young, and joyous. And it was all so simple, she had contended; why should not their faith be as her faith—the faith of food and blanket? The faith of trail and hunting camp? The faith with which strong clean men faced the quick danger and sudden death by field and flood? Why not? The faith of Jacob Welse? Of Matt McCarthy? Of the Indian boys she had played with? Of the Indian girls she had led to Amazonian war? Of the very wolf-dogs straining in the harnesses and running with her across the snow? It was healthy, it was real, it was good, she thought, and she was glad.

The rich notes of a robin saluted her from the birch wood, and opened her ears to the day. A partridge boomed afar in the forest, and a tree-squirrel launched unerringly into space above her head, and went on, from limb to limb and tree to tree, scolding graciously the while. From the hidden river rose the shouts of the toiling adventurers, already parted from sleep and fighting their way towards the Pole.

Frona arose, shook back her hair, and took instinctively the old path between the trees to the camp of Chief George and the Dyea tribesmen. She came upon a boy, breech-clouted and bare, like a copper god. He was gathering wood, and looked at her keenly over his bronze shoulder. She bade him good-morning, blithely, in the Dyea tongue; but he shook his head, and laughed insultingly, and paused in his work to hurl shameful words after her. She did not understand, for this was not the old way, and when she passed a great and glowering Sitkan buck she kept her tongue between her teeth. At the fringe of the forest, the camp confronted her. And she was startled. It was not the old camp of a score or more of lodges clustering and huddling together in the open as though for company, but a mighty camp. It began at the very forest, and flowed in and out among the scattered tree-clumps on the flat, and spilled over and down to the river bank where the long canoes were lined up ten and twelve deep. It was a gathering of the tribes, like unto none in all the past, and a thousand miles of coast made up the tally. They were all strange Indians, with wives and chattels and dogs. She rubbed shoulders with Juneau and Wrangel men, and was jostled by wild-eyed Sticks from over the Passes, fierce Chilcats, and Queen Charlotte Islanders. And the looks they cast upon her were black and frowning, save—and far worse—where the merrier souls leered patronizingly into her face and chuckled unmentionable things.

She was not frightened by this insolence, but angered; for it hurt her, and embittered the pleasurable home-coming. Yet she quickly grasped the significance of it: the old patriarchal status of her father's time had passed away, and civilization, in a scorching blast, had swept down upon this people in a day. Glancing under the raised flaps of a tent, she saw haggard-faced bucks squatting in a circle on the floor. By the door a heap of broken bottles advertised the vigils of the night. A white man, low of visage and shrewd, was dealing cards about, and gold and silver coins leaped into heaping bets upon the blanket board. A few steps farther on she heard the cluttering whirl of a wheel of fortune, and saw the Indians, men and women, chancing eagerly their sweat-earned wages for the gaudy prizes of the game. And from tepee and lodge rose the cracked and crazy strains of cheap music-boxes.

An old squaw, peeling a willow pole in the sunshine of an open doorway, raised her head and uttered a shrill cry.

"Hee-Hee! Tenas Hee-Hee!" she muttered as well and as excitedly as her toothless gums would permit.

Frona thrilled at the cry. Tenas Hee-Hee! Little Laughter! Her name of the long gone Indian past! She turned and went over to the old woman.

"And hast thou so soon forgotten, Tenas Hee-Hee?" she mumbled. "And thine eyes so young and sharp! Not so soon does Neepoosa forget."

"It is thou, Neepoosa?" Frona cried, her tongue halting from the disuse of years.

"Ay, it is Neepoosa," the old woman replied, drawing her inside the tent, and despatching a boy, hot-footed, on some errand. They sat down together on the floor, and she patted Frona's hand lovingly, peering, meanwhile, bleareyed and misty, into her face. "Ay, it is Neepoosa, grown old quickly after the manner of our women. Neepoosa, who dandled thee in her arms when thou wast a child. Neepoosa, who gave thee thy name, Tenas Hee-Hee. Who fought for thee with Death when thou wast ailing; and gathered growing things from the woods and grasses of the earth and made of them tea, and gave thee to drink. But I mark little change, for I knew thee at once. It was thy very shadow on the ground that made me lift my head. A little change, mayhap. Tall thou art, and like a slender willow in thy grace, and the sun has kissed thy cheeks more lightly of the years; but there is the old hair, flying wild and of the color of the brown seaweed floating on the tide, and the mouth, quick to laugh and loth to cry. And the eyes are as clear and true as in the days when Neepoosa chid thee for wrong-doing, and thou wouldst not put false words upon thy tongue. Ai! Ai! Not as thou art the other women who come now into the land!"

"And why is a white woman without honor among you?" Frona demanded. "Your men say evil things to me in the camp, and as I came through the woods, even the boys. Not in the old days, when I played with them, was this shame so."

"Ai! Ai!" Neepoosa made answer. "It is so. But do not blame them. Pour not thine anger upon their heads. For it is true it is the fault of thy women who come into the land these days. They can point to no man and say, 'That is my man.' And it is not good that women should he thus. And they look upon all men, bold-eyed and shameless, and their tongues are unclean, and their hearts bad. Wherefore are thy women without honor among us. As for the boys, they are but boys. And the men; how should they know?"

The tent-flaps were poked aside and an old man came in. He grunted to Frona and sat down. Only a certain eager alertness showed the delight he took in her presence.

"So Tenas Hee-Hee has come back in these bad days," he vouchsafed in a shrill, quavering voice.

"And why bad days, Muskim?" Frona asked. "Do not the women wear brighter colors? Are not the bellies fuller with flour and bacon and white man's grub? Do not the young men contrive great wealth what of their pack-straps and paddles? And art thou not remembered with the ancient offerings of meat and fish and blanket? Why bad days, Muskim?"

"True," he replied in his fine, priestly way, a reminiscent flash of the old fire lighting his eyes. "It is very true. The women wear brighter colors.

But they have found favor, in the eyes of thy white men, and they look no more upon the young men of their own blood. Wherefore the tribe does not increase, nor do the little children longer clutter the way of our feet. It is so. The bellies are fuller with the white man's grub; but also are they fuller with the white man's bad whiskey. Nor could it be otherwise that the young men contrive great wealth; but they sit by night over the cards, and it passes from them, and they speak harsh words one to another, and in anger blows are struck, and there is bad blood between them. As for old Muskim, there are few offerings of meat and fish and blanket. For the young women have turned aside from the old paths, nor do the young men longer honor the old totems and the old gods. So these are bad days, Tenas Hee-Hee, and they behold old Muskim go down in sorrow to the grave."

"Ai! Ai! It is so!" wailed Neepoosa.

"Because of the madness of thy people have my people become mad," Muskim continued. "They come over the salt sea like the waves of the sea, thy people, and they go—ah! who knoweth where?"

"Ai! Who knoweth where?" Neepoosa lamented, rocking slowly back and forth.

"Ever they go towards the frost and cold; and ever do they come, more people, wave upon wave!"

"Ai! Ai! Into the frost and cold! It is a long way, and dark and cold!" She shivered, then laid a sudden hand on Frona's arm. "And thou goest?"

Frona nodded.

"And Tenas Hee-Hee goest! Ai! Ai! Ai!"

The tent-flap lifted, and Matt McCarthy peered in. "It's yourself,

Frona, is it? With breakfast waitin' this half-hour on ye, an' old

Andy fumin' an' frettin' like the old woman he is. Good-mornin' to ye,

Neepoosa," he addressed Frona's companions, "an' to ye, Muskim, though, belike ye've little mimory iv me face."

The old couple grunted salutation and remained stolidly silent.

"But hurry with ye, girl," turning back to Frona. "Me steamer starts by mid-day, an' it's little I'll see iv ye at the best. An' likewise there's Andy an' the breakfast pipin' hot, both iv them."

CHAPTER III

Frona waved her hand to Andy and swung out on the trail. Fastened tightly to her back were her camera and a small travelling satchel. In addition, she carried for alpenstock the willow pole of Neepoosa. Her dress was of the mountaineering sort, short-skirted and scant, allowing the greatest play with the least material, and withal gray of color and modest.

Her outfit, on the backs of a dozen Indians and in charge of Del Bishop, had got under way hours before. The previous day, on her return with Matt McCarthy from the Siwash camp, she had found Del Bishop at the store waiting her. His business was quickly transacted, for the proposition he made was terse and to the point. She was going into the country. He was intending to go in. She would need somebody. If she had not picked any one yet, why he was just the man. He had forgotten to tell her the day he took her ashore that he had been in the country years before and knew all about it. True, he hated the water, and it was mainly a water journey; but he was not afraid of it. He was afraid of nothing. Further, he would fight for her at the drop of the hat. As for pay, when they got to Dawson, a good word from her to Jacob Welse, and a year's outfit would be his. No, no; no grub-stake about it, no strings on him! He would pay for the outfit later on when his sack was dusted. What did she think about it, anyway? And Frona did think about it, for ere she had finished breakfast he was out hustling the packers together.

She found herself making better speed than the majority of her fellows, who were heavily laden and had to rest their packs every few hundred yards. Yet she found herself hard put to keep the pace of a bunch of Scandinavians ahead of her. They were huge strapping blond-haired giants, each striding along with a hundred pounds on his back, and all harnessed to a go-cart which carried fully six hundred more. Their faces were as laughing suns, and the joy of life was in them. The toil seemed child's play and slipped from them lightly. They joked with one another, and with the passers-by, in a meaningless tongue, and their great chests rumbled with cavern-echoing laughs. Men stood aside for them, and looked after them enviously; for they took the rises of the trail on the run, and rattled down the counter slopes, and ground the iron-rimmed wheels harshly over the rocks. Plunging through a dark stretch of woods, they came out upon the river at the ford. A drowned man lay on his back on the sand-bar, staring upward, unblinking, at the sun. A man, in irritated tones, was questioning over and over, "Where's his pardner? Ain't he got a pardner?" Two more men had thrown off their packs and were coolly taking an inventory of the dead man's possessions. One called aloud the various articles, while the other checked them off on a piece of dirty wrapping-paper. Letters and receipts, wet and pulpy, strewed the sand. A few gold coins were heaped carelessly on a white handkerchief. Other men, crossing back and forth in canoes and skiffs, took no notice.

The Scandinavians glanced at the sight, and their faces sobered for a moment. "Where's his pardner? Ain't he got a pardner?" the irritated man demanded of them. They shook their heads. They did not understand English. They stepped into the water and splashed onward. Some one called warningly from the opposite bank, whereat they stood still and conferred together. Then they started on again. The two men taking the inventory turned to watch. The current rose nigh to their hips, but it was swift and they staggered, while now and again the cart slipped sideways with the stream. The worst was over, and Frona found herself holding her breath. The water had sunk to the knees of the two foremost men, when a strap snapped on one nearest the cart. His pack swung suddenly to the side, overbalancing him. At the same instant the man next to him slipped, and each jerked the other under. The next two were whipped off their feet, while the cart, turning over, swept from the bottom of the ford into the deep water. The two men who had almost emerged threw themselves backward on the pull-ropes. The effort was heroic, but giants though they were, the task was too great and they were dragged, inch by inch, downward and under.

Their packs held them to the bottom, save him whose strap had broken. This one struck out, not to the shore, but down the stream, striving to keep up with his comrades. A couple of hundred feet below, the rapid dashed over a toothed-reef of rocks, and here, a minute later, they appeared. The cart, still loaded, showed first, smashing a wheel and turning over and over into the next plunge. The men followed in a miserable tangle. They were beaten against the submerged rocks and swept on, all but one. Frona, in a canoe (a dozen canoes were already in pursuit), saw him grip the rock with bleeding fingers. She saw his white face and the agony of the effort; but his hold relaxed and he was jerked away, just as his free comrade, swimming mightily, was reaching for him. Hidden from sight, they took the next plunge, showing for a second, still struggling, at the shallow foot of the rapid.

A canoe picked up the swimming man, but the rest disappeared in a long stretch of swift, deep water. For a quarter of an hour the canoes plied fruitlessly about, then found the dead men gently grounded in an eddy. A tow-rope was requisitioned from an up-coming boat, and a pair of horses from a pack-train on the bank, and the ghastly jetsam hauled ashore. Frona looked at the five young giants lying in the mud, broken-boned, limp, uncaring. They were still harnessed to the cart, and the poor worthless packs still clung to their backs, The sixth sat in the midst, dry-eyed and stunned. A dozen feet away the steady flood of life flowed by and Frona melted into it and went on.

The dark spruce-shrouded mountains drew close together in the Dyea Canyon, and the feet of men churned the wet sunless earth into mire and bog-hole. And when they had done this they sought new paths, till there were many paths. And on such a path Frona came upon a man spread carelessly in the mud. He lay on his side, legs apart and one arm buried beneath him, pinned down by a bulky pack. His cheek was pillowed restfully in the ooze, and on his face there was an expression of content. He brightened when he saw her, and his eyes twinkled cheerily.

"'Bout time you hove along," he greeted her. "Been waitin' an hour on you as it is."

"That's it," as Frona bent over him. "Just unbuckle that strap. The pesky thing! 'Twas just out o' my reach all the time."

"Are you hurt?" she asked.

He slipped out of his straps, shook himself, and felt the twisted arm. "Nope. Sound as a dollar, thank you. And no kick to register, either." He reached over and wiped his muddy hands on a low-bowed spruce. "Just my luck; but I got a good rest, so what's the good of makin' a beef about it? You see, I tripped on that little root there, and slip! slump! slam! and slush!—there I was, down and out, and the buckle just out o' reach. And there I lay for a blasted hour, everybody hitting the lower path."

"But why didn't you call out to them?"

"And make 'em climb up the hill to me? Them all tuckered out with their own work? Not on your life! Wasn't serious enough. If any other man 'd make me climb up just because he'd slipped down, I'd take him out o' the mud all right, all right, and punch and punch him back into the mud again. Besides, I knew somebody was bound to come along my way after a while."

"Oh, you'll do!" she cried, appropriating Del Bishop's phrase. "You'll do for this country!"

"Yep," he called back, shouldering his pack and starting off at a lively clip. "And, anyway, I got a good rest."

The trail dipped through a precipitous morass to the river's brink. A slender pine-tree spanned the screaming foam and bent midway to touch the water. The surge beat upon the taper trunk and gave it a rhythmical swaying motion, while the feet of the packers had worn smooth its wave-washed surface. Eighty feet it stretched in ticklish insecurity. Frona stepped upon it, felt it move beneath her, heard the bellowing of the water, saw the mad rush—and shrank back. She slipped the knot of her shoe-laces and pretended great care in the tying thereof as a bunch of Indians came out of the woods above and down through the mud. Three or four bucks led the way, followed by many squaws, all bending in the head-straps to the heavy packs. Behind came the children burdened according to their years, and in the rear half a dozen dogs, tongues lagging out and dragging forward painfully under their several loads.

The men glanced at her sideways, and one of them said something in an undertone. Frona could not hear, but the snicker which went down the line brought the flush of shame to her brow and told her more forcibly than could the words. Her face was hot, for she sat disgraced in her own sight; but she gave no sign. The leader stood aside, and one by one, and never more than one at a time, they made the perilous passage. At the bend in the middle their weight forced the tree under, and they felt for their footing, up to the ankles in the cold, driving torrent. Even the little children made it without hesitancy, and then the dogs whining and reluctant but urged on by the man. When the last had crossed over, he turned to Frona.

"Um horse trail," he said, pointing up the mountain side. "Much better you take um horse trail. More far; much better."

But she shook her head and waited till he reached the farther bank; for she felt the call, not only upon her own pride, but upon the pride of her race; and it was a greater demand than her demand, just as the race was greater than she. So she put foot upon the log, and, with the eyes of the alien people upon her, walked down into the foam-white swirl.

She came upon a man weeping by the side of the trail. His pack, clumsily strapped, sprawled on the ground. He had taken off a shoe, and one naked foot showed swollen and blistered.

"What is the matter?" she asked, halting before him.

He looked up at her, then down into the depths where the Dyea River cut the gloomy darkness with its living silver. The tears still welled in his eyes, and he sniffled.

"What is the matter?" she repeated. "Can I be of any help?"

"No," he replied. "How can you help? My feet are raw, and my back is nearly broken, and I am all tired out. Can you help any of these things?"

"Well," judiciously, "I am sure it might be worse. Think of the men who have just landed on the beach. It will take them ten days or two weeks to back-trip their outfits as far as you have already got yours."

"But my partners have left me and gone on," he moaned, a sneaking appeal for pity in his voice. "And I am all alone, and I don't feel able to move another step. And then think of my wife and babies. I left them down in the States. Oh, if they could only see me now! I can't go back to them, and I can't go on. It's too much for me. I can't stand it, this working like a horse. I was not made to work like a horse. I'll die, I know I will, if I do. Oh, what shall I do? What shall I do?"

"Why did your comrades leave you?"

"Because I was not so strong as they; because I could not pack as much or as long. And they laughed at me and left me."

"Have you ever roughed it?" Frona asked.

"No."

"You look well put up and strong. Weigh probably one hundred and sixty-five?"

"One hundred-and seventy," he corrected.

"You don't look as though you had ever been troubled with sickness. Never an invalid?"

"N-no."

"And your comrades? They are miners?"

"Never mining in their lives. They worked in the same establishment with me. That's what makes it so hard, don't you see! We'd known one another for years! And to go off and leave me just because I couldn't keep up!"

"My friend," and Frona knew she was speaking for the race, "you are strong as they. You can work just as hard as they; pack as much. But you are weak of heart. This is no place for the weak of heart. You cannot work like a horse because you will not. Therefore the country has no use for you. The north wants strong men,—strong of soul, not body. The body does not count. So go back to the States. We do not want you here. If you come you will die, and what then of your wife and babies? So sell out your outfit and go back. You will be home in three weeks. Good-by."

She passed through Sheep Camp. Somewhere above, a mighty glacier, under the pent pressure of a subterranean reservoir, had burst asunder and hurled a hundred thousand tons of ice and water down the rocky gorge. The trail was yet slippery with the slime of the flood, and men were rummaging disconsolately in the rubbish of overthrown tents and caches. But here and there they worked with nervous haste, and the stark corpses by the trail-side attested dumbly to their labor. A few hundred yards beyond, the work of the rush went on uninterrupted. Men rested their packs on jutting stones, swapped escapes whilst they regained their breath, then stumbled on to their toil again.

The mid-day sun beat down upon the stone "Scales." The forest had given up the struggle, and the dizzying heat recoiled from the unclothed rock. On either hand rose the ice-marred ribs of earth, naked and strenuous in their nakedness. Above towered storm-beaten Chilcoot. Up its gaunt and ragged front crawled a slender string of men. But it was an endless string. It came out of the last fringe of dwarfed shrub below, drew a black line across a dazzling stretch of ice, and filed past Frona where she ate her lunch by the way. And it went on, up the pitch of the steep, growing fainter and smaller, till it squirmed and twisted like a column of ants and vanished over the crest of the pass.

Even as she looked, Chilcoot was wrapped in rolling mist and whirling cloud, and a storm of sleet and wind roared down upon the toiling pigmies. The light was swept out of the day, and a deep gloom prevailed; but Frona knew that somewhere up there, clinging and climbing and immortally striving, the long line of ants still twisted towards the sky. And she thrilled at the thought, strong with man's ancient love of mastery, and stepped into the line which came out of the storm behind and disappeared into the storm before.

She blew through the gap of the pass in a whirlwind of vapor, with hand and foot clambered down the volcanic ruin of Chilcoot's mighty father, and stood on the bleak edge of the lake which filled the pit of the crater. The lake was angry and white-capped, and though a hundred caches were waiting ferriage, no boats were plying back and forth. A rickety skeleton of sticks, in a shell of greased canvas, lay upon the rocks. Frona sought out the owner, a bright-faced young fellow, with sharp black eyes and a salient jaw. Yes, he was the ferryman, but he had quit work for the day. Water too rough for freighting. He charged twenty-five dollars for passengers, but he was not taking passengers to-day. Had he not said it was too rough? That was why.

"But you will take me, surely?" she asked.

He shook his head and gazed out over the lake. "At the far end it's rougher than you see it here. Even the big wooden boats won't tackle it. The last that tried, with a gang of packers aboard, was blown over on the west shore. We could see them plainly. And as there's no trail around from there, they'll have to camp it out till the blow is over."

"But they're better off than I am. My camp outfit is at Happy Camp, and I can't very well stay here," Frona smiled winsomely, but there was no appeal in the smile; no feminine helplessness throwing itself on the strength and chivalry of the male. "Do reconsider and take me across."

"No."

"I'll give you fifty."

"No, I say."

"But I'm not afraid, you know."

The young fellow's eyes flashed angrily. He turned upon her suddenly, but on second thought did not utter the words forming on his lips. She realized the unintentional slur she had cast, and was about to explain. But on second thought she, too, remained silent; for she read him, and knew that it was perhaps the only way for her to gain her point. They stood there, bodies inclined to the storm in the manner of seamen on sloped decks, unyieldingly looking into each other's eyes. His hair was plastered in wet ringlets on his forehead, while hers, in longer wisps, beat furiously about her face.

"Come on, then!" He flung the boat into the water with an angry jerk, and tossed the oars aboard. "Climb in! I'll take you, but not for your fifty dollars. You pay the regulation price, and that's all."

A gust of the gale caught the light shell and swept it broadside for a score of feet. The spray drove inboard in a continuous stinging shower, and Frona at once fell to work with the bailing-can.

"I hope we're blown ashore," he shouted, stooping forward to the oars. "It would be embarrassing—for you." He looked up savagely into her face.

"No," she modified; "but it would be very miserable for both of us,—a night without tent, blankets, or fire. Besides, we're not going to blow ashore."

She stepped out on the slippery rocks and helped him heave up the canvas craft and tilt the water out. On either side uprose bare wet walls of rock. A heavy sleet was falling steadily, through which a few streaming caches showed in the gathering darkness.

"You'd better hurry up," he advised, thanking her for the assistance

and relaunching the boat. "Two miles of stiff trail from here to Happy

Camp. No wood until you get there, so you'd best hustle along.

Good-by."

Frona reached out and took his hand, and said, "You are a brave man."

"Oh, I don't know." He returned the grip with usury and looked his admiration.

A dozen tents held grimly to their pegs on the extreme edge of the timber line at Happy Camp. Frona, weary with the day, went from tent to tent. Her wet skirts clung heavily to her tired limbs, while the wind buffeted her brutally about. Once, through a canvas wall, she heard a man apostrophizing gorgeously, and felt sure that it was Del Bishop. But a peep into the interior told a different tale; so she wandered fruitlessly on till she reached the last tent in the camp. She untied the flap and looked in. A spluttering candle showed the one occupant, a man, down on his knees and blowing lustily into the firebox of a smoky Yukon stove.

CHAPTER IV

She cast off the lower flap-fastenings and entered. The man still blew into the stove, unaware of his company. Frona coughed, and he raised a pair of smoke-reddened eyes to hers.

"Certainly," he said, casually enough. "Fasten the flaps and make yourself comfortable." And thereat returned to his borean task.

"Hospitable, to say the least," she commented to herself, obeying his command and coming up to the stove.

A heap of dwarfed spruce, gnarled and wet and cut to proper stove-length, lay to one side. Frona knew it well, creeping and crawling and twisting itself among the rocks of the shallow alluvial deposit, unlike its arboreal prototype, rarely lifting its head more than a foot from the earth. She looked into the oven, found it empty, and filled it with the wet wood. The man arose to his feet, coughing from the smoke which had been driven into his lungs, and nodding approval.

When he had recovered his breath, "Sit down and dry your skirts. I'll get supper."

He put a coffee-pot on the front lid of the stove, emptied the bucket into it, and went out of the tent after more water. As his back disappeared, Frona dived for her satchel, and when he returned a moment later he found her with a dry skirt on and wringing the wet one out. While he fished about in the grub-box for dishes and eating utensils, she stretched a spare bit of rope between the tent-poles and hung the skirt on it to dry. The dishes were dirty, and, as he bent over and washed them, she turned her back and deftly changed her stockings. Her childhood had taught her the value of well-cared feet for the trail. She put her wet shoes on a pile of wood at the back of the stove, substituting for them a pair of soft and dainty house-moccasins of Indian make. The fire had now grown strong, and she was content to let her under-garments dry on her body.

During all this time neither had spoken a word. Not only had the man remained silent, but he went about his work in so preoccupied a way that it seemed to Frona that he turned a deaf ear to the words of explanation she would have liked to utter. His whole bearing conveyed the impression that it was the most ordinary thing under the sun for a young woman to come in out of the storm and night and partake of his hospitality. In one way, she liked this; but in so far as she did not comprehend it, she was troubled. She had a perception of a something being taken for granted which she did not understand. Once or twice she moistened her lips to speak, but he appeared so oblivious of her presence that she withheld.

After opening a can of corned beef with the axe, he fried half a dozen thick slices of bacon, set the frying-pan back, and boiled the coffee. From the grub-box he resurrected the half of a cold heavy flapjack. He looked at it dubiously, and shot a quick glance at her. Then he threw the sodden thing out of doors and dumped the contents of a sea-biscuit bag upon a camp cloth. The sea-biscuit had been crumbled into chips and fragments and generously soaked by the rain till it had become a mushy, pulpy mass of dirty white.

"It's all I have in the way of bread," he muttered; "but sit down and we will make the best of it."

"One moment—" And before he could protest, Frona had poured the sea-biscuit into the frying-pan on top of the grease and bacon. To this she added a couple of cups of water and stirred briskly over the fire. When it had sobbed and sighed with the heat for some few minutes, she sliced up the corned beef and mixed it in with the rest. And by the time she had seasoned it heavily with salt and black pepper, a savory steam was rising from the concoction.

"Must say it's pretty good stuff," he said, balancing his plate on his knee and sampling the mess avidiously. "What do you happen to call it?"

"Slumgullion," she responded curtly, and thereafter the meal went on in silence.

Frona helped him to the coffee, studying him intently the while. And not only was it not an unpleasant face, she decided, but it was strong. Strong, she amended, potentially rather than actually. A student, she added, for she had seen many students' eyes and knew the lasting impress of the midnight oil long continued; and his eyes bore the impress. Brown eyes, she concluded, and handsome as the male's should be handsome; but she noted with surprise, when she refilled his plate with slumgullion, that they were not at all brown in the ordinary sense, but hazel-brown. In the daylight, she felt certain, and in times of best health, they would seem gray, and almost blue-gray. She knew it well; her one girl chum and dearest friend had had such an eye.

His hair was chestnut-brown, glinting in the candle-light to gold, and the hint of waviness in it explained the perceptible droop to his tawny moustache. For the rest, his face was clean-shaven and cut on a good masculine pattern. At first she found fault with the more than slight cheek-hollows under the cheek-bones, but when she measured his well-knit, slenderly muscular figure, with its deep chest and heavy shoulders, she discovered that she preferred the hollows; at least they did not imply lack of nutrition. The body gave the lie to that; while they themselves denied the vice of over-feeding. Height, five feet, nine, she summed up from out of her gymnasium experience; and age anywhere between twenty-five and thirty, though nearer the former most likely.

"Haven't many blankets," he said abruptly, pausing to drain his cup and set it over on the grub-box. "I don't expect my Indians back from Lake Linderman till morning, and the beggars have packed over everything except a few sacks of flour and the bare camp outfit. However, I've a couple of heavy ulsters which will serve just as well."

He turned his back, as though he did not expect a reply, and untied a rubber-covered roll of blankets. Then he drew the two ulsters from a clothes-bag and threw them down on the bedding.

"Vaudeville artist, I suppose?"

He asked the question seemingly without interest, as though to keep the conversation going, and, in fact, as if he knew the stereotyped answer beforehand. But to Frona the question was like a blow in the face. She remembered Neepoosa's philippic against the white women who were coming into the land, and realized the falseness of her position and the way in which he looked upon her.

But he went on before she could speak. "Last night I had two vaudeville queens, and three the night before. Only there was more bedding then. It's unfortunate, isn't it, the aptitude they display in getting lost from their outfits? Yet somehow I have failed to find any lost outfits so far. And they are all queens, it seems. No under-studies or minor turns about them,—no, no. And I presume you are a queen, too?"

The too-ready blood sprayed her cheek, and this made her angrier than did he; for whereas she was sure of the steady grip she had on herself, her flushed face betokened a confusion which did not really possess her.

"No," she answered, coolly; "I am not a vaudeville artist."

He tossed several sacks of flour to one side of the stove, without replying, and made of them the foundation of a bed; and with the remaining sacks he duplicated the operation on the opposite side of the stove.

"But you are some kind of an artist, then," he insisted when he had finished, with an open contempt on the "artist."

"Unfortunately, I am not any kind of an artist at all."

He dropped the blanket he was folding and straightened his back. Hitherto he had no more than glanced at her; but now he scrutinized her carefully, every inch of her, from head to heel and back again, the cut of her garments and the very way she did her hair. And he took his time about it.

"Oh! I beg pardon," was his verdict, followed by another stare. "Then you are a very foolish woman dreaming of fortune and shutting your eyes to the dangers of the pilgrimage. It is only meet that two kinds of women come into this country. Those who by virtue of wifehood and daughterhood are respectable, and those who are not respectable. Vaudeville stars and artists, they call themselves for the sake of decency; and out of courtesy we countenance it. Yes, yes, I know. But remember, the women who come over the trail must be one or the other. There is no middle course, and those who attempt it are bound to fail. So you are a very, very foolish girl, and you had better turn back while there is yet a chance. If you will view it in the light of a loan from a stranger, I will advance your passage back to the States, and start an Indian over the trail with you to-morrow for Dyea."

Once or twice Frona had attempted to interrupt him, but he had waved her imperatively to silence with his hand.

"I thank you," she began; but he broke in,—

"Oh, not at all, not at all."

"I thank you," she repeated; but it happens that—a—that you are mistaken. I have just come over the trail from Dyea and expect to meet my outfit already in camp here at Happy Camp. They started hours ahead of me, and I can't understand how I passed them—yes I do, too! A boat was blown over to the west shore of Crater Lake this afternoon, and they must have been in it. That is where I missed them and came on. As for my turning back, I appreciate your motive for suggesting it, but my father is in Dawson, and I have not seen him for three years. Also, I have come through from Dyea this day, and am tired, and I would like to get some rest. So, if you still extend your hospitality, I'll go to bed."

"Impossible!" He kicked the blankets to one side, sat down on the flour sacks, and directed a blank look upon her.

"Are—are there any women in the other tents?" she asked, hesitatingly.

"I did not see any, but I may have overlooked."

"A man and his wife were, but they pulled stakes this morning. No; there are no other women except—except two or three in a tent, which—er—which will not do for you."

"Do you think I am afraid of their hospitality?" she demanded, hotly.

"As you said, they are women."

"But I said it would not do," he answered, absently, staring at the straining canvas and listening to the roar of the storm. "A man would die in the open on a night like this.

"And the other tents are crowded to the walls," he mused. "I happen to know. They have stored all their caches inside because of the water, and they haven't room to turn around. Besides, a dozen other strangers are storm-bound with them. Two or three asked to spread their beds in here to-night if they couldn't pinch room elsewhere. Evidently they have; but that does not argue that there is any surplus space left. And anyway—"

He broke off helplessly. The inevitableness of the situation was growing.

"Can I make Deep Lake to-night?" Frona asked, forgetting herself to sympathize with him, then becoming conscious of what she was doing and bursting into laughter.

"But you couldn't ford the river in the dark." He frowned at her levity. "And there are no camps between."

"Are you afraid?" she asked with just the shadow of a sneer.

"Not for myself."

"Well, then, I think I'll go to bed."

"I might sit up and keep the fire going," he suggested after a pause.

"Fiddlesticks!" she cried. "As though your foolish little code were saved in the least! We are not in civilization. This is the trail to the Pole. Go to bed."

He elevated his shoulders in token of surrender. "Agreed. What shall I do then?"

"Help me make my bed, of course. Sacks laid crosswise! Thank you, sir, but I have bones and muscles that rebel. Here— Pull them around this way."

Under her direction he laid the sacks lengthwise in a double row. This left an uncomfortable hollow with lumpy sack-corners down the middle; but she smote them flat with the side of the axe, and in the same manner lessened the slope to the walls of the hollow. Then she made a triple longitudinal fold in a blanket and spread it along the bottom of the long depression.

"Hum!" he soliloquized. "Now I see why I sleep so badly. Here goes!"

And he speedily flung his own sacks into shape.

"It is plain you are unused to the trail," she informed him, spreading the topmost blanket and sitting down.

"Perhaps so," he made answer. "But what do you know about this trail life?" he growled a little later.

"Enough to conform," she rejoined equivocally, pulling out the dried wood from the oven and replacing it with wet.

"Listen to it! How it storms!" he exclaimed. "It's growing worse, if worse be possible."

The tent reeled under the blows of the wind, the canvas booming hollowly at every shock, while the sleet and rain rattled overhead like skirmish-fire grown into a battle. In the lulls they could hear the water streaming off at the side-walls with the noise of small cataracts. He reached up curiously and touched the wet roof. A burst of water followed instantly at the point of contact and coursed down upon the grub-box.

"You mustn't do that!" Frona cried, springing to her feet. She put her finger on the spot, and, pressing tightly against the canvas, ran it down to the side-wall. The leak at once stopped. "You mustn't do it, you know," she reproved.

"Jove!" was his reply. "And you came through from Dyea to-day! Aren't you stiff?"

"Quite a bit," she confessed, candidly, "and sleepy."

"Good-night," she called to him several minutes later, stretching her body luxuriously in the warm blankets. And a quarter of an hour after that, "Oh, I say! Are you awake?"

"Yes," his voice came muffled across the stove. "What is it?"

"Have you the shavings cut?"

"Shavings?" he queried, sleepily. "What shavings?"

"For the fire in the morning, of course. So get up and cut them."

He obeyed without a word; but ere he was done she had ceased to hear him.

The ubiquitous bacon was abroad on the air when she opened her eyes. Day had broken, and with it the storm. The wet sun was shining cheerily over the drenched landscape and in at the wide-spread flaps. Already work had begun, and groups of men were filing past under their packs. Frona turned over on her side. Breakfast was cooked. Her host had just put the bacon and fried potatoes in the oven, and was engaged in propping the door ajar with two sticks of firewood.

"Good-morning," she greeted.

"And good-morning to you," he responded, rising to his feet and picking up the water-bucket. "I don't hope that you slept well, for I know you did."

Frona laughed.

"I'm going out after some water," he vouchsafed. "And when I return I shall expect you ready for breakfast."

After breakfast, basking herself in the sun, Frona descried a familiar bunch of men rounding the tail of the glacier in the direction of Crater Lake. She clapped her hands.

"There comes my outfit, and Del Bishop as shame-faced as can be, I'm sure, at his failure to connect." Turning to the man, and at the same time slinging camera and satchel over her shoulder, "So I must say good-by, not forgetting to thank you for your kindness."

"Oh, not at all, not at all. Pray don't mention it. I'd do the same for any—"

"Vaudeville artist!"

He looked his reproach, but went on. "I don't know your name, nor do I wish to know it."

"Well, I shall not be so harsh, for I do know your name, MISTER VANCE

CORLISS! I saw it on the shipping tags, of course," she explained.

"And I want you to come and see me when you get to Dawson. My name is

Frona Welse. Good-by."

"Your father is not Jacob Welse?" he called after her as she ran lightly down towards the trail.

She turned her head and nodded.

But Del Bishop was not shamefaced, nor even worried. "Trust a Welse to land on their feet on a soft spot," he had consoled himself as he dropped off to sleep the night before. But he was angry—"madder 'n hops," in his own vernacular.

"Good-mornin'," he saluted. "And it's plain by your face you had a comfortable night of it, and no thanks to me."

"You weren't worried, were you?" she asked.

"Worried? About a Welse? Who? Me? Not on your life. I was too busy tellin' Crater Lake what I thought of it. I don't like the water. I told you so. And it's always playin' me scurvy—not that I'm afraid of it, though."

"Hey, you Pete!" turning to the Indians. "Hit 'er up! Got to make

Linderman by noon!"

"Frona Welse?" Vance Corliss was repeating to himself.

The whole thing seemed a dream, and he reassured himself by turning and looking after her retreating form. Del Bishop and the Indians were already out of sight behind a wall of rock. Frona was just rounding the base. The sun was full upon her, and she stood out radiantly against the black shadow of the wall beyond. She waved her alpenstock, and as he doffed his cap, rounded the brink and disappeared.

CHAPTER V

The position occupied by Jacob Welse was certainly an anomalous one. He was a giant trader in a country without commerce, a ripened product of the nineteenth century flourishing in a society as primitive as that of the Mediterranean vandals. A captain of industry and a splendid monopolist, he dominated the most independent aggregate of men ever drawn together from the ends of the earth. An economic missionary, a commercial St. Paul, he preached the doctrines of expediency and force. Believing in the natural rights of man, a child himself of democracy, he bent all men to his absolutism. Government of Jacob Welse, for Jacob Welse and the people, by Jacob Welse, was his unwritten gospel. Single-handed he had carved out his dominion till he gripped the domain of a dozen Roman provinces. At his ukase the population ebbed and flowed over a hundred thousand miles of territory, and cities sprang up or disappeared at his bidding.

Yet he was a common man. The air of the world first smote his lungs on the open prairie by the River Platte, the blue sky over head, and beneath, the green grass of the earth pressing against his tender nakedness. On the horses his eyes first opened, still saddled and gazing in mild wonder on the miracle; for his trapper father had but turned aside from the trail that the wife might have quiet and the birth be accomplished. An hour or so and the two, which were now three, were in the saddle and overhauling their trapper comrades. The party had not been delayed; no time lost. In the morning his mother cooked the breakfast over the camp-fire, and capped it with a fifty-mile ride into the next sun-down.

The trapper father had come of the sturdy Welsh stock which trickled into early Ohio out of the jostling East, and the mother was a nomadic daughter of the Irish emigrant settlers of Ontario. From both sides came the Wanderlust of the blood, the fever to be moving, to be pushing on to the edge of things. In the first year of his life, ere he had learned the way of his legs, Jacob Welse had wandered a-horse through a thousand miles of wilderness, and wintered in a hunting-lodge on the head-waters of the Red River of the North. His first foot-gear was moccasins, his first taffy the tallow from a moose. His first generalizations were that the world was composed of great wastes and white vastnesses, and populated with Indians and white hunters like his father. A town was a cluster of deer-skin lodges; a trading-post a seat of civilization; and a factor God Almighty Himself. Rivers and lakes existed chiefly for man's use in travelling. Viewed in this light, the mountains puzzled him; but he placed them away in his classification of the Inexplicable and did not worry. Men died, sometimes. But their meat was not good to eat, and their hides worthless,—perhaps because they did not grow fur. Pelts were valuable, and with a few bales a man might purchase the earth. Animals were made for men to catch and skin. He did not know what men were made for, unless, perhaps, for the factor.

As he grew older he modified these concepts, but the process was a continual source of naive apprehension and wonderment. It was not until he became a man and had wandered through half the cities of the States that this expression of childish wonder passed out of his eyes and left them wholly keen and alert. At his boy's first contact with the cities, while he revised his synthesis of things, he also generalized afresh. People who lived in cities were effeminate. They did not carry the points of the compass in their heads, and they got lost easily. That was why they elected to stay in the cities. Because they might catch cold and because they were afraid of the dark, they slept under shelter and locked their doors at night. The women were soft and pretty, but they could not lift a snowshoe far in a day's journey. Everybody talked too much. That was why they lied and were unable to work greatly with their hands. Finally, there was a new human force called "bluff." A man who made a bluff must be dead sure of it, or else be prepared to back it up. Bluff was a very good thing—when exercised with discretion.

Later, though living his life mainly in the woods and mountains, he came to know that the cities were not all bad; that a man might live in a city and still be a man. Accustomed to do battle with natural forces, he was attracted by the commercial battle with social forces. The masters of marts and exchanges dazzled but did not blind him, and he studied them, and strove to grasp the secrets of their strength. And further, in token that some good did come out of Nazareth, in the full tide of manhood he took to himself a city-bred woman. But he still yearned for the edge of things, and the leaven in his blood worked till they went away, and above the Dyea Beach, on the rim of the forest, built the big log trading-post. And here, in the mellow of time, he got a proper focus on things and unified the phenomena of society precisely as he had already unified the phenomena of nature. There was naught in one which could not be expressed in terms of the other. The same principles underlaid both; the same truths were manifest of both. Competition was the secret of creation. Battle was the law and the way of progress. The world was made for the strong, and only the strong inherited it, and through it all there ran an eternal equity. To be honest was to be strong. To sin was to weaken. To bluff an honest man was to be dishonest. To bluff a bluffer was to smite with the steel of justice. The primitive strength was in the arm; the modern strength in the brain. Though it had shifted ground, the struggle was the same old struggle. As of old time, men still fought for the mastery of the earth and the delights thereof. But the sword had given way to the ledger; the mail-clad baron to the soft-garbed industrial lord, and the centre of imperial political power to the seat of commercial exchanges. The modern will had destroyed the ancient brute. The stubborn earth yielded only to force. Brain was greater than body. The man with the brain could best conquer things primitive.

He did not have much education as education goes. To the three R's his mother taught him by camp-fire and candle-light, he had added a somewhat miscellaneous book-knowledge; but he was not burdened with what he had gathered. Yet he read the facts of life understandingly, and the sobriety which comes of the soil was his, and the clear earth-vision.

And so it came about that Jacob Welse crossed over the Chilcoot in an early day, and disappeared into the vast unknown. A year later he emerged at the Russian missions clustered about the mouth of the Yukon on Bering Sea. He had journeyed down a river three thousand miles long, he had seen things, and dreamed a great dream. But he held his tongue and went to work, and one day the defiant whistle of a crazy stern-wheel tub saluted the midnight sun on the dank river-stretch by Fort o' Yukon. It was a magnificent adventure. How he achieved it only Jacob Welse can tell; but with the impossible to begin with, plus the impossible, he added steamer to steamer and heaped enterprise upon enterprise. Along many a thousand miles of river and tributary he built trading-posts and warehouses. He forced the white man's axe into the hands of the aborigines, and in every village and between the villages rose the cords of four-foot firewood for his boilers. On an island in Bering Sea, where the river and the ocean meet, he established a great distributing station, and on the North Pacific he put big ocean steamships; while in his offices in Seattle and San Francisco it took clerks by the score to keep the order and system of his business.

Men drifted into the land. Hitherto famine had driven them out, but Jacob Welse was there now, and his grub-stores; so they wintered in the frost and groped in the frozen muck for gold. He encouraged them, grub-staked them, carried them on the books of the company. His steamers dragged them up the Koyokuk in the old days of Arctic City. Wherever pay was struck he built a warehouse and a store. The town followed. He explored; he speculated; he developed. Tireless, indomitable, with the steel-glitter in his dark eyes, he was everywhere at once, doing all things. In the opening up of a new river he was in the van; and at the tail-end also, hurrying forward the grub. On the Outside he fought trade-combinations; made alliances with the corporations of the earth, and forced discriminating tariffs from the great carriers. On the Inside he sold flour, and blankets, and tobacco; built saw-mills, staked townsites, and sought properties in copper, iron, and coal; and that the miners should be well-equipped, ransacked the lands of the Arctic even as far as Siberia for native-made snow-shoes, muclucs, and *parkas*.

He bore the country on his shoulders; saw to its needs; did its work. Every ounce of its dust passed through his hands; every post-card and letter of credit. He did its banking and exchange; carried and distributed its mails. He frowned upon competition; frightened out predatory capital; bluffed militant syndicates, and when they would not, backed his bluff and broke them. And for all, yet found time and place to remember his motherless girl, and to love her, and to fit her for the position he had made.

CHAPTER VI

"So I think, captain, you will agree that we must exaggerate the seriousness of the situation." Jacob Welse helped his visitor into his fur greatcoat and went on. "Not that it is not serious, but that it may not become more serious. Both you and I have handled famines before. We must frighten them, and frighten them now, before it is too late. Take five thousand men out of Dawson and there will be grub to last. Let those five thousand carry their tale of famine to Dyea and Skaguay, and they will prevent five thousand more coming in over the ice."

"Quite right! And you may count on the hearty co-operation of the police, Mr. Welse." The speaker, a strong-faced, grizzled man, heavy-set and of military bearing, pulled up his collar and rested his hand on the door-knob. "I see already, thanks to you, the newcomers are beginning to sell their outfits and buy dogs. Lord! won't there be a stampede out over the ice as soon as the river closes down! And each that sells a thousand pounds of grub and goes lessens the proposition by one empty stomach and fills another that remains. When does the Laura start?"

"This morning, with three hundred grubless men aboard. Would that they were three thousand!"

Amen to that! And by the way, when does your daughter arrive?"

"'Most any day, now." Jacob Welse's eyes warmed. "And I want you to dinner when she does, and bring along a bunch of your young bucks from the Barracks. I don't know all their names, but just the same extend the invitation as though from me personally. I haven't cultivated the social side much,—no time, but see to it that the girl enjoys herself. Fresh from the States and London, and she's liable to feel lonesome. You understand."

Jacob Welse closed the door, tilted his chair back, and cocked his feet on the guard-rail of the stove. For one half-minute a girlish vision wavered in the shimmering air above the stove, then merged into a woman of fair Saxon type.

The door opened. "Mr. Welse, Mr. Foster sent me to find out if he is to go on filling signed warehouse orders?"

"Certainly, Mr. Smith. But tell him to scale them down by half. If a man holds an order for a thousand pounds, give him five hundred."

He lighted a cigar and tilted back again in his chair.

"Captain McGregor wants to see you, sir."

"Send him in."

Captain McGregor strode in and remained standing before his employer. The rough hand of the New World had been laid upon the Scotsman from his boyhood; but sterling honesty was written in every line of his bitter-seamed face, while a prognathous jaw proclaimed to the onlooker that honesty was the best policy,—for the onlooker at any rate, should he wish to do business with the owner of the jaw. This warning was backed up by the nose, side-twisted and broken, and by a long scar which ran up the forehead and disappeared in the gray-grizzled hair.

"We throw off the lines in an hour, sir; so I've come for the last word."

"Good." Jacob Welse whirled his chair about. "Captain McGregor."

"Ay."

"I had other work cut out for you this winter; but I have changed my mind and chosen you to go down with the Laura. Can you guess why?"

Captain McGregor swayed his weight from one leg to the other, and a shrewd chuckle of a smile wrinkled the corners of his eyes. "Going to be trouble," he grunted.

"And I couldn't have picked a better man. Mr. Bally will give you detailed instructions as you go aboard. But let me say this: If we can't scare enough men out of the country, there'll be need for every pound of grub at Fort Yukon. Understand?"

"Ay."

"So no extravagance. You are taking three hundred men down with you. The chances are that twice as many more will go down as soon as the river freezes. You'll have a thousand to feed through the winter. Put them on rations,—working rations,—and see that they work. Cordwood, six dollars per cord, and piled on the bank where steamers can make a landing. No work, no rations. Understand?"

"Ay."

"A thousand men can get ugly, if they are idle. They can get ugly anyway. Watch out they don't rush the caches. If they do,—do your duty."

The other nodded grimly. His hands gripped unconsciously, while the scar on his forehead took on a livid hue.

"There are five steamers in the ice. Make them safe against the spring break-up. But first transfer all their cargoes to one big cache. You can defend it better, and make the cache impregnable. Send a messenger down to Fort Burr, asking Mr. Carter for three of his men. He doesn't need them. Nothing much is doing at Circle City. Stop in on the way down and take half of Mr. Burdwell's men. You'll need them. There'll be gun-fighters in plenty to deal with. Be stiff. Keep things in check from the start. Remember, the man who shoots first comes off with the whole hide. And keep a constant eye on the grub."

"And on the forty-five-nineties," Captain McGregor rumbled back as he passed out the door.

"John Melton—Mr. Melton, sir. Can he see you?"

"See here, Welse, what's this mean?" John Melton followed wrathfully on the heels of the clerk, and he almost walked over him as he flourished a paper before the head of the company. "Read that! What's it stand for?"

Jacob Welse glanced over it and looked up coolly. "One thousand pounds of grub."

"That's what I say, but that fellow you've got in the warehouse says no,— five hundred's all it's good for."

"He spoke the truth."

"But—"

"It stands for one thousand pounds, but in the warehouse it is only good for five hundred."

"That your signature?" thrusting the receipt again into the other's line of vision.

"Yes."

"Then what are you going to do about it?"

"Give you five hundred. What are you going to do about it?"

"Refuse to take it."

"Very good. There is no further discussion."

"Yes there is. I propose to have no further dealings with you. I'm rich enough to freight my own stuff in over the Passes, and I will next year. Our business stops right now and for all time."

"I cannot object to that. You have three hundred thousand dollars in dust deposited with me. Go to Mr. Atsheler and draw it at once."

The man fumed impotently up and down. "Can't I get that other five hundred? Great God, man! I've paid for it! You don't intend me to starve?"

"Look here, Melton." Jacob Welse paused to knock the ash from his cigar. "At this very moment what are you working for? What are you trying to get?"

"A thousand pounds of grub."

"For your own stomach?"

The Bonanzo king nodded his head.

"Just so." The lines showed more sharply on Jacob Welse's forehead. "You are working for your own stomach. I am working for the stomachs of twenty thousand."

"But you filled Tim McReady's thousand pounds yesterday all right."

"The scale-down did not go into effect until to-day."

"But why am I the one to get it in the neck hard?"

"Why didn't you come yesterday, and Tim McReady to-day?"

Melton's face went blank, and Jacob Welse answered his own question with shrugging shoulders.

"That's the way it stands, Melton. No favoritism. If you hold me responsible for Tim McReady, I shall hold you responsible for not coming yesterday. Better we both throw it upon Providence. You went through the Forty Mile Famine. You are a white man. A Bonanzo property, or a block of Bonanzo properties, does not entitle you to a pound more than the oldest penniless 'sour-dough' or the newest baby born. Trust me. As long as I have a pound of grub you shall not starve. Stiffen up. Shake hands. Get a smile on your face and make the best of it."

Still savage of spirit, though rapidly toning down, the king shook hands and flung out of the room. Before the door could close on his heels, a loose-jointed Yankee shambled in, thrust a moccasined foot to the side and hooked a chair under him, and sat down.

"Say," he opened up, confidentially, "people's gittin' scairt over the grub proposition, I guess some."

"Hello, Dave. That you?"

"S'pose so. But ez I was saying there'll be a lively stampede fer the

Outside soon as the river freezes."

"Think so?"

"Unh huh."

"Then I'm glad to hear it. It's what the country needs. Going to join them?"

"Not in a thousand years." Dave Harney threw his head back with smug complacency. "Freighted my truck up to the mine yesterday. Wa'n't a bit too soon about it, either. But say . . . Suthin' happened to the sugar. Had it all on the last sled, an' jest where the trail turns off the Klondike into Bonanzo, what does that sled do but break through the ice! I never seen the beat of it—the last sled of all, an' all the sugar! So I jest thought I'd drop in to-day an' git a hundred pounds or so. White or brown, I ain't pertickler."

Jacob Welse shook his head and smiled, but Harney hitched his chair closer.

"The clerk of yourn said he didn't know, an' ez there wa'n't no call to pester him, I said I'd jest drop round an' see you. I don't care what it's wuth. Make it a hundred even; that'll do me handy.

"Say," he went on easily, noting the decidedly negative poise of the other's head. "I've got a tolerable sweet tooth, I have. Recollect the taffy I made over on Preacher Creek that time? I declare! how time does fly! That was all of six years ago if it's a day. More'n that, surely. Seven, by the Jimcracky! But ez I was sayin', I'd ruther do without my plug of 'Star' than sugar. An' about that sugar? Got my dogs outside. Better go round to the warehouse an' git it, eh? Pretty good idea."

But he saw the "No" shaping on Jacob Welse's lips, and hurried on before it could be uttered.

"Now, I don't want to hog it. Wouldn't do that fer the world. So if yer short, I can put up with seventy-five—" (he studied the other's face), "an' I might do with fifty. I 'preciate your position, an' I ain't low-down critter enough to pester—"

"What's the good of spilling words, Dave? We haven't a pound of sugar to spare—"

"Ez I was sayin', I ain't no hog; an' seein' 's it's you, Welse, I'll make to scrimp along on twenty-five—"

"Not an ounce!"

"Not the least leetle mite? Well, well, don't git het up. We'll jest fergit I ast you fer any, an' I'll drop round some likelier time. So long. Say!" He threw his jaw to one side and seemed to stiffen the muscles of his ear as he listened intently. "That's the Laura's whistle. She's startin' soon. Goin' to see her off? Come along."

Jacob Welse pulled on his bearskin coat and mittens, and they passed through the outer offices into the main store. So large was it, that the tenscore purchasers before the counters made no apparent crowd. Many were serious-faced, and more than one looked darkly at the head of the company as he passed. The clerks were selling everything except grub, and it was grub that was in demand. "Holding it for a rise. Famine prices," a red-whiskered miner sneered. Jacob Welse heard it, but took no notice. He expected to hear it many times and more unpleasantly ere the scare was over.

On the sidewalk he stopped to glance over the public bulletins posted against the side of the building. Dogs lost, found, and for sale occupied some space, but the rest was devoted to notices of sales of outfits. The timid were already growing frightened. Outfits of five hundred pounds were offering at a dollar a pound, without flour; others, with flour, at a dollar and a half. Jacob Welse saw Melton talking with an anxious-faced newcomer, and the satisfaction displayed by the Bonanzo king told that he had succeeded in filling his winter's cache.

"Why don't you smell out the sugar, Dave?" Jacob Welse asked, pointing to the bulletins.

Dave Harney looked his reproach. "Mebbe you think I ain't ben smellin'. I've clean wore my dogs out chasin' round from Klondike City to the Hospital. Can't git yer fingers on it fer love or money."

They walked down the block-long sidewalk, past the warehouse doors and the long teams of waiting huskies curled up in wolfish comfort in the snow. It was for this snow, the first permanent one of the fall, that the miners up-creek had waited to begin their freighting.

"Curious, ain't it?" Dave hazarded suggestively, as they crossed the main street to the river bank. "Mighty curious—me ownin' two five-hundred-foot Eldorado claims an' a fraction, wuth five millions if I'm wuth a cent, an' no sweetenin' fer my coffee or mush! Why, gosh-dang-it! this country kin go to blazes! I'll sell out! I'll quit it cold! I'll—I'll—go back to the States!"

"Oh, no, you won't," Jacob Welse answered. "I've heard you talk before. You put in a year up Stuart River on straight meat, if I haven't forgotten. And you ate salmon-belly and dogs up the Tanana, to say nothing of going through two famines; and you haven't turned your back on the country yet. And you never will. And you'll die here as sure as that's the Laura's spring being hauled aboard. And I look forward confidently to the day when I shall ship you out in a lead-lined box and burden the San Francisco end with the trouble of winding up your estate. You are a fixture, and you know it."

As he talked he constantly acknowledged greetings from the passers-by. Those who knew him were mainly old-timers and he knew them all by name, though there was scarcely a newcomer to whom his face was not familiar.

"I'll jest bet I'll be in Paris in 1900," the Eldorado king protested feebly.

But Jacob Welse did not hear. There was a jangling of gongs as McGregor saluted him from the pilot-house and the Laura slipped out from the bank. The men on the shore filled the air with good-luck farewells and last advice, but the three hundred grubless ones, turning their backs on the golden dream, were moody and dispirited, and made small response. The Laura backed out through a channel cut in the shore-ice, swung about in the current, and with a final blast put on full steam ahead.

The crowd thinned away and went about its business, leaving Jacob Welse the centre of a group of a dozen or so. The talk was of the famine, but it was the talk of men. Even Dave Harney forgot to curse the country for its sugar shortage, and waxed facetious over the newcomers,—*chechaquos*, he called them, having recourse to the Siwash tongue. In the midst of his remarks his quick eye lighted on a black speck floating down with the mush-ice of the river. "Jest look at that!" he cried. "A Peterborough canoe runnin' the ice!"

Twisting and turning, now paddling, now shoving clear of the floating cakes, the two men in the canoe worked in to the rim-ice, along the edge of which they drifted, waiting for an opening. Opposite the channel cut out by the steamer, they drove their paddles deep and darted into the calm dead water. The waiting group received them with open arms, helping them up the bank and carrying their shell after them.

In its bottom were two leather mail-pouches, a couple of blankets, coffee-pot and frying-pan, and a scant grub-sack. As for the men, so frosted were they, and so numb with the cold, that they could hardly stand. Dave Harney proposed whiskey, and was for haling them away at once; but one delayed long enough to shake stiff hands with Jacob Welse.

"She's coming," he announced. "Passed her boat an hour back. It ought to be round the bend any minute. I've got despatches for you, but I'll see you later. Got to get something into me first." Turning to go with Harney, he stopped suddenly and pointed up stream. "There she is now. Just coming out past the bluff."

"Run along, boys, an' git yer whiskey," Harney admonished him and his mate. "Tell 'm it's on me, double dose, an' jest excuse me not drinkin' with you, fer I'm goin' to stay."

The Klondike was throwing a thick flow of ice, partly mush and partly solid, and swept the boat out towards the middle of the Yukon. They could see the struggle plainly from the bank,—four men standing up and poling a way through the jarring cakes. A Yukon stove aboard was sending up a trailing pillar of blue smoke, and, as the boat drew closer, they could see a woman in the stern working the long steering-sweep. At sight of this there was a snap and sparkle in Jacob Welse's eyes. It was the first omen, and it was good, he thought. She was still a Welse; a struggler and a fighter. The years of her culture had not weakened her. Though tasting of the fruits of the first remove from the soil, she was not afraid of the soil; she could return to it gleefully and naturally.

So he mused till the boat drove in, ice-rimed and battered, against the edge of the rim-ice. The one white man aboard sprang out, painter in hand, to slow it down and work into the channel. But the rim-ice was formed of the night, and the front of it shelved off with him into the current. The nose of the boat sheered out under the pressure of a heavy cake, so that he came up at the stern. The woman's arm flashed over the side to his collar, and at the same instant, sharp and authoritative, her voice rang out to the Indian oarsmen to back water. Still holding the man's head above water, she threw her body against the sweep and guided the boat stern-foremost into the opening. A few more strokes and it grounded at the foot of the bank. She passed the collar of the chattering man to Dave Harney, who dragged him out and started him off on the trail of the mail-carriers.

Frona stood up, her cheeks glowing from the quick work. Jacob Welse hesitated. Though he stood within reach of the gunwale, a gulf of three years was between. The womanhood of twenty, added unto the girl of seventeen, made a sum more prodigious than he had imagined. He did not know whether to bear-hug the radiant young creature or to take her hand and help her ashore. But there was no apparent hitch, for she leaped beside him and was into his arms. Those above looked away to a man till the two came up the bank hand in hand.

"Gentlemen, my daughter." There was a great pride in his face.

Frona embraced them all with a comrade smile, and each man felt that for an instant her eyes had looked straight into his.

CHAPTER VII

That Vance Corliss wanted to see more of the girl he had divided blankets with, goes with the saying. He had not been wise enough to lug a camera into the country, but none the less, by a yet subtler process, a sun-picture had been recorded somewhere on his cerebral tissues. In the flash of an instant it had been done. A wave message of light and color, a molecular agitation and integration, a certain minute though definite corrugation in a brain recess,—and there it was, a picture complete! The blazing sunlight on the beetling black; a slender gray form, radiant, starting forward to the vision from the marge where light and darkness met; a fresh young morning smile wreathed in a flame of burning gold.

It was a picture he looked at often, and the more he looked the greater was his desire, to see Frona Welse again. This event he anticipated with a thrill, with the exultancy over change which is common of all life. She was something new, a fresh type, a woman unrelated to all women he had met. Out of the fascinating unknown a pair of hazel eyes smiled into his, and a hand, soft of touch and strong of grip, beckoned him. And there was an allurement about it which was as the allurement of sin.

Not that Vance Corliss was anybody's fool, nor that his had been an anchorite's existence; but that his upbringing, rather, had given his life a certain puritanical bent. Awakening intelligence and broader knowledge had weakened the early influence of an austere mother, but had not wholly eradicated it. It was there, deep down, very shadowy, but still a part of him. He could not get away from it. It distorted, ever so slightly, his concepts of things. It gave a squint to his perceptions, and very often, when the sex feminine was concerned, determined his classifications. He prided himself on his largeness when he granted that there were three kinds of women. His mother had only admitted two. But he had outgrown her. It was incontestable that there were three kinds,—the good, the bad, and the partly good and partly bad. That the last usually went bad, he believed firmly. In its very nature such a condition could not be permanent. It was the intermediary stage, marking the passage from high to low, from best to worst.

All of which might have been true, even as he saw it; but with definitions for premises, conclusions cannot fail to be dogmatic. What was good and bad? There it was. That was where his mother whispered with dead lips to him. Nor alone his mother, but divers conventional generations, even back to the sturdy ancestor who first uplifted from the soil and looked down. For Vance Corliss was many times removed from the red earth, and, though he did not know it, there was a clamor within him for a return lest he perish.

Not that he pigeon-holed Frona according to his inherited definitions. He refused to classify her at all. He did not dare. He preferred to pass judgment later, when he had gathered more data. And there was the allurement, the gathering of the data; the great critical point where purity reaches dreamy hands towards pitch and refuses to call it pitch—till defiled. No; Vance Corliss was not a cad. And since purity is merely a relative term, he was not pure. That there was no pitch under his nails was not because he had manicured diligently, but because it had not been his luck to run across any pitch. He was not good because he chose to be, because evil was repellant; but because he had not had opportunity to become evil. But from this, on the other hand, it is not to be argued that he would have gone bad had he had a chance.

He was a product of the sheltered life. All his days had been lived in a sanitary dwelling; the plumbing was excellent. The air he had breathed had been mostly ozone artificially manufactured. He had been sun-bathed in balmy weather, and brought in out of the wet when it rained. And when he reached the age of choice he had been too fully occupied to deviate from the straight path, along which his mother had taught him to creep and toddle, and along which he now proceeded to walk upright, without thought of what lay on either side.

Vitality cannot be used over again. If it be expended on one thing, there is none left for the other thing. And so with Vance Corliss. Scholarly lucubrations and healthy exercises during his college days had consumed all the energy his normal digestion extracted from a wholesome omnivorous diet.

When he did discover a bit of surplus energy, he worked it off in the society of his mother and of the conventional minds and prim teas she surrounded herself with. Result: A very nice young man, of whom no maid's mother need ever be in trepidation; a very strong young man, whose substance had not been wasted in riotous living; a very learned young man, with a Freiberg mining engineer's diploma and a B.A. sheepskin from Yale; and, lastly, a very self-centred, self-possessed young man.

Now his greatest virtue lay in this: he had not become hardened in the mould baked by his several forbears and into which he had been pressed by his mother's hands. Some atavism had been at work in the making of him, and he had reverted to that ancestor who sturdily uplifted. But so far this portion of his heritage had lain dormant. He had simply remained adjusted to a stable environment. There had been no call upon the adaptability which was his. But whensoever the call came, being so constituted, it was manifest that he should adapt, should adjust himself to the unwonted pressure of new conditions. The maxim of the rolling stone may be all true; but notwithstanding, in the scheme of life, the inability to become fixed is an excellence par excellence. Though he did not know it, this inability was Vance Corliss's most splendid possession.

But to return. He looked forward with great sober glee to meeting Frona Welse, and in the meanwhile consulted often the sun-picture he carried of her. Though he went over the Pass and down the lakes and river with a push of money behind him (London syndicates are never niggardly in such matters). Frona beat him into Dawson by a fortnight. While on his part money in the end overcame obstacles, on hers the name of Welse was a talisman greater than treasure. After his arrival, a couple of weeks were consumed in buying a cabin, presenting his letters of introduction, and settling down. But all things come in the fulness of time, and so, one night after the river closed, he pointed his moccasins in the direction of Jacob Welse's house. Mrs. Schoville, the Gold Commissioner's wife, gave him the honor of her company.

Corliss wanted to rub his eyes. Steam-heating apparatus in the Klondike! But the next instant he had passed out of the hall through the heavy portieres and stood inside the drawing-room. And it was a drawing-room. His moose-hide moccasins sank luxuriantly into the deep carpet, and his eyes were caught by a Turner sunrise on the opposite wall. And there were other paintings and things in bronze. Two Dutch fireplaces were roaring full with huge back-logs of spruce. There was a piano; and somebody was singing. Frona sprang from the stool and came forward, greeting him with both hands. He had thought his sun-picture perfect, but this fire-picture, this young creature with the flush and warmth of ringing life, quite eclipsed it. It was a whirling moment, as he held her two hands in his, one of those moments when an incomprehensible orgasm quickens the blood and dizzies the brain. Though the first syllables came to him faintly, Mrs. Schoville's voice brought him back to himself.

"Oh!" she cried. "You know him!"

And Frona answered, "Yes, we met on the Dyea Trail; and those who meet on the Dyea Trail can never forget."

"How romantic!"

The Gold Commissioner's wife clapped her hands. Though fat and forty, and phlegmatic of temperament, between exclamations and hand-clappings her waking existence was mostly explosive. Her husband secretly averred that did God Himself design to meet her face to face, she would smite together her chubby hands and cry out, "How romantic!"

"How did it happen?" she continued. "He didn't rescue you over a cliff, or that sort of thing, did he? Do say that he did! And you never said a word about it, Mr. Corliss. Do tell me. I'm just dying to know!"

"Oh, nothing like that," he hastened to answer. "Nothing much. I, that is we—"

He felt a sinking as Frona interrupted. There was no telling what this remarkable girl might say.

"He gave me of his hospitality, that was all," she said. "And I can vouch for his fried potatoes; while for his coffee, it is excellent—when one is very hungry."

"Ingrate!" he managed to articulate, and thereby to gain a smile, ere he was introduced to a cleanly built lieutenant of the Mounted Police, who stood by the fireplace discussing the grub proposition with a dapper little man very much out of place in a white shirt and stiff collar.

Thanks to the particular niche in society into which he happened to be born, Corliss drifted about easily from group to group, and was much envied therefore by Del Bishop, who sat stiffly in the first chair he had dropped into, and who was waiting patiently for the first person to take leave that he might know how to compass the manoeuvre. In his mind's eye he had figured most of it out, knew just how many steps required to carry him to the door, was certain he would have to say good-by to Frona, but did not know whether or not he was supposed to shake hands all around. He had just dropped in to see Frona and say "Howdee," as he expressed it, and had unwittingly found himself in company.

Corliss, having terminated a buzz with a Miss Mortimer on the decadence of the French symbolists, encountered Del Bishop. But the pocket-miner remembered him at once from the one glimpse he had caught of Corliss standing by his tent-door in Happy Camp. Was almighty obliged to him for his night's hospitality to Miss Frona, seein' as he'd ben side-tracked down the line; that any kindness to her was a kindness to him; and that he'd remember it, by God, as long as he had a corner of a blanket to pull over him. Hoped it hadn't put him out. Miss Frona'd said that bedding was scarce, but it wasn't a cold night (more blowy than crisp), so he reckoned there couldn't 'a' ben much shiverin'. All of which struck Corliss as perilous, and he broke away at the first opportunity, leaving the pocket-miner yearning for the door.

But Dave Harney, who had not come by mistake, avoided gluing himself to the first chair. Being an Eldorado king, he had felt it incumbent to assume the position in society to which his numerous millions entitled him; and though unused all his days to social amenities other than the out-hanging latch-string and the general pot, he had succeeded to his own satisfaction as a knight of the carpet. Quick to take a cue, he circulated with an aplomb which his striking garments and long shambling gait only heightened, and talked choppy and disconnected fragments with whomsoever he ran up against. The Miss Mortimer, who spoke Parisian French, took him aback with her symbolists; but he evened matters up with a goodly measure of the bastard lingo of the Canadian *voyageurs*, and left her gasping and meditating over a proposition to sell him twenty-five pounds of sugar, white or brown. But she was not unduly favored, for with everybody he adroitly turned the conversation to grub, and then led up to the eternal proposition. "Sugar or bust," he would conclude gayly each time and wander on to the next.

But he put the capstone on his social success by asking Frona to sing the touching ditty, "I Left My Happy Home for You." This was something beyond her, though she had him hum over the opening bars so that she could furnish the accompaniment. His voice was more strenuous than sweet, and Del Bishop, discovering himself at last, joined in raucously on the choruses. This made him feel so much better that he disconnected himself from the chair, and when he finally got home he kicked up his sleepy tent-mate to tell him about the high time he'd had over at the Welse's. Mrs. Schoville tittered and thought it all so unique, and she thought it so unique several times more when the lieutenant of Mounted Police and a couple of compatriots roared "Rule Britannia" and "God Save the Queen," and the Americans responded with "My Country, 'Tis of Thee" and "John Brown." Then big Alec Beaubien, the Circle City king, demanded the "Marseillaise," and the company broke up chanting "Die Wacht am Rhein" to the frosty night.

"Don't come on these nights," Frona whispered to Corliss at parting.

"We haven't spoken three words, and I know we shall be good friends. Did Dave Harney succeed in getting any sugar out of you?"

They mingled their laughter, and Corliss went home under the aurora borealis, striving to reduce his impressions to some kind of order.

CHAPTER VIII

"And why should I not be proud of my race?"

Frona's cheeks were flushed and her eyes sparkling. They had both been harking back to childhood, and she had been telling Corliss of her mother, whom she faintly remembered. Fair and flaxen-haired, typically Saxon, was the likeness she had drawn, filled out largely with knowledge gained from her father and from old Andy of the Dyea Post. The discussion had then turned upon the race in general, and Frona had said things in the heat of enthusiasm which affected the more conservative mind of Corliss as dangerous and not solidly based on fact. He deemed himself too large for race egotism and insular prejudice, and had seen fit to laugh at her immature convictions.

"It's a common characteristic of all peoples," he proceeded, "to consider themselves superior races,—a naive, natural egoism, very healthy and very good, but none the less manifestly untrue. The Jews conceived themselves to be God's chosen people, and they still so conceive themselves—"

"And because of it they have left a deep mark down the page of history," she interrupted.

"But time has not proved the stability of their conceptions. And you must also view the other side. A superior people must look upon all others as inferior peoples. This comes home to you. To be a Roman were greater than to be a king, and when the Romans rubbed against your savage ancestors in the German forests, they elevated their brows and said, 'An inferior people, barbarians.'"

"But we are here, now. We are, and the Romans are not. The test is time. So far we have stood the test; the signs are favorable that we shall continue to stand it. We are the best fitted!"

"Egotism."

"But wait. Put it to the test."

As she spoke her hand flew out impulsively to his. At the touch his heart pulsed upward, there was a rush Of blood and a tightening across the temples. Ridiculous, but delightful, he thought. At this rate he could argue with her the night through.

"The test," she repeated, withdrawing her hand without embarrassment. "We are a race of doers and fighters, of globe-encirclers and zone-conquerors. We toil and struggle, and stand by the toil and struggle no matter how hopeless it may be. While we are persistent and resistant, we are so made that we fit ourselves to the most diverse conditions. Will the Indian, the Negro, or the Mongol ever conquer the Teuton? Surely not! The Indian has persistence without variability; if he does not modify he dies, if he does try to modify he dies anyway. The Negro has adaptability, but he is servile and must be led. As for the Chinese, they are permanent. All that the other races are not, the Anglo-Saxon, or Teuton if you please, is. All that the other races have not, the Teuton has. What race is to rise up and overwhelm us?"

"Ah, you forget the Slav," Corliss suggested slyly.

"The Slav!" Her face fell. "True, the Slav! The only stripling in this world of young men and gray-beards! But he is still in the future, and in the future the decision rests. In the mean time we prepare. If may be we shall have such a start that we shall prevent him growing. You know, because he was better skilled in chemistry, knew how to manufacture gunpowder, that the Spaniard destroyed the Aztec. May not we, who are possessing ourselves of the world and its resources, and gathering to ourselves all its knowledge, may not we nip the Slav ere he grows a thatch to his lip?"

Vance Corliss shook his head non-committally, and laughed.

"Oh! I know I become absurd and grow over-warm!" she exclaimed. "But after all, one reason that we are the salt of the earth is because we have the courage to say so."

"And I am sure your warmth spreads," he responded. "See, I'm beginning to glow myself. We are not God's, but Nature's chosen people, we Angles, and Saxons, and Normans, and Vikings, and the earth is our heritage. Let us arise and go forth!"

"Now you are laughing at me, and, besides, we have already gone forth. Why have you fared into the north, if not to lay hands on the race legacy?"

She turned her head at the sound of approaching footsteps, and cried for greeting, "I appeal to you, Captain Alexander! I summon you to bear witness!"

The captain of police smiled in his sternly mirthful fashion as he shook hands with Frona and Corliss. "Bear witness?" he questioned. "Ah, yes!

"'Bear witness, O my comrades, what a hard-bit gang were we,—

The servants of the sweep-head, but the masters of the sea!'"

He quoted the verse with a savage solemnity exulting through his deep voice. This, and the appositeness of it, quite carried Frona away, and she had both his hands in hers on the instant. Corliss was aware of an inward wince at the action. It was uncomfortable. He did not like to see her so promiscuous with those warm, strong hands of hers. Did she so favor all men who delighted her by word or deed? He did not mind her fingers closing round his, but somehow it seemed wanton when shared with the next comer. By the time he had thought thus far, Frona had explained the topic under discussion, and Captain Alexander was testifying.

"I don't know much about your Slav and other kin, except that they are good workers and strong; but I do know that the white man is the greatest and best *breed* in the world. Take the Indian, for instance. The white man comes along and beats him at all his games, outworks him, out-roughs him, out-fishes him, out-hunts him. As far back as their myths go, the Alaskan Indians have packed on their backs. But the gold-rushers, as soon as they had learned the tricks of the trade, packed greater loads and packed them farther than did the Indians. Why, last May, the Queen's birthday, we had sports on the river. In the one, two, three, four, and five men canoe races we beat the Indians right and left. Yet they had been born to the paddle, and most of us had never seen a canoe until man-grown."

"But why is it?" Corliss queried.

"I do not know why. I only know that it is. I simply bear witness. I do know that we do what they cannot do, and what they can do, we do better."

Frona nodded her head triumphantly at Corliss. "Come, acknowledge your defeat, so that we may go in to dinner. Defeat for the time being, at least. The concrete facts of paddles and pack-straps quite overcome your dogmatics. Ah, I thought so. More time? All the time in the world. But let us go in. We'll see what my father thinks of it,—and Mr. Kellar. A symposium on Anglo-Saxon supremacy!"

Frost and enervation are mutually repellant. The Northland gives a keenness and zest to the blood which cannot be obtained in warmer climes. Naturally so, then, the friendship which sprang up between Corliss and Frona was anything but languid. They met often under her father's roof-tree, and went many places together. Each found a pleasurable attraction in the other, and a satisfaction which the things they were not in accord with could not mar. Frona liked the man because he was a man. In her wildest flights she could never imagine linking herself with any man, no matter how exalted spiritually, who was not a man physically. It was a delight to her and a joy to look upon the strong males of her kind, with bodies comely in the sight of God and muscles swelling with the promise of deeds and work. Man, to her, was preeminently a fighter. She believed in natural selection and in sexual selection, and was certain that if man had thereby become possessed of faculties and functions, they were for him to use and could but tend to his good. And likewise with instincts. If she felt drawn to any person or thing, it was good for her to be so drawn, good for herself. If she felt impelled to joy in a well-built frame and well-shaped muscle, why should she restrain? Why should she not love the body, and without shame? The history of the race, and of all races, sealed her choice with approval. Down all time, the weak and effeminate males had vanished from the world-stage. Only the strong could inherit the earth. She had been born of the strong, and she chose to cast her lot with the strong.

Yet of all creatures, she was the last to be deaf and blind to the things of the spirit. But the things of the spirit she demanded should be likewise strong. No halting, no stuttered utterance, tremulous waiting, minor wailing! The mind and the soul must be as quick and definite and certain as the body. Nor was the spirit made alone for immortal dreaming. Like the flesh, it must strive and toil. It must be workaday as well as idle day. She could understand a weakling singing sweetly and even greatly, and in so far she could love him for his sweetness and greatness; but her love would have fuller measure were he strong of body as well. She believed she was just. She gave the flesh its due and the spirit its due; but she had, over and above, her own choice, her own individual ideal. She liked to see the two go hand in hand. Prophecy and dyspepsia did not affect her as a felicitous admixture. A splendid savage and a weak-kneed poet! She could admire the one for his brawn and the other for his song; but she would prefer that they had been made one in the beginning.

As to Vance Corliss. First, and most necessary of all, there was that physiological affinity between them that made the touch of his hand a pleasure to her. Though souls may rush together, if body cannot endure body, happiness is reared on sand and the structure will be ever unstable and tottery. Next, Corliss had the physical potency of the hero without the grossness of the brute. His muscular development was more qualitative than quantitative, and it is the qualitative development which gives rise to beauty of form. A giant need not be proportioned in the mould; nor a thew be symmetrical to be massive.

And finally,—none the less necessary but still finally,—Vance Corliss was neither spiritually dead nor decadent. He affected her as fresh and wholesome and strong, as reared above the soil but not scorning the soil. Of course, none of this she reasoned out otherwise than by subconscious processes. Her conclusions were feelings, not thoughts.

Though they quarrelled and disagreed on innumerable things, deep down, underlying all, there was a permanent unity. She liked him for a certain stern soberness that was his, and for his saving grace of humor. Seriousness and banter were not incompatible. She liked him for his gallantry, made to work with and not for display. She liked the spirit of his offer at Happy Camp, when he proposed giving her an Indian guide and passage-money back to the United States. He could *do* as well as talk. She liked him for his outlook, for his innate liberality, which she felt to be there, somehow, no matter that often he was narrow of expression. She liked him for his mind. Though somewhat academic, somewhat tainted with latter-day scholasticism, it was still a mind which permitted him to be classed with the "Intellectuals." He was capable of divorcing sentiment and emotion from reason. Granted that he included all the factors, he could not go wrong. And here was where she found chief fault with him,—his narrowness which precluded all the factors; his narrowness which gave the lie to the breadth she knew was really his. But she was aware that it was not an irremediable defect, and that the new life he was leading was very apt to rectify it. He was filled with culture; what he needed was a few more of life's facts.

And she liked him for himself, which is quite different from liking the parts which went to compose him. For it is no miracle for two things, added together, to produce not only the sum of themselves, but a third thing which is not to be found in either of them. So with him. She liked him for himself, for that something which refused to stand out as a part, or a sum of parts; for that something which is the corner-stone of Faith and which has ever baffled Philosophy and Science. And further, to like, with Frona Welse, did not mean to love.

First, and above all, Vance Corliss was drawn to Frona Welse because of the clamor within him for a return to the soil. In him the elements were so mixed that it was impossible for women many times removed to find favor in his eyes. Such he had met constantly, but not one had ever drawn from him a superfluous heart-beat. Though there had been in him a growing instinctive knowledge of lack of unity,—the lack of unity which must precede, always, the love of man and woman,—not one of the daughters of Eve he had met had flashed irresistibly in to fill the void. Elective affinity, sexual affinity, or whatsoever the intangible essence known as love is, had never been manifest. When he met Frona it had at once sprung, full-fledged, into existence. But he quite misunderstood it, took it for a mere attraction towards the new and unaccustomed.

Many men, possessed of birth and *breed*ing, have yielded to this clamor for return. And giving the apparent lie to their own sanity and moral stability, many such men have married peasant girls or barmaids, And those to whom evil apportioned itself have been prone to distrust the impulse they obeyed, forgetting that nature makes or mars the individual for the sake, always, of the type. For in every such case of return, the impulse was sound,—only that time and space interfered, and propinquity determined whether the object of choice should be bar-maid or peasant girl.

Happily for Vance Corliss, time and space were propitious, and in Frona he found the culture he could not do without, and the clean sharp tang of the earth he needed. In so far as her education and culture went, she was an astonishment. He had met the scientifically smattered young woman before, but Frona had something more than smattering. Further, she gave new life to old facts, and her interpretations of common things were coherent and vigorous and new. Though his acquired conservatism was alarmed and cried danger, he could not remain cold to the charm of her philosophizing, while her scholarly attainments were fully redeemed by her enthusiasm. Though he could not agree with much that she passionately held, he yet recognized that the passion of sincerity and enthusiasm was good.

But her chief fault, in his eyes, was her unconventionality. Woman was something so inexpressibly sacred to him, that he could not bear to see any good woman venturing where the footing was precarious. Whatever good woman thus ventured, overstepping the metes and bounds of sex and status, he deemed did so of wantonness. And wantonness of such order was akin to—well, he could not say it when thinking of Frona, though she hurt him often by her unwise acts. However, he only felt such hurts when away from her. When with her, looking into her eyes which always looked back, or at greeting and parting pressing her hand which always pressed honestly, it seemed certain that there was in her nothing but goodness and truth.

And then he liked her in many different ways for many different things. For her impulses, and for her passions which were always elevated. And already, from breathing the Northland air, he had come to like her for that comradeship which at first had shocked him. There were other acquired likings, her lack of prudishness, for instance, which he awoke one day to find that he had previously confounded with lack of modesty. And it was only the day before that day that he drifted, before he thought, into a discussion with her of "Camille." She had seen Bernhardt, and dwelt lovingly on the recollection. He went home afterwards, a dull pain gnawing at his heart, striving to reconcile Frona with the ideal impressed upon him by his mother that innocence was another term for ignorance. Notwithstanding, by the following day he had worked it out and loosened another finger of the maternal grip.

He liked the flame of her hair in the sunshine, the glint of its gold by the firelight, and the waywardness of it and the glory. He liked her neat-shod feet and the gray-gaitered calves,—alas, now hidden in long-skirted Dawson. He liked her for the strength of her slenderness; and to walk with her, swinging her step and stride to his, or to merely watch her come across a room or down the street, was a delight. Life and the joy of life romped through her blood, abstemiously filling out and rounding off each shapely muscle and soft curve. And he liked it all. Especially he liked the swell of her forearm, which rose firm and strong and tantalizing and sought shelter all too quickly under the loose-flowing sleeve.

The co-ordination of physical with spiritual beauty is very strong in normal men, and so it was with Vance Corliss. That he liked the one was no reason that he failed to appreciate the other. He liked Frona for both, and for herself as well. And to like, with him, though he did not know it, was to love.

CHAPTER IX

Vance Corliss proceeded at a fair rate to adapt himself to the Northland life, and he found that many adjustments came easy. While his own tongue was alien to the brimstone of the Lord, he became quite used to strong language on the part of other men, even in the most genial conversation. Carthey, a little Texan who went to work for him for a while, opened or closed every second sentence, on an average, with the mild expletive, "By damn!" It was also his invariable way of expressing surprise, disappointment, consternation, or all the rest of the tribe of sudden emotions. By pitch and stress and intonation, the protean oath was made to perform every function of ordinary speech. At first it was a constant source of irritation and disgust to Corliss, but erelong he grew not only to tolerate it, but to like it, and to wait for it eagerly. Once, Carthey's wheel-dog lost an ear in a hasty contention with a dog of the Hudson Bay, and when the young fellow bent over the animal and discovered the loss, the blended endearment and pathos of the "by damn" which fell from his lips was a relation to Corliss. All was not evil out of Nazareth, he concluded sagely, and, like Jacob Welse of old, revised his philosophy of life accordingly.

Again, there were two sides to the social life of Dawson. Up at the Barracks, at the Welse's, and a few other places, all men of standing were welcomed and made comfortable by the womenkind of like standing. There were teas, and dinners, and dances, and socials for charity, and the usual run of things; all of which, however, failed to wholly satisfy the men. Down in the town there was a totally different though equally popular other side. As the country was too young for club-life, the masculine portion of the community expressed its masculinity by herding together in the saloons,— the ministers and missionaries being the only exceptions to this mode of expression. Business appointments and deals were made and consummated in the saloons, enterprises projected, shop talked, the latest news discussed, and a general good fellowship maintained. There all life rubbed shoulders, and kings and dog-drivers, old-timers and *chechaquos*, met on a common level. And it so happened, probably because saw-mills and house-space were scarce, that the saloons accommodated the gambling tables and the polished dance-house floors. And here, because he needs must bend to custom, Corliss's adaptation went on rapidly. And as Carthey, who appreciated him, soliloquized, "The best of it is he likes it damn well, by damn!"

But any adjustment must have its painful periods, and while Corliss's general change went on smoothly, in the particular case of Frona it was different. She had a code of her own, quite unlike that of the community, and perhaps believed woman might do things at which even the saloon-inhabiting males would be shocked. And because of this, she and Corliss had their first disagreeable disagreement.

Frona loved to run with the dogs through the biting frost, cheeks tingling, blood bounding, body thrust forward, and limbs rising and falling ceaselessly to the pace. And one November day, with the first cold snap on and the spirit thermometer frigidly marking sixty-five below, she got out the sled, harnessed her team of huskies, and flew down the river trail. As soon as she cleared the town she was off and running. And in such manner, running and riding by turns, she swept through the Indian village below the bluffs, made an eight-mile circle up Moosehide Creek and back, crossed the river on the ice, and several hours later came flying up the west bank of the Yukon opposite the town. She was aiming to tap and return by the trail for the wood-sleds which crossed thereabout, but a mile away from it she ran into the soft snow and brought the winded dogs to a walk.

Along the rim of the river and under the frown of the overhanging cliffs, she directed the path she was breaking. Here and there she made detours to avoid the out-jutting talus, and at other times followed the ice in against the precipitous walls and hugged them closely around the abrupt bends. And so, at the head of her huskies, she came suddenly upon a woman sitting in the snow and gazing across the river at smoke-canopied Dawson. She had been crying, and this was sufficient to prevent Frona's scrutiny from wandering farther. A tear, turned to a globule of ice, rested on her cheek, and her eyes were dim and moist; there was an-expression of hopeless, fathomless woe.

"Oh!" Frona cried, stopping the dogs and coming up to her. "You are hurt? Can I help you?" she queried, though the stranger shook her head. "But you mustn't sit there. It is nearly seventy below, and you'll freeze in a few minutes. Your cheeks are bitten already." She rubbed the afflicted parts vigorously with a mitten of snow, and then looked down on the warm returning glow.

"I beg pardon." The woman rose somewhat stiffly to her feet. "And I thank you, but I am perfectly warm, you see" (settling the fur cape more closely about her with a snuggling movement), "and I had just sat down for the moment."

Frona noted that she was very beautiful, and her woman's eye roved over and took in the splendid furs, the make of the gown, and the bead-work of the moccasins which peeped from beneath. And in view of all this, and of the fact that the face was unfamiliar, she felt an instinctive desire to shrink back.

"And I haven't hurt myself," the woman went on. "Just a mood, that was all, looking out over the dreary endless white."

"Yes," Frona replied, mastering herself; "I can understand. There must be much of sadness in such a landscape, only it never comes that way to me. The sombreness and the sternness of it appeal to me, but not the sadness."

"And that is because the lines of our lives have been laid in different places," the other ventured, reflectively. "It is not what the landscape is, but what we are. If we were not, the landscape would remain, but without human significance. That is what we invest it with.

"'Truth is within ourselves; it takes no rise

From outward things, whate'er you may believe.'"

Frona's eyes brightened, and she went on to complete the passage:

"'There is an inmost centre in us all,

Where truth abides in fulness; and around.'

"And—and—how does it go? I have forgotten."

"'Wall upon wall, the gross flesh hems it in—'"

The woman ceased abruptly, her voice trilling off into silvery laughter with a certain bitter reckless ring to it which made Frona inwardly shiver. She moved as though to go back to her dogs, but the woman's hand went out in a familiar gesture,—twin to Frona's own,—which went at once to Frona's heart.

"Stay a moment," she said, with an undertone of pleading in the words, "and talk with me. It is long since I have met a woman"—she paused while her tongue wandered for the word—"who could quote 'Paracelsus.' You are,—I know you, you see,—you are Jacob Welse's daughter, Frona Welse, I believe."

Frona nodded her identity, hesitated, and looked at the woman with secret intentness. She was conscious of a great and pardonable curiosity, of a frank out-reaching for fuller knowledge. This creature, so like, so different; old as the oldest race, and young as the last rose-tinted babe; flung far as the farthermost fires of men, and eternal as humanity itself—where were they unlike, this woman and she? Her five senses told her not; by every law of life they were no; only, only by the fast-drawn lines of social caste and social wisdom were they not the same. So she thought, even as for one searching moment she studied the other's face. And in the situation she found an uplifting awfulness, such as comes when the veil is thrust aside and one gazes on the mysteriousness of Deity. She remembered: "Her feet take hold of hell; her house is the way to the grave, going down to the chamber of death," and in the same instant strong upon her was the vision of the familiar gesture with which the woman's hand had gone out in mute appeal, and she looked aside, out over the dreary endless white, and for her, too, the day became filled with sadness.

She gave an involuntary, half-nervous shiver, though she said, naturally enough, "Come, let us walk on and get the blood moving again. I had no idea it was so cold till I stood still." She turned to the dogs: "Mush-on! King! You Sandy! Mush!" And back again to the woman, "I am quite chilled, and as for you, you must be—"

"Quite warm, of course. You have been running and your clothes are wet against you, while I have kept up the needful circulation and no more. I saw you when you leaped off the sled below the hospital and vanished down the river like a Diana of the snows. How I envied you! You must enjoy it."

"Oh, I do," Frona answered, simply. "I was raised with the dogs."

"It savors of the Greek."

Frona did not reply, and they walked on in silence. Yet Frona wished, though she dared not dare, that she could give her tongue free rein, and from out of the other's bitter knowledge, for her own soul's sake and sanity, draw the pregnant human generalizations which she must possess. And over her welled a wave of pity and distress; and she felt a discomfort, for she knew not what to say or how to voice her heart. And when the other's speech broke forth, she hailed it with a great relief.

"Tell me," the woman demanded, half-eagerly, half-masterly, "tell me about yourself. You are new to the Inside. Where were you before you came in? Tell me."

So the difficulty was solved, in a way, and Frona talked on about herself, with a successfully feigned girlhood innocence, as though she did not appreciate the other or understand her ill-concealed yearning for that which she might not have, but which was Frona's.

"There is the trail you are trying to connect with." They had rounded the last of the cliffs, and Frona's companion pointed ahead to where the walls receded and wrinkled to a gorge, out of which the sleds drew the firewood across the river to town. "I shall leave you there," she concluded.

"But are you not going back to Dawson?" Frona queried. "It is growing late, and you had better not linger."

"No . . . I . . ."

Her painful hesitancy brought Frona to a realization of her own thoughtlessness. But she had made the step, and she knew she could not retrace it.

"We will go back together," she said, bravely. And in candid all-knowledge of the other, "I do not mind."

Then it was that the blood surged into the woman's cold face, and her hand went out to the girl in the old, old way.

"No, no, I beg of you," she stammered. "I beg of you . . . I . . . I prefer to continue my walk a little farther. See! Some one is coming now!"

By this time they had reached the wood-trail, and Frona's face was flaming as the other's had flamed. A light sled, dogs a-lope and swinging down out of the gorge, was just upon them. A man was running with the team, and he waved his hand to the two women.

"Vance!" Frona exclaimed, as he threw his lead-dogs in the snow and brought the sled to a halt. "What are you doing over here? Is the syndicate bent upon cornering the firewood also?"

"No. We're not so bad as that." His face was full of smiling happiness at the meeting as he shook hands with her. "But Carthey is leaving me,—going prospecting somewhere around the North Pole, I believe,—and I came across to look up Del Bishop, if he'll serve."

He turned his head to glance expectantly at her companion, and she saw the smile go out of his face and anger come in. Frona was helplessly aware that she had no grip over the situation, and, though a rebellion at the cruelty and injustice of it was smouldering somewhere deep down, she could only watch the swift culmination of the little tragedy. The woman met his gaze with a half-shrinking, as from an impending blow, and with a softness of expression which entreated pity. But he regarded her long and coldly, then deliberately turned his back. As he did this, Frona noted her face go tired and gray, and the hardness and recklessness of her laughter were there painted in harsh tones, and a bitter devil rose up and lurked in her eyes. It was evident that the same bitter devil rushed hotly to her tongue. But it chanced just then that she glanced at Frona, and all expression was brushed from her face save the infinite tiredness. She smiled wistfully at the girl, and without a word turned and went down the trail.

And without a word Frona sprang upon her sled and was off. The way was wide, and Corliss swung in his dogs abreast of hers. The smouldering rebellion flared up, and she seemed to gather to herself some of the woman's recklessness.

"You brute!"

The words left her mouth, sharp, clear-cut, breaking the silence like the lash of a whip. The unexpectedness of it, and the savagery, took Corliss aback. He did not know what to do or say.

"Oh, you coward! You coward!"

"Frona! Listen to me—"

But she cut him off. "No. Do not speak. You can have nothing to say. You have behaved abominably. I am disappointed in you. It is horrible! horrible!"

"Yes, it was horrible,—horrible that she should walk with you, have speech with you, be seen with you."

"'Not until the sun excludes you, do I exclude you,'" she flung back at him.

"But there is a fitness of things—"

"Fitness!" She turned upon him and loosed her wrath. "If she is unfit, are you fit? May you cast the first stone with that smugly sanctimonious air of yours?"

"You shall not talk to me in this fashion. I'll not have it."

He clutched at her sled, and even in the midst of her anger she noticed it with a little thrill of pleasure.

"Shall not? You coward!"

He reached out as though to lay hands upon her, and she raised her coiled whip to strike. But to his credit he never flinched; his white face calmly waited to receive the blow. Then she deflected the stroke, and the long lash hissed out and fell among the dogs. Swinging the whip briskly, she rose to her knees on the sled and called frantically to the animals. Hers was the better team, and she shot rapidly away from Corliss. She wished to get away, not so much from him as from herself, and she encouraged the huskies into wilder and wilder speed. She took the steep river-bank in full career and dashed like a whirlwind through the town and home. Never in her life had she been in such a condition; never had she experienced such terrible anger. And not only was she already ashamed, but she was frightened and afraid of herself.

CHAPTER X

The next morning Corliss was knocked out of a late bed by Bash, one of Jacob Welse's Indians. He was the bearer of a brief little note from Frona, which contained a request for the mining engineer to come and see her at his first opportunity. That was all that was said, and he pondered over it deeply. What did she wish to say to him? She was still such an unknown quantity,—and never so much as now in the light of the day before,—that he could not guess. Did she desire to give him his dismissal on a definite, well-understood basis? To take advantage of her sex and further humiliate him? To tell him what she thought of him in coolly considered, cold-measured terms? Or was she penitently striving to make amends for the unmerited harshness she had dealt him? There was neither contrition nor anger in the note, no clew, nothing save a formally worded desire to see him.

So it was in a rather unsettled and curious frame of mind that he walked in upon her as the last hour of the morning drew to a close. He was neither on his dignity nor off, his attitude being strictly non-committal against the moment she should disclose hers. But without beating about the bush, in that way of hers which he had come already to admire, she at once showed her colors and came frankly forward to him. The first glimpse of her face told him, the first feel of her hand, before she had said a word, told him that all was well.

"I am glad you have come," she began. "I could not be at peace with myself until I had seen you and told you how sorry I am for yesterday, and how deeply ashamed I—"

"There, there. It's not so bad as all that." They were still standing, and he took a step nearer to her. "I assure you I can appreciate your side of it; and though, looking at it theoretically, it was the highest conduct, demanding the fullest meed of praise, still, in all frankness, there is much to—to—"

"Yes."

"Much to deplore in it from the social stand-point. And unhappily, we cannot leave the social stand-point out of our reckoning. But so far as I may speak for myself, you have done nothing to feel sorry for or be ashamed of."

"It is kind of you," she cried, graciously. "Only it is not true, and you know it is not true. You know that you acted for the best; you know that I hurt you, insulted you; you know that I behaved like a fish-wife, and you do know that I disgusted you—"

"No, no!" He raised his hand as though to ward from her the blows she dealt herself.

"But yes, yes. And I have all reason in the world to be ashamed. I can only say this in defence: the woman had affected me deeply—so deeply that I was close to weeping. Then you came on the scene,—you know what you did,—and the sorrow for her bred an indignation against you, and—well, I worked myself into a nervous condition such as I had never experienced in my life. It was hysteria, I suppose. Anyway, I was not myself."

"We were neither of us ourselves."

"Now you are untrue. I did wrong, but you were yourself, as much so then as now. But do be seated. Here we stand as though you were ready to run away at first sign of another outbreak."

"Surely you are not so terrible!" he laughed, adroitly pulling his chair into position so that the light fell upon her face.

"Rather, you are not such a coward. I must have been terrible yesterday. I—I almost struck you. And you were certainly brave when the whip hung over you. Why, you did not even attempt to raise a hand and shield yourself."

"I notice the dogs your whip falls among come nevertheless to lick your hand and to be petted."

"Ergo?" she queried, audaciously.

"Ergo, it all depends," he equivocated.

"And, notwithstanding, I am forgiven?"

"As I hope to be forgiven."

"Then I am glad—only, you have done nothing to be forgiven for. You acted according to your light, and I to mine, though it must be acknowledged that mine casts the broader flare. Ah! I have it," clapping her hands in delight, "I was not angry with you yesterday; nor did I behave rudely to you, or even threaten you. It was utterly impersonal, the whole of it. You simply stood for society, for the type which aroused my indignation and anger; and, as its representative, you bore the brunt of it. Don't you see?"

"I see, and cleverly put; only, while you escape the charge of maltreating me yesterday; you throw yourself open to it to-day. You make me out all that is narrow-minded and mean and despicable, which is very unjust. Only a few minutes past I said that your way of looking at it, theoretically considered, was irreproachable. But not so when we include society."

"But you misunderstand me, Vance. Listen." Her hand went out to his, and he was content to listen. "I have always upheld that what is is well. I grant the wisdom of the prevailing social judgment in this matter. Though I deplore it, I grant it; for the human is so made. But I grant it socially only. I, as an individual, choose to regard such things differently. And as between individuals so minded, why should it not be so regarded? Don't you see? Now I find you guilty. As between you and me, yesterday, on the river, you did not so regard it. You behaved as narrow-mindedly as would have the society you represent."

"Then you would preach two doctrines?" he retaliated. "One for the elect and one for the herd? You would be a democrat in theory and an aristocrat in practice? In fact, the whole stand you are making is nothing more or less than Jesuitical."

"I suppose with the next breath you will be contending that all men are born free and equal, with a bundle of natural rights thrown in? You are going to have Del Bishop work for you; by what equal free-born right will he work for you, or you suffer him to work?"

"No," he denied. "I should have to modify somewhat the questions of equality and rights."

"And if you modify, you are lost!" she exulted. "For you can only modify in the direction of my position, which is neither so Jesuitical nor so harsh as you have defined it. But don't let us get lost in dialectics. I want to see what I can see, so tell me about this woman."

"Not a very tasteful topic," Corliss objected.

"But I seek knowledge."

"Nor can it be wholesome knowledge."

Frona tapped her foot impatiently, and studied him.

"She is beautiful, very beautiful," she suggested. "Do you not think so?"

"As beautiful as hell."

"But still beautiful," she insisted.

"Yes, if you will have it so. And she is as cruel, and hard, and hopeless as she is beautiful."

"Yet I came upon her, alone, by the trail, her face softened, and tears in her eyes. And I believe, with a woman's ken, that I saw a side of her to which you are blind. And so strongly did I see it, that when you appeared my mind was blank to all save the solitary wail, *Oh, the pity of it! The pity of it!* And she is a woman, even as I, and I doubt not that we are very much alike. Why, she even quoted Browning—"

"And last week," he cut her short, "in a single sitting, she gambled away thirty thousand of Jack Dorsey's dust,—Dorsey, with two mortgages already on his dump! They found him in the snow next morning, with one chamber empty in his revolver."

Frona made no reply, but, walking over to the candle, deliberately thrust her finger into the flame. Then she held it up to Corliss that he might see the outraged skin, red and angry.

"And so I point the parable. The fire is very good, but I misuse it, and I am punished."

"You forget," he objected. "The fire works in blind obedience to natural law. Lucile is a free agent. That which she has chosen to do, that she has done."

"Nay, it is you who forget, for just as surely Dorsey was a free agent.

But you said Lucile. Is that her name? I wish I knew her better."

Corliss winced. "Don't! You hurt me when you say such things."

"And why, pray?"

"Because—because—"

"Yes?"

"Because I honor woman highly. Frona, you have always made a stand for frankness, and I can now advantage by it. It hurts me because of the honor in which I hold you, because I cannot bear to see taint approach you. Why, when I saw you and that woman together on the trail, I—you cannot understand what I suffered."

"Taint?" There was a tightening about her lips which he did not notice, and a just perceptible lustre of victory lighted her eyes.

"Yes, taint,—contamination," he reiterated. "There are some things which it were not well for a good woman to understand. One cannot dabble with mud and remain spotless."

"That opens the field wide." She clasped and unclasped her hands gleefully. "You have said that her name was Lucile; you display a knowledge of her; you have given me facts about her; you doubtless retain many which you dare not give; in short, if one cannot dabble and remain spotless, how about you?"

"But I am—"

"A man, of course. Very good. Because you are a man, you may court contamination. Because I am a woman, I may not. Contamination contaminates, does it not? Then you, what do you here with me? Out upon you!"

Corliss threw up his hands laughingly. "I give in. You are too much for me with your formal logic. I can only fall back on the higher logic, which you will not recognize."

"Which is—"

"Strength. What man wills for woman, that will he have."

"I take you, then, on your own ground," she rushed on. "What of Lucile? What man has willed that he has had. So you, and all men, have willed since the beginning of time. So poor Dorsey willed. You cannot answer, so let me speak something that occurs to me concerning that higher logic you call strength. I have met it before. I recognized it in you, yesterday, on the sleds."

"In me?"

"In you, when you reached out and clutched at me. You could not down the primitive passion, and, for that matter, you did not know it was uppermost. But the expression on your face, I imagine, was very like that of a woman-stealing cave-man. Another instant, and I am sure you would have laid violent hands upon me."

"Then I ask your pardon. I did not dream—"

"There you go, spoiling it all! I—I quite liked you for it. Don't you remember, I, too, was a cave-woman, brandishing the whip over your head?

"But I am not done with you yet, Sir Doubleface, even if you have dropped out of the battle." Her eyes were sparkling mischievously, and the wee laughter-creases were forming on her cheek. "I purpose to unmask you."

"As clay in the hands of the potter," he responded, meekly.

"Then you must remember several things. At first, when I was very humble and apologetic, you made it easier for me by saying that you could only condemn my conduct on the ground of being socially unwise. Remember?"

Corliss nodded.

"Then, just after you branded me as Jesuitical, I turned the conversation to Lucile, saying that I wished to see what I could see."

Again he nodded.

"And just as I expected, I saw. For in only a few minutes you began to talk about taint, and contamination, and dabbling in mud,—and all in relation to me. There are your two propositions, sir. You may only stand on one, and I feel sure that you stand on the last one. Yes, I am right. You do. And you were insincere, confess, when you found my conduct unwise only from the social point of view. I like sincerity."

"Yes," he began, "I was unwittingly insincere. But I did not know it until further analysis, with your help, put me straight. Say what you will, Frona, my conception of woman is such that she should not court defilement."

"But cannot we be as gods, knowing good and evil?"

"But we are not gods," he shook his head, sadly.

"Only the men are?"

"That is new-womanish talk," he frowned. "Equal rights, the ballot, and all that."

"Oh! Don't!" she protested. "You won't understand me; you can't. I am no woman's rights' creature; and I stand, not for the new woman, but for the new womanhood. Because I am sincere; because I desire to be natural, and honest, and true; and because I am consistent with myself, you choose to misunderstand it all and to lay wrong strictures upon me. I do try to be consistent, and I think I fairly succeed; but you can see neither rhyme nor reason in my consistency. Perhaps it is because you are unused to consistent, natural women; because, more likely, you are only familiar with the hot-house *breed*s,—pretty, helpless, well-rounded, stall-fatted little things, blissfully innocent and criminally ignorant. They are not natural or strong; nor can they mother the natural and strong."

She stopped abruptly. They heard somebody enter the hall, and a heavy, soft-moccasined tread approaching.

"We are friends," she added hurriedly, and Corliss answered with his eyes.

"Ain't intrudin', am I?" Dave Harney grinned broad insinuation and looked about ponderously before coming up to shake hands.

"Not at all," Corliss answered. "We've bored each other till we were pining for some one to come along. If you hadn't, we would soon have been quarrelling, wouldn't we, Miss Welse?"

"I don't think he states the situation fairly," she smiled back. "In fact, we had already begun to quarrel."

"You do look a mite flustered," Harney criticised, dropping his loose-jointed frame all over the pillows of the lounging couch.

"How's the famine?" Corliss asked. "Any public relief started yet?"

"Won't need any public relief. Miss Frona's old man was too forehanded fer 'em. Scairt the daylights out of the critters, I do b'lieve. Three thousand went out over the ice hittin' the high places, an' half ez many again went down to the caches, and the market's loosened some considerable. Jest what Welse figgered on, everybody speculated on a rise and held all the grub they could lay hand to. That helped scare the shorts, and away they stampeded fer Salt Water, the whole caboodle, a-takin' all the dogs with 'em. Say!" he sat up solemnly, "corner dogs! They'll rise suthin' unheard on in the spring when freightin' gits brisk. I've corralled a hundred a'ready, an' I figger to clear a hundred dollars clean on every hide of 'em."

"Think so?"

"Think so! I guess yes. Between we three, confidential, I'm startin' a couple of lads down into the Lower Country next week to buy up five hundred of the best huskies they kin spot. Think so! I've limbered my jints too long in the land to git caught nappin'."

Frona burst out laughing. "But you got pinched on the sugar, Dave."

"Oh, I dunno," he responded, complacently. "Which reminds me. I've got a noospaper, an' only four weeks' old, the *Seattle Post-Intelligencer*."

"Has the United States and Spain—"

"Not so fast, not so fast!" The long Yankee waved his arms for silence, cutting off Frona's question which was following fast on that of Corliss.

"But have you read it?" they both demanded.

"Unh huh, every line, advertisements an' all."

"Then do tell me," Frona began. "Has—"

"Now you keep quiet, Miss Frona, till I tell you about it reg'lar. That noospaper cost me fifty dollars—caught the man comin' in round the bend above Klondike City, an' bought it on the spot. The dummy could a-got a hundred fer it, easy, if he'd held on till he made town—"

"But what does it say? Has—"

"Ez I was sayin', that noospaper cost me fifty dollars. It's the only one that come in. Everybody's jest dyin' to hear the noos. So I invited a select number of 'em to come here to yer parlors to-night, Miss Frona, ez the only likely place, an' they kin read it out loud, by shifts, ez long ez they want or till they're tired—that is, if you'll let 'em have the use of the place."

"Why, of course, they are welcome. And you are very kind to—"

He waved her praise away. "Jest ez I kalkilated. Now it so happens, ez you said, that I was pinched on sugar. So every mother's son and daughter that gits a squint at that paper to-night got to pony up five cups of sugar. Savve? Five cups,—big cups, white, or brown, or cube,—an' I'll take their IOU's, an' send a boy round to their shacks the day followin' to collect."

Frona's face went blank at the telling, then the laughter came back into it. "Won't it be jolly? I'll do it if it raises a scandal. To-night, Dave? Sure to-night?"

"Sure. An' you git a complimentary, you know, fer the loan of yer parlor."

"But papa must pay his five cups. You must insist upon it, Dave."

Dave's eyes twinkled appreciatively. "I'll git it back on him, you bet!"

"And I'll make him come," she promised, "at the tail of Dave Harney's chariot."

"Sugar cart," Dave suggested. "An' to-morrow night I'll take the paper down to the Opery House. Won't be fresh, then, so they kin git in cheap; a cup'll be about the right thing, I reckon." He sat up and cracked his huge knuckles boastfully. "I ain't ben a-burnin' daylight sence navigation closed; an' if they set up all night they won't be up early enough in the mornin' to git ahead of Dave Harney—even on a sugar proposition."

CHAPTER XI

Over in the corner Vance Corliss leaned against the piano, deep in conversation with Colonel Trethaway. The latter, keen and sharp and wiry, for all his white hair and sixty-odd years, was as young in appearance as a man of thirty. A veteran mining engineer, with a record which put him at the head of his profession, he represented as large American interests as Corliss did British. Not only had a cordial friendship sprung up between them, but in a business way they had already been of large assistance to each other. And it was well that they should stand together,—a pair who held in grip and could direct at will the potent capital which two nations had contributed to the development of the land under the Pole.

The crowded room was thick with tobacco smoke. A hundred men or so, garbed in furs and warm-colored wools, lined the walls and looked on. But the mumble of their general conversation destroyed the spectacular feature of the scene and gave to it the geniality of common comradeship. For all its *bizarre* appearance, it was very like the living-room of the home when the members of the household come together after the work of the day. Kerosene lamps and tallow candles glimmered feebly in the murky atmosphere, while large stoves roared their red-hot and white-hot cheer.

On the floor a score of couples pulsed rhythmically to the swinging waltz-time music. Starched shirts and frock coats were not. The men wore their wolf- and beaver-skin caps, with the gay-tasselled ear-flaps flying free, while on their feet were the moose-skin moccasins and walrus-hide muclucs of the north. Here and there a woman was in moccasins, though the majority danced in frail ball-room slippers of silk and satin. At one end of the hall a great open doorway gave glimpse of another large room where the crowd was even denser. From this room, in the lulls in the music, came the pop of corks and the clink of glasses, and as an undertone the steady click and clatter of chips and roulette balls.

The small door at the rear opened, and a woman, befurred and muffled, came in on a wave of frost. The cold rushed in with her to the warmth, taking form in a misty cloud which hung close to the floor, hiding the feet of the dancers, and writhing and twisting until vanquished by the heat.

"A veritable frost queen, my Lucile," Colonel Trethaway addressed her.

She tossed her head and laughed, and, as she removed her capes and street-moccasins, chatted with him gayly. But of Corliss, though he stood within a yard of her, she took no notice. Half a dozen dancing men were waiting patiently at a little distance till she should have done with the colonel. The piano and violin played the opening bars of a schottische, and she turned to go; but a sudden impulse made Corliss step up to her. It was wholly unpremeditated; he had not dreamed of doing it.

"I am very sorry," he said.

Her eyes flashed angrily as she turned upon him.

"I mean it," he repeated, holding out his hand. "I am very sorry. I was a brute and a coward. Will you forgive me?"

She hesitated, and, with the wisdom bought of experience, searched him for the ulterior motive. Then, her face softened, and she took his hand. A warm mist dimmed her eyes.

"Thank you," she said.

But the waiting men had grown impatient, and she was whirled away in the arms of a handsome young fellow, conspicuous in a cap of yellow Siberian wolf-skin. Corliss came back to his companion, feeling unaccountably good and marvelling at what he had done.

"It's a damned shame." The colonel's eye still followed Lucile, and Vance understood. "Corliss, I've lived my threescore, and lived them well, and do you know, woman is a greater mystery than ever. Look at them, look at them all!" He embraced the whole scene with his eyes. "Butterflies, bits of light and song and laughter, dancing, dancing down the last tail-reach of hell. Not only Lucile, but the rest of them. Look at May, there, with the brow of a Madonna and the tongue of a gutter-devil. And Myrtle—for all the world one of Gainsborough's old English beauties stepped down from the canvas to riot out the century in Dawson's dance-halls. And Laura, there, wouldn't she make a mother? Can't you see the child in the curve of her arm against her breast! They're the best of the boiling, I know,—a new country always gathers the best,—but there's something wrong, Corliss, something wrong. The heats of life have passed with me, and my vision is truer, surer. It seems a new Christ must arise and preach a new salvation—economic or sociologic—in these latter days, it matters not, so long as it is preached. The world has need of it."

The room was wont to be swept by sudden tides, and notably between the dances, when the revellers ebbed through the great doorway to where corks popped and glasses tinkled. Colonel Trethaway and Corliss followed out on the next ebb to the bar, where fifty men and women were lined up. They found themselves next to Lucile and the fellow in the yellow wolf-skin cap. He was undeniably handsome, and his looks were enhanced by a warm overplus of blood in the cheeks and a certain mellow fire in the eyes. He was not technically drunk, for he had himself in perfect physical control; but his was the soul-exhilaration which comes of the juice of the grape. His voice was raised the least bit and joyous, and his tongue made quick and witty—just in the unstable condition when vices and virtues are prone to extravagant expression.

As he raised his glass, the man next to him accidentally jostled his arm. He shook the wine from his sleeve and spoke his mind. It was not a nice word, but one customarily calculated to rouse the fighting blood. And the other man's blood roused, for his fist landed under the wolf-skin cap with force sufficient to drive its owner back against Corliss. The insulted man followed up his attack swiftly. The women slipped away, leaving a free field for the men, some of whom were for crowding in, and some for giving room and fair play.

The wolf-skin cap did not put up a fight or try to meet the wrath he had invoked, but, with his hands shielding his face, strove to retreat. The crowd called upon him to stand up and fight. He nerved himself to the attempt, but weakened as the man closed in on him, and dodged away.

"Let him alone. He deserves it," the colonel called to Vance as he showed signs of interfering. "He won't fight. If he did, I think I could almost forgive him."

"But I can't see him pummelled," Vance objected. "If he would only stand up, it wouldn't seem so brutal."

The blood was streaming from his nose and from a slight cut over one eye, when Corliss sprang between. He attempted to hold the two men apart, but pressing too hard against the truculent individual, overbalanced him and threw him to the floor. Every man has friends in a bar-room fight, and before Vance knew what was taking place he was staggered by a blow from a chum of the man he had downed. Del Bishop, who had edged in, let drive promptly at the man who had attacked his employer, and the fight became general. The crowd took sides on the moment and went at it.

Colonel Trethaway forgot that the heats of life had passed, and swinging a three-legged stool, danced nimbly into the fray. A couple of mounted police, on liberty, joined him, and with half a dozen others safeguarded the man with the wolf-skin cap.

Fierce though it was, and noisy, it was purely a local disturbance. At the far end of the bar the barkeepers still dispensed drinks, and in the next room the music was on and the dancers afoot. The gamblers continued their play, and at only the near tables did they evince any interest in the affair.

"Knock'm down an' drag'm out!" Del Bishop grinned, as he fought for a brief space shoulder to shoulder with Corliss.

Corliss grinned back, met the rush of a stalwart dog-driver with a clinch, and came down on top of him among the stamping feet. He was drawn close, and felt the fellow's teeth sinking into his ear. Like a flash, he surveyed his whole future and saw himself going one-eared through life, and in the same dash, as though inspired, his thumbs flew to the man's eyes and pressed heavily on the balls. Men fell over him and trampled upon him, but it all seemed very dim and far away. He only knew, as he pressed with his thumbs, that the man's teeth wavered reluctantly. He added a little pressure (a little more, and the man would have been eyeless), and the teeth slackened and slipped their grip.

After that, as he crawled out of the fringe of the melee and came to his feet by the side of the bar, all distaste for fighting left him. He had found that he was very much like other men after all, and the imminent loss of part of his anatomy had scraped off twenty years of culture. Gambling without stakes is an insipid amusement, and Corliss discovered, likewise, that the warm blood which rises from hygienic gymnasium work is something quite different from that which pounds hotly along when thew matches thew and flesh impacts on flesh and the stake is life and limb. As he dragged himself to his feet by means of the bar-rail, he saw a man in a squirrel-skin *parka* lift a beer-mug to hurl at Trethaway, a couple of paces off. And the fingers, which were more used to test-tubes and water colors, doubled into a hard fist which smote the mug-thrower cleanly on the point of the jaw. The man merely dropped the glass and himself on the floor. Vance was dazed for the moment, then he realized that he had knocked the man unconscious,—the first in his life,—and a pang of delight thrilled through him.

Colonel Trethaway thanked him with a look, and shouted, "Get on the outside! Work to the door, Corliss! Work to the door!"

Quite a struggle took place before the storm-doors could be thrown open; but the colonel, still attached to the three-legged stool, effectually dissipated the opposition, and the Opera House disgorged its turbulent contents into the street. This accomplished, hostilities ceased, after the manner of such fights, and the crowd scattered. The two policemen went back to keep order, accompanied by the rest of the allies, while Corliss and the colonel, followed by the Wolf-Skin Cap and Del Bishop, proceeded up the street.

"Blood and sweat! Blood and sweat!" Colonel Trethaway exulted. "Talk about putting the vim into one! Why, I'm twenty years younger if I'm a day! Corliss, your hand. I congratulate you, I do, I heartily do. Candidly, I didn't think it was in you. You're a surprise, sir, a surprise!"

"And a surprise to myself," Corliss answered. The reaction had set in, and he was feeling sick and faint. "And you, also, are a surprise. The way you handled that stool—"

"Yes, now! I flatter myself I did fairly well with it. Did you see—well, look at that!" He held up the weapon in question, still tightly clutched, and joined in the laugh against himself.

"Whom have I to thank, gentlemen?"

They had come to a pause at the corner, and the man they had rescued was holding out his hand.

"My name is St. Vincent," he went on, "and—"

"What name?" Del Bishop queried with sudden interest.

"St. Vincent, Gregory St. Vincent—"

Bishop's fist shot out, and Gregory St. Vincent pitched heavily into the snow. The colonel instinctively raised the stool, then helped Corliss to hold the pocket-miner back.

"Are you crazy, man?" Vance demanded.

"The skunk! I wish I'd hit 'm harder!" was the response. Then, "Oh, that's all right. Let go o' me. I won't hit 'm again. Let go o' me, I'm goin' home. Good-night."

As they helped St. Vincent to his feet, Vance could have sworn he heard the colonel giggling. And he confessed to it later, as he explained, "It was so curious and unexpected." But he made amends by taking it upon himself to see St. Vincent home.

"But why did you hit him?" Corliss asked, unavailingly, for the fourth time after he had got into his cabin.

"The mean, crawlin' skunk!" the pocket-miner gritted in his blankets.

"What'd you stop me for, anyway? I wish I'd hit 'm twice as hard!"

CHAPTER XII

"Mr. Harney, pleased to meet you. Dave, I believe, Dave Harney?" Dave Harney nodded, and Gregory St. Vincent turned to Frona. "You see, Miss Welse, the world is none so large. Mr. Harney and I are not strangers after all."

The Eldorado king studied the other's face until a glimmering intelligence came to him. "Hold on!" he cried, as St. Vincent started to speak, "I got my finger on you. You were smooth-faced then. Let's see,—'86, fall of '87, summer of '88,—yep, that's when. Summer of '88 I come floatin' a raft out of Stewart River, loaded down with quarters of moose an' strainin' to make the Lower Country 'fore they went bad. Yep, an' down the Yukon you come, in a Linderman boat. An' I was holdin' strong, ez it was Wednesday, an' my pardner ez it was Friday, an' you put us straight—Sunday, I b'lieve it was. Yep, Sunday. I declare! Nine years ago! And we swapped moose-steaks fer flour an' bakin' soda, an'—an'—an' sugar! By the Jimcracky! I'm glad to see you!"

He shoved out his hand and they shook again.

"Come an' see me," he invited, as he moved away. "I've a right tidy little shack up on the hill, and another on Eldorado. Latch-string's always out. Come an' see me, an' stay ez long ez you've a mind to. Sorry to quit you cold, but I got to traipse down to the Opery House and collect my taxes,—sugar. Miss Frona'll tell you."

"You are a surprise, Mr. St. Vincent." Frona switched back to the point of interest, after briefly relating Harney's saccharine difficulties. "The country must indeed have been a wilderness nine years ago, and to think that you went through it at that early day! Do tell me about it."

Gregory St. Vincent shrugged his shoulders, "There is very little to tell. It was an ugly failure, filled with many things that are not nice, and containing nothing of which to be proud."

"But do tell me, I enjoy such things. They seem closer and truer to life than the ordinary every-day happenings. A failure, as you call it, implies something attempted. What did you attempt?"

He noted her frank interest with satisfaction. "Well, if you will, I can tell you in few words all there is to tell. I took the mad idea into my head of breaking a new path around the world, and in the interest of science and journalism, particularly journalism, I proposed going through Alaska, crossing the Bering Straits on the ice, and journeying to Europe by way of Northern Siberia. It was a splendid undertaking, most of it being virgin ground, only I failed. I crossed the Straits in good order, but came to grief in Eastern Siberia—all because of Tamerlane is the excuse I have grown accustomed to making."

"A Ulysses!" Mrs. Schoville clapped her hands and joined them. "A modern Ulysses! How romantic!"

"But not an Othello," Frona replied. "His tongue is a sluggard. He leaves one at the most interesting point with an enigmatical reference to a man of a bygone age. You take an unfair advantage of us, Mr. St. Vincent, and we shall be unhappy until you show how Tamerlane brought your journey to an untimely end."

He laughed, and with an effort put aside his reluctance to speak of his travels. "When Tamerlane swept with fire and sword over Eastern Asia, states were disrupted, cities overthrown, and tribes scattered like star-dust. In fact, a vast people was hurled broadcast over the land. Fleeing before the mad lust of the conquerors, these refugees swung far into Siberia, circling to the north and east and fringing the rim of the polar basin with a spray of Mongol tribes—am I not tiring you?"

"No, no!" Mrs. Schoville exclaimed. "It is fascinating! Your method of narration is so vivid! It reminds me of—of—"

"Of Macaulay," St. Vincent laughed, good-naturedly. "You know I am a journalist, and he has strongly influenced my style. But I promise you I shall tone down. However, to return, had it not been for these Mongol tribes, I should not have been halted in my travels. Instead of being forced to marry a greasy princess, and to become proficient in interclannish warfare and reindeer-stealing, I should have travelled easily and peaceably to St. Petersburg."

"Oh, these heroes! Are they not exasperating, Frona? But what about the reindeer-stealing and the greasy princesses?"

The Gold Commissioner's wife beamed upon him, and glancing for permission to Frona, he went on.

"The coast people were Esquimo stock, merry-natured and happy, and inoffensive. They called themselves the Oukilion, or the Sea Men. I bought dogs and food from them, and they treated me splendidly. But they were subject to the Chow Chuen, or interior people, who were known as the Deer Men. The Chow Chuen were a savage, indomitable breed, with all the fierceness of the untamed Mongol, plus double his viciousness. As soon as I left the coast they fell upon me, confiscated my goods, and made me a slave."

"But were there no Russians?" Mrs. Schoville asked.

"Russians? Among the Chow Chuen?" He laughed his amusement. "Geographically, they are within the White Tsar's domain; but politically, no. I doubt if they ever heard of him. Remember, the interior of North-Eastern Siberia is hidden in the polar gloom, a terra incognita, where few men have gone and none has returned."

"But you—"

"I chance to be the exception. Why I was spared, I do not know. It just so happened. At first I was vilely treated, beaten by the women and children, clothed in vermin-infested mangy furs, and fed on refuse. They were utterly heartless. How I managed to survive is beyond me; but I know that often and often, at first, I meditated suicide. The only thing that saved me during that period from taking my own life was the fact that I quickly became too stupefied and bestial, what of my suffering and degradation. Half-frozen, half-starved, undergoing untold misery and hardship, beaten many and many a time into insensibility, I became the sheerest animal.

"On looking back much of it seems a dream. There are gaps which my memory cannot fill. I have vague recollections of being lashed to a sled and dragged from camp to camp and tribe to tribe. Carted about for exhibition purposes, I suppose, much as we do lions and elephants and wild men. How far I so journeyed up and down that bleak region I cannot guess, though it must have been several thousand miles. I do know that when consciousness returned to me and I really became myself again, I was fully a thousand miles to the west of the point where I was captured.

"It was springtime, and from out of a forgotten past it seemed I suddenly opened my eyes. A reindeer thong was about my waist and made fast to the tail-end of a sled. This thong I clutched with both hands, like an organ-grinder's monkey; for the flesh of my body was raw and in great sores from where the thong had cut in.

"A low cunning came to me, and I made myself agreeable and servile. That night I danced and sang, and did my best to amuse them, for I was resolved to incur no more of the maltreatment which had plunged me into darkness. Now the Deer Men traded with the Sea Men, and the Sea Men with the whites, especially the whalers. So later I discovered a deck of cards in the possession of one of the women, and I proceeded to mystify the Chow Chuen with a few commonplace tricks. Likewise, with fitting solemnity, I perpetrated upon them the little I knew of parlor legerdemain. Result: I was appreciated at once, and was better fed and better clothed.

"To make a long story short, I gradually became a man of importance. First the old people and the women came to me for advice, and later the chiefs. My slight but rough and ready knowledge of medicine and surgery stood me in good stead, and I became indispensable. From a slave, I worked myself to a seat among the head men, and in war and peace, so soon as I had learned their ways, was an unchallenged authority. Reindeer was their medium of exchange, their unit of value as it were, and we were almost constantly engaged in cattle forays among the adjacent clans, or in protecting our own herds from their inroads. I improved upon their methods, taught them better strategy and tactics, and put a snap and go into their operations which no neighbor tribe could withstand.

"But still, though I became a power, I was no nearer my freedom. It was laughable, for I had over-reached myself and made myself too valuable. They cherished me with exceeding kindness, but they were jealously careful. I could go and come and command without restraint, but when the trading parties went down to the coast I was not permitted to accompany them. That was the one restriction placed upon my movements.

"Also, it is very tottery in the high places, and when I began altering their political structures I came to grief again. In the process of binding together twenty or more of the neighboring tribes in order to settle rival claims, I was given the over-lordship of the federation. But Old Pi-Une was the greatest of the under-chiefs,—a king in a way,—and in relinquishing his claim to the supreme leadership he refused to forego all the honors. The least that could be done to appease him was for me to marry his daughter Ilswunga. Nay, he demanded it. I offered to abandon the federation, but he would not hear of it. And—"

"And?" Mrs. Schoville murmured ecstatically.

"And I married Ilswunga, which is the Chow Chuen name for Wild Deer.

Poor Ilswunga! Like Swinburne's Iseult of Brittany, and I Tristram!

The last I saw of her she was playing solitaire in the Mission of

Irkutsky and stubbornly refusing to take a bath."

"Oh, mercy! It's ten o'clock!" Mrs. Schoville suddenly cried, her husband having at last caught her eye from across the room. "I'm so sorry I can't hear the rest, Mr. St. Vincent, how you escaped and all that. But you must come and see me. I am just dying to hear!"

"And I took you for a tenderfoot, a *chechaquo*," Frona said meekly, as St. Vincent tied his ear-flaps and turned up his collar preparatory to leaving.

"I dislike posing," he answered, matching her meekness. "It smacks of insincerity; it really is untrue. And it is so easy to slip into it. Look at the old-timers,—'sour-doughs' as they proudly call themselves. Just because they have been in the country a few years, they let themselves grow wild and woolly and glorify in it. They may not know it, but it is a pose. In so far as they cultivate salient peculiarities, they cultivate falseness to themselves and live lies."

"I hardly think you are wholly just," Frona said, in defence of her chosen heroes. "I do like what you say about the matter in general, and I detest posing, but the majority of the old-timers would be peculiar in any country, under any circumstances. That peculiarity is their own; it is their mode of expression. And it is, I am sure, just what makes them go into new countries. The normal man, of course, stays at home."

"Oh, I quite agree with you, Miss Welse," he temporized easily. "I did not intend it so sweepingly. I meant to brand that sprinkling among them who are *poseurs*. In the main, as you say, they are honest, and sincere, and natural."

"Then we have no quarrel. But Mr. St. Vincent, before you go, would you care to come to-morrow evening? We are getting up theatricals for Christmas. I know you can help us greatly, and I think it will not be altogether unenjoyable to you. All the younger people are interested,—the officials, officers of police, mining engineers, gentlemen rovers, and so forth, to say nothing of the nice women. You are bound to like them."

"I am sure I shall," as he took her hand. "Tomorrow, did you say?"

"To-morrow evening. Good-night."

A brave man, she told herself as she went bade from the door, and a splendid type of the race.

CHAPTER XIII

Gregory St. Vincent swiftly became an important factor in the social life of Dawson. As a representative of the Amalgamated Press Association, he had brought with him the best credentials a powerful influence could obtain, and over and beyond, he was well qualified socially by his letters of introduction. It developed in a quiet way that he was a wanderer and explorer of no small parts, and that he had seen life and strife pretty well all over the earth's crust. And withal, he was so mild and modest about it, that nobody, not even among the men, was irritated by his achievements. Incidentally, he ran across numerous old acquaintances. Jacob Welse he had met at St. Michael's in the fall of '88, just prior to his crossing Bering Straits on the ice. A month or so later, Father Barnum (who had come up from the Lower River to take charge of the hospital) had met him a couple of hundred miles on his way north of St. Michael's. Captain Alexander, of the Police, had rubbed shoulders with him in the British Legation at Peking. And Bettles, another old-timer of standing, had met him at Fort o' Yukon nine years before.

So Dawson, ever prone to look askance at the casual comer, received him with open arms. Especially was he a favorite with the women. As a promoter of pleasures and an organizer of amusements he took the lead, and it quickly came to pass that no function was complete without him. Not only did he come to help in the theatricals, but insensibly, and as a matter of course, he took charge. Frona, as her friends charged, was suffering from a stroke of Ibsen, so they hit upon the "Doll's House," and she was cast for Nora. Corliss, who was responsible, by the way, for the theatricals, having first suggested them, was to take Torvald's part; but his interest seemed to have died out, or at any rate he begged off on the plea of business rush. So St. Vincent, without friction, took Torvald's lines. Corliss did manage to attend one rehearsal. It might have been that he had come tired from forty miles with the dogs, and it might have been that Torvald was obliged to put his arm about Nora at divers times and to toy playfully with her ear; but, one way or the other, Corliss never attended again.

Busy he certainly was, and when not away on trail he was closeted almost continually with Jacob Welse and Colonel Trethaway. That it was a deal of magnitude was evidenced by the fact that Welse's mining interests involved alone mounted to several millions. Corliss was primarily a worker and doer, and on discovering that his thorough theoretical knowledge lacked practical experience, he felt put upon his mettle and worked the harder. He even marvelled at the silliness of the men who had burdened him with such responsibilities, simply because of his pull, and he told Trethaway as much. But the colonel, while recognizing his shortcomings, liked him for his candor, and admired him for his effort and for the quickness with which he came to grasp things actual.

Del Bishop, who had refused to play any hand but his own, had gone to work for Corliss because by so doing he was enabled to play his own hand better. He was practically unfettered, while the opportunities to further himself were greatly increased. Equipped with the best of outfits and a magnificent dog-team, his task was mainly to run the various creeks and keep his eyes and ears open. A pocket-miner, first, last, and always, he was privately on the constant lookout for pockets, which occupation did not interfere in the least with the duty he owed his employer. And as the days went by he stored his mind with miscellaneous data concerning the nature of the various placer deposits and the lay of the land, against the summer when the thawed surface and the running water would permit him to follow a trace from creek-bed to side-slope and source.

Corliss was a good employer, paid well, and considered it his right to work men as he worked himself. Those who took service with him either strengthened their own manhood and remained, or quit and said harsh things about him. Jacob Welse noted this trait with appreciation, and he sounded the mining engineer's praises continually. Frona heard and was gratified, for she liked the things her father liked; and she was more gratified because the man was Corliss. But in his rush of business she saw less of him than formerly, while St. Vincent came to occupy a greater and growing portion of her time. His healthful, optimistic spirit pleased her, while he corresponded well to her idealized natural man and favorite racial type. Her first doubt—that if what he said was true—had passed away. All the evidence had gone counter. Men who at first questioned the truth of his wonderful adventures gave in after hearing him talk. Those to any extent conversant with the parts of the world he made mention of, could not but acknowledge that he knew what he talked about. Young Soley, representing Bannock's News Syndicate, and Holmes of the Fairweather, recollected his return to the world in '91, and the sensation created thereby. And Sid Winslow, Pacific Coast journalist, had made his acquaintance at the Wanderers' Club shortly after he landed from the United States revenue cutter which had brought him down from the north. Further, as Frona well saw, he bore the ear-marks of his experiences; they showed their handiwork in his whole outlook on life. Then the primitive was strong in him, and his was a passionate race pride which fully matched hers. In the absence of Corliss they were much together, went out frequently with the dogs, and grew to know each other thoroughly.

All of which was not pleasant to Corliss, especially when the brief intervals he could devote to her were usually intruded upon by the correspondent. Naturally, Corliss was not drawn to him, and other men, who knew or had heard of the Opera House occurrence, only accepted him after a tentative fashion. Trethaway had the indiscretion, once or twice, to speak slightingly of him, but so fiercely was he defended by his admirers that the colonel developed the good taste to thenceforward keep his tongue between his teeth. Once, Corliss, listening to an extravagant panegyric bursting from the lips of Mrs. Schoville, permitted himself the luxury of an incredulous smile; but the quick wave of color in Frona's face, and the gathering of the brows, warned him.

At another time he was unwise enough and angry enough to refer to the Opera House broil. He was carried away, and what he might have said of that night's happening would have redounded neither to St. Vincent's credit nor to his own, had not Frona innocently put a seal upon his lips ere he had properly begun.

"Yes," she said. "Mr. St. Vincent told me about it. He met you for the first time that night, I believe. You all fought royally on his side,—you and Colonel Trethaway. He spoke his admiration unreservedly and, to tell the truth, with enthusiasm."

Corliss made a gesture of depreciation.

"No! no! From what he said you must have behaved splendidly. And I was most pleased to hear. It must be great to give the brute the rein now and again, and healthy, too. Great for us who have wandered from the natural and softened to sickly ripeness. Just to shake off artificiality and rage up and down! and yet, the inmost mentor, serene and passionless, viewing all and saying: 'This is my other self. Behold! I, who am now powerless, am the power behind and ruleth still! This other self, mine ancient, violent, elder self, rages blindly as the beast, but 'tis I, sitting apart, who discern the merit of the cause and bid him rage or bid him cease!' Oh, to be a man!"

Corliss could not help a humoring smile, which put Frona upon defence at once.

"Tell me, Vance, how did it feel? Have I not described it rightly? Were the symptoms yours? Did you not hold aloof and watch yourself play the brute?"

He remembered the momentary daze which came when he stunned the man with his fist, and nodded.

"And pride?" she demanded, inexorably. "Or shame?"

"A—a little of both, and more of the first than the second," he confessed. "At the time I suppose I was madly exultant; then afterwards came the shame, and I tossed awake half the night."

"And finally?"

"Pride, I guess. I couldn't help it, couldn't down it. I awoke in the morning feeling as though I had won my spurs. In a subconscious way I was inordinately proud of myself, and time and again, mentally, I caught myself throwing chests. Then came the shame again, and I tried to reason back my self-respect. And last of all, pride. The fight was fair and open. It was none of my seeking. I was forced into it by the best of motives. I am not sorry, and I would repeat it if necessary."

"And rightly so." Frona's eyes were sparkling. "And how did Mr. St.

Vincent acquit himself?"

"He? . . . . Oh, I suppose all right, creditably. I was too busy watching my other self to take notice."

"But he saw you."

"Most likely so. I acknowledge my negligence. I should have done better, the chances are, had I thought it would have been of interest to you—pardon me. Just my bungling wit. The truth is, I was too much of a greenhorn to hold my own and spare glances on my neighbors."

So Corliss went away, glad that he had not spoken, and keenly appreciating St. Vincent's craft whereby he had so adroitly forestalled adverse comment by telling the story in his own modest, self-effacing way.

Two men and a woman! The most potent trinity of factors in the creating of human pathos and tragedy! As ever in the history of man, since the first father dropped down from his arboreal home and walked upright, so at Dawson. Necessarily, there were minor factors, not least among which was Del Bishop, who, in his aggressive way, stepped in and accelerated things. This came about in a trail-camp on the way to Miller Creek, where Corliss was bent on gathering in a large number of low-grade claims which could only be worked profitably on a large scale.

"I'll not be wastin' candles when I make a strike, savve!" the pocket-miner remarked savagely to the coffee, which he was settling with a chunk of ice. "Not on your life, I guess rather not!"

"Kerosene?" Corliss queried, running a piece of bacon-rind round the frying-pan and pouring in the batter.

"Kerosene, hell! You won't see my trail for smoke when I get a gait on for God's country, my wad in my poke and the sunshine in my eyes. Say! How'd a good juicy tenderloin strike you just now, green onions, fried potatoes, and fixin's on the side? S'help me, that's the first proposition I'll hump myself up against. Then a general whoop-la! for a week—Seattle or 'Frisco, I don't care a rap which, and then—"

113

"Out of money and after a job."

"Not on your family tree!" Bishop roared. "Cache my sack before I go on the tear, sure pop, and then, afterwards, Southern California. Many's the day I've had my eye on a peach of a fruit farm down there—forty thousand'll buy it. No more workin' for grub-stakes and the like. Figured it out long; ago,—hired men to work the ranch, a manager to run it, and me ownin' the game and livin' off the percentage. A stable with always a couple of bronchos handy; handy to slap the packs and saddles on and be off and away whenever the fever for chasin' pockets came over me. Great pocket country down there, to the east and along the desert."

"And no house on the ranch?"

"Cert! With sweet peas growin' up the sides, and in back a patch for vegetables—string-beans and spinach and radishes, cucumbers and 'sparagrass, turnips, carrots, cabbage, and such. And a woman inside to draw me back when I get to runnin' loco after the pockets. Say, you know all about minin'. Did you ever go snoozin' round after pockets? No? Then just steer clear. They're worse than whiskey, horses, or cards. Women, when they come afterwards, ain't in it. Whenever you get a hankerin' after pockets, go right off and get married. It's the only thing'll save you; and even then, mebbe, it won't. I ought 'a' done it years ago. I might 'a' made something of myself if I had. Jerusalem! the jobs I've jumped and the good things chucked in my time, just because of pockets! Say, Corliss, you want to get married, you do, and right off. I'm tellin' you straight. Take warnin' from me and don't stay single any longer than God'll let you, sure!"

Corliss laughed.

"Sure, I mean it. I'm older'n you, and know what I'm talkin'. Now there's a bit of a thing down in Dawson I'd like to see you get your hands on. You was made for each other, both of you."

Corliss was past the stage when he would have treated Bishop's meddling as an impertinence. The trail, which turns men into the same blankets and makes them brothers, was the great leveller of distinctions, as he had come to learn. So he flopped a flapjack and held his tongue.

"Why don't you waltz in and win?" Del demanded, insistently. "Don't you cotton to her? I know you do, or you wouldn't come back to cabin, after bein' with her, a-walkin'-like on air. Better waltz in while you got a chance. Why, there was Emmy, a tidy bit of flesh as women go, and we took to each other on the jump. But I kept a-chasin' pockets and chasin' pockets, and delayin'. And then a big black lumberman, a Kanuck, began sidlin' up to her, and I made up my mind to speak—only I went off after one more pocket, just one more, and when I got back she was Mrs. Somebody Else.

"So take warnin'. There's that writer-guy, that skunk I poked outside the Opera House. He's walkin' right in and gettin' thick; and here's you, just like me, a-racin' round all creation and lettin' matrimony slide. Mark my words, Corliss! Some fine frost you'll come slippin' into camp and find 'em housekeepin'. Sure! With nothin' left for you in life but pocketing!"

The picture was so unpleasant that Corliss turned surly and ordered him to shut up.

"Who? Me?" Del asked so aggrievedly that Corliss laughed.

"What would you do, then?" he asked.

"Me? In all kindness I'll tell you. As soon as you get back you go and see her. Make dates with her ahead till you got to put 'em on paper to remember 'em all. Get a cinch on her spare time ahead so as to shut the other fellow out. Don't get down in the dirt to her,—she's not that kind,—but don't be too high and mighty, neither. Just so-so—savve? And then, some time when you see she's feelin' good, and smilin' at you in that way of hers, why up and call her hand. Of course I can't say what the showdown'll be. That's for you to find out. But don't hold off too long about it. Better married early than never. And if that writer-guy shoves in, poke him in the breadbasket—hard! That'll settle him plenty. Better still, take him off to one side and talk to him. Tell'm you're a bad man, and that you staked that claim before he was dry behind the ears, and that if he comes nosin' around tryin' to file on it you'll beat his head off."

Bishop got up, stretched, and went outside to feed the dogs. "Don't forget to beat his head off," he called back. "And if you're squeamish about it, just call on me. I won't keep 'm waitin' long."

CHAPTER XIV

"Ah, the salt water, Miss Welse, the strong salt water and the big waves and the heavy boats for smooth or rough—that I know. But the fresh water, and the little canoes, egg-shells, fairy bubbles; a big breath, a sigh, a heart-pulse too much, and pouf! over you go; not so, that I do not know." Baron Courbertin smiled self-commiseratingly and went on. "But it is delightful, magnificent. I have watched and envied. Some day I shall learn."

"It is not so difficult," St. Vincent interposed. "Is it, Miss Welse?"

Just a sure and delicate poise of mind and body—"

"Like the tight-rope dancer?"

"Oh, you are incorrigible," Frona laughed. "I feel certain that you know as much about canoes as we."

"And you know?—a woman?" Cosmopolitan as the Frenchman was, the independence and ability for doing of the Yankee women were a perpetual wonder to him. "How?"

"When I was a very little girl, at Dyea, among the Indians. But next spring, after the river breaks, we'll give you your first lessons, Mr. St. Vincent and I. So you see, you will return to civilization with accomplishments. And you will surely love it."

"Under such charming tutorship," he murmured, gallantly. "But you, Mr. St. Vincent, do you think I shall be so successful that I may come to love it? Do you love it?—you, who stand always in the background, sparing of speech, inscrutable, as though able but unwilling to speak from out the eternal wisdom of a vast experience." The baron turned quickly to Frona. "We are old friends, did I not tell you? So I may, what you Americans call, *josh* with him. Is it not so, Mr. St. Vincent?"

Gregory nodded, and Frona said, "I am sure you met at the ends of the earth somewhere."

"Yokohama," St. Vincent cut in shortly; "eleven years ago, in cherry-blossom time. But Baron Courbertin does me an injustice, which stings, unhappily, because it is not true. I am afraid, when I get started, that I talk too much about myself."

"A martyr to your friends," Frona conciliated. "And such a teller of good tales that your friends cannot forbear imposing upon you."

"Then tell us a canoe story," the baron begged. "A good one! A—what you Yankees call—a *hair-raiser!*"

They drew up to Mrs. Schoville's fat wood-burning stove, and St. Vincent told of the great whirlpool in the Box Canyon, of the terrible corkscrew in the mane of the White Horse Rapids, and of his cowardly comrade, who, walking around, had left him to go through alone—nine years before when the Yukon was virgin.

Half an hour later Mrs. Schoville bustled in, with Corliss in her wake.

"That hill! The last of my breath!" she gasped, pulling off her mittens. "Never saw such luck!" she declared none the less vehemently the next moment.

"This play will never come off! I never shall be Mrs. Linden! How can I? Krogstad's gone on a stampede to Indian River, and no one knows when he'll be back! Krogstad" (to Corliss) "is Mr. Maybrick, you know. And Mrs. Alexander has the neuralgia and can't stir out. So there's no rehearsal to-day, that's flat!" She attitudinized dramatically: "'*Yes, in my first terror! But a day has passed, and in that day I have seen incredible things in this house! Helmer must know everything! There must be an end to this unhappy secret! O Krogstad, you need me, and I—I need you,*' and you are over on the Indian River making sour-dough bread, and I shall never see you more!"

They clapped their applause.

"My only reward for venturing out and keeping you all waiting was my meeting with this ridiculous fellow." She shoved Corliss forward. "Oh! you have not met! Baron Courbertin, Mr. Corliss. If you strike it rich, baron, I advise you to sell to Mr. Corliss. He has the money-bags of Croesus, and will buy anything so long as the title is good. And if you don't strike, sell anyway. He's a professional philanthropist, you know.

"But would you believe it!" (addressing the general group) "this ridiculous fellow kindly offered to see me up the hill and gossip along the way—gossip! though he refused point-blank to come in and watch the rehearsal. But when he found there wasn't to be any, he changed about like a weather-vane. So here he is, claiming to have been away to Miller Creek; but between ourselves there is no telling what dark deeds—"

"Dark deeds! Look!" Frona broke in, pointing to the tip of an amber mouth-piece which projected from Vance's outside breast-pocket. "A pipe! My congratulations."

She held out her hand and he shook good-humoredly.

"All Del's fault," he laughed. "When I go before the great white throne, it is he who shall stand forth and be responsible for that particular sin."

"An improvement, nevertheless," she argued. "All that is wanting is a good round swear-word now and again."

"Oh, I assure you I am not unlearned," he retorted. "No man can drive dogs else. I can swear from hell to breakfast, by damn, and back again, if you will permit me, to the last link of perdition. By the bones of Pharaoh and the blood of Judas, for instance, are fairly efficacious with a string of huskies; but the best of my dog-driving nomenclature, more's the pity, women cannot stand. I promise you, however, in spite of hell and high water—"

"Oh! Oh!" Mrs. Schoville screamed, thrusting her fingers into her ears.

"Madame," Baron Courbertin spoke up gravely, "it is a fact, a lamentable fact, that the dogs of the north are responsible for more men's souls than all other causes put together. Is it not so? I leave it to the gentlemen."

Both Corliss and St. Vincent solemnly agreed, and proceeded to detonate the lady by swapping heart-rending and apposite dog tales.

St. Vincent and the baron remained behind to take lunch with the Gold Commissioner's wife, leaving Frona and Corliss to go down the hill together. Silently consenting, as though to prolong the descent, they swerved to the right, cutting transversely the myriad foot-paths and sled roads which led down into the town. It was a mid-December day, clear and cold; and the hesitant high-noon sun, having laboriously dragged its pale orb up from behind the southern land-rim, balked at the great climb to the zenith, and began its shamefaced slide back beneath the earth. Its oblique rays refracted from the floating frost particles till the air was filled with glittering jewel-dust—resplendent, blazing, flashing light and fire, but cold as outer space.

They passed down through the scintillant, magical sheen, their moccasins rhythmically crunching the snow and their breaths wreathing mysteriously from their lips in sprayed opalescence. Neither spoke, nor cared to speak, so wonderful was it all. At their feet, under the great vault of heaven, a speck in the midst of the white vastness, huddled the golden city—puny and sordid, feebly protesting against immensity, man's challenge to the infinite!

Calls of men and cries of encouragement came sharply to them from close at hand, and they halted. There was an eager yelping, a scratching of feet, and a string of ice-rimed wolf-dogs, with hot-lolling tongues and dripping jaws, pulled up the slope and turned into the path ahead of them. On the sled, a long and narrow box of rough-sawed spruce told the nature of the freight. Two dog-drivers, a woman walking blindly, and a black-robed priest, made up the funeral cortege. A few paces farther on the dogs were again put against the steep, and with whine and shout and clatter the unheeding clay was hauled on and upward to its ice-hewn hillside chamber.

"A zone-conqueror," Frona broke voice.

Corliss found his thought following hers, and answered, "These battlers of frost and fighters of hunger! I can understand how the dominant races have come down out of the north to empire. Strong to venture, strong to endure, with infinite faith and infinite patience, is it to be wondered at?"

Frona glanced at him in eloquent silence.

"'We smote with our swords,'" he chanted; "'to me it was a joy like having my bright bride by me on the couch.' 'I have marched with my bloody sword, and the raven has followed me. Furiously we fought; the fire passed over the dwellings of men; we slept in the blood of those who kept the gates.'"

"But do you feel it, Vance?" she cried, her hand flashing out and resting on his arm.

"I begin to feel, I think. The north has taught me, is teaching me. The old thing's come back with new significance. Yet I do not know. It seems a tremendous egotism, a magnificent dream."

"But you are not a negro or a Mongol, nor are you descended from the negro or Mongol."

"Yes," he considered, "I am my father's son, and the line goes back to the sea-kings who never slept under the smoky rafters of a roof or drained the ale-horn by inhabited hearth. There must be a reason for the dead-status of the black, a reason for the Teuton spreading over the earth as no other race has ever spread. There must be something in race heredity, else I would not leap at the summons."

"A great race, Vance. Half of the earth its heritage, and all of the sea! And in threescore generations it has achieved it all—think of it! threescore generations!—and to-day it reaches out wider-armed than ever. The smiter and the destroyer among nations! the builder and the law-giver! Oh, Vance, my love is passionate, but God will forgive, for it is good. A great race, greatly conceived; and if to perish, greatly to perish! Don't you remember:

"'*Trembles Yggdrasil's ash yet standing; groans that ancient tree, and the Jotun Loki is loosed. The shadows groan on the ways of Hel, until the fire of Surt has consumed the tree. Hrym steers from the east, the waters rise, the mundane snake is coiled in jotun-rage. The worm heats the water, and the eagle screams; the pale of beak tears carcases; the ship Naglfar is loosed. Surt from the south comes with flickering flame; shines from his sword the Val-god's sun.*'"

Swaying there like a furred Valkyrie above the final carnage of men and gods, she touched his imagination, and the blood surged exultingly along unknown channels, thrilling and uplifting.

"'*The stony hills are dashed together, the giantesses totter; men tread the path of Hel, and heaven is cloven. The sun darkens, earth in ocean sinks, fall from heaven the bright stars, fire's breath assails the all-nourishing tree, towering fire plays against heaven itself.*'"

Outlined against the blazing air, her brows and lashes white with frost, the jewel-dust striking and washing against hair and face, and the south-sun lighting her with a great redness, the man saw her as the genius of the race. The traditions of the blood laid hold of him, and he felt strangely at one with the white-skinned, yellow-haired giants of the younger world. And as he looked upon her the mighty past rose before him, and the caverns of his being resounded with the shock and tumult of forgotten battles. With bellowing of storm-winds and crash of smoking North Sea waves, he saw the sharp-beaked fighting galleys, and the sea-flung Northmen, great-muscled, deep-chested, sprung from the elements, men of sword and sweep, marauders and scourgers of the warm south-lands! The din of twenty centuries of battle was roaring in his ear, and the clamor for return to type strong upon him. He seized her hands passionately.

"Be the bright bride by me, Frona! Be the bright bride by me on the couch!"

She started and looked down at him, questioningly. Then the import of it reached her and she involuntarily drew back. The sun shot a last failing flicker across the earth and vanished. The fire went out of the air, and the day darkened. Far above, the hearse-dogs howled mournfully.

"No," he interrupted, as words formed on her lips. "Do not speak. I know my answer, your answer . . . now . . . I was a fool . . . Come, let us go down."

It was not until they had left the mountain behind them, crossed the flat, and come out on the river by the saw-mill, that the bustle and skurry of human life made it seem possible for them to speak. Corliss had walked with his eyes moodily bent to the ground; and Frona, with head erect and looking everywhere, stealing an occasional glance to his face. Where the road rose over the log run-way of the mill the footing was slippery, and catching at her to save her from falling, their eyes met.

"I—I am grieved," she hesitated. And then, in unconscious self-defence, "It was so . . . I had not expected it—just then."

"Else you would have prevented?" he asked, bitterly.

"Yes. I think I should have. I did not wish to give you pain—"

"Then you expected it, some time?"

"And feared it. But I had hoped . . . I . . . Vance, I did not come into the Klondike to get married. I liked you at the beginning, and I have liked you more and more,—never so much as to-day,—but—"

"But you had never looked upon me in the light of a possible husband—that is what you are trying to say."

As he spoke, he looked at her side-wise, and sharply; and when her eyes met his with the same old frankness, the thought of losing her maddened him.

"But I have," she answered at once. "I have looked upon you in that light, but somehow it was not convincing. Why, I do not know. There was so much I found to like in you, so much—"

He tried to stop her with a dissenting gesture, but she went on.

"So much to admire. There was all the warmth of friendship, and closer friendship,—a growing *camaraderie*, in fact; but nothing more. Though I did not wish more, I should have welcomed it had it come."

"As one welcomes the unwelcome guest."

"Why won't you help me, Vance, instead of making it harder? It is hard on you, surely, but do you imagine that I am enjoying it? I feel because of your pain, and, further, I know when I refuse a dear friend for a lover the dear friend goes from me. I do not part with friends lightly."

"I see; doubly bankrupt; friend and lover both. But they are easily replaced. I fancy I was half lost before I spoke. Had I remained silent, it would have been the same anyway. Time softens; new associations, new thoughts and faces; men with marvellous adventures—"

She stopped him abruptly.

"It is useless, Vance, no matter what you may say. I shall not quarrel with you. I can understand how you feel—"

"If I am quarrelsome, then I had better leave you." He halted suddenly, and she stood beside him. "Here comes Dave Harney. He will see you home. It's only a step."

"You are doing neither yourself nor me kindness." She spoke with final firmness. "I decline to consider this the end. We are too close to it to understand it fairly. You must come and see me when we are both calmer. I refuse to be treated in this fashion. It is childish of you." She shot a hasty glance at the approaching Eldorado king. "I do not think I deserve it at your hands. I refuse to lose you as a friend. And I insist that you come and see me, that things remain on the old footing."

He shook his head.

"Hello!" Dave Harney touched his cap and slowed down loose-jointedly.

"Sorry you didn't take my tip? Dogs gone up a dollar a pound since

yesterday, and still a-whoopin'. Good-afternoon, Miss Frona, and Mr.

Corliss. Goin' my way?"

"Miss Welse is." Corliss touched the visor of his cap and half-turned on his heel.

"Where're you off to?" Dave demanded.

"Got an appointment," he lied.

"Remember," Frona called to him, "you must come and see me."

"Too busy, I'm afraid, just now. Good-by. So long, Dave."

"Jemimy!" Dave remarked, staring after him; "but he's a hustler. Always busy—with big things, too. Wonder why he didn't go in for dogs?"

CHAPTER XV

But Corliss did go back to see her, and before the day was out. A little bitter self-communion had not taken long to show him his childishness. The sting of loss was hard enough, but the thought, now they could be nothing to each other, that her last impressions of him should be bad, hurt almost as much, and in a way, even more. And further, putting all to the side, he was really ashamed. He had thought that he could have taken such a disappointment more manfully, especially since in advance he had not been at all sure of his footing.

So he called upon her, walked with her up to the Barracks, and on the way, with her help, managed to soften the awkwardness which the morning had left between them. He talked reasonably and meekly, which she countenanced, and would have apologized roundly had she not prevented him.

"Not the slightest bit of blame attaches to you," she said. "Had I been in your place, I should probably have done the same and behaved much more outrageously. For you were outrageous, you know."

"But had you been in my place, and I in yours," he answered, with a weak attempt at humor, "there would have been no need."

She smiled, glad that he was feeling less strongly about it.

"But, unhappily, our social wisdom does not permit such a reversal," he added, more with a desire to be saying something.

"Ah!" she laughed. "There's where my Jesuitism comes in. I can rise above our social wisdom."

"You don't mean to say,—that—?"

"There, shocked as usual! No, I could not be so crude as to speak outright, but I might *finesse*, as you whist-players say. Accomplish the same end, only with greater delicacy. After all, a distinction without a difference."

"Could you?" he asked.

"I know I could,—if the occasion demanded. I am not one to let what I might deem life-happiness slip from me without a struggle. That" (judicially) "occurs only in books and among sentimentalists. As my father always says, I belong to the strugglers and fighters. That which appeared to me great and sacred, that would I battle for, though I brought heaven tumbling about my ears."

"You have made me very happy, Vance," she said at parting by the Barracks gates. "And things shall go along in the same old way. And mind, not a bit less of you than formerly; but, rather, much more."

But Corliss, after several perfunctory visits, forgot the way which led to Jacob Welse's home, and applied himself savagely to his work. He even had the hypocrisy, at times, to felicitate himself upon his escape, and to draw bleak fireside pictures of the dismal future which would have been had he and Frona incompatibly mated. But this was only at times. As a rule, the thought of her made him hungry, in a way akin to physical hunger; and the one thing he found to overcome it was hard work and plenty of it. But even then, what of trail and creek, and camp and survey, he could only get away from her in his waking hours. In his sleep he was ignobly conquered, and Del Bishop, who was with him much, studied his restlessness and gave a ready ear to his mumbled words.

The pocket-miner put two and two together, and made a correct induction from the different little things which came under his notice. But this did not require any great astuteness. The simple fact that he no longer called on Frona was sufficient evidence of an unprospering suit. But Del went a step farther, and drew the corollary that St. Vincent was the cause of it all. Several times he had seen the correspondent with Frona, going one place and another, and was duly incensed thereat.

"I'll fix 'm yet!" he muttered in camp one evening, over on Gold Bottom.

"Whom?" Corliss queried.

"Who? That newspaper man, that's who!"

"What for?"

"Aw—general principles. Why'n't you let me paste 'm that night at the Opera House?"

Corliss laughed at the recollection. "Why did you strike him, Del?"

"General principles," Del snapped back and shut up.

But Del Bishop, for all his punitive spirit, did not neglect the main chance, and on the return trip, when they came to the forks of Eldorado and Bonanza, he called a halt.

"Say, Corliss," he began at once, "d'you know what a hunch is?" His employer nodded his comprehension. "Well, I've got one. I ain't never asked favors of you before, but this once I want you to lay over here till to-morrow. Seems to me my fruit ranch is 'most in sight. I can damn near smell the oranges a-ripenin'."

"Certainly," Corliss agreed. "But better still, I'll run on down to Dawson, and you can come in when you've finished hunching."

"Say!" Del objected. "I said it was a hunch; and I want to ring you in on it, savve? You're all right, and you've learned a hell of a lot out of books. You're a regular high-roller when it comes to the laboratory, and all that; but it takes yours truly to get down and read the face of nature without spectacles. Now I've got a theory—"

Corliss threw up his hands in affected dismay, and the pocket-miner began to grow angry.

"That's right! Laugh! But it's built right up on your own pet theory of erosion and changed riverbeds. And I didn't pocket among the Mexicans two years for nothin'. Where d'you s'pose this Eldorado gold came from?—rough, and no signs of washin'? Eh? There's where you need your spectacles. Books have made you short-sighted. But never mind how. 'Tisn't exactly pockets, neither, but I know what I'm spelling about. I ain't been keepin' tab on traces for my health. I can tell you mining sharps more about the lay of Eldorado

Creek in one minute than you could figure out in a month of Sundays. But never mind, no offence. You lay over with me till to-morrow, and you can buy a ranch 'longside of mine, sure." "Well, all right. I can rest up and look over my notes while you're hunting your ancient river-bed."

"Didn't I tell you it was a hunch?" Del reproachfully demanded.

"And haven't I agreed to stop over? What more do you want?"

"To give you a fruit ranch, that's what! Just to go with me and nose round a bit, that's all."

"I do not want any of your impossible fruit ranches. I'm tired and worried; can't you leave me alone? I think I am more than fair when I humor you to the extent of stopping over. You may waste your time nosing around, but I shall stay in camp. Understand?"

"Burn my body, but you're grateful! By the Jumpin' Methuselah, I'll quit my job in two minutes if you don't fire me. Me a-layin' 'wake nights and workin' up my theory, and calculatin' on lettin' you in, and you a-snorin' and Frona-this and Frona-that—"

"That'll do! Stop it!"

"The hell it will! If I didn't know more about gold-mining than you do about courtin'—"

Corliss sprang at him, but Del dodged to one side and put up his fists. Then he ducked a wild right and left swing and side-stepped his way into firmer footing on the hard trail.

"Hold on a moment," he cried, as Corliss made to come at him again.

"Just a second. If I lick you, will you come up the hillside with me?"

"Yes."

"And if I don't, you can fire me. That's fair. Come on."

Vance had no show whatever, as Del well knew, who played with him, feinting, attacking, retreating, dazzling, and disappearing every now and again out of his field of vision in a most exasperating way. As Vance speedily discovered, he possessed very little correlation between mind and body, and the next thing he discovered was that he was lying in the snow and slowly coming back to his senses.

"How—how did you do it?" he stammered to the pocket-miner, who had his head on his knee and was rubbing his forehead with snow.

"Oh, you'll do!" Del laughed, helping him limply to his feet. "You're the right stuff. I'll show you some time. You've got lots to learn yet what you won't find in books. But not now. We've got to wade in and make camp, then you're comin' up the hill with me."

"Hee! hee!" he chuckled later, as they fitted the pipe of the Yukon stove. "Slow sighted and short. Couldn't follow me, eh? But I'll show you some time, oh, I'll show you all right, all right!"

"Grab an axe an' come on," he commanded when the camp was completed.

He led the way up Eldorado, borrowed a pick, shovel, and pan at a cabin, and headed up among the benches near the mouth of French Creek. Vance, though feeling somewhat sore, was laughing at himself by this time and enjoying the situation. He exaggerated the humility with which he walked at the heel of his conqueror, while the extravagant servility which marked his obedience to his hired man made that individual grin.

"You'll do. You've got the makin's in you!" Del threw down the tools and scanned the run of the snow-surface carefully. "Here, take the axe, shinny up the hill, and lug me down some *skookum* dry wood."

By the time Corliss returned with the last load of wood, the pocket-miner had cleared away the snow and moss in divers spots, and formed, in general design, a rude cross.

"Cuttin' her both ways," he explained. "Mebbe I'll hit her here, or over there, or up above; but if there's anything in the hunch, this is the place. Bedrock dips in above, and it's deep there and most likely richer, but too much work. This is the rim of the bench. Can't be more'n a couple of feet down. All we want is indications; afterwards we can tap in from the side."

As he talked, he started fires here and there on the uncovered spaces. "But look here, Corliss, I want you to mind this ain't pocketin'. This is just plain ordinary 'prentice work; but pocketin'"—he straightened up his back and spoke reverently—"but pocketin' is the deepest science and the finest art. Delicate to a hair's-breadth, hand and eye true and steady as steel. When you've got to burn your pan blue-black twice a day, and out of a shovelful of gravel wash down to the one wee speck of flour gold,—why, that's washin', that's what it is. Tell you what, I'd sooner follow a pocket than eat."

"And you would sooner fight than do either." Bishop stopped to consider. He weighed himself with care equal to that of retaining the one wee speck of flour gold. "No, I wouldn't, neither. I'd take pocketin' in mine every time. It's as bad as dope; Corliss, sure. If it once gets a-hold of you, you're a goner. You'll never shake it. Look at me! And talk about pipe-dreams; they can't burn a candle 'longside of it."

He walked over and kicked one of the fires apart. Then he lifted the pick, and the steel point drove in and stopped with a metallic clang, as though brought up by solid cement.

"Ain't thawed two inches," he muttered, stooping down and groping with his fingers in the wet muck. The blades of last year's grass had been burned away, but he managed to gather up and tear away a handful of the roots.

"Hell!"

"What's the matter?" Corliss asked.

"Hell!" he repeated in a passionless way, knocking the dirt-covered roots against the pan.

Corliss went over and stooped to closer inspection. "Hold on!" he cried, picking up two or three grimy bits of dirt and rubbing them with his fingers. A bright yellow flashed forth.

"Hell!" the pocket-miner reiterated tonelessly. "First rattle out the box. Begins at the grass roots and goes all the way down."

Head turned to the side and up, eyes closed, nostrils distended and quivering, he rose suddenly to his feet and sniffed the air. Corliss looked up wonderingly.

"Huh!" the pocket-miner grunted. Then he drew a deep breath. "Can't you smell them oranges?"

CHAPTER XVI

The stampede to French Hill was on by the beginning of Christmas week. Corliss and Bishop had been in no hurry to record for they looked the ground over carefully before blazing their stakes, and let a few close friends into the secret,—Harney, Welse, Trethaway, a Dutch *chechaquo* who had forfeited both feet to the frost, a couple of the mounted police, an old pal with whom Del had prospected through the Black Hills Country, the washerwoman at the Forks, and last, and notably, Lucile. Corliss was responsible for her getting in on the lay, and he drove and marked her stakes himself, though it fell to the colonel to deliver the invitation to her to come and be rich.

In accordance with the custom of the country, those thus benefited offered to sign over half-interests to the two discoverers. Corliss would not tolerate the proposition. Del was similarly minded, though swayed by no ethical reasons. He had enough as it stood. "Got my fruit ranch paid for, double the size I was calculatin' on," he explained; "and if I had any more, I wouldn't know what to do with it, sure."

After the strike, Corliss took it upon himself as a matter of course to look about for another man; but when he brought a keen-eyed Californian into camp, Del was duly wroth.

"Not on your life," he stormed.

"But you are rich now," Vance answered, "and have no need to work."

"Rich, hell!" the pocket-miner rejoined. "Accordin' to covenant, you can't fire me; and I'm goin' to hold the job down as long as my sweet will'll let me. Savve?"

On Friday morning, early, all interested parties appeared before the Gold Commissioner to record their claims. The news went abroad immediately. In five minutes the first stampeders were hitting the trail. At the end of half an hour the town was afoot. To prevent mistakes on their property,—jumping, moving of stakes, and mutilation of notices,—Vance and Del, after promptly recording, started to return. But with the government seal attached to their holdings, they took it leisurely, the stampeders sliding past them in a steady stream. Midway, Del chanced to look behind. St. Vincent was in sight, footing it at a lively pace, the regulation stampeding pack on his shoulders. The trail made a sharp bend at that place, and with the exception of the three of them no one was in sight.

"Don't speak to me. Don't recognize me," Del cautioned sharply, as he spoke, buttoning his nose-strap across his face, which served to quite hide his identity. "There's a water-hole over there. Get down on your belly and make a blind at gettin' a drink. Then go on by your lonely to the claims; I've business of my own to handle. And for the love of your bother don't say a word to me or to the skunk. Don't let 'm see your face."

Corliss obeyed wonderingly, stepping aside from the beaten path, lying down in the snow, and dipping into the water-hole with an empty condensed milk-can. Bishop bent on one knee and stooped as though fastening his moccasin. Just as St. Vincent came up with him he finished tying the knot, and started forward with the feverish haste of a man trying to make up for lost time.

"I say, hold on, my man," the correspondent called out to him.

Bishop shot a hurried glance at him and pressed on. St. Vincent broke into a run till they were side by side again.

"Is this the way—"

"To the benches of French Hill?" Del snapped him short. "Betcher your life. That's the way I'm headin'. So long."

He ploughed forward at a tremendous rate, and the correspondent, half-running, swung in behind with the evident intention of taking the pace. Corliss, still in the dark, lifted his head and watched them go; but when he saw the pocket-miner swerve abruptly to the right and take the trail up Adams Creek, the light dawned upon him and he laughed softly to himself.

Late that night Del arrived in camp on Eldorado exhausted but jubilant.

"Didn't do a thing to him," he cried before he was half inside the tent-flaps. "Gimme a bite to eat" (grabbing at the teapot and running a hot flood down his throat),—"cookin'-fat, slush, old moccasins, candle-ends, anything!"

Then he collapsed upon the blankets and fell to rubbing his stiff leg-muscles while Corliss fried bacon and dished up the beans.

"What about 'm?" he exulted between mouthfuls. "Well, you can stack your chips that he didn't get in on the French Hill benches. *How far is it, my man?*" (in the well-mimicked, patronizing tones of St. Vincent). "*How far is it?*" with the patronage left out. "*How far to French Hill?*" weakly. "*How far do you think it is?*" very weakly, with a tremolo which hinted of repressed tears. "*How far—*"

The pocket-miner burst into roars of laughter, which were choked by a misdirected flood of tea, and which left him coughing and speechless.

"Where'd I leave 'm?" when he had recovered. "Over on the divide to Indian River, winded, plum-beaten, done for. Just about able to crawl into the nearest camp, and that's about all. I've covered fifty stiff miles myself, so here's for bed. Good-night. Don't call me in the mornin'."

He turned into the blankets all-standing, and as he dozed off Vance could hear him muttering, "*How far is it, my man? I say, how far is it?*"

Regarding Lucile, Corliss was disappointed. "I confess I cannot understand her," he said to Colonel Trethaway. "I thought her bench claim would make her independent of the Opera House."

"You can't get a dump out in a day," the colonel interposed.

"But you can mortgage the dirt in the ground when it prospects as hers does. Yet I took that into consideration, and offered to advance her a few thousand, non-interest bearing, and she declined. Said she didn't need it,—in fact, was really grateful; thanked me, and said that any time I was short to come and see her."

Trethaway smiled and played with his watch-chain. "What would you? Life, even here, certainly means more to you and me than a bit of grub, a piece of blanket, and a Yukon stove. She is as gregarious as the rest of us, and probably a little more so. Suppose you cut her off from the Opera House,— what then? May she go up to the Barracks and consort with the captain's lady, make social calls on Mrs. Schoville, or chum with Frona? Don't you see? Will you escort her, in daylight, down the public street?"

"Will you?" Vance demanded.

"Ay," the colonel replied, unhesitatingly, "and with pleasure."

"And so will I; but—" He paused and gazed gloomily into the fire. "But see how she is going on with St. Vincent. As thick as thieves they are, and always together."

"Puzzles me," Trethaway admitted. "I can grasp St. Vincent's side of it. Many irons in the fire, and Lucile owns a bench claim on the second tier of French Hill. Mark me, Corliss, we can tell infallibly the day that Frona consents to go to his bed and board,—if she ever does consent."

"And that will be?"

"The day St. Vincent breaks with Lucile."

Corliss pondered, and the colonel went on.

"But I can't grasp Lucile's side of it. What she can see in St. Vincent—"

"Her taste is no worse than—than that of the rest of the women," Vance broke in hotly. "I am sure that—"

"Frona could not display poor taste, eh?" Corliss turned on his heel and walked out, and left Colonel Trethaway smiling grimly.

Vance Corliss never knew how many people, directly and indirectly, had his cause at heart that Christmas week. Two men strove in particular, one for him and one for the sake of Frona. Pete Whipple, an old-timer in the land, possessed an Eldorado claim directly beneath French Hill, also a woman of the country for a wife,—a swarthy *breed*, not over pretty, whose Indian mother had mated with a Russian fur-trader some thirty years before at Kutlik on the Great Delta. Bishop went down one Sunday morning to yarn away an hour or so with Whipple, but found the wife alone in the cabin. She talked a bastard English gibberish which was an anguish to hear, so the pocket-miner resolved to smoke a pipe and depart without rudeness. But he got her tongue wagging, and to such an extent that he stopped and smoked many pipes, and whenever she lagged, urged her on again. He grunted and chuckled and swore in undertones while he listened, punctuating her narrative regularly with *hells*! which adequately expressed the many shades of interest he felt.

In the midst of it, the woman fished an ancient leather-bound volume, all scarred and marred, from the bottom of a dilapidated chest, and thereafter it lay on the table between them. Though it remained unopened, she constantly referred to it by look and gesture, and each time she did so a greedy light blazed in Bishop's eyes. At the end, when she could say no more and had repeated herself from two to half a dozen times, he pulled out his sack. Mrs. Whipple set up the gold scales and placed the weights, which he counterbalanced with a hundred dollars' worth of dust. Then he departed up the hill to the tent, hugging the purchase closely, and broke in on Corliss, who sat in the blankets mending moccasins.

"I'll fix 'm yet," Del remarked casually, at the same time patting the book and throwing it down on the bed.

Corliss looked up inquiringly and opened it. The paper was yellow with age and rotten from the weather-wear of trail, while the text was printed in Russian. "I didn't know you were a Russian scholar, Del," he quizzed. "But I can't read a line of it."

"Neither can I, more's the pity; nor does Whipple's woman savve the lingo. I got it from her. But her old man—he was full Russian, you know—he used to read it aloud to her. But she knows what she knows and what her old man knew, and so do I."

"And what do the three of you know?"

"Oh, that's tellin'," Bishop answered, coyly. "But you wait and watch my smoke, and when you see it risin', you'll know, too."

Matt McCarthy came in over the ice Christmas week, summed up the situation so far as Frona and St. Vincent were concerned, and did not like it. Dave Harney furnished him with full information, to which he added that obtained from Lucile, with whom he was on good terms. Perhaps it was because he received the full benefit of the sum of their prejudice; but no matter how, he at any rate answered roll-call with those who looked upon the correspondent with disfavor. It was impossible for them to tell why they did not approve of the man, but somehow St. Vincent was never much of a success with men. This, in turn, might have been due to the fact that he shone so resplendently with women as to cast his fellows in eclipse; for otherwise, in his intercourse with men, he was all that a man could wish. There was nothing domineering or over-riding about him, while he manifested a good fellowship at least equal to their own.

Yet, having withheld his judgment after listening to Lucile and Harney, Matt McCarthy speedily reached a verdict upon spending an hour with St. Vincent at Jacob Welse's,—and this in face of the fact that what Lucile had said had been invalidated by Matt's learning of her intimacy with the man in question. Strong of friendship, quick of heart and hand, Matt did not let the grass grow under his feet. "'Tis I'll be takin' a social fling meself, as befits a mimber iv the noble Eldorado Dynasty," he explained, and went up the hill to a whist party in Dave Harney's cabin. To himself he added, "An' belike, if Satan takes his eye off his own, I'll put it to that young cub iv his."

But more than once during the evening he discovered himself challenging his own judgment. Probe as he would with his innocent wit, Matt found himself baffled. St. Vincent certainly rang true. Simple, light-hearted, unaffected, joking and being joked in all good-nature, thoroughly democratic. Matt failed to catch the faintest echo of insincerity.

"May the dogs walk on me grave," he communed with himself while studying a hand which suffered from a plethora of trumps. "Is it the years are tellin', puttin' the frost in me veins and chillin' the blood? A likely lad, an' is it for me to misjudge because his is a-takin' way with the ladies? Just because the swate creatures smile on the lad an' flutter warm at the sight iv him? Bright eyes and brave men! 'Tis the way they have iv lovin' valor. They're shuddered an' shocked at the cruel an' bloody dades iv war, yet who so quick do they lose their hearts to as the brave butcher-bye iv a sodger? Why not? The lad's done brave things, and the girls give him the warm soft smile. Small reason, that, for me to be callin' him the devil's own cub. Out upon ye, Matt McCarthy, for a crusty old sour-dough, with vitals frozen an' summer gone from yer heart! 'Tis an ossification ye've become! But bide a wee, Matt, bide a wee," he supplemented. "Wait till ye've felt the fale iv his flesh."

The opportunity came shortly, when St. Vincent, with Frona opposite, swept in the full thirteen tricks.

"A rampse!" Matt cried. "Vincent, me lad, a rampse! Yer hand on it, me brave!"

It was a stout grip, neither warm nor clammy, but Matt shook his head dubiously. "What's the good iv botherin'?" he muttered to himself as he shuffled the cards for the next deal. "Ye old fool! Find out first how Frona darlin' stands, an' if it's pat she is, thin 'tis time for doin'."

"Oh, McCarthy's all hunky," Dave Harney assured them later on, coming to the rescue of St. Vincent, who was getting the rough side of the Irishman's wit. The evening was over and the company was putting on its wraps and mittens. "Didn't tell you 'bout his visit to the cathedral, did he, when he was on the Outside? Well, it was suthin' like this, ez he was explainin' it to me. He went to the cathedral durin' service, an' took in the priests and choir-boys in their surplices,—*parkas*, he called 'em,—an' watched the burnin' of the holy incense. 'An' do ye know, Dave, he sez to me, 'they got in an' made a smudge, and there wa'n't a darned mosquito in sight.'"

"True, ivery word iv it." Matt unblushingly fathered Harney's yarn. "An' did ye niver hear tell iv the time Dave an' me got drunk on condensed milk?"

"Oh! Horrors!" cried Mrs. Schoville. "But how? Do tell us."

"'Twas durin' the time iv the candle famine at Forty Mile. Cold snap on, an' Dave slides into me shack to pass the time o' day, and glues his eyes on me case iv condensed milk. 'How'd ye like a sip iv Moran's good whiskey?' he sez, eyin' the case iv milk the while. I confiss me mouth went wet at the naked thought iv it. 'But what's the use iv likin'?' sez I, with me sack bulgin' with emptiness.' 'Candles worth tin dollars the dozen,' sez he, 'a dollar apiece. Will ye give six cans iv milk for a bottle iv the old stuff?' 'How'll ye do it?' sez I. 'Trust me,' sez he. 'Give me the cans. 'Tis cold out iv doors, an' I've a pair iv candle-moulds.'

"An' it's the sacred truth I'm tellin' ye all, an' if ye run across Bill Moran he'll back me word; for what does Dave Harney do but lug off me six cans, freeze the milk into his candle-moulds, an' trade them in to bill Moran for a bottle iv tanglefoot!"

As soon as he could be heard through the laughter, Harney raised his voice. "It's true, as McCarthy tells, but he's only told you the half. Can't you guess the rest, Matt?"

Matt shook his head.

"Bein' short on milk myself, an' not over much sugar, I doctored three of your cans with water, which went to make the candles. An' by the bye, I had milk in my coffee for a month to come."

"It's on me, Dave," McCarthy admitted. "'Tis only that yer me host, or I'd be shockin' the ladies with yer nortorious disgraces. But I'll lave ye live this time, Dave. Come, spade the partin' guests; we must be movin'."

"No ye don't, ye young laddy-buck," he interposed, as St. Vincent started to take Frona down the hill, "'Tis her foster-daddy sees her home this night."

McCarthy laughed in his silent way and offered his arm to Frona, while St. Vincent joined in the laugh against himself, dropped back, and joined Miss Mortimer and Baron Courbertin.

"What's this I'm hearin' about you an' Vincent?" Matt bluntly asked as soon as they had drawn apart from the others.

He looked at her with his keen gray eyes, but she returned the look quite as keenly.

"How should I know what you have been hearing?" she countered.

"Whin the talk goes round iv a maid an' a man, the one pretty an' the other not unhandsome, both young an' neither married, does it 'token aught but the one thing?"

"Yes?"

"An' the one thing the greatest thing in all the world."

"Well?" Frona was the least bit angry, and did not feel inclined to help him.

"Marriage, iv course," he blurted out. "'Tis said it looks that way with the pair of ye."

"But is it said that it *is* that way?"

"Isn't the looks iv it enough ?" he demanded.

"No; and you are old enough to know better. Mr. St. Vincent and I—we enjoy each other as friends, that is all. But suppose it is as you say, what of it?"

"Well," McCarthy deliberated, "there's other talk goes round, 'Tis said Vincent is over-thick with a jade down in the town—Lucile, they speak iv her."

"All of which signifies?"

She waited, and McCarthy watched her dumbly.

"I know Lucile, and I like her," Frona continued, filling the gap of his silence, and ostentatiously manoeuvring to help him on. "Do you know her? Don't you like her?"

Matt started to speak, cleared his throat, and halted. At last, in desperation, he blurted out, "For two cents, Frona, I'd lay ye acrost me knee."

She laughed. "You don't dare. I'm not running barelegged at Dyea."

"Now don't be tasin'," he blarneyed.

"I'm not teasing. Don't you like her?—Lucile?"

"An' what iv it?" he challenged, brazenly.

"Just what I asked,—what of it?"

"Thin I'll tell ye in plain words from a man old enough to be yer father. 'Tis undacent, damnably undacent, for a man to kape company with a good young girl—"

"Thank you," she laughed, dropping a courtesy. Then she added, half in bitterness, "There have been others who—"

"Name me the man!" he cried hotly.

"There, there, go on. You were saying?"

"That it's a crying shame for a man to kape company with—with you, an' at the same time be chake by jowl with a woman iv her stamp."

"And why?"

"To come drippin' from the muck to dirty yer claneness! An' ye can ask why?"

"But wait, Matt, wait a moment. Granting your premises—"

"Little I know iv primises," he growled. "'Tis facts I'm dalin' with."

Frona bit her lip. "Never mind. Have it as you will; but let me go on and I will deal with facts, too. When did you last see Lucile?"

"An' why are ye askin'?" he demanded, suspiciously.

"Never mind why. The fact."

"Well, thin, the fore part iv last night, an' much good may it do ye."

"And danced with her?"

"A rollickin' Virginia reel, an' not sayin' a word iv a quadrille or so. Tis at square dances I excel meself."

Frona walked on in a simulated brown study, no sound going up from the twain save the complaint of the snow from under their moccasins.

"Well, thin?" he questioned, uneasily.

"An' what iv it?" he insisted after another silence.

"Oh, nothing," she answered. "I was just wondering which was the muckiest, Mr. St. Vincent or you—or myself, with whom you have both been cheek by jowl."

Now, McCarthy was unversed in the virtues of social wisdom, and, though he felt somehow the error of her position, he could not put it into definite thought; so he steered wisely, if weakly, out of danger.

"It's gettin' mad ye are with yer old Matt," he insinuated, "who has yer own good at heart, an' because iv it makes a fool iv himself."

"No, I'm not."

"But ye are."

"There!" leaning swiftly to him and kissing him. "How could I remember the Dyea days and be angry?"

"Ah, Frona darlin', well may ye say it. I'm the dust iv the dirt under yer feet, an' ye may walk on me—anything save get mad. I cud die for ye, swing for ye, to make ye happy. I cud kill the man that gave ye sorrow, were it but a thimbleful, an' go plump into hell with a smile on me face an' joy in me heart."

They had halted before her door, and she pressed his arm gratefully. "I am not angry, Matt. But with the exception of my father you are the only person I would have permitted to talk to me about this—this affair in the way you have. And though I like you, Matt, love you better than ever, I shall nevertheless be very angry if you mention it again. You have no right. It is something that concerns me alone. And it is wrong of you—"

"To prevint ye walkin' blind into danger?"

"If you wish to put it that way, yes."

He growled deep down in his throat.

"What is it you are saying?" she asked.

"That ye may shut me mouth, but that ye can't bind me arm."

"But you mustn't, Matt, dear, you mustn't."

Again he answered with a subterranean murmur.

"And I want you to promise me, now, that you will not interfere in my life that way, by word or deed."

"I'll not promise."

"But you must."

"I'll not. Further, it's gettin' cold on the stoop, an' ye'll be frostin' yer toes, the pink little toes I fished splinters out iv at Dyea. So it's in with ye, Frona girl, an' good-night."

He thrust her inside and departed. When he reached the corner he stopped suddenly and regarded his shadow on the snow. "Matt McCarthy, yer a damned fool! Who iver heard iv a Welse not knowin' their own mind? As though ye'd niver had dalin's with the stiff-necked breed, ye calamitous son iv misfortune!"

Then he went his way, still growling deeply, and at every growl the curious wolf-dog at his heels bristled and bared its fangs.

CHAPTER XVII

"Tired?"

Jacob Welse put both hands on Frona's shoulders, and his eyes spoke the love his stiff tongue could not compass. The tree and the excitement and the pleasure were over with, a score or so of children had gone home frostily happy across the snow, the last guest had departed, and Christmas Eve and Christmas Day were blending into one.

She returned his fondness with glad-eyed interest, and they dropped into huge comfortable chairs on either side the fireplace, in which the backlog was falling to ruddy ruin.

"And this time next year?" He put the question seemingly to the glowing log, and, as if in ominous foreshadow, it flared brightly and crumbled away in a burst of sparks.

"It is marvellous," he went on, dismissing the future in an effort to shake himself into a wholesomer frame of mind. "It has been one long continuous miracle, the last few months, since you have been with me. We have seen very little of each other, you know, since your childhood, and when I think upon it soberly it is hard to realize that you are really mine, sprung from me, bone of my bone and flesh of my flesh. As the tangle-haired wild young creature of Dyea,—a healthy, little, natural animal and nothing more,—it required no imagination to accept you as one of the breed of Welse. But as Frona, the woman, as you were to-night, as you are now as I look at you, as you have been since you came down the Yukon, it is hard . . . I cannot realize . . . I . . ." He faltered and threw up his hands helplessly. "I almost wish that I had given you no education, that I had kept you with me, faring with me, adventuring with me, achieving with me, and failing with me. I would have known you, now, as we sit by the fire. As it is, I do not. To that which I did know there has been added, somehow (what shall I call it?), a subtlety; complexity,—favorite words of yours,—which is beyond me.

"No." He waved the speech abruptly from her lips. She came over and knelt at his feet, resting her head on his knee and clasping his hand in firm sympathy. "No, that is not true. Those are not the words. I cannot find them. I fail to say what I feel. Let me try again. Underneath all you do carry the stamp of the breed. I knew I risked the loss of that when I sent you away, but I had faith in the persistence of the blood and I took the chance; doubted and feared when you were gone; waited and prayed dumbly, and hoped oftentimes hopelessly; and then the day dawned, the day of days! When they said your boat was coming, death rose and walked on the one hand of me, and on the other life everlasting. *Made or marred; made or marred,*—the words rang through my brain till they maddened me. Would the Welse remain the Welse? Would the blood persist? Would the young shoot rise straight and tall and strong, green with sap and fresh and vigorous? Or would it droop limp and lifeless, withered by the heats of the world other than the little simple, natural Dyea world?

"It was the day of days, and yet it was a lingering, watching, waiting tragedy. You know I had lived the years lonely, fought the lone fight, and you, away, the only kin. If it had failed . . . But your boat shot from the bluffs into the open, and I was half-afraid to look. Men have never called me coward, but I was nearer the coward then than ever and all before. Ay, that moment I had faced death easier. And it was foolish, absurd. How could I know whether it was for good or ill when you drifted a distant speck on the river? Still, I looked, and the miracle began, for I did know. You stood at the steering-sweep. You were a Welse. It seems so little; in truth it meant so much. It was not to be expected of a mere woman, but of a Welse, yes. And when Bishop went over the side, and you gripped the situation as imperatively as the sweep, and your voice rang out, and the Siwashes bent their backs to your will,—then was it the day of days."

"I tried always, and remembered," Frona whispered. She crept up softly till her arm was about his neck and her head against his breast. He rested one arm lightly on her body, and poured her bright hair again and again from his hand in glistening waves.

"As I said, the stamp of the breed was unmarred, but there was yet a difference. There is a difference. I have watched it, studied it, tried to make it out. I have sat at table, proud by the side of you, but dwarfed. When you talked of little things I was large enough to follow; when of big things, too small. I knew you, had my hand on you, when *presto*! and you were away, gone—I was lost. He is a fool who knows not his own ignorance; I was wise enough to know mine. Art, poetry, music,—what do I know of them? And they were the great things, are the great things to you, mean more to you than the little things I may comprehend. And I had hoped, blindly, foolishly, that we might be one in the spirit as well as the one flesh. It has been bitter, but I have faced it, and understand. But to see my own red blood get away from me, elude me, rise above me! It stuns. God! I have heard you read from your Browning—no, no; do not speak—and watched the play of your face, the uplift and the passion of it, and all the while the words droning in upon me, meaningless, musical, maddening. And Mrs. Schoville sitting there, nursing an expression of idiotic ecstasy, and understanding no more than I. I could have strangled her.

"Why, I have stolen away, at night, with your Browning, and locked myself in like a thief in fear. The text was senseless, I have beaten my head with my fist like a wild man, to try and knock some comprehension into it. For my life had worked itself out along one set groove, deep and narrow. I was in the rut. I had done those things which came to my hand and done them well; but the time was past; I could not turn my hand anew. I, who am strong and dominant, who have played large with destiny, who could buy body and soul a thousand painters and versifiers, was baffled by a few paltry cents' worth of printed paper!"

He spilled her hair for a moment's silence.

"To come back. I had attempted the impossible, gambled against the inevitable. I had sent you from me to get that which I had not, dreaming that we would still be one. As though two could be added to two and still remain two. So, to sum up, the breed still holds, but you have learned an alien tongue. When you speak it I am deaf. And bitterest of all, I know that the new tongue is the greater. I do not know why I have said all this, made my confession of weakness—"

"Oh, father mine, greatest of men!" She raised her head and laughed into his eyes, the while brushing back the thick iron-gray hair which thatched the dome of his forehead. "You, who have wrestled more mightily, done greater things than these painters and versifiers. You who know so well the law of change. Might not the same plaint fall from your father's lips were he to sit now beside you and look upon your work and you?"

"Yes, yes. I have said that I understand. Do not let us discuss it . . . a moment's weakness. My father was a great man."

"And so mine."

"A struggler to the end of his days. He fought the great lone fight—"

"And so mine."

"And died fighting."

"And so shall mine. So shall we all, we Welses."

He shook her playfully, in token of returning spirits. "But I intend to sell out,—mines, Company, everything,—and study Browning."

"Still the fight. You can't discount the blood, father."

"Why were you not a boy?" he demanded, abruptly. "You would have been a splendid one. As it is, a woman, made to be the delight of some man, you must pass from me—to-morrow, next day, this time next year, who knows how soon? Ah? now I know the direction my thought has been trending. Just as I know you do, so do I recognize the inevitableness of it and the justness. But the man, Frona, the man?"

"Don't," she demurred. "Tell me of your father's fight, the last fight, the great lone fight at Treasure City. Ten to one it was, and well fought. Tell me."

"No, Frona. Do you realize that for the first time in our lives we talk together seriously, as father and daughter,—for the first time? You have had no mother to advise; no father, for I trusted the blood, and wisely, and let you go. But there comes a time when the mother's counsel is needed, and you, you who never knew one?"

Frona yielded, in instant recognition, and waiting, snuggled more closely to him.

"This man, St. Vincent—how is it between you?"

"I . . . I do not know. How do you mean?"

"Remember always, Frona, that you have free choice, yours is the last word. Still, I would like to understand. I could . . . perhaps . . . I might be able to suggest. But nothing more. Still, a suggestion . . ."

There was something inexpressibly sacred about it, yet she found herself tongue-tied. Instead of the one definite thing to say, a muddle of ideas fluttered in her brain. After all, could he understand? Was there not a difference which prevented him from comprehending the motives which, for her, were impelling? For all her harking back to the primitive and stout defence of its sanity and truth, did his native philosophy give him the same code which she drew from her acquired philosophy? Then she stood aside and regarded herself and the queries she put, and drew apart from them, for they breathed of treason.

"There is nothing between us, father," she spoke up resolutely. "Mr. St. Vincent has said nothing, nothing. We are good friends, we like each other, we are very good friends. I think that is all."

"But you like each other; you like him. Is it in the way a woman must like a man before she can honestly share her life with him, lose herself in him? Do you feel with Ruth, so that when the time comes you can say, 'Thy people are my people, and thy God my God'?"

"N——o. It may be; but I cannot, dare not face it, say it or not say it, think it or not think it—now. It is the great affirmation. When it comes it must come, no one may know how or why, in a great white flash, like a revelation, hiding nothing, revealing everything in dazzling, blinding truth. At least I so imagine."

Jacob Welse nodded his head with the slow meditation of one who understands, yet stops to ponder and weigh again.

"But why have you asked, father? Why has Mr. St. Vincent been raised? I have been friends with other men."

"But I have not felt about other men as I do of St. Vincent. We may be truthful, you and I, and forgive the pain we give each other. My opinion counts for no more than another's. Fallibility is the commonest of curses. Nor can I explain why I feel as I do—I oppose much in the way you expect to when your great white flash sears your eyes. But, in a word, I do not like St. Vincent."

"A very common judgment of him among the men," Frona interposed, driven irresistibly to the defensive.

"Such consensus of opinion only makes my position stronger," he returned, but not disputatively. "Yet I must remember that I look upon him as men look. His popularity with women must proceed from the fact that women look differently than men, just as women do differ physically and spiritually from men. It is deep, too deep for me to explain. I but follow my nature and try to be just."

"But have you nothing more definite?" she asked, groping for better comprehension of his attitude. "Can you not put into some sort of coherence some one certain thing of the things you feel?"

"I hardly dare. Intuitions can rarely be expressed in terms of thought. But let me try. We Welses have never known a coward. And where cowardice is, nothing can endure. It is like building on sand, or like a vile disease which rots and rots and we know not when it may break forth."

"But it seems to me that Mr. St. Vincent is the last man in the world with whom cowardice may be associated. I cannot conceive of him in that light."

The distress in her face hurt him. "I know nothing against St. Vincent. There is no evidence to show that he is anything but what he appears. Still, I cannot help feeling it, in my fallible human way. Yet there is one thing I have heard, a sordid pot-house brawl in the Opera House. Mind you, Frona, I say nothing against the brawl or the place,—men are men, but it is *said* that he did not act as a man ought that night."

"But as you say, father, men are men. We would like to have them other than they are, for the world surely would be better; but we must take them as they are. Lucile—"

"No, no; you misunderstand. I did not refer to her, but to the fight. He did not . . . he was cowardly."

"But as you say, it is *said*. He told me about it, not long afterwards, and I do not think he would have dared had there been anything—"

"But I do not make it as a charge," Jacob Welse hastily broke in. "Merely hearsay, and the prejudice of the men would be sufficient to account for the tale. And it has no bearing, anyway. I should not have brought it up, for I have known good men funk in my time—buck fever, as it were. And now let us dismiss it all from our minds. I merely wished to suggest, and I suppose I have bungled. But understand this, Frona," turning her face up to his, "understand above all things and in spite of them, first, last, and always, that you are my daughter, and that I believe your life is sacredly yours, not mine, yours to deal with and to make or mar. Your life is yours to live, and in so far that I influence it you will not have lived your life, nor would your life have been yours. Nor would you have been a Welse, for there was never a Welse yet who suffered dictation. They died first, or went away to pioneer on the edge of things.

"Why, if you thought the dance house the proper or natural medium for self-expression, I might be sad, but to-morrow I would sanction your going down to the Opera House. It would be unwise to stop you, and, further, it is not our way. The Welses have ever stood by, in many a lost cause and forlorn hope, knee to knee and shoulder to shoulder. Conventions are worthless for such as we. They are for the swine who without them would wallow deeper. The weak must obey or be crushed; not so with the strong. The mass is nothing; the individual everything; and it is the individual, always, that rules the mass and gives the law. A fig for what the world says! If the Welse should procreate a bastard line this day, it would be the way of the Welse, and you would be a daughter of the Welse, and in the face of hell and heaven, of God himself, we would stand together, we of the one blood, Frona, you and I."

"You are larger than I," she whispered, kissing his forehead, and the caress of her lips seemed to him the soft impact of a leaf falling through the still autumn air.

And as the heat of the room ebbed away, he told of her foremother and of his, and of the sturdy Welse who fought the great lone fight, and died, fighting, at Treasure City.

CHAPTER XVIII

The "Doll's House" was a success. Mrs. Schoville ecstasized over it in terms so immeasurable, so unqualifiable, that Jacob Welse, standing near, bent a glittering gaze upon her plump white throat and unconsciously clutched and closed his hand on an invisible windpipe. Dave Harney proclaimed its excellence effusively, though he questioned the soundness of Nora's philosophy and swore by his Puritan gods that Torvald was the longest-eared Jack in two hemispheres. Even Miss Mortimer, antagonistic as she was to the whole school, conceded that the players had redeemed it; while Matt McCarthy announced that he didn't blame Nora darlin' the least bit, though he told the Gold Commissioner privately that a song or so and a skirt dance wouldn't have hurt the performance.

"Iv course the Nora girl was right," he insisted to Harney, both of whom were walking on the heels of Frona and St. Vincent. "I'd be seein'—"

"Rubber—"

"Rubber yer gran'mother!" Matt wrathfully exclaimed.

"Ez I was sayin'," Harney continued, imperturbably, "rubber boots is goin' to go sky-high 'bout the time of wash-up. Three ounces the pair, an' you kin put your chips on that for a high card. You kin gather 'em in now for an ounce a pair and clear two on the deal. A cinch, Matt, a dead open an' shut."

"The devil take you an' yer cinches! It's Nora darlin' I have in me mind the while."

They bade good-by to Frona and St. Vincent and went off disputing under the stars in the direction of the Opera House.

Gregory St. Vincent heaved an audible sigh. "At last."

"At last what?" Frona asked, incuriously.

"At last the first opportunity for me to tell you how well you did. You carried off the final scene wonderfully; so well that it seemed you were really passing out of my life forever."

"What a misfortune!"

"It was terrible."

"No."

"But, yes. I took the whole condition upon myself. You were not Nora, you were Frona; nor I Torvald, but Gregory. When you made your exit, capped and jacketed and travelling-bag in hand, it seemed I could not possibly stay and finish my lines. And when the door slammed and you were gone, the only thing that saved me was the curtain. It brought me to myself, or else I would have rushed after you in the face of the audience."

"It is strange how a simulated part may react upon one," Frona speculated.

"Or rather?" St. Vincent suggested.

Frona made no answer, and they walked on without speech. She was still under the spell of the evening, and the exaltation which had come to her as Nora had not yet departed. Besides, she read between the lines of St. Vincent's conversation, and was oppressed by the timidity which comes over woman when she faces man on the verge of the greater intimacy.

It was a clear, cold night, not over-cold,—not more than forty below,— and the land was bathed in a soft, diffused flood of light which found its source not in the stars, nor yet in the moon, which was somewhere over on the other side of the world. From the south-east to the northwest a pale-greenish glow fringed the rim of the heavens, and it was from this the dim radiance was exhaled.

Suddenly, like the ray of a search-light, a band of white light ploughed overhead. Night turned to ghostly day on the instant, then blacker night descended. But to the southeast a noiseless commotion was apparent. The glowing greenish gauze was in a ferment, bubbling, uprearing, downfalling, and tentatively thrusting huge bodiless hands into the upper ether. Once more a cyclopean rocket twisted its fiery way across the sky, from horizon to zenith, and on, and on, in tremendous flight, to horizon again. But the span could not hold, and in its wake the black night brooded. And yet again, broader, stronger, deeper, lavishly spilling streamers to right and left, it flaunted the midmost zenith with its gorgeous flare, and passed on and down to the further edge of the world. Heaven was bridged at last, and the bridge endured!

At this flaming triumph the silence of earth was broken, and ten thousand wolf-dogs, in long-drawn unisoned howls, sobbed their dismay and grief. Frona shivered, and St. Vincent passed his arm about her waist. The woman in her was aware of the touch of man, and of a slight tingling thrill of vague delight; but she made no resistance. And as the wolf-dogs mourned at her feet and the aurora wantoned overhead, she felt herself drawn against him closely.

"Need I tell my story?" he whispered.

She drooped her head in tired content on his shoulder, and together they watched the burning vault wherein the stars dimmed and vanished. Ebbing, flowing, pulsing to some tremendous rhythm, the prism colors hurled themselves in luminous deluge across the firmament. Then the canopy of heaven became a mighty loom, wherein imperial purple and deep sea-green blended, wove, and interwove, with blazing woof and flashing warp, till the most delicate of tulles, fluorescent and bewildering, was daintily and airily shaken in the face of the astonished night.

Without warning the span was sundered by an arrogant arm of black. The arch dissolved in blushing confusion. Chasms of blackness yawned, grew, and rushed together. Broken masses of strayed color and fading fire stole timidly towards the sky-line. Then the dome of night towered imponderable, immense, and the stars came back one by one, and the wolf-dogs mourned anew.

"I can offer you so little, dear," the man said with a slightly perceptible bitterness. "The precarious fortunes of a gypsy wanderer."

And the woman, placing his hand and pressing it against her heart, said, as a great woman had said before her, "A tent and a crust of bread with you, Richard."

CHAPTER XIX

How-ha was only an Indian woman, bred of a long line of fish-eating, meat-rending carnivores, and her ethics were as crude and simple as her blood. But long contact with the whites had given her an insight into their way of looking at things, and though she grunted contemptuously in her secret soul, she none the less understood their way perfectly. Ten years previous she had cooked for Jacob Welse, and served him in one fashion or another ever since; and when on a dreary January morning she opened the front door in response to the deep-tongued knocker, even her stolid presence was shaken as she recognized the visitor. Not that the average man or woman would have so recognized. But How-ha's faculties of observing and remembering details had been developed in a hard school where death dealt his blow to the lax and life saluted the vigilant.

How-ha looked up and down the woman who stood before her. Through the heavy veil she could barely distinguish the flash of the eyes, while the hood of the *parka* effectually concealed the hair, and the *parka* proper the particular outlines of the body. But How-ha paused and looked again. There was something familiar in the vague general outline. She quested back to the shrouded head again, and knew the unmistakable poise. Then How-ha's eyes went blear as she traversed the simple windings of her own brain, inspecting the bare shelves taciturnly stored with the impressions of a meagre life. No disorder; no confused mingling of records; no devious and interminable impress of complex emotions, tangled theories, and bewildering abstractions—nothing but simple facts, neatly classified and conveniently collated. Unerringly from the stores of the past she picked and chose and put together in the instant present, till obscurity dropped from the woman before her, and she knew her, word and deed and look and history.

"Much better you go 'way quickety-quick," How-ha informed her.

"Miss Welse. I wish to see her."

The strange woman spoke in firm, even tones which betokened the will behind, but which failed to move How-ha.

"Much better you go," she repeated, stolidly.

"Here, take this to Frona Welse, and—ah! would you!" (thrusting her knee between the door and jamb) "and leave the door open."

How-ha scowled, but took the note; for she could not shake off the grip of the ten years of servitude to the superior race.

May I see you?

LUCILE.

So the note ran. Frona glanced up expectantly at the Indian woman.

"Um kick toes outside," How-ha explained. "Me tell um go 'way quickety-quick? Eh? You t'ink yes? Um no good. Um—"

"No. Take her,"—Frona was thinking quickly,—"no; bring her up here."

"Much better—"

"Go!"

How-ha grunted, and yielded up the obedience she could not withhold; though, as she went down the stairs to the door, in a tenebrous, glimmering way she wondered that the accident of white skin or swart made master or servant as the case might be.

In the one sweep of vision, Lucile took in Frona smiling with extended hand in the foreground, the dainty dressing-table, the simple finery, the thousand girlish evidences; and with the sweet wholesomeness of it pervading her nostrils, her own girlhood rose up and smote her. Then she turned a bleak eye and cold ear on outward things.

"I am glad you came," Frona was saying. "I have *so* wanted to see you again, and—but do get that heavy *parka* off, please. How thick it is, and what splendid fur and workmanship!"

"Yes, from Siberia." A present from St. Vincent, Lucile felt like adding, but said instead, "The Siberians have not yet learned to scamp their work, you know."

She sank down into the low-seated rocker with a native grace which could not escape the beauty-loving eye of the girl, and with proud-poised head and silent tongue listened to Frona as the minutes ticked away, and observed with impersonal amusement Frona's painful toil at making conversation.

"What has she come for?" Frona asked herself, as she talked on furs and weather and indifferent things.

"If you do not say something, Lucile, I shall get nervous, soon," she ventured at last in desperation. "Has anything happened?"

Lucile went over to the mirror and picked up, from among the trinkets beneath, a tiny open-work miniature of Frona. "This is you? How old were you?"

"Sixteen."

"A sylph, but a cold northern one."

"The blood warms late with us," Frona reproved; "but is—"

"None the less warm for that," Lucile laughed. "And how old are you now?"

"Twenty."

"Twenty," Lucile repeated, slowly. "Twenty," and resumed her seat.

"You are twenty. And I am twenty-four."

"So little difference as that!"

"But our blood warms early." Lucile voiced her reproach across the unfathomable gulf which four years could not plumb.

Frona could hardly hide her vexation. Lucile went over and looked at the miniature again and returned.

"What do you think of love?" she asked abruptly, her face softening unheralded into a smile.

"Love?" the girl quavered.

"Yes, love. What do you know about it? What do you think of it?"

A flood of definitions, glowing and rosy, sped to her tongue, but Frona swept them aside and answered, "Love is immolation."

"Very good—sacrifice. And, now, does it pay?"

"Yes, it pays. Of course it pays. Who can doubt it?"

Lucile's eyes twinkled amusedly.

"Why do you smile?" Frona asked.

"Look at me, Frona." Lucile stood up and her face blazed. "I am twenty-four. Not altogether a fright; not altogether a dunce. I have a heart. I have good red blood and warm. And I have loved. I do not remember the pay. I know only that I have paid."

"And in the paying were paid," Frona took up warmly. "The price was the reward. If love be fallible, yet you have loved; you have done, you have served. What more would you?"

"The whelpage love," Lucile sneered.

"Oh! You are unfair."

"I do you justice," Lucile insisted firmly. "You would tell me that you know; that you have gone unveiled and seen clear-eyed; that without placing more than lips to the brim you have divined the taste of the dregs, and that the taste is good. Bah! The whelpage love! And, oh, Frona, I know; you are full womanly and broad, and lend no ear to little things, but"—she tapped a slender finger to forehead—"it is all here. It is a heady brew, and you have smelled the fumes overmuch. But drain the dregs, turn down the glass, and say that it is good. No, God forbid!" she cried, passionately. "There are good loves. You should find no masquerade, but one fair and shining."

Frona was up to her old trick,—their common one,—and her hand slid down Lucile's arm till hand clasped in hand. "You say things which I feel are wrong, yet may not answer. I can, but how dare I? I dare not put mere thoughts against your facts. I, who have lived so little, cannot in theory give the lie to you who have lived so much—"

"'For he who lives more lives than one, more lives than one must die.'"

From out of her pain, Lucile spoke the words of her pain, and Frona, throwing arms about her, sobbed on her breast in understanding. As for Lucile, the slight nervous ingathering of the brows above her eyes smoothed out, and she pressed the kiss of motherhood, lightly and secretly, on the other's hair. For a space,—then the brows ingathered, the lips drew firm, and she put Frona from her.

"You are going to marry Gregory St. Vincent?"

Frona was startled. It was only a fortnight old, and not a word had been breathed. "How do you know?"

"You have answered." Lucile watched Frona's open face and the bold running advertisement, and felt as the skilled fencer who fronts a tyro, weak of wrist, each opening naked to his hand. "How do I know?" She laughed harshly. "When a man leaves one's arms suddenly, lips wet with last kisses and mouth areek with last lies!"

"And—?"

"Forgets the way back to those arms."

"So?" The blood of the Welse pounded up, and like a hot sun dried the mists from her eyes and left them flashing. "Then that is why you came. I could have guessed it had I given second thought to Dawson's gossip."

"It is not too late." Lucile's lip curled. "And it is your way."

"And I am mindful. What is it? Do you intend telling me what he has done, what he has been to you. Let me say that it is useless. He is a man, as you and I are women."

"No," Lucile lied, swallowing her astonishment.

"I had not thought that any action of his would affect you. I knew you were too great for that. But—have you considered me?"

Frona caught her breath for a moment. Then she straightened out her arms to hold the man in challenge to the arms of Lucile.

"Your father over again," Lucile exclaimed. "Oh, you impossible Welses!"

"But he is not worthy of you, Frona Welse," she continued; "of me, yes. He is not a nice man, a great man, nor a good. His love cannot match with yours. Bah! He does not possess love; passion, of one sort and another, is the best he may lay claim to. That you do not want. It is all, at the best, he can give you. And you, pray what may you give him? Yourself? A prodigious waste! But your father's yellow—"

"Don't go on, or I shall refuse to listen. It is wrong of you." So Frona made her cease, and then, with bold inconsistency, "And what may the woman Lucile give him?"

"Some few wild moments," was the prompt response; "a burning burst of happiness, and the regrets of hell—which latter he deserves, as do I. So the balance is maintained, and all is well."

"But—but—"

"For there is a devil in him," she held on, "a most alluring devil, which delights me, on my soul it does, and which, pray God, Frona, you may never know. For you have no devil; mine matches his and mates. I am free to confess that the whole thing is only an attraction. There is nothing permanent about him, nor about me. And there's the beauty, the balance is preserved."

Frona lay back in her chair and lazily regarded her visitor, Lucile waited for her to speak. It was very quiet.

"Well?" Lucile at last demanded, in a low, curious tone, at the same time rising to slip into her parka.

"Nothing. I was only waiting."

"I am done."

"Then let me say that I do not understand you," Frona summed up, coldly. "I cannot somehow just catch your motive. There is a flat ring to what you have said. However, of this I am sure: for some unaccountable reason you have been untrue to yourself to-day. Do not ask me, for, as I said before, I do not know where or how; yet I am none the less convinced. This I do know, you are not the Lucile I met by the wood trail across the river. That was the true Lucile, little though I saw of her. The woman who is here to-day is a strange woman. I do not know her. Sometimes it has seemed she was Lucile, but rarely. This woman has lied, lied to me, and lied to me about herself. As to what she said of the man, at the worst that is merely an opinion. It may be she has lied about him likewise. The chance is large that she has. What do you think about it?"

"That you are a very clever girl, Frona. That you speak sometimes more truly than you know, and that at others you are blinder than you dream."

"There is something I could love in you, but you have hidden it away so that I cannot find it."

Lucile's lips trembled on the verge of speech. But she settled her *parka* about her and turned to go.

Frona saw her to the door herself, and How-ha pondered over the white who made the law and was greater than the law.

When the door had closed, Lucile spat into the street. "Faugh! St. Vincent! I have defiled my mouth with your name!" And she spat again.

"Come in."

At the summons Matt McCarthy pulled the latch-string, pushed the door open, and closed it carefully behind him.

"Oh, it is you!" St. Vincent regarded his visitor with dark abstraction, then, recollecting himself, held out his hand. "Why, hello, Matt, old man.

My mind was a thousand miles away when you entered. Take a stool and make yourself comfortable. There's the tobacco by your hand. Take a try at it and give us your verdict."

"An' well may his mind be a thousand miles away," Matt assured himself; for in the dark he had passed a woman on the trail who looked suspiciously like Lucile. But aloud, "Sure, an' it's day-dramin' ye mane. An' small wondher."

"How's that?" the correspondent asked, cheerily.

"By the same token that I met Lucile down the trail a piece, an' the heels iv her moccasins pointing to yer shack. It's a bitter tongue the jade slings on occasion," Matt chuckled.

"That's the worst of it." St. Vincent met him frankly. "A man looks sidewise at them for a passing moment, and they demand that the moment be eternal."

Off with the old love's a stiff proposition, eh?"

"I should say so. And you understand. It's easy to see, Matt, you've had some experience in your time."

"In me time? I'll have ye know I'm not too old to still enjoy a bit iv a fling."

"Certainly, certainly. One can read it in your eyes. The warm heart and the roving eye, Matt!" He slapped his visitor on the shoulder with a hearty laugh.

"An' I've none the best iv ye, Vincent. 'Tis a wicked lad ye are,

with a takin' way with the ladies—as plain as the nose on yer face.

Manny's the idle kiss ye've given, an' manny's the heart ye've broke.

But, Vincent, bye, did ye iver know the rale thing?"

"How do you mean?"

"The rale thing, the rale thing—that is—well, have ye been iver a father?"

St. Vincent shook his head.

"And niver have I. But have ye felt the love iv a father, thin?"

"I hardly know. I don't think so."

"Well, I have. An' it's the rale thing, I'll tell ye. If iver a man suckled a child, I did, or the next door to it. A girl child at that, an' she's woman grown, now, an' if the thing is possible, I love her more than her own blood-father. Bad luck, exciptin' her, there was niver but one woman I loved, an' that woman had mated beforetime. Not a soul did I brathe a word to, trust me, nor even herself. But she died. God's love be with her."

His chin went down upon his chest and he quested back to a flaxen-haired Saxon woman, strayed like a bit of sunshine into the log store by the Dyea River. He looked up suddenly, and caught St. Vincent's stare bent blankly to the floor as he mused on other things.

"A truce to foolishness, Vincent."

The correspondent returned to himself with an effort and found the

Irishman's small blue eyes boring into him.

"Are ye a brave man, Vincent?"

For a second's space they searched each other's souls. And in that space Matt could have sworn he saw the faintest possible flicker or flutter in the man's eyes.

He brought his fist down on the table with a triumphant crash. "By

God, yer not!"

The correspondent pulled the tobacco jug over to him and rolled a cigarette. He rolled it carefully, the delicate rice paper crisping in his hand without a tremor; but all the while a red tide mounting up from beneath the collar of his shirt, deepening in the hollows of the cheeks and thinning against the cheekbones above, creeping, spreading, till all his face was aflame.

"'Tis good. An' likely it saves me fingers a dirty job. Vincent, man, the girl child which is woman grown slapes in Dawson this night. God help us, you an' me, but we'll niver hit again the pillow as clane an' pure as she! Vincent, a word to the wise: ye'll niver lay holy hand or otherwise upon her."

The devil, which Lucile had proclaimed, began to quicken,—a fuming, fretting, irrational devil.

"I do not like ye. I kape me raysons to meself. It is sufficient. But take this to heart, an' take it well: should ye be mad enough to make her yer wife, iv that damned day ye'll niver see the inding, nor lay eye upon the bridal bed. Why, man, I cud bate ye to death with me two fists if need be. But it's to be hoped I'll do a nater job. Rest aisy. I promise ye."

"You Irish pig!"

So the devil burst forth, and all unaware, for McCarthy found himself eye-high with the muzzle of a Colt's revolver.

"Is it loaded?" he asked. "I belave ye. But why are ye lingerin'?

Lift the hammer, will ye?"

The correspondent's trigger-finger moved and there was a warning click.

"Now pull it. Pull it, I say. As though ye cud, with that flutter to yer eye."

St. Vincent attempted to turn his head aside.

"Look at me, man!" McCarthy commanded. "Kape yer eyes on me when ye do it."

Unwillingly the sideward movement was arrested, and his eyes returned and met the Irishman's.

"Now!"

St. Vincent ground his teeth and pulled the trigger—at least he thought he did, as men think they do things in dreams. He willed the deed, flashed the order forth; but the flutter of his soul stopped it.

"'Tis paralyzed, is it, that shaky little finger?" Matt grinned into the face of the tortured man. "Now turn it aside, so, an' drop it, gently . . . gently . . . gently." His voice crooned away in soothing diminuendo.

When the trigger was safely down, St. Vincent let the revolver fall from his hand, and with a slight audible sigh sank nervelessly upon a stool. He tried to straighten himself, but instead dropped down upon the table and buried his face in his palsied hands. Matt drew on his mittens, looking down upon him pityingly the while, and went out, closing the door softly behind him.

CHAPTER XX

Where nature shows the rough hand, the sons of men are apt to respond with kindred roughness. The amenities of life spring up only in mellow lands, where the sun is warm and the earth fat. The damp and soggy climate of Britain drives men to strong drink; the rosy Orient lures to the dream splendors of the lotus. The big-bodied, white-skinned northern dweller, rude and ferocious, bellows his anger uncouthly and drives a gross fist into the face of his foe. The supple south-sojourner, silken of smile and lazy of gesture, waits, and does his work from behind, when no man looketh, gracefully and without offence. Their ends are one; the difference lies in their ways, and therein the climate, and the cumulative effect thereof, is the determining factor. Both are sinners, as men born of women have ever been; but the one does his sin openly, in the clear sight of God; the other—as though God could not see—veils his iniquity with shimmering fancies, hiding it like it were some splendid mystery.

These be the ways of men, each as the sun shines upon him and the wind blows against him, according to his kind, and the seed of his father, and the milk of his mother. Each is the resultant of many forces which go to make a pressure mightier than he, and which moulds him in the predestined shape. But, with sound legs under him, he may run away, and meet with a new pressure. He may continue running, each new pressure prodding him as he goes, until he dies and his final form will be that predestined of the many pressures. An exchange of cradle-babes, and the base-born slave may wear the purple imperially, and the royal infant begs an alms as wheedlingly or cringe to the lash as abjectly as his meanest subject. A Chesterfield, with an empty belly, chancing upon good fare, will gorge as faithfully as the swine in the next sty. And an Epicurus, in the dirt-igloo of the Eskimos, will wax eloquent over the whale oil and walrus blubber, or die.

Thus, in the young Northland, frosty and grim and menacing, men stripped off the sloth of the south and gave battle greatly. And they stripped likewise much of the veneer of civilization—all of its follies, most of its foibles, and perhaps a few of its virtues. Maybe so; but they reserved the great traditions and at least lived frankly, laughed honestly, and looked one another in the eyes.

And so it is not well for women, born south of fifty-three and reared gently, to knock loosely about the Northland, unless they be great of heart. They may be soft and tender and sensitive, possessed of eyes which have not lost the lustre and the wonder, and of ears used only to sweet sounds; but if their philosophy is sane and stable, large enough to understand and to forgive, they will come to no harm and attain comprehension. If not, they will see things and hear things which hurt, and they will suffer greatly, and lose faith in man—which is the greatest evil that may happen them. Such should be sedulously cherished, and it were well to depute this to their men-folk, the nearer of kin the better. In line, it were good policy to seek out a cabin on the hill overlooking Dawson, or—best of all—across the Yukon on the western bank. Let them not move abroad unheralded and unaccompanied; and the hillside back of the cabin may be recommended as a fit field for stretching muscles and breathing deeply, a place where their ears may remain undefiled by the harsh words of men who strive to the utmost.

Vance Corliss wiped the last tin dish and filed it away on the shelf, lighted his pipe, and rolled over on his back on the bunk to contemplate the moss-chinked roof of his French Hill cabin. This French Hill cabin stood on the last dip of the hill into Eldorado Creek, close to the main-travelled trail; and its one window blinked cheerily of nights at those who journeyed late.

The door was kicked open, and Del Bishop staggered in with a load of fire-wood. His breath had so settled on his face in a white rime that he could not speak. Such a condition was ever a hardship with the man, so he thrust his face forthwith into the quivering heat above the stove. In a trice the frost was started and the thawed streamlets dancing madly on the white-hot surface beneath. Then the ice began to fall from is beard in chunks, rattling on the lid-tops and simmering spitefully till spurted upward in clouds of steam.

"And so you witness an actual phenomenon, illustrative of the three forms of matter," Vance laughed, mimicking the monotonous tones of the demonstrator; "solid, liquid, and vapor. In another moment you will have the gas."

"Th—th—that's all very well," Bishop spluttered, wrestling with an obstructing piece of ice until it was wrenched from his upper lip and slammed stoveward with a bang.

"How cold do you make it, Del? Fifty?"

"Fifty?" the pocket-miner demanded with unutterable scorn, wiping his face. "Quicksilver's been solid for hours, and it's been gittin' colder an' colder ever since. Fifty? I'll bet my new mittens against your old moccasins that it ain't a notch below seventy."

"Think so?"

"D'ye want to bet?"

Vance nodded laughingly.

"Centigrade or Fahrenheit?" Bishop asked, suddenly suspicious.

"Oh, well, if you want my old moccasins so badly," Vance rejoined, feigning to be hurt by the other's lack of faith, "why, you can have them without betting."

Del snorted and flung himself down on the opposite bunk. "Think yer funny, don't you?" No answer forthcoming, he deemed the retort conclusive, rolled over, and fell to studying the moss chinks.

Fifteen minutes of this diversion sufficed. "Play you a rubber of crib before bed," he challenged across to the other bunk.

"I'll go you." Corliss got up, stretched, and moved the kerosene lamp from the shelf to the table, "Think it will hold out?" he asked, surveying the oil-level through the cheap glass.

Bishop threw down the crib-board and cards, and measured the contents of the lamp with his eye. "Forgot to fill it, didn't I? Too late now. Do it tomorrow. It'll last the rubber out, sure."

Corliss took up the cards, but paused in the shuffling. "We've a big trip before us, Del, about a month from now, the middle of March as near as I can plan it,—up the Stuart River to McQuestion; up McQuestion and back again down the Mayo; then across country to Mazy May, winding up at Henderson Creek—"

"On the Indian River?"

"No," Corliss replied, as he dealt the hands; "just below where the

Stuart taps the Yukon. And then back to Dawson before the ice breaks."

The pocket-miner's eyes sparkled. "Keep us hustlin'; but, say, it's a trip, isn't it! Hunch?"

"I've received word from the Parker outfit on the Mayo, and McPherson isn't asleep on Henderson—you don't know him. They're keeping quiet, and of course one can't tell, but . . ."

Bishop nodded his head sagely, while Corliss turned the trump he had cut. A sure vision of a "twenty-four" hand was dazzling him, when there was a sound of voices without and the door shook to a heavy knock.

"Come in!" he bawled. "An' don't make such a row about it! Look at that"—to Corliss, at the same time facing his hand—"fifteen-eight, fifteen-sixteen, and eight are twenty-four. Just my luck!"

Corliss started swiftly to his feet. Bishop jerked his head about. Two women and a man had staggered clumsily in through the door, and were standing just inside, momentarily blinded by the light.

"By all the Prophets! Cornell!" The pocket-miner wrung the man's hand and led him forward. "You recollect Cornell, Corliss? Jake Cornell, Thirty-Seven and a Half Eldorado."

"How could I forget?" the engineer acknowledged warmly, shaking his hand. "That was a miserable night you put us up last fall, about as miserable as the moose-steak was good that you gave us for breakfast."

Jake Cornell, hirsute and cadaverous of aspect, nodded his head with emphasis and deposited a corpulent demijohn on the table. Again he nodded his head, and glared wildly about him. The stove caught his eye and he strode over to it, lifted a lid, and spat out a mouthful of amber-colored juice. Another stride and he was back.

"'Course I recollect the night," he rumbled, the ice clattering from his hairy jaws. "And I'm danged glad to see you, that's a fact." He seemed suddenly to remember himself, and added a little sheepishly, "The fact is, we're all danged glad to see you, ain't we, girls?" He twisted his head about and nodded his companions up. "Blanche, my dear, Mr. Corliss—hem—it gives me . . . hem . . . it gives me pleasure to make you acquainted. Cariboo Blanche, sir. Cariboo Blanche."

"Pleased to meet you." Cariboo Blanche put out a frank hand and looked him over keenly. She was a fair-featured, blondish woman, originally not unpleasing of appearance, but now with lines all deepened and hardened as on the faces of men who have endured much weather-beat.

Congratulating himself upon his social proficiency, Jake Cornell cleared his throat and marshalled the second woman to the front. "Mr. Corliss, the Virgin; I make you both acquainted. Hem!" in response to the query in Vance's eyes—"Yes, the Virgin. That's all, just the Virgin."

She smiled and bowed, but did not shake hands. "A toff" was her secret comment upon the engineer; and from her limited experience she had been led to understand that it was not good form among "toffs" to shake hands.

Corliss fumbled his hand, then bowed, and looked at her curiously. She was a pretty, low-browed creature; darkly pretty, with a well-favored body, and for all that the type was mean, he could not escape the charm of her over-brimming vitality. She seemed bursting with it, and every quick, spontaneous movement appeared to spring from very excess of red blood and superabundant energy.

"Pretty healthy proposition, ain't she?" Jake Cornell demanded, following his host's gaze with approval.

"None o' your gammon, Jake," the Virgin snapped back, with lip curled contemptuously for Vance's especial benefit. "I fancy it'd be more in keeping if you'd look to pore Blanche, there."

"Fact is, we're plum ding dong played out," Jake said. "An' Blanche went through the ice just down the trail, and her feet's like to freezin'."

Blanche smiled as Corliss piloted her to a stool by the fire, and her stern mouth gave no indication of the pain she was suffering. He turned away when the Virgin addressed herself to removing the wet footgear, while Bishop went rummaging for socks and moccasins.

"Didn't go in more'n to the ankles," Cornell explained confidentially; "but that's plenty a night like this."

Corliss agreed with a nod of the head.

"Spotted your light, and—hem—and so we come. Don't mind, do you?"

"Why, certainly not—"

"No intrudin'?"

Corliss reassured him by laying hand on his shoulder and cordially pressing him to a seat. Blanche sighed luxuriously. Her wet stockings were stretched up and already steaming, and her feet basking in the capacious warmth of Bishop's Siwash socks. Vance shoved the tobacco canister across, but Cornell pulled out a handful of cigars and passed them around.

"Uncommon bad piece of trail just this side of the turn," he remarked stentoriously, at the same time flinging an eloquent glance at the demijohn. "Ice rotten from the springs and no sign till you're into it." Turning to the woman by the stove, "How're you feeling, Blanche?"

"Tony," she responded, stretching her body lazily and redisposing her feet; "though my legs ain't as limber as when we pulled out."

Looking to his host for consent, Cornell tilted the demijohn over his arm and partly filled the four tin mugs and an empty jelly glass.

"Wot's the matter with a toddy?" the Virgin broke in; "or a punch?"

"Got any lime juice?" she demanded of Corliss.

"You 'ave? Jolly!" She directed her dark eyes towards Del. "'Ere, you, cookie! Trot out your mixing-pan and sling the kettle for 'ot water. Come on! All hands! Jake's treat, and I'll show you 'ow! Any sugar, Mr. Corliss? And nutmeg? Cinnamon, then? O.K. It'll do. Lively now, cookie!"

"Ain't she a peach?" Cornell confided to Vance, watching her with mellow eyes as she stirred the steaming brew.

But the Virgin directed her attentions to the engineer. "Don't mind 'im, sir," she advised. "'E's more'n arf-gorn a'ready, a-'itting the jug every blessed stop."

"Now, my dear—" Jake protested.

"Don't you my-dear me," she sniffed. "I don't like you."

"Why?"

"Cos . . ." She ladled the punch carefully into the mugs and meditated. "Cos you chew tobacco. Cos you're whiskery. Wot I take to is smooth-faced young chaps."

"Don't take any stock in her nonsense," the Fraction King warned, "She just does it a-purpose to get me mad."

"Now then!" she commanded, sharply. "Step up to your licker! 'Ere's 'ow!"

"What'll it be?" cried Blanche from the stove.

The elevated mugs wavered and halted.

"The Queen, Gawd bless 'er!" the Virgin toasted promptly.

"And Bill!" Del Bishop interrupted.

Again the mugs wavered.

"Bill 'oo?" the Virgin asked, suspiciously.

"McKinley."

She favored him with a smile. "Thank you, cookie, you're a trump. Now! 'Ere's a go, gents! Take it standing. The Queen, Gawd bless 'er, and Bill McKinley!"

"Bottoms up!" thundered Jake Cornell, and the mugs smote the table with clanging rims.

Vance Corliss discovered himself amused and interested. According to Frona, he mused ironically,—this was learning life, was adding to his sum of human generalizations. The phrase was hers, and he rolled it over a couple of times. Then, again, her engagement with St. Vincent crept into his thought, and he charmed the Virgin by asking her to sing. But she was coy, and only after Bishop had rendered the several score stanzas of "Flying Cloud" did she comply. Her voice, in a weakly way, probably registered an octave and a half; below that point it underwent strange metamorphoses, while on the upper levels it was devious and rickety. Nevertheless she sang "Take Back Your Gold" with touching effect, which brought a fiery moisture into the eyes of the Fraction King, who listened greedily, for the time being experiencing unwonted ethical yearnings.

The applause was generous, followed immediately by Bishop, who toasted the singer as the "Enchantress of Bow Bells," to the reverberating "bottoms up!" of Jake Cornell.

Two hours later, Frona Welse rapped. It was a sharp, insistent rap, penetrating the din within and bringing Corliss to the door.

She gave a glad little cry when she saw who it was. "Oh; it is you,

Vance! I didn't know you lived here."

He shook hands and blocked the doorway with his body. Behind him the Virgin was laughing and Jake Cornell roaring:

"Oh, cable this message along the track;

The Prod's out West, but he's coming back;

Put plenty of veal for one on the rack,

Trolla lala, la la la, la la!"

"What is it?" Vance questioned. "Anything up?"

"I think you might ask me in." There was a hint of reproach in Frona's voice, and of haste. "I blundered through the ice, and my feet are freezing."

"O Gawd!" in the exuberant tones of the Virgin, came whirling over Vance's shoulder, and the voices of Blanche and Bishop joining in a laugh against Cornell, and that worthy's vociferous protestations. It seemed to him that all the blood of his body had rushed into his face. "But you can't come in, Frona. Don't you hear them?"

"But I must," she insisted. "My feet are freezing."

With a gesture of resignation he stepped aside and closed the door after her. Coming suddenly in from the darkness, she hesitated a moment, but in that moment recovered her sight and took in the scene. The air was thick with tobacco smoke, and the odor of it, in the close room, was sickening to one fresh from the pure outside. On the table a column of steam was ascending from the big mixing-pan. The Virgin, fleeing before Cornell, was defending herself with a long mustard spoon. Evading him and watching her chance, she continually daubed his nose and cheeks with the yellow smear. Blanche had twisted about from the stove to see the fun, and Del Bishop, with a mug at rest half-way to his lips, was applauding the successive strokes. The faces of all were flushed.

Vance leaned nervelessly against the door. The whole situation seemed so unthinkably impossible. An insane desire to laugh came over him, which resolved itself into a coughing fit. But Frona, realizing her own pressing need by the growing absence of sensation in her feet, stepped forward.

"Hello, Del!" she called.

The mirth froze on his face at the familiar sound and he slowly and unwilling turned his head to meet her. She had slipped the hood of her *parka* back, and her face, outlined against the dark fur, rosy with the cold and bright, was like a shaft of the sun shot into the murk of a boozing-ken. They all knew her, for who did not know Jacob Welse's daughter? The Virgin dropped the mustard-spoon with a startled shriek, while Cornell, passing a dazed hand across his yellow markings and consummating the general smear, collapsed on the nearest stool. Cariboo Blanche alone retained her self-possession, and laughed softly.

Bishop managed to articulate "Hello!" but was unable to stave off the silence which settled down.

Frona waited a second, and then said, "Good-evening, all."

"This way." Vance had recovered himself, and seated her by the stove opposite Blanche. "Better get your things off quickly, and be careful of the heat. I'll see what I can find for you."

"Some cold water, please," she asked. "It will take the frost out.

Del will get it."

"I hope it is not serious?"

"No." She shook her head and smiled up to him, at the same time working away at her ice-coated moccasins. "There hasn't been time for more than surface-freezing. At the worst the skin will peel off."

An unearthly silence brooded in the cabin, broken only by Bishop filling a basin from the water-bucket, and by Corliss seeking out his smallest and daintiest house-moccasins and his warmest socks.

Frona, rubbing her feet vigorously, paused and looked up. "Don't let me chill the festivities just because I'm cold," she laughed. "Please go on."

Jake Cornell straightened up and cleared his throat inanely, and the Virgin looked over-dignified; but Blanche came over and took the towel out of Frona's hands.

"I wet my feet in the same place," she said, kneeling down and bringing a glow to the frosted feet.

"I suppose you can manage some sort of a fit with them. Here!" Vance tossed over the house-moccasins and woollen wrappings, which the two women, with low laughs and confidential undertones, proceeded to utilize.

"But what in the world were you doing on trail, alone, at this time of night?" Vance asked. In his heart he was marvelling at the coolness and pluck with which she was carrying off the situation.

"I know beforehand that you will censure me," she replied, helping Blanche arrange the wet gear over the fire. "I was at Mrs. Stanton's; but first, you must know, Miss Mortimer and I are staying at the Pently's for a week. Now, to start fresh again. I intended to leave Mrs. Stanton's before dark; but her baby got into the kerosene, her husband had gone down to Dawson, and—well, we weren't sure of the baby up to half an hour ago. She wouldn't hear of me returning alone; but there was nothing to fear; only I had not expected soft ice in such a snap."

"How'd you fix the kid?" Del asked, intent on keeping the talk going now that it had started.

"Chewing tobacco." And when the laughter had subsided, she went on:

"There wasn't any mustard, and it was the best I could think of.

Besides, Matt McCarthy saved my life with it once, down at Dyea when I had the croup. But you were singing when I came in," she suggested.

"Do go on."

Jake Cornell hawed prodigiously. "And I got done."

"Then you, Del. Sing 'Flying Cloud' as you used to coming down the river."

"Oh, 'e 'as!" said the Virgin.

"Then you sing. I am sure you do."

She smiled into the Virgin's eyes, and that lady delivered herself of a coster ballad with more art than she was aware. The chill of Frona's advent was quickly dissipated, and song and toast and merriment went round again. Nor was Frona above touching lips to the jelly glass in fellowship; and she contributed her quota by singing "Annie Laurie" and "Ben Bolt." Also, but privily, she watched the drink saturating the besotted souls of Cornell and the Virgin. It was an experience, and she was glad of it, though sorry in a way for Corliss, who played the host lamely.

But he had little need of pity. "Any other woman—" he said to himself a score of times, looking at Frona and trying to picture numerous women he had known by his mother's teapot, knocking at the door and coming in as Frona had done. Then, again, it was only yesterday that it would have hurt him, Blanche's rubbing her feet; but now he gloried in Frona's permitting it, and his heart went out in a more kindly way to Blanche. Perhaps it was the elevation of the liquor, but he seemed to discover new virtues in her rugged face.

Frona had put on her dried moccasins and risen to her feet, and was listening patiently to Jake Cornell, who hiccoughed a last incoherent toast.

"To the—hic—man," he rumbled, cavernously, "the man—hic—that made—that made—"

"The blessed country," volunteered the Virgin.

"True, my dear—hic. To the man that made the blessed country. To—hic—to Jacob Welse!"

"And a rider!" Blanche cried. "To Jacob Welse's daughter!"

"Ay! Standing! And bottoms up!"

"Oh! she's a jolly good fellow," Del led off, the drink ruddying his cheek.

"I'd like to shake hands with you, just once," Blanche said in a low voice, while the rest were chorusing.

Frona slipped her mitten, which she had already put on, and the pressure was firm between them.

"No," she said to Corliss, who had put on his cap and was tying the ear-flaps; "Blanche tells me the Pently's are only half a mile from here. The trail is straight. I'll not hear of any one accompanying me.

"No!" This time she spoke so authoritatively that he tossed his cap into the bunk. "Good-night, all!" she called, sweeping the roisterers with a smile.

But Corliss saw her to the door and stepped outside. She glanced up to him. Her hood was pulled only partly up, and her face shone alluringly under the starlight.

"I—Frona . . . I wish—"

"Don't be alarmed," she whispered. "I'll not tell on you, Vance."

He saw the mocking glint in her eyes, but tried to go on. "I wish to explain just how—"

"No need. I understand. But at the same time I must confess I do not particularly admire your taste—"

"Frona!" The evident pain in his voice reached her.

"Oh, you big foolish!" she laughed. "Don't I know? Didn't Blanche tell me she wet her feet?"

Corliss bowed his head. "Truly, Frona, you are the most consistent woman I ever met. Furthermore," with a straightening of his form and a dominant assertion in his voice, "this is not the last."

She tried to stop him, but he continued. "I feel, I know that things will turn out differently. To fling your own words back at you, all the factors have not been taken into consideration. As for St. Vincent . . . I'll have you yet. For that matter, now could not be too soon!"

He flashed out hungry arms to her, but she read quicker than he moved, and, laughing, eluded him and ran lightly down the trail.

"Come back, Frona! Come back!" he called, "I am sorry."

"No, you're not," came the answer. "And I'd be sorry if you were.

Good-night."

He watched her merge into the shadows, then entered the cabin. He had utterly forgotten the scene within, and at the first glance it startled him. Cariboo Blanche was crying softly to herself. Her eyes were luminous and moist, and, as he looked, a lone tear stole down her cheek. Bishop's face had gone serious. The Virgin had sprawled head and shoulders on the table, amid overturned mugs and dripping lees, and Cornell was tittubating over her, hiccoughing, and repeating vacuously, "You're all right, my dear. You're all right."

But the Virgin was inconsolable. "O Gawd! Wen I think on wot is, an' was . . . an' no fault of mine. No fault of mine, I tell you!" she shrieked with quick fierceness. "'Ow was I born, I ask? Wot was my old man? A drunk, a chronic. An' my old woman? Talk of Whitechapel! 'Oo guv a cent for me, or 'ow I was dragged up? 'Oo cared a rap? I say? 'Oo cared a rap?"

A sudden revulsion came over Corliss. "Hold your tongue!" he ordered.

The Virgin raised her head, her loosened hair streaming about her like a Fury's. "Wot is she?" she sneered. "Sweet'eart?"

Corliss whirled upon her savagely, face white and voice shaking with passion.

The Virgin cowered down and instinctively threw up her hands to protect her face. "Don't 'it me, sir!" she whined. "Don't 'it me!"

He was frightened at himself, and waited till he could gather control.

"Now," he said, calmly, "get into your things and go. All of you.

Clear out. Vamose."

"You're no man, you ain't," the Virgin snarled, discovering that physical assault was not imminent.

But Corliss herded her particularly to the door, and gave no heed.

"A-turning ladies out!" she sniffed, with a stumble over the threshold;

"No offence," Jake Cornell muttered, pacifically; "no offence."

"Good-night. Sorry," Corliss said to Blanche, with the shadow of a forgiving smile, as she passed out.

"You're a toff! That's wot you are, a bloomin' toff!" the Virgin howled back as he shut the door.

He looked blankly at Del Bishop and surveyed the sodden confusion on the table. Then he walked over and threw himself down on his bunk. Bishop leaned an elbow on the table and pulled at his wheezy pipe. The lamp smoked, flickered, and went out; but still he remained, filling his pipe again and again and striking endless matches.

"Del! Are you awake?" Corliss called at last.

Del grunted.

"I was a cur to turn them out into the snow. I am ashamed."

"Sure," was the affirmation.

A long silence followed. Del knocked the ashes out and raised up.

"'Sleep?" he called.

There was no reply, and he walked to the bunk softly and pulled the blankets over the engineer.

CHAPTER XXI

"Yes; what does it all mean?" Corliss stretched lazily, and cocked up his feet on the table. He was not especially interested, but Colonel Trethaway persisted in talking seriously.

"That's it! The very thing—the old and ever young demand which man slaps into the face of the universe." The colonel searched among the scraps in his note-book. "See," holding up a soiled slip of typed paper, "I copied this out years ago. Listen. 'What a monstrous spectre is this man, this disease of the agglutinated dust, lifting alternate feet or lying drugged with slumber; killing, feeding, growing, bringing forth small copies of himself; grown up with hair like grass, fitted with eyes that glitter in his face; a thing to set children screaming. Poor soul, here for so little, cast among so many hardships, filled with desires so incommensurate and so inconsistent; savagely surrounded, savagely descended, irremediably condemned to prey upon his fellow-lives. Infinitely childish, often admirably valiant, often touchingly kind; sitting down to debate of right or wrong and the attributes of the deity; rising up to battle for an egg or die for an idea!'

"And all to what end?" he demanded, hotly, throwing down the paper, "this disease of the agglutinated dust?"

Corliss yawned in reply. He had been on trail all day and was yearning for between-blankets.

"Here am I, Colonel Trethaway, modestly along in years, fairly well preserved, a place in the community, a comfortable bank account, no need to ever exert myself again, yet enduring life bleakly and working ridiculously with a zest worthy of a man half my years. And to what end? I can only eat so much, smoke so much, sleep so much, and this tail-dump of earth men call Alaska is the worst of all possible places in the matter of grub, tobacco, and blankets."

"But it is the living strenuously which holds you," Corliss interjected.

"Frona's philosophy," the colonel sneered.

"And my philosophy, and yours."

"And of the agglutinated dust—"

"Which is quickened with a passion you do not take into account,—the passion of duty, of race, of God!"

"And the compensation?" Trethaway demanded.

"Each breath you draw. The Mayfly lives an hour."

"I don't see it."

"Blood and sweat! Blood and sweat! You cried that after the rough and tumble in the Opera House, and every word of it was receipt in full."

"Frona's philosophy."

"And yours and mine."

The colonel threw up his shoulders, and after a pause confessed. "You see, try as I will, I can't make a pessimist out of myself. We are all compensated, and I more fully than most men. What end? I asked, and the answer forthcame: Since the ultimate end is beyond us, then the immediate. More compensation, here and now!"

"Quite hedonistic."

"And rational. I shall look to it at once. I can buy grub and blankets for a score; I can eat and sleep for only one; ergo, why not for two?"

Corliss took his feet down and sat up. "In other words?"

"I shall get married, and—give the community a shock. Communities like shocks. That's one of their compensations for being agglutinative."

"I can't think of but one woman," Corliss essayed tentatively, putting out his hand.

Trethaway shook it slowly. "It is she."

Corliss let go, and misgiving shot into his face. "But St. Vincent?"

"Is your problem, not mine."

"Then Lucile—?"

"Certainly not. She played a quixotic little game of her own and botched it beautifully."

"I—I do not understand." Corliss brushed his brows in a dazed sort of way.

Trethaway parted his lips in a superior smile. "It is not necessary that you should. The question is, Will you stand up with me?"

"Surely. But what a confoundedly long way around you took. It is not your usual method."

"Nor was it with her," the colonel declared, twisting his moustache proudly.

A captain of the North-West Mounted Police, by virtue of his magisterial office, may perform marriages in time of stress as well as execute exemplary justice. So Captain Alexander received a call from Colonel Trethaway, and after he left jotted down an engagement for the next morning. Then the impending groom went to see Frona. Lucile did not make the request, he hastened to explain, but—well, the fact was she did not know any women, and, furthermore, he (the colonel) knew whom Lucile would like to ask, did she dare. So he did it upon his own responsibility. And coming as a surprise, he knew it would be a great joy to her.

Frona was taken aback by the suddenness of it. Only the other day, it was, that Lucile had made a plea to her for St. Vincent, and now it was Colonel Trethaway! True, there had been a false quantity somewhere, but now it seemed doubly false. Could it be, after all, that Lucile was mercenary? These thoughts crowded upon her swiftly, with the colonel anxiously watching her face the while. She knew she must answer quickly, yet was distracted by an involuntary admiration for his bravery. So she followed, perforce, the lead of her heart, and consented.

Yet the whole thing was rather strained when the four of them came together, next day, in Captain Alexander's private office. There was a gloomy chill about it. Lucile seemed ready to cry, and showed a repressed perturbation quite unexpected of her; while, try as she would, Frona could not call upon her usual sympathy to drive away the coldness which obtruded intangibly between them. This, in turn, had a consequent effect on Vance, and gave a certain distance to his manner which forced him out of touch even with the colonel.

Colonel Trethaway seemed to have thrown twenty years off his erect shoulders, and the discrepancy in the match which Frona had felt vanished as she looked at him. "He has lived the years well," she thought, and prompted mysteriously, almost with vague apprehension she turned her eyes to Corliss. But if the groom had thrown off twenty years, Vance was not a whit behind. Since their last meeting he had sacrificed his brown moustache to the frost, and his smooth face, smitten with health and vigor, looked uncommonly boyish; and yet, withal, the naked upper lip advertised a stiffness and resolution hitherto concealed. Furthermore, his features portrayed a growth, and his eyes, which had been softly firm, were now firm with the added harshness or hardness which is bred of coping with things and coping quickly,—the stamp of executiveness which is pressed upon men who do, and upon all men who do, whether they drive dogs, buck the sea, or dictate the policies of empires.

When the simple ceremony was over, Frona kissed Lucile; but Lucile felt that there was a subtle something wanting, and her eyes filled with unshed tears. Trethaway, who had felt the aloofness from the start, caught an opportunity with Frona while Captain Alexander and Corliss were being pleasant to Mrs. Trethaway.

"What's the matter, Frona?" the colonel demanded, bluntly. "I hope you did not come under protest. I am sorry, not for you, because lack of frankness deserves nothing, but for Lucile. It is not fair to her."

"There has been a lack of frankness throughout." Her voice trembled. "I tried my best,—I thought I could do better,—but I cannot feign what I do not feel. I am sorry, but I . . . I am disappointed. No, I cannot explain, and to you least of all."

"Let's be above-board, Frona. St. Vincent's concerned?"

She nodded.

"And I can put my hand right on the spot. First place," he looked to the side and saw Lucile stealing an anxious glance to him,—"first place, only the other day she gave you a song about St. Vincent. Second place, and therefore, you think her heart's not in this present proposition; that she doesn't care a rap for me; in short, that she's marrying me for reinstatement and spoils. Isn't that it?"

"And isn't it enough? Oh, I am disappointed, Colonel Trethaway, grievously, in her, in you, in myself."

"Don't be a fool! I like you too well to see you make yourself one. The play's been too quick, that is all. Your eye lost it. Listen. We've kept it quiet, but she's in with the elect on French Hill. Her claim's prospected the richest of the outfit. Present indication half a million at least. In her own name, no strings attached. Couldn't she take that and go anywhere in the world and reinstate herself? And for that matter, you might presume that I am marrying her for spoils. Frona, she cares for me, and in your ear, she's too good for me. My hope is that the future will make up. But never mind that—haven't got the time now.

"You consider her affection sudden, eh? Let me tell you we've been growing into each other from the time I came into the country, and with our eyes open. St. Vincent? Pshaw! I knew it all the time. She got it into her head that the whole of him wasn't worth a little finger of you, and she tried to break things up. You'll never know how she worked with him. I told her she didn't know the Welse, and she said so, too, after. So there it is; take it or leave it."

"But what do you think about St. Vincent?"

"What I think is neither here nor there; but I'll tell you honestly that I back her judgment. But that's not the point. What are you going to do about it? about her? now?"

She did not answer, but went back to the waiting group. Lucile saw her coming and watched her face.

"He's been telling you—?"

"That I am a fool," Frona answered. "And I think I am." And with a smile, "I take it on faith that I am, anyway. I—I can't reason it out just now, but. . ."

Captain Alexander discovered a prenuptial joke just about then, and led the way over to the stove to crack it upon the colonel, and Vance went along to see fair play.

"It's the first time," Lucile was saying, "and it means more to me, so much more, than to . . . most women. I am afraid. It is a terrible thing for me to do. But I do love him, I do!" And when the joke had been duly digested and they came back, she was sobbing, "Dear, dear Frona."

It was just the moment, better than he could have chosen; and capped and mittened, without knocking, Jacob Welse came in.

"The uninvited guest," was his greeting. "Is it all over? So?" And he swallowed Lucile up in his huge bearskin. "Colonel, your hand, and your pardon for my intruding, and your regrets for not giving me the word. Come, out with them! Hello, Corliss! Captain Alexander, a good day."

"What have I done?" Frona wailed, received the bear-hug, and managed to press his hand till it almost hurt.

"Had to back the game," he whispered; and this time his hand did hurt.

"Now, colonel, I don't know what your plans are, and I don't care. Call them off. I've got a little spread down to the house, and the only honest case of champagne this side of Circle. Of course, you're coming, Corliss, and—" His eye roved past Captain Alexander with hardly a pause.

"Of course," came the answer like a flash, though the Chief Magistrate of the Northwest had had time to canvass the possible results of such unofficial action. "Got a hack?"

Jacob Welse laughed and held up a moccasined foot. "Walking be—chucked!" The captain started impulsively towards the door. "I'll have the sleds up before you're ready. Three of them, and bells galore!"

So Trethaway's forecast was correct, and Dawson vindicated its agglutinativeness by rubbing its eyes when three sleds, with three scarlet-tuniced policemen swinging the whips, tore down its main street; and it rubbed its eyes again when it saw the occupants thereof.

"We shall live quietly," Lucile told Frona. "The Klondike is not all the world, and the best is yet to come."

But Jacob Welse said otherwise. "We've got to make this thing go," he said to Captain Alexander, and Captain Alexander said that he was unaccustomed to backing out.

Mrs. Schoville emitted preliminary thunders, marshalled the other women, and became chronically seismic and unsafe.

Lucile went nowhere save to Frona's. But Jacob Welse, who rarely went anywhere, was often to be found by Colonel Trethaway's fireside, and not only was he to be found there, but he usually brought somebody along. "Anything on hand this evening?" he was wont to say on casual meeting. "No? Then come along with me." Sometimes he said it with lamb-like innocence, sometimes with a challenge brooding under his bushy brows, and rarely did he fail to get his man. These men had wives, and thus were the germs of dissolution sown in the ranks of the opposition.

Then, again, at Colonel Trethaway's there was something to be found besides weak tea and small talk; and the correspondents, engineers, and gentlemen rovers kept the trail well packed in that direction, though it was the Kings, to a man, who first broke the way. So the Trethaway cabin became the centre of things, and, backed commercially, financially, and officially, it could not fail to succeed socially.

The only bad effect of all this was to make the lives of Mrs. Schoville and divers others of her sex more monotonous, and to cause them to lose faith in certain hoary and inconsequent maxims. Furthermore, Captain Alexander, as highest official, was a power in the land, and Jacob Welse was the Company, and there was a superstition extant concerning the unwisdom of being on indifferent terms with the Company. And the time was not long till probably a bare half-dozen remained in outer cold, and they were considered a warped lot, anyway.

CHAPTER XXII

Quite an exodus took place in Dawson in the spring. Men, because they had made stakes, and other men, because they had made none, bought up the available dogs and rushed out for Dyea over the last ice. Incidentally, it was discovered that Dave Harney possessed most of these dogs.

"Going out?" Jacob Welse asked him on a day when the meridian sun for the first time felt faintly warm to the naked skin.

"Well, I calkilate not. I'm clearin' three dollars a pair on the moccasins I cornered, to say nothing but saw wood on the boots. Say, Welse, not that my nose is out of joint, but you jest cinched me everlastin' on sugar, didn't you?"

Jacob Welse smiled.

"And by the Jimcracky I'm squared! Got any rubber boots?"

"No; went out of stock early in the winter." Dave snickered slowly.

"And I'm the pertickler party that hocus-pocused 'em."

"Not you. I gave special orders to the clerks. They weren't sold in lots."

"No more they wa'n't. One man to the pair and one pair to the man, and a couple of hundred of them; but it was my dust they chucked into the scales an nobody else's. Drink? Don't mind. Easy! Put up your sack. Call it rebate, for I kin afford it. . . Goin' out? Not this year, I guess. Wash-up's comin'."

A strike on Henderson the middle of April, which promised to be sensational, drew St. Vincent to Stewart River. And a little later, Jacob Welse, interested on Gallagher Gulch and with an eye riveted on the copper mines of White River, went up into the same district, and with him went Frona, for it was more vacation than business. In the mean time, Corliss and Bishop, who had been on trail for a month or more running over the Mayo and McQuestion Country, rounded up on the left fork of Henderson, where a block of claims waited to be surveyed.

But by May, spring was so far advanced that travel on the creeks became perilous, and on the last of the thawing ice the miners travelled down to the bunch of islands below the mouth of the Stewart, where they went into temporary quarters or crowded the hospitality of those who possessed cabins. Corliss and Bishop located on Split-up Island (so called through the habit parties from the Outside had of dividing there and going several ways), where Tommy McPherson was comfortably situated. A couple of days later, Jacob Welse and Frona arrived from a hazardous trip out of White River, and pitched tent on the high ground at the upper end of Split-up. A few *chechaquos*, the first of the spring rush, strung in exhausted and went into camp against the breaking of the river. Also, there were still men going out who, barred by the rotten ice, came ashore to build poling-boats and await the break-up or to negotiate with the residents for canoes. Notably among these was the Baron Courbertin.

"Ah! Excruciating! Magnificent! Is it not?"

So Frona first ran across him on the following day. "What?" she asked, giving him her hand.

"You! You!" doffing his cap. "It is a delight!"

"I am sure—" she began.

"No! No!" He shook his curly mop warmly. "It is not you. See!" He turned to a Peterborough, for which McPherson had just mulcted him of thrice its value. "The canoe! Is it not—not—what you Yankees call—a bute?"

"Oh, the canoe," she repeated, with a falling inflection of chagrin.

"No! No! Pardon!" He stamped angrily upon the ground. "It is not so. It is not you. It is not the canoe. It is—ah! I have it now! It is your promise. One day, do you not remember, at Madame Schoville's, we talked of the canoe, and of my ignorance, which was sad, and you promised, you said—"

"I would give you your first lesson?"

"And is it not delightful? Listen! Do you not hear? The rippling—ah! the rippling!—deep down at the heart of things! Soon will the water run free. Here is the canoe! Here we meet! The first lesson! Delightful! Delightful!"

The next island below Split-up was known as Roubeau's Island, and was separated from the former by a narrow back-channel. Here, when the bottom had about dropped out of the trail, and with the dogs swimming as often as not, arrived St. Vincent—the last man to travel the winter trail. He went into the cabin of John Borg, a taciturn, gloomy individual, prone to segregate himself from his kind. It was the mischance of St. Vincent's life that of all cabins he chose Borg's for an abiding-place against the break-up.

"All right," the man said, when questioned by him. "Throw your blankets into the corner. Bella'll clear the litter out of the spare bunk."

Not till evening did he speak again, and then, "You're big enough to do your own cooking. When the woman's done with the stove you can fire away."

The woman, or Bella, was a comely Indian girl, young, and the prettiest St. Vincent had run across. Instead of the customary greased swarthiness of the race, her skin was clear and of a light-bronze tone, and her features less harsh, more felicitously curved, than those common to the blood.

After supper, Borg, both elbows on table and huge misshapen hands supporting chin and jaws, sat puffing stinking Siwash tobacco and staring straight before him. It would have seemed ruminative, the stare, had his eyes been softer or had he blinked; as it was, his face was set and trance-like.

"Have you been in the country long?" St. Vincent asked, endeavoring to make conversation.

Borg turned his sullen-black eyes upon him, and seemed to look into him and through him and beyond him, and, still regarding him, to have forgotten all about him. It was as though he pondered some great and weighty matter—probably his sins, the correspondent mused nervously, rolling himself a cigarette. When the yellow cube had dissipated itself in curling fragrance, and he was deliberating about rolling a second, Borg suddenly spoke.

"Fifteen years," he said, and returned to his tremendous cogitation.

Thereat, and for half an hour thereafter, St. Vincent, fascinated, studied his inscrutable countenance. To begin with, it was a massive head, abnormal and top-heavy, and its only excuse for being was the huge bull-throat which supported it. It had been cast in a mould of elemental generousness, and everything about it partook of the asymmetrical crudeness of the elemental. The hair, rank of growth, thick and unkempt, matted itself here and there into curious splotches of gray; and again, grinning at age, twisted itself into curling locks of lustreless black—locks of unusual thickness, like crooked fingers, heavy and solid. The shaggy whiskers, almost bare in places, and in others massing into bunchgrass-like clumps, were plentifully splashed with gray. They rioted monstrously over his face and fell raggedly to his chest, but failed to hide the great hollowed cheeks or the twisted mouth. The latter was thin-lipped and cruel, but cruel only in a passionless sort of way. But the forehead was the anomaly,—the anomaly required to complete the irregularity of the face. For it was a perfect forehead, full and broad, and rising superbly strong to its high dome. It was as the seat and bulwark of some vast intelligence; omniscience might have brooded there.

Bella, washing the dishes and placing them away on the shelf behind Borg's back, dropped a heavy tin cup. The cabin was very still, and the sharp rattle came without warning. On the instant, with a brute roar, the chair was overturned and Borg was on his feet, eyes blazing and face convulsed. Bella gave an inarticulate, animal-like cry of fear and cowered at his feet. St. Vincent felt his hair bristling, and an uncanny chill, like a jet of cold air, played up and down his spine. Then Borg righted the chair and sank back into his old position, chin on hands and brooding ponderously. Not a word was spoken, and Bella went on unconcernedly with the dishes, while St. Vincent rolled, a shaky cigarette and wondered if it had been a dream.

Jacob Welse laughed when the correspondent told him. "Just his way," he said; "for his ways are like his looks,—unusual. He's an unsociable beast. Been in the country more years than he can number acquaintances. Truth to say, I don't think he has a friend in all Alaska, not even among the Indians, and he's chummed thick with them off and on. 'Johnny Sorehead,' they call him, but it might as well be 'Johnny Break-um-head,' for he's got a quick temper and a rough hand. Temper! Some little misunderstanding popped up between him and the agent at Arctic City. He was in the right, too,—agent's mistake,—but he tabooed the Company on the spot and lived on straight meat for a year. Then I happened to run across him at Tanana Station, and after due explanations he consented to buy from us again."

"Got the girl from up the head-waters of the White," Bill Brown told St. Vincent. "Welse thinks he's pioneering in that direction, but Borg could give him cards and spades on it and then win out. He's been over the ground years ago. Yes, strange sort of a chap. Wouldn't hanker to be bunk-mates with him."

But St. Vincent did not mind the eccentricities of the man, for he spent most of his time on Split-up Island with Frona and the Baron. One day, however, and innocently, he ran foul of him. Two Swedes, hunting tree-squirrels from the other end of Roubeau Island, had stopped to ask for matches and to yarn a while in the warm sunshine of the clearing. St. Vincent and Borg were accommodating them, the latter for the most part in meditative monosyllables. Just to the rear, by the cabin-door, Bella was washing clothes. The tub was a cumbersome home-made affair, and half-full of water, was more than a fair match for an ordinary woman. The correspondent noticed her struggling with it, and stepped back quickly to her aid.

With the tub between them, they proceeded to carry it to one side in order to dump it where the ground drained from the cabin. St. Vincent slipped in the thawing snow and the soapy water splashed up. Then Bella slipped, and then they both slipped. Bella giggled and laughed, and St. Vincent laughed back. The spring was in the air and in their blood, and it was very good to be alive. Only a wintry heart could deny a smile on such a day. Bella slipped again, tried to recover, slipped with the other foot, and sat down abruptly. Laughing gleefully, both of them, the correspondent caught her hands to pull her to her feet. With a bound and a bellow, Borg was upon them. Their hands were torn apart and St. Vincent thrust heavily backward. He staggered for a couple of yards and almost fell. Then the scene of the cabin was repeated. Bella cowered and grovelled in the muck, and her lord towered wrathfully over her.

"Look you," he said in stifled gutturals, turning to St. Vincent. "You sleep in my cabin and you cook. That is enough. Let my woman alone."

Things went on after that as though nothing had happened; St. Vincent gave Bella a wide berth and seemed to have forgotten her existence. But the Swedes went back to their end of the island, laughing at the trivial happening which was destined to be significant.

CHAPTER XXIII

Spring, smiting with soft, warm hands, had come like a miracle, and now lingered for a dreamy spell before bursting into full-blown summer. The snow had left the bottoms and valleys and nestled only on the north slopes of the ice-scarred ridges. The glacial drip was already in evidence, and every creek in roaring spate. Each day the sun rose earlier and stayed later. It was now chill day by three o'clock and mellow twilight at nine. Soon a golden circle would be drawn around the sky, and deep midnight become bright as high noon. The willows and aspens had long since budded, and were now decking themselves in liveries of fresh young green, and the sap was rising in the pines.

Mother nature had heaved her waking sigh and gone about her brief business. Crickets sang of nights in the stilly cabins, and in the sunshine mosquitoes crept from out hollow logs and snug crevices among the rocks,— big, noisy, harmless fellows, that had procreated the year gone, lain frozen through the winter, and were now rejuvenated to buzz through swift senility to second death. All sorts of creeping, crawling, fluttering life came forth from the warming earth and hastened to mature, reproduce, and cease. Just a breath of balmy air, and then the long cold frost again—ah! they knew it well and lost no time. Sand martins were driving their ancient tunnels into the soft clay banks, and robins singing on the spruce-garbed islands. Overhead the woodpecker knocked insistently, and in the forest depths the partridge boom-boomed and strutted in virile glory.

But in all this nervous haste the Yukon took no part. For many a thousand miles it lay cold, unsmiling, dead. Wild fowl, driving up from the south in wind-jamming wedges, halted, looked vainly for open water, and quested dauntlessly on into the north. From bank to bank stretched the savage ice. Here and there the water burst through and flooded over, but in the chill nights froze solidly as ever. Tradition has it that of old time the Yukon lay unbroken through three long summers, and on the face of it there be traditions less easy of belief.

So summer waited for open water, and the tardy Yukon took to stretching of days and cracking its stiff joints. Now an air-hole ate into the ice, and ate and ate; or a fissure formed, and grew, and failed to freeze again. Then the ice ripped from the shore and uprose bodily a yard. But still the river was loth to loose its grip. It was a slow travail, and man, used to nursing nature with pigmy skill, able to burst waterspouts and harness waterfalls, could avail nothing against the billions of frigid tons which refused to run down the hill to Bering Sea.

On Split-up Island all were ready for the break-up. Waterways have ever been first highways, and the Yukon was the sole highway in all the land. So those bound up-river pitched their poling-boats and shod their poles with iron, and those bound down caulked their scows and barges and shaped spare sweeps with axe and drawing-knife. Jacob Welse loafed and joyed in the utter cessation from work, and Frona joyed with him in that it was good. But Baron Courbertin was in a fever at the delay. His hot blood grew riotous after the long hibernation, and the warm sunshine dazzled him with warmer fancies.

"Oh! Oh! It will never break! Never!" And he stood gazing at the surly ice and raining politely phrased anathema upon it. "It is a conspiracy, poor La Bijou, a conspiracy!" He caressed La Bijou like it were a horse, for so he had christened the glistening Peterborough canoe.

Frona and St. Vincent laughed and preached him the gospel of patience, which he proceeded to tuck away into the deepest abysses of perdition till interrupted by Jacob Welse.

"Look, Courbertin! Over there, south of the bluff. Do you make out anything? Moving?"

"Yes; a dog."

"It moves too slowly for a dog. Frona, get the glasses."

Courbertin and St. Vincent sprang after them, but the latter knew their abiding-place and returned triumphant. Jacob Welse put the binoculars to his eyes and gazed steadily across the river. It was a sheer mile from the island to the farther bank, and the sunglare on the ice was a sore task to the vision.

"It is a man." He passed the glasses to the Baron and strained absently with his naked eyes. "And something is up."

"He creeps!" the baron exclaimed. "The man creeps, he crawls, on hand and knee! Look! See!" He thrust the glasses tremblingly into Frona's hands.

Looking across the void of shimmering white, it was difficult to discern a dark object of such size when dimly outlined against an equally dark background of brush and earth. But Frona could make the man out with fair distinctness; and as she grew accustomed to the strain she could distinguish each movement, and especially so when he came to a wind-thrown pine. Sue watched painfully. Twice, after tortuous effort, squirming and twisting, he failed in breasting the big trunk, and on the third attempt, after infinite exertion, he cleared it only to topple helplessly forward and fall on his face in the tangled undergrowth.

"It is a man." She turned the glasses over to St. Vincent. "And he is crawling feebly. He fell just then this side of the log."

"Does he move?" Jacob Welse asked, and, on a shake of St. Vincent's head, brought his rifle from the tent.

He fired six shots skyward in rapid succession. "He moves!" The correspondent followed him closely. "He is crawling to the bank. Ah! . . . No; one moment . . . Yes! He lies on the ground and raises his hat, or something, on a stick. He is waving it." (Jacob Welse fired six more shots.) "He waves again. Now he has dropped it and lies quite still."

All three looked inquiringly to Jacob Welse.

He shrugged his shoulders. "How should I know? A white man or an Indian; starvation most likely, or else he is injured."

"But he may be dying," Frona pleaded, as though her father, who had done most things, could do all things.

"We can do nothing."

"Ah! Terrible! terrible!" The baron wrung his hands. "Before our very eyes, and we can do nothing! No!" he exclaimed, with swift resolution, "it shall not be! I will cross the ice!"

He would have started precipitately down the bank had not Jacob Welse caught his arm.

"Not such a rush, baron. Keep your head."

"But—"

"But nothing. Does the man want food, or medicine, or what? Wait a moment. We will try it together."

"Count me in," St. Vincent volunteered promptly, and Frona's eyes sparkled.

While she made up a bundle of food in the tent, the men provided and rigged themselves with sixty or seventy feet of light rope. Jacob Welse and St. Vincent made themselves fast to it at either end, and the baron in the middle. He claimed the food as his portion, and strapped it to his broad shoulders. Frona watched their progress from the bank. The first hundred yards were easy going, but she noticed at once the change when they had passed the limit of the fairly solid shore-ice. Her father led sturdily, feeling ahead and to the side with his staff and changing direction continually.

St. Vincent, at the rear of the extended line, was the first to go through, but he fell with the pole thrust deftly across the opening and resting on the ice. His head did not go under, though the current sucked powerfully, and the two men dragged him out after a sharp pull. Frona saw them consult together for a minute, with much pointing and gesticulating on the part of the baron, and then St. Vincent detach himself and turn shoreward.

"Br-r-r-r," he shivered, coming up the bank to her. "It's impossible."

"But why didn't they come in?" she asked, a slight note of displeasure manifest in her voice.

"Said they were going to make one more try, first. That Courbertin is hot-headed, you know."

"And my father just as bull-headed," she smiled. "But hadn't you better change? There are spare things in the tent."

"Oh, no." He threw himself down beside her. "It's warm in the sun."

For an hour they watched the two men, who had become mere specks of black in the distance; for they had managed to gain the middle of the river and at the same time had worked nearly a mile up-stream. Frona followed them closely with the glasses, though often they were lost to sight behind the ice-ridges.

"It was unfair of them," she heard St. Vincent complain, "to say they were only going to have one more try. Otherwise I should not have turned back. Yet they can't make it—absolutely impossible."

"Yes . . . No . . . Yes! They're turning back," she announced. "But listen! What is that?"

A hoarse rumble, like distant thunder, rose from the midst of the ice.

She sprang to her feet. "Gregory, the river can't be breaking!"

"No, no; surely not. See, it is gone." The noise which had come from above had died away downstream.

"But there! There!"

Another rumble, hoarser and more ominous than before, lifted itself and hushed the robins and the squirrels. When abreast of them, it sounded like a railroad train on a distant trestle. A third rumble, which approached a roar and was of greater duration, began from above and passed by.

"Oh, why don't they hurry!"

The two specks had stopped, evidently in conversation. She ran the glasses hastily up and down the river. Though another roar had risen, she could make out no commotion. The ice lay still and motionless. The robins resumed their singing, and the squirrels were chattering with spiteful glee.

"Don't fear, Frona." St. Vincent put his arm about her protectingly. "If there is any danger, they know it better than we, and they are taking their time."

"I never saw a big river break up," she confessed, and resigned herself to the waiting.

The roars rose and fell sporadically, but there were no other signs of disruption, and gradually the two men, with frequent duckings, worked inshore. The water was streaming from them and they were shivering severely as they came up the bank.

"At last!" Frona had both her father's hands in hers. "I thought you would never come back."

"There, there. Run and get dinner," Jacob Welse laughed. "There was no danger."

"But what was it?"

"Stewart River's broken and sending its ice down under the Yukon ice.

We could hear the grinding plainly out there."

"Ah! And it was terrible! terrible!" cried the baron. "And that poor, poor man, we cannot save him!"

"Yes, we can. We'll have a try with the dogs after dinner. Hurry, Frona."

But the dogs were a failure. Jacob Welse picked out the leaders as the more intelligent, and with grub-packs on them drove them out from the bank. They could not grasp what was demanded of them. Whenever they tried to return they were driven back with sticks and clods and imprecations. This only bewildered them, and they retreated out of range, whence they raised their wet, cold paws and whined pitifully to the shore.

"If they could only make it once, they would understand, and then it would go like clock-work. Ah! Would you? Go on! Chook, Miriam! Chook! The thing is to get the first one across."

Jacob Welse finally succeeded in getting Miriam, lead-dog to Frona's team, to take the trail left by him and the baron. The dog went on bravely, scrambling over, floundering through, and sometimes swimming; but when she had gained the farthest point reached by them, she sat down helplessly. Later on, she cut back to the shore at a tangent, landing on the deserted island above; and an hour afterwards trotted into camp minus the grub-pack. Then the two dogs, hovering just out of range, compromised matters by devouring each other's burdens; after which the attempt was given over and they were called in.

During the afternoon the noise increased in frequency, and by nightfall was continuous, but by morning it had ceased utterly. The river had risen eight feet, and in many places was running over its crust. Much crackling and splitting were going on, and fissures leaping into life and multiplying in all directions.

"The under-tow ice has jammed below among the islands," Jacob Welse explained. "That's what caused the rise. Then, again, it has jammed at the mouth of the Stewart and is backing up. When that breaks through, it will go down underneath and stick on the lower jam."

"And then? and then?" The baron exulted.

"La Bijou will swim again."

As the light grew stronger, they searched for the man across the river.

He had not moved, but in response to their rifle-shots waved feebly.

"Nothing for it till the river breaks, baron, and then a dash with La Bijou. St. Vincent, you had better bring your blankets up and sleep here to-night. We'll need three paddles, and I think we can get McPherson."

"No need," the correspondent hastened to reply. "The back-channel is like adamant, and I'll be up by daybreak."

"But I? Why not?" Baron Courbertin demanded. Frona laughed.

"Remember, we haven't given you your first lessons yet."

"And there'll hardly be time to-morrow," Jacob Welse added. "When she goes, she goes with a rush. St. Vincent, McPherson, and I will have to make the crew, I'm afraid. Sorry, baron. Stay with us another year and you'll be fit."

But Baron Courbertin was inconsolable, and sulked for a full half-hour.

CHAPTER XXIV

"Awake! You dreamers, wake!"

Frona was out of her sleeping-furs at Del Bishop's first call; but ere she had slipped a skirt on and bare feet into moccasins, her father, beyond the blanket-curtain, had thrown back the flaps of the tent and stumbled out.

The river was up. In the chill gray light she could see the ice rubbing softly against the very crest of the bank; it even topped it in places, and the huge cakes worked inshore many feet. A hundred yards out the white field merged into the dim dawn and the gray sky. Subdued splits and splutters whispered from out the obscureness, and a gentle grinding could be heard.

"When will it go?" she asked of Del.

"Not a bit too lively for us. See there!" He pointed with his toe to the water lapping out from under the ice and creeping greedily towards them. "A foot rise every ten minutes."

"Danger?" he scoffed. "Not on your life. It's got to go. Them islands"—waving his hand indefinitely down river—"can't hold up under more pressure. If they don't let go the ice, the ice'll scour them clean out of the bed of the Yukon. Sure! But I've got to be chasin' back. Lower ground down our way. Fifteen inches on the cabin floor, and McPherson and Corliss hustlin' perishables into the bunks."

"Tell McPherson to be ready for a call," Jacob Welse shouted after him. And then to Frona, "Now's the time for St. Vincent to cross the back-channel."

The baron, shivering barefooted, pulled out his watch. "Ten minutes to three," he chattered.

"Hadn't you better go back and get your moccasins?" Frona asked.

"There will be time."

"And miss the magnificence? Hark!"

From nowhere in particular a brisk crackling arose, then died away. The ice was in motion. Slowly, very slowly, it proceeded down stream. There was no commotion, no ear-splitting thunder, no splendid display of force; simply a silent flood of white, an orderly procession of tight-packed ice—packed so closely that not a drop of water was in evidence. It was there, somewhere, down underneath; but it had to be taken on faith. There was a dull hum or muffled grating, but so low in pitch that the ear strained to catch it.

"Ah! Where is the magnificence? It is a fake!"

The baron shook his fists angrily at the river, and Jacob Welse's thick brows seemed to draw down in order to hide the grim smile in his eyes.

"Ha! ha! I laugh! I snap my fingers! See! I defy!"

As the challenge left his lips. Baron Courbertin stepped upon a cake which rubbed lightly past at his feet. So unexpected was it, that when Jacob Welse reached after him he was gone.

The ice was picking up in momentum, and the hum growing louder and more threatening. Balancing gracefully, like a circus-rider, the Frenchman whirled away along the rim of the bank. Fifty precarious feet he rode, his mount becoming more unstable every instant, and he leaped neatly to the shore. He came back laughing, and received for his pains two or three of the choicest phrases Jacob Welse could select from the essentially masculine portion of his vocabulary.

"And for why?" Courbertin demanded, stung to the quick.

"For why?" Jacob Welse mimicked wrathfully, pointing into the sleek stream sliding by.

A great cake had driven its nose into the bed of the river thirty feet below and was struggling to up-end. All the frigid flood behind crinkled and bent back like so much paper. Then the stalled cake turned completely over and thrust its muddy nose skyward. But the squeeze caught it, while cake mounted cake at its back, and its fifty feet of muck and gouge were hurled into the air. It crashed upon the moving mass beneath, and flying fragments landed at the feet of those that watched. Caught broadside in a chaos of pressures, it crumbled into scattered pieces and disappeared.

"God!" The baron spoke the word reverently and with awe.

Frona caught his hand on the one side and her father's on the other. The ice was now leaping past in feverish haste. Somewhere below a heavy cake butted into the bank, and the ground swayed under their feet. Another followed it, nearer the surface, and as they sprang back, upreared mightily, and, with a ton or so of soil on its broad back, bowled insolently onward. And yet another, reaching inshore like a huge hand, ripped three careless pines out by the roots and bore them away.

Day had broken, and the driving white gorged the Yukon from shore to shore. What of the pressure of pent water behind, the speed of the flood had become dizzying. Down all its length the bank was being gashed and gouged, and the island was jarring and shaking to its foundations.

"Oh, great! Great!" Frona sprang up and down between the men. "Where is your fake, baron?"

"Ah!" He shook his head. "Ah! I was wrong. I am miserable. But the magnificence! Look!"

He pointed down to the bunch of islands which obstructed the bend. There the mile-wide stream divided and subdivided again,—which was well for water, but not so well for packed ice. The islands drove their wedged heads into the frozen flood and tossed the cakes high into the air. But cake pressed upon cake and shelved out of the water, out and up, sliding and grinding and climbing, and still more cakes from behind, till hillocks and mountains of ice upreared and crashed among the trees.

"A likely place for a jam," Jacob Welse said. "Get the glasses, Frona." He gazed through them long and steadily. "It's growing, spreading out. A cake at the right time and the right place . . ."

"But the river is falling!" Frona cried.

The ice had dropped six feet below the top of the bank, and the Baron Courbertin marked it with a stick.

"Our man's still there, but he doesn't move."

It was clear day, and the sun was breaking forth in the north-east.

They took turn about with the glasses in gazing across the river.

"Look! Is it not marvellous?" Courbertin pointed to the mark he had made. The water had dropped another foot. "Ah! Too bad! too bad! The jam; there will be none!"

Jacob Welse regarded him gravely.

"Ah! There will be?" he asked, picking up hope.

Frona looked inquiringly at her father.

"Jams are not always nice," he said, with a short laugh. "It all depends where they take place and where you happen to be."

"But the river! Look! It falls; I can see it before my eyes."

"It is not too late." He swept the island-studded bend and saw the ice-mountains larger and reaching out one to the other. "Go into the tent, Courbertin, and put on the pair of moccasins you'll find by the stove. Go on. You won't miss anything. And you, Frona, start the fire and get the coffee under way."

Half an hour after, though the river had fallen twenty feet, they found the ice still pounding along.

"Now the fun begins. Here, take a squint, you hot-headed Gaul. The left-hand channel, man. Now she takes it!"

Courbertin saw the left-hand channel close, and then a great white barrier heave up and travel from island to island. The ice before them slowed down and came to rest. Then followed the instant rise of the river. Up it came in a swift rush, as though nothing short of the sky could stop it. As when they

205

were first awakened, the cakes rubbed and slid inshore over the crest of the bank, the muddy water creeping in advance and marking the way.

"Mon Dieu! But this is not nice!"

"But magnificent, baron," Frona teased. "In the meanwhile you are getting your feet wet."

He retreated out of the water, and in time, for a small avalanche of cakes rattled down upon the place he had just left. The rising water had forced the ice up till it stood breast-high above the island like a wall.

"But it will go down soon when the jam breaks. See, even now it comes up not so swift. It has broken."

Frona was watching the barrier. "No, it hasn't," she denied.

"But the water no longer rises like a race-horse."

"Nor does it stop rising."

He was puzzled for the nonce. Then his face brightened. "Ah! I have it! Above, somewhere, there is another jam. Most excellent, is it not?"

She caught his excited hand in hers and detained him. "But, listen.

Suppose the upper jam breaks and the lower jam holds?"

He looked at her steadily till he grasped the full import. His face flushed, and with a quick intake of the breath he straightened up and threw back his head. He made a sweeping gesture as though to include the island. "Then you, and I, the tent, the boats, cabins, trees, everything, and La Bijou! Pouf! and all are gone, to the devil!"

Frona shook her head. "It is too bad."

"Bad? Pardon. Magnificent!"

"No, no, baron; not that. But that you are not an Anglo-Saxon. The race could well be proud of you."

"And you, Frona, would you not glorify the French!"

"At it again, eh? Throwing bouquets at yourselves." Del Bishop grinned at them, and made to depart as quickly as he had come. "But twist yourselves. Some sick men in a cabin down here. Got to get 'em out. You're needed. And don't be all day about it," he shouted over his shoulder as he disappeared among the trees.

The river was still rising, though more slowly, and as soon as they left the high ground they were splashing along ankle-deep in the water. Winding in and out among the trees, they came upon a boat which had been hauled out the previous fall. And three *chechaquos*, who had managed to get into the country thus far over the ice, had piled themselves into it, also their tent, sleds, and dogs. But the boat was perilously near the ice-gorge, which growled and wrestled and over-topped it a bare dozen feet away.

"Come! Get out of this, you fools!" Jacob Welse shouted as he went past.

Del Bishop had told them to "get the hell out of there" when he ran by, and they could not understand. One of them turned up an unheeding, terrified face. Another lay prone and listless across the thwarts as though bereft of strength; while the third, with the face of a clerk, rocked back and forth and moaned monotonously, "My God! My God!"

The baron stopped long enough to shake him. "Damn!" he cried. "Your legs, man!—not God, but your legs! Ah! ah!—hump yourself! Yes, hump! Get a move on! Twist! Get back from the bank! The woods, the trees, anywhere!"

He tried to drag him out, but the man struck at him savagely and held back.

"How one collects the vernacular," he confided proudly to Frona as they hurried on. "Twist! It is a strong word, and suitable."

"You should travel with Del," she laughed. "He'd increase your stock in no time."

"You don't say so."

"Yes, but I do."

"Ah! Your idioms. I shall never learn." And he shook his head despairingly with both his hands.

They came out in a clearing, where a cabin stood close to the river. On its flat earth-roof two sick men, swathed in blankets, were lying, while Bishop, Corliss, and Jacob Welse were splashing about inside the cabin after the clothes-bags and general outfit. The mean depth of the flood was a couple of feet, but the floor of the cabin had been dug out for purposes of warmth, and there the water was to the waist.

"Keep the tobacco dry," one of the sick men said feebly from the roof.

"Tobacco, hell!" his companion advised. "Look out for the flour. And the sugar," he added, as an afterthought.

"That's 'cause Bill he don't smoke, miss," the first man explained.

"But keep an eye on it, won't you?" he pleaded.

"Here. Now shut up." Del tossed the canister beside him, and the man clutched it as though it were a sack of nuggets.

"Can I be of any use?" she asked, looking up at them.

"Nope. Scurvy. Nothing'll do 'em any good but God's country and raw potatoes." The pocket-miner regarded her for a moment. "What are you doing here, anyway? Go on back to high ground."

But with a groan and a crash, the ice-wall bulged in. A fifty-ton cake ended over, splashing them with muddy water, and settled down before the door. A smaller cake drove against the out-jutting corner-logs and the cabin reeled. Courbertin and Jacob Welse were inside.

"After you," Frona heard the baron, and then her father's short amused laugh; and the gallant Frenchman came out last, squeezing his way between the cake and the logs.

"Say, Bill, if that there lower jam holds, we're goners;" the man with the canister called to his partner.

"Ay, that it will," came the answer. "Below Nulato I saw Bixbie Island swept clean as my old mother's kitchen floor."

The men came hastily together about Frona.

"This won't do. We've got to carry them over to your shack, Corliss." As he spoke, Jacob Welse clambered nimbly up the cabin and gazed down at the big barrier. "Where's McPherson?" he asked.

"Petrified astride the ridge-pole this last hour."

Jacob Welse waved his arm. "It's breaking! There she goes!"

"No kitchen floor this time. Bill, with my respects to your old woman," called he of the tobacco.

"Ay," answered the imperturbable Bill.

The whole river seemed to pick itself up and start down the stream. With the increasing motion the ice-wall broke in a hundred places, and from up and down the shore came the rending and crashing of uprooted trees.

Corliss and Bishop laid hold of Bill and started off to McPherson's, and Jacob Welse and the baron were just sliding his mate over the eaves, when a huge block of ice rammed in and smote the cabin squarely. Frona saw it, and cried a warning, but the tiered logs were overthrown like a house of cards. She saw Courbertin and the sick man hurled clear of the wreckage, and her father go down with it. She sprang to the spot, but he did not rise. She pulled at him to get his mouth above water, but at full stretch his head, barely showed. Then she let go and felt about with her hands till she found his right arm jammed between the logs. These she could not move, but she thrust between them one of the roof-poles which had underlaid the dirt and moss. It was a rude handspike and hardly equal to the work, for when she threw her weight upon the free end it bent and crackled. Heedful of the warning, she came in a couple of feet and swung upon it tentatively and carefully till something gave and Jacob Welse shoved his muddy face into the air.

He drew half a dozen great breaths, and burst out, "But that tastes good!" And then, throwing a quick glance about him, Frona, Del Bishop is a most veracious man."

"Why?" she asked, perplexedly.

"Because he said you'd do, you know."

He kissed her, and they both spat the mud from their lips, laughing.

Courbertin floundered round a corner of the wreckage.

"Never was there such a man!" he cried, gleefully. "He is mad, crazy! There is no appeasement. His skull is cracked by the fall, and his tobacco is gone. It is chiefly the tobacco which is lamentable."

But his skull was not cracked, for it was merely a slit of the scalp of five inches or so.

"You'll have to wait till the others come back. I can't carry." Jacob Welse pointed to his right arm, which hung dead. "Only wrenched," he explained. "No bones broken."

The baron struck an extravagant attitude and pointed down at Frona's foot. "Ah! the water, it is gone, and there, a jewel of the flood, a pearl of price!"

Her well-worn moccasins had gone rotten from the soaking, and a little white toe peeped out at the world of slime.

"Then I am indeed wealthy, baron; for I have nine others."

"And who shall deny? who shall deny?" he cried, fervently.

"What a ridiculous, foolish, lovable fellow it is!"

"I kiss your hand." And he knelt gallantly in the muck.

She jerked her hand away, and, burying it with its mate in his curly mop, shook his head back and forth. "What shall I do with him, father?"

Jacob Welse shrugged his shoulders and laughed; and she turned Courbertin's face up and kissed him on the lips. And Jacob Welse knew that his was the larger share in that manifest joy.

The river, fallen to its winter level, was pounding its ice-glut steadily along. But in falling it had rimmed the shore with a twenty-foot wall of stranded floes. The great blocks were spilled inland among the thrown and standing trees and the slime-coated flowers and grasses like the titanic vomit of some Northland monster. The sun was not idle, and the steaming thaw washed the mud and foulness from the bergs till they blazed like heaped diamonds in the brightness, or shimmered opalescent-blue. Yet they were reared hazardously one on another, and ever and anon flashing towers and rainbow minarets crumbled thunderously into the flood. By one of the gaps so made lay La Bijou, and about it, saving *chechaquos* and sick men, were grouped the denizens of Split-up.

"Na, na, lad; twa men'll be a plenty." Tommy McPherson sought about him with his eyes for corroboration. "Gin ye gat three i' the canoe 'twill be ower comfortable."

"It must be a dash or nothing," Corliss spoke up. "We need three men,

Tommy, and you know it."

"Na, na; twa's a plenty, I'm tellin' ye."

"But I'm afraid we'll have to do with two."

The Scotch-Canadian evinced his satisfaction openly. "Mair'd be a bother; an' I doot not ye'll mak' it all richt, lad."

"And you'll make one of those two, Tommy," Corliss went on, inexorably.

"Na; there's ithers a plenty wi'oot coontin' me."

"No, there's not. Courbertin doesn't know the first thing. St. Vincent evidently cannot cross the slough. Mr. Welse's arm puts him out of it. So it's only you and I, Tommy."

"I'll not be inqueesitive, but yon son of Anak's a likely mon. He maun pit oop a guid stroke." While the Scot did not lose much love for the truculent pocket-miner, he was well aware of his grit, and seized the chance to save himself by shoving the other into the breach.

Del Bishop stepped into the centre of the little circle, paused, and looked every man in the eyes before he spoke.

"Is there a man here'll say I'm a coward?" he demanded without preface. Again he looked each one in the eyes. "Or is there a man who'll even hint that I ever did a curlike act?" And yet again he searched the circle. "Well and good. I hate the water, but I've never been afraid of it. I don't know how to swim, yet I've been over the side more times than it's good to remember. I can't pull an oar without batting my back on the bottom of the boat. As for steering—well, authorities say there's thirty-two points to the compass, but there's at least thirty more when I get started. And as sure as God made little apples, I don't know my elbow from my knee about a paddle. I've capsized damn near every canoe I ever set foot in. I've gone right through the bottom of two. I've turned turtle in the Canyon and been pulled out below the White Horse. I can only keep stroke with one man, and that man's yours truly. But, gentlemen, if the call comes, I'll take my place in La Bijou and take her to hell if she don't turn over on the way."

Baron Courbertin threw his arms about him, crying, "As sure as God made little apples, thou art a man!"

Tommy's face was white, and he sought refuge in speech from the silence which settled down. "I'll deny I lift a guid paddle, nor that my wind is fair; but gin ye gang a tithe the way the next jam'll be on us. For my pairt I conseeder it ay rash. Bide a wee till the river's clear, say I."

"It's no go, Tommy," Jacob Welse admonished. "You can't cash excuses here."

"But, mon! It doesna need discreemeenation—"

"That'll do!" from Corliss. "You're coming."

"I'll naething o' the sort. I'll—"

"Shut up!" Del had come into the world with lungs of leather and larynx of brass, and when he thus jerked out the stops the Scotsman quailed and shrank down.

"Oyez! Oyez!" In contrast to Del's siren tones, Frona's were purest silver as they rippled down-island through the trees. "Oyez! Oyez! Open water! Open water! And wait a minute. I'll be with you."

Three miles up-stream, where the Yukon curved grandly in from the west, a bit of water appeared. It seemed too marvellous for belief, after the granite winter; but McPherson, untouched of imagination, began a crafty retreat.

"Bide a wee, bide a wee," he protested, when collared by the pocket-miner. "A've forgot my pipe."

"Then you'll bide with us, Tommy," Del sneered. "And I'd let you have a draw of mine if your own wasn't sticking out of your pocket."

"'Twas the baccy I'd in mind."

"Then dig into this." He shoved his pouch into McPherson's shaking hands. "You'd better shed your coat. Here! I'll help you. And private, Tommy, if you don't act the man, I won't do a thing to you. Sure."

Corliss had stripped his heavy flannel shirt for freedom; and it was plain, when Frona joined them, that she also had been shedding. Jacket and skirt were gone, and her underskirt of dark cloth ceased midway below the knee.

"You'll do," Del commended.

Jacob Welse looked at her anxiously, and went over to where she was testing the grips of the several paddles. "You're not—?" he began.

She nodded.

"You're a guid girl," McPherson broke in. "Now, a've a wumman to home, to say naething o' three bairns—"

"All ready!" Corliss lifted the bow of La Bijou and looked back.

The turbid water lashed by on the heels of the ice-run. Courbertin took the stern in the steep descent, and Del marshalled Tommy's reluctant rear. A flat floe, dipping into the water at a slight incline, served as the embarking-stage.

"Into the bow with you, Tommy!"

The Scotsman groaned, felt Bishop breathe heavily at his back, and obeyed; Frona meeting his weight by slipping into the stern.

"I can steer," she assured Corliss, who for the first time was aware that she was coming.

He glanced up to Jacob Welse, as though for consent, and received it.

"Hit 'er up! Hit 'er up!" Del urged impatiently. "You're burnin' daylight!"

CHAPTER XXV

La Bijou was a perfect expression of all that was dainty and delicate in the boat-builder's soul. Light as an egg-shell, and as fragile, her three-eighths-inch skin offered no protection from a driving chunk of ice as small as a man's head. Nor, though the water was open, did she find a clear way, for the river was full of scattered floes which had crumbled down from the rim-ice. And here, at once, through skilful handling, Corliss took to himself confidence in Frona.

It was a great picture: the river rushing blackly between its crystalline walls; beyond, the green woods stretching upward to touch the cloud-flecked summer sky; and over all, like a furnace blast, the hot sun beating down. A great picture, but somehow Corliss's mind turned to his mother and her perennial tea, the soft carpets, the prim New England maid-servants, the canaries singing in the wide windows, and he wondered if she could understand. And when he thought of the woman behind him, and felt the *dip and lift, dip and lift,* of her paddle, his mother's women came back to him, one by one, and passed in long review,—pale, glimmering ghosts, he thought, caricatures of the stock which had replenished the earth, and which would continue to replenish the earth.

La Bijou skirted a pivoting floe, darted into a nipping channel, and shot out into the open with the walls grinding together behind. Tommy groaned.

"Well done!" Corliss encouraged.

"The fule wumman!" came the backward snarl. "Why couldna she bide a bit?"

Frona caught his words and flung a laugh defiantly. Vance darted a glance over his shoulder to her, and her smile was witchery. Her cap, perched precariously, was sliding off, while her flying hair, aglint in the sunshine, framed her face as he had seen it framed on the Dyea Trail.

"How I should like to sing, if it weren't for saving one's breath. Say the 'Song of the Sword,' or the 'Anchor Chanty.'"

"Or the 'First Chanty,'" Corliss answered. "'Mine was the woman, darkling I found her,'" he hummed, significantly.

She flashed her paddle into the water on the opposite side in order to go wide of a jagged cake, and seemed not to hear. "I could go on this way forever."

"And I," Corliss affirmed, warmly.

But she refused to take notice, saying, instead, "Vance, do you know I'm glad we're friends?"

"No fault of mine we're not more."

"You're losing your stroke, sir," she reprimanded; and he bent silently to the work.

La Bijou was driving against the current at an angle of forty-five degrees, and her resultant course was a line at right angles to the river. Thus, she would tap the western bank directly opposite the starting-point, where she could work up-stream in the slacker flood. But a mile of indented shore, and then a hundred yards of bluffs rising precipitously from out a stiff current would still lie between them and the man to be rescued.

"Now let us ease up," Corliss advised, as they slipped into an eddy and drifted with the back-tide under the great wall of rim-ice.

"Who would think it mid-May?" She glanced up at the carelessly poised cakes. "Does it seem real to you, Vance?"

He shook his head.

"Nor to me. I know that I, Frona, in the flesh, am here, in a Peterborough, paddling for dear life with two men; year of our Lord eighteen hundred and ninety-eight, Alaska, Yukon River; this is water, that is ice; my arms are tired, my heart up a few beats, and I am sweating,—and yet it seems all a dream. Just think! A year ago I was in Paris!" She drew a deep breath and looked out over the water to the further shore, where Jacob Welse's tent, like a snowy handkerchief, sprawled against the deep green of the forest. "I do not believe there is such a place," she added. "There is no Paris."

"And I was in London a twelvemonth past," Corliss meditated. "But I have undergone a new incarnation. London? There is no London now. It is impossible. How could there be so many people in the world? This is the world, and we know of fact that there are very few people in it, else there could not be so much ice and sea and sky. Tommy, here, I know, thinks fondly of a place he calls Toronto. He mistakes. It exists only in his mind,—a memory of a former life he knew. Of course, he does not think so. That is but natural; for he is no philosopher, nor does he bother—"

"Wheest, will ye!" Tommy fiercely whispered. "Your gabble'll bring it doon aboot oor heads."

Life is brief in the Northland, and fulfilment ever clutters the heels of prophecy. A premonitory tremor sighed down the air, and the rainbow wall swayed above them. The three paddles gripped the water with common accord. La Bijou leaped out from under. Broadside after broadside flared and crashed, and a thousand frigid tons thundered down behind them. The displaced water surged outward in a foamy, upstanding circle, and La Bijou, striving wildly to rise, ducked through the stiff overhang of the crest and wallowed, half-full, in the trough.

"Dinna I tell ye, ye gabbling fules!"

"Sit still, and bail!" Corliss checked him sharply. "Or you'll not have the comfort of telling us anything."

He shook his head at Frona, and she winked back; then they both chuckled, much like children over an escapade which looks disastrous but turns out well.

Creeping timidly under the shadow of the impending avalanches, La Bijou slipped noiselessly up the last eddy. A corner of the bluff rose savagely from the river—a monstrous mass of naked rock, scarred and battered of the centuries; hating the river that gnawed it ever; hating the rain that graved its grim face with unsightly seams; hating the sun that refused to mate with it, whereof green life might come forth and hide its hideousness. The whole force of the river hurled in against it, waged furious war along its battlements, and caromed off into mid-stream again. Down all its length the stiff waves stood in serried rows, and its crevices and water-worn caverns were a-bellow with unseen strife.

"Now! Bend to it! Your best!"

It was the last order Corliss could give, for in the din they were about to enter a man's voice were like a cricket's chirp amid the growling of an earthquake. La Bijou sprang forward, cleared the eddy with a bound, and plunged into the thick. *Dip and lift, dip and lift,* the paddles worked with rhythmic strength. The water rippled and tore, and pulled all ways at once; and the fragile shell, unable to go all ways at once, shook and quivered with the shock of resistance. It veered nervously to the right and left, but Frona held it with a hand of steel. A yard away a fissure in the rock grinned at them. La Bijou leaped and shot ahead, and the water, slipping away underneath, kept her always in one place. Now they surged out from the fissure, now in; ahead for half a yard, then back again; and the fissure mocked their toil.

Five minutes, each of which sounded a separate eternity, and the fissure was past. Ten minutes, and it was a hundred feet astern. *Dip and lift,* dip and lift, till sky and earth and river were blotted out, and consciousness dwindled to a thin line,—a streak of foam, fringed on the one hand with sneering rock, on the other with snarling water. That thin line summed up all. Somewhere below was the beginning of things; somewhere above, beyond the roar and traffic, was the end of things; and for that end they strove.

And still Frona held the egg-shell with a hand of steel. What they gained they held, and fought for more, inch by inch, dip and lift; and all would have been well but for the flutter of Tommy's soul. A cake of ice, sucked beneath by the current, rose under his paddle with a flurry of foam, turned over its toothed edge, and was dragged back into the depths. And in that sight he saw himself, hair streaming upward and drowned hands clutching emptiness, going feet first, down and down. He stared, wide-eyed, at the portent, and his poised paddle refused to strike. On the instant the fissure grinned in their faces, and the next they were below the bluffs, drifting gently in the eddy.

Frona lay, head thrown back, sobbing at the sun; amidships Corliss sprawled panting; and forward, choking and gasping and nerveless, the Scotsman drooped his head upon his knees. La Bijou rubbed softly against the rim-ice and came to rest. The rainbow-wall hung above like a fairy pile; the sun, flung backward from innumerable facets, clothed it in jewelled splendor. Silvery streams tinkled down its crystal slopes; and in its clear depths seemed to unfold, veil on veil, the secrets of life and death and mortal striving,—vistas of pale-shimmering azure opening like dream-visions, and promising, down there in the great cool heart, infinite rest, infinite cessation and rest.

The topmost tower, delicately massive, a score of feet above them, swayed to and fro, gently, like the ripple of wheat in light summer airs. But Corliss gazed at it unheeding. Just to lie there, on the marge of the mystery, just to lie there and drink the air in great gulps, and do nothing!—he asked no more. A dervish, whirling on heel till all things blur, may grasp the essence of the universe and prove the Godhead indivisible; and so a man, plying a paddle, and plying and plying, may shake off his limitations and rise above time and space. And so Corliss.

But gradually his blood ceased its mad pounding, and the air was no longer nectar-sweet, and a sense of things real and pressing came back to him.

"We've got to get out of this," he said. His voice sounded like a man's whose throat has been scorched by many and long potations. It frightened him, but he limply lifted a shaking paddle and shoved off.

"Yes; let us start, by all means," Frona said in a dim voice, which seemed to come to him from a far distance.

Tommy lifted his head and gazed about. "A doot we'll juist hae to gie it oop."

"Bend to it!"

"Ye'll no try it anither?"

"Bend to it!" Corliss repeated.

"Till your heart bursts, Tommy," Frona added.

Once again they fought up the thin line, and all the world vanished, save the streak of foam, and the snarling water, and the grinning fissure. But they passed it, inch by inch, and the broad bend welcomed them from above, and only a rocky buttress of implacable hate, around whose base howled the tides of an equal hate, stood between. Then La Bijou leaped and throbbed and shook again, and the current slid out from under, and they remained ever in one place. *Dip and lift, dip and lift,* through an infinity of time and torture and travail, till even the line dimmed and faded and the struggle lost its meaning. Their souls became merged in the rhythm of the toil. Ever lifting, ever falling, they seemed to have become great pendulums of time. And before and behind glimmered the eternities, and between the eternities, ever lifting, ever falling, they pulsed in vast rhythmical movement. They were no longer humans, but rhythms. They surged in till their paddles touched the bitter rock, but they did not know; surged out, where chance piloted them unscathed through the lashing ice, but they did not see. Nor did they feel the shock of the smitten waves, nor the driving spray that cooled their faces. . .

La Bijou veered out into the stream, and their paddles, flashing mechanically in the sunshine, held her to the return angle across the river. As time and matter came back to them, and Split-up Island dawned upon their eyes like the foreshore of a new world, they settled down to the long easy stroke wherein breath and strength may be recovered.

"A third attempt would have been useless," Corliss said, in a dry, cracked whisper.

And Frona answered, "Yes; our hearts would have surely broken."

Life, and the pleasant camp-fire, and the quiet rest in the noonday shade, came back to Tommy as the shore drew near, and more than all, blessed Toronto, its houses that never moved, and its jostling streets. Each time his head sank forward and he reached out and clutched the water with his paddle, the streets enlarged, as though gazing through a telescope and adjusting to a nearer focus. And each time the paddle drove clear and his head was raised, the island bounded forward. His head sank, and the streets were of the size of life; it raised, and Jacob Welse and the two men stood on the bank three lengths away.

"Dinna I tell ye!" he shouted to them, triumphantly.

But Frona jerked the canoe parallel with the bank, and he found himself gazing at the long up-stream stretch. He arrested a stroke midway, and his paddle clattered in the bottom.

"Pick it up!" Corliss's voice was sharp and relentless.

"I'll do naething o' the kind." He turned a rebellious face on his tormentor, and ground his teeth in anger and disappointment.

The canoe was drifting down with the current, and Frona merely held it in place. Corliss crawled forward on his knees.

"I don't want to hurt you, Tommy," he said in a low, tense voice, "so . . . well, just pick it up, that's a good fellow."

"I'll no."

"Then I shall kill you," Corliss went on, in the same calm, passionless way, at the same time drawing his hunting-knife from its sheath.

"And if I dinna?" the Scotsman queried stoutly, though cowering away.

Corliss pressed gently with the knife. The point of the steel entered Tommy's back just where the heart should be, passed slowly through the shirt, and bit into the skin. Nor did it stop there; neither did it quicken, but just as slowly held on its way. He shrank back, quivering.

"There! there! man! Pit it oop!" he shrieked. "I maun gie in!"

Frona's face was quite pale, but her eyes were hard, brilliantly hard, and she nodded approval.

"We're going to try this side, and shoot across from above," she called to her father. "What? I can't hear. Tommy? Oh, his heart's weak. Nothing serious." She saluted with her paddle. "We'll be back in no time, father mine. In no time."

Stewart River was wide open, and they ascended it a quarter of a mile before they shot its mouth and continued up the Yukon. But when they were well abreast of the man on the opposite bank a new obstacle faced them. A mile above, a wreck of an island clung desperately to the river bed. Its tail dwindled to a sand-spit which bisected the river as far down as the impassable bluffs. Further, a few hundred thousand tons of ice had grounded upon the spit and upreared a glittering ridge.

"We'll have to portage," Corliss said, as Frona turned the canoe from the bank.

La Bijou darted across the narrower channel to the sand-spit and slipped up a little ice ravine, where the walls were less precipitous. They landed on an out-jutting cake, which, without support, overhung the water for sheer thirty feet. How far its other end could be buried in the mass was matter for conjecture. They climbed to the summit, dragging the canoe after them, and looked out over the dazzle. Floe was piled on floe in titanic confusion. Huge blocks topped and overtopped one another, only to serve as pedestals for great white masses, which blazed and scintillated in the sun like monstrous jewels.

"A bonny place for a bit walk," Tommy sneered, "wi' the next jam fair to come ony time." He sat down resolutely. "No, thank ye kindly, I'll no try it."

Frona and Corliss clambered on, the canoe between them.

"The Persians lashed their slaves into battle," she remarked, looking back. "I never understood before. Hadn't you better go back after him?"

Corliss kicked him up, whimpering, and forced him to go on in advance. The canoe was an affair of little weight, but its bulk, on the steep rises and sharp turns, taxed their strength. The sun burned down upon them. Its white glare hurt their eyes, the sweat oozed out from every pore, and they panted for breath.

"Oh, Vance, do you know . . ."

"What?" He swept the perspiration from his forehead and flung it from him with a quick flirt of the hand.

"I wish I had eaten more breakfast."

He grunted sympathetically. They had reached the midmost ridge and could see the open river, and beyond, quite clearly, the man and his signal of distress. Below, pastoral in its green quiet, lay Split-up Island. They looked up to the broad bend of the Yukon, smiling lazily, as though it were not capable at any moment of spewing forth a flood of death. At their feet the ice sloped down into a miniature gorge, across which the sun cast a broad shadow.

"Go on, Tommy," Frona bade. "We're half-way over, and there's water down there."

"It's water ye'd be thinkin' on, is it?" he snarled, "and you a-leadin' a buddie to his death!"

"I fear you have done some great sin, Tommy," she said, with a reproving shake of the head, "or else you would not be so afraid of death." She sighed and picked up her end of the canoe. "Well, I suppose it is natural. You do not know how to die—"

"No more do I want to die," he broke in fiercely.

"But there come times for all men to die,—times when to die is the only thing to do. Perhaps this is such a time."

Tommy slid carefully over a glistening ledge and dropped his height to a broad foothold. "It's a' vera guid," he grinned up; "but dinna ye think a've suffeecient discreemeenation to judge for mysel'? Why should I no sing my ain sang?"

"Because you do not know how. The strong have ever pitched the key for such as you. It is they that have taught your kind when and how to die, and led you to die, and lashed you to die."

"Ye pit it fair," he rejoined. "And ye do it weel. It doesna behoove me to complain, sic a michty fine job ye're makin' on it."

"You are doing well," Corliss chuckled, as Tommy dropped out of sight and landed into the bed of the gorge. "The cantankerous brute! he'd argue on the trail to Judgment."

"Where did you learn to paddle?" she asked.

"College—exercise," he answered, shortly. "But isn't that fine? Look!"

The melting ice had formed a pool in the bottom of the gorge. Frona stretched out full length, and dipped her hot mouth in its coolness. And lying as she did, the soles of her dilapidated moccasins, or rather the soles of her feet (for moccasins and stockings had gone in shreds), were turned upward. They were very white, and from contact with the ice were bruised and cut. Here and there the blood oozed out, and from one of the toes it streamed steadily.

"So wee, and pretty, and salt-like," Tommy gibed. "One wouldna think they could lead a strong man to hell."

"By the way you grumble, they're leading you fast enough," Corliss answered angrily.

"Forty mile an hour," Tommy retorted, as he walked away, gloating over having the last word.

"One moment. You've two shirts. Lend me one."

The Scotsman's face lighted inquisitively, till he comprehended. Then he shook his head and started on again.

Frona scrambled to her feet. "What's the matter?"

"Nothing. Sit down."

"But what is the matter?"

Corliss put his hands on her shoulders and pressed her back. "Your feet. You can't go on in such shape. They're in ribbons. See!" He brushed the sole of one of them and held up a blood-dripping palm. "Why didn't you tell me?"

"Oh, they didn't bother—much."

"Give me one of your skirts," he demanded.

"I . . ." She faltered. "I only have one."

He looked about him. Tommy had disappeared among the ice-floes.

"We must be getting on," Frona said, attempting to rise.

But he held her back. "Not another step till I fix you. Here goes, so shut your eyes."

She obeyed, and when she opened them he was naked to the waist, and his undershirt, torn in strips, was being bound about her feet.

"You were in the rear, and I did not know—"

"Don't apologize, pray," she interrupted. "I could have spoken."

"I'm not; I'm reproaching you. Now, the other one. Put it up!"

The nearness to her bred a madness, and he touched his lips lightly to the same white little toe that had won the Baron Courbertin a kiss.

Though she did not draw back, her face flushed, and she thrilled as she had thrilled once before in her life. "You take advantage of your own goodness," she rebuked him.

"Then I will doubly advantage myself."

"Please don't," she begged.

"And why not? It is a custom of the sea to broach the spirits as the ship prepares to sink. And since this is a sort of a forlorn hope, you know, why not?"

"But . . ."

"But what, Miss Prim?"

"Oh! Of all things, you know I do not deserve that! If there were nobody else to be considered, why, under the circumstances . . ."

He drew the last knot tight and dropped her foot. "Damn St. Vincent, anyway! Come on!"

"So would I, were I you," she laughed, taking up her end of the canoe. "But how you have changed, Vance. You are not the same man I met on the Dyea Trail. You hadn't learned to swear, then, among other things."

"No, I'm not the same; for which I thank God and you. Only I think I am honester than you. I always live up to my philosophy."

"Now confess that's unfair. You ask too much under the circumstances—"

"Only a little toe."

"Or else, I suppose, you just care for me in a kind, big-brotherly way.

In which case, if you really wish it, you may—"

"Do keep quiet," he broke in, roughly, "or I'll be making a gorgeous fool of myself."

"Kiss all my toes," she finished.

He grunted, but did not deign a reply. The work quickly took their breath, and they went on in silence till they descended the last steep to where McPherson waited by the open river.

"Del hates St. Vincent," she said boldly. "Why?"

"Yes, it seems that way." He glanced back at her curiously. "And wherever he goes, Del lugs an old Russian book, which he can't read but which he nevertheless regards, in some sort of way, as St. Vincent's Nemesis. And do you know, Frona, he has such faith in it that I can't help catching a little myself. I don't know whether you'll come to me, or whether I'll go to you, but—"

She dropped her end of the canoe and broke out in laughter. He was annoyed, and a hurt spread of blood ruddied his face.

"If I have—" he began.

"Stupid!" she laughed. "Don't be silly! And above all don't be dignified. It doesn't exactly become you at the present moment,—your hair all tangled, a murderous knife in your belt, and naked to the waist like a pirate stripped for battle. Be fierce, frown, swear, anything, but please don't be dignified. I do wish I had my camera. In after years I could say: 'This, my friends, is Corliss, the great Arctic explorer, just as he looked at the conclusion of his world-famous trip *Through Darkest Alaska.*'"

He pointed an ominous finger at her and said sternly, "Where is your skirt?"

She involuntarily looked down. But its tatterdemalion presence relieved her, and her face jerked up scarlet.

"You should be ashamed!"

"Please, please do not be dignified," he laughed. "Very true, it doesn't exactly become you at the present moment. Now, if I had my camera—"

"Do be quiet and go on," she said. "Tommy is waiting. I hope the sun takes the skin all off your back," she panted vindictively, as they slid the canoe down the last shelf and dropped it into the water.

Ten minutes later they climbed the ice-wall, and on and up the bank, which was partly a hillside, to where the signal of distress still fluttered. Beneath it, on the ground, lay stretched the man. He lay very quietly, and the fear that they were too late was upon them, when he moved his head slightly and moaned. His rough clothes were in rags, and the black, bruised flesh of his feet showed through the remnants of his moccasins. His body was thin and gaunt, without flesh-pads or muscles, while the bones seemed ready to break through the tight-stretched skin. As Corliss felt his pulse, his eyes fluttered open and stared glassily. Frona shuddered.

"Man, it's fair gruesome," McPherson muttered, running his hand up a shrunken arm.

"You go on to the canoe, Frona," Corliss said. "Tommy and I will carry him down."

But her lips set firmly. Though the descent was made easier by her aid, the man was well shaken by the time they laid him in the bottom of the canoe,—so well shaken that some last shreds of consciousness were aroused.

He opened his eyes and whispered hoarsely, "Jacob Welse . . . despatches . . . from the Outside." He plucked feebly at his open shirt, and across his emaciated chest they saw the leather strap, to which, doubtless, the despatch-pouch was slung.

At either end of the canoe there was room to spare, but amidships Corliss was forced to paddle with the man between his knees. La Bijou swung out blithely from the bank. It was down-stream at last, and there was little need for exertion.

Vance's arms and shoulders and back, a bright scarlet, caught Frona's attention. "My hopes are realized," she exulted, reaching out and softly stroking a burning arm. "We shall have to put cold cream on it when we get back."

"Go ahead," he encouraged. "That feels awfully good."

She splashed his hot back with a handful of the ice-cold water from over-side. He caught his breath with a gasp, and shivered. Tommy turned about to look at them.

"It's a guid deed we'll 'a doon this day," he remarked, pleasantly.

"To gie a hand in distress is guid i' the sight of God."

"Who's afeared ?" Frona laughed.

"Weel," he deliberated, "I was a bit fashed, no doot, but—"

His utterance ceased, and he seemed suddenly to petrify. His eyes fixed themselves in a terrible stare over Frona's shoulder. And then, slowly and dreamily, with the solemnity fitting an invocation of Deity, murmured, "Guid Gawd Almichty!"

They whirled their heads about. A wall of ice was sweeping round the bend, and even as they looked the right-hand flank, unable to compass the curve, struck the further shore and flung up a ridge of heaving mountains.

"Guid Gawd! Guid Gawd! Like rats i' the trap!" Tommy jabbed his paddle futilely in the water.

"Get the stroke!" Corliss hissed in his ear, and La Bijou sprang away.

Frona steered straight across the current, at almost right angles, for Split-up; but when the sandspit, over which they had portaged, crashed at the impact of a million tons, Corliss glanced at her anxiously. She smiled and shook her head, at the same time slacking off the course.

"We can't make it," she whispered, looking back at the ice a couple of hundred feet away. "Our only chance is to run before it and work in slowly."

She cherished every inward inch jealously, holding the canoe up as sharply as she dared and at the same time maintaining a constant distance ahead of the ice-rim.

"I canna stand the pace," Tommy whimpered once; but the silence of

Corliss and Frona seemed ominous, and he kept his paddle going.

At the very fore of the ice was a floe five or six feet thick and a couple of acres in extent. Reaching out in advance of the pack, it clove through the water till on either side there formed a bore like that of a quick flood-tide in an inland passage. Tommy caught sight of it, and would have collapsed had not Corliss prodded him, between strokes, with the point of his paddle.

"We can keep ahead," Frona panted; "but we must get time to make the landing?"

"When the chance comes, drive her in, bow on," Corliss counselled; "and when she strikes, jump and run for it."

"Climb, rather. I'm glad my skirt is short."

Repulsed by the bluffs of the left bank, the ice was forced towards the right. The big floe, in advance, drove in upon the precise point of Split-up Island.

"If you look back, I'll brain you with the paddle," Corliss threatened.

"Ay," Tommy groaned.

But Corliss looked back, and so did Frona. The great berg struck the land with an earthquake shock. For fifty feet the soft island was demolished. A score of pines swayed frantically and went down, and where they went down rose up a mountain of ice, which rose, and fell, and rose again. Below, and but a few feet away, Del Bishop ran out to the bank, and above the roar they could hear faintly his "Hit 'er up! Hit 'er up!" Then the ice-rim wrinkled up and he sprang back to escape it.

"The first opening," Corliss gasped.

Frona's lips spread apart; she tried to speak but failed, then nodded her head that she had heard. They swung along in rapid rhythm under the rainbow-wall, looking for a place where it might be quickly cleared. And down all the length of Split-up Island they raced vainly, the shore crashing behind them as they fled.

As they darted across the mouth of the back-channel to Roubeau Island they found themselves heading directly for an opening in the rim-ice. La Bijou drove into it full tilt, and went half her length out of water on a shelving cake. The three leaped together, but while the two of them gripped the canoe to run it up, Tommy, in the lead, strove only to save himself. And he would have succeeded had he not slipped and fallen midway in the climb. He half arose, slipped, and fell again. Corliss, hauling on the bow of the canoe, trampled over him. He reached up and clutched the gunwale. They did not have the strength, and this clog brought them at once to a standstill. Corliss looked back and yelled for him to leave go, but he only turned upward a piteous face, like that of a drowning man, and clutched more tightly. Behind them the ice was thundering. The first flurry of coming destruction was upon them. They endeavored desperately to drag up the canoe, but the added burden was too much, and they fell on their knees. The sick man sat up suddenly and laughed wildly. "Blood of my soul!" he ejaculated, and laughed again.

Roubeau Island swayed to the first shock, and the ice was rocking under their feet. Frona seized a paddle and smashed the Scotsman's knuckles; and the instant he loosed his grip, Corliss carried the canoe up in a mad rush, Frona clinging on and helping from behind. The rainbow-wall curled up like a scroll, and in the convolutions of the scroll, like a bee in the many folds of a magnificent orchid, Tommy disappeared.

They fell, breathless, on the earth. But a monstrous cake shoved up from the jam and balanced above them. Frona tried to struggle to her feet, but sank on her knees; and it remained for Corliss to snatch her and the canoe out from underneath. Again they fell, this time under the trees, the sun sifting down upon them through the green pine needles, the robins singing overhead, and a colony of crickets chirping in the warmth.

CHAPTER XXVI

Frona woke, slowly, as though from a long dream. She was lying where she had fallen, across Corliss's legs, while he, on his back, faced the hot sun without concern. She crawled up to him. He was breathing regularly, with closed eyes, which opened to meet hers. He smiled, and she sank down again. Then he rolled over on his side, and they looked at each other.

"Vance."

"Yes."

She reached out her hand; his closed upon it, and their eyelids fluttered and drooped down. The river still rumbled en, somewhere in the infinite distance, but it came to them like the murmur of a world forgotten. A soft languor encompassed them. The golden sunshine dripped down upon them through the living green, and all the life of the warm earth seemed singing. And quiet was very good. Fifteen long minutes they drowsed, and woke again.

Frona sat up. "I—I was afraid," she said.

"Not you."

"Afraid that I might be afraid," she amended, fumbling with her hair.

"Leave it down. The day merits it."

She complied, with a toss of the head which circled it with a nimbus of rippling yellow.

"Tommy's gone," Corliss mused, the race with the ice coming slowly back.

"Yes," she answered. "I rapped him on the knuckles. It was terrible. But the chance is we've a better man in the canoe, and we must care for him at once. Hello! Look there!" Through the trees, not a score of feet away, she saw the wall of a large cabin. "Nobody in sight. It must be deserted, or else they're visiting, whoever they are. You look to our man, Vance,—I'm more presentable,—and I'll go and see."

She skirted the cabin, which was a large one for the Yukon country, and came around to where it fronted on the river. The door stood open, and, as she paused to knock, the whole interior flashed upon her in an astounding picture,—a cumulative picture, or series of pictures, as it were. For first she was aware of a crowd of men, and of some great common purpose upon which all were seriously bent. At her knock they instinctively divided, so that a lane opened up, flanked by their pressed bodies, to the far end of the room. And there, in the long bunks on either side, sat two grave rows of men. And midway between, against the wall, was a table. This table seemed the centre of interest. Fresh from the sun-dazzle, the light within was dim and murky, but she managed to make out a bearded American sitting by the table and hammering it with a heavy caulking-mallet. And on the opposite side sat St. Vincent. She had time to note his worn and haggard face, before a man of Scandinavian appearance slouched up to the table.

The man with the mallet raised his right hand and said glibly, "You do most solemnly swear that what you are about to give before the court—" He abruptly stopped and glowered at the man before him. "Take off your hat!" he roared, and a snicker went up from the crowd as the man obeyed.

Then he of the mallet began again. "You do most solemnly swear that what you are about to give before the court shall be the truth, the whole truth, and nothing but the truth, so help you God?"

The Scandinavian nodded and dropped his hand.

"One moment, gentlemen." Frona advanced up the lane, which closed behind her.

St. Vincent sprang to his feet and stretched out his arms to her.

"Frona," he cried, "oh, Frona, I am innocent!"

It struck her like a blow, the unexpectedness of it, and for the instant, in the sickly light, she was conscious only of the ring of white faces, each face set with eyes that burned. Innocent of what? she thought, and as she looked at St. Vincent, arms still extended, she was aware, in a vague, troubled way, of something distasteful. Innocent of what? He might have had more reserve. He might have waited till he was charged. She did not know that he was charged with anything.

"Friend of the prisoner," the man with the mallet said authoritatively.

"Bring a stool for'ard, some of you."

"One moment . . ." She staggered against the table and rested a hand on it. "I do not understand. This is all new . . ." But her eyes happened to come to rest on her feet, wrapped in dirty rags, and she knew that she was clad in a short and tattered skirt, that her arm peeped forth through a rent in her sleeve, and that her hair was down and flying. Her cheek and neck on one side seemed coated with some curious substance. She brushed it with her hand, and caked mud rattled to the floor.

"That will do," the man said, not unkindly. "Sit down. We're in the same box. We do not understand. But take my word for it, we're here to find out. So sit down."

She raised her hand. "One moment—"

"Sit down!" he thundered. "The court cannot be disturbed."

A hum went up from the crowd, words of dissent, and the man pounded the table for silence. But Frona resolutely kept her feet.

When the noise had subsided, she addressed the man in the chair. "Mr. Chairman: I take it that this is a miners' meeting." (The man nodded.)

"Then, having an equal voice in the managing of this community's affairs, I demand to be heard. It is important that I should be heard."

"But you are out of order. Miss—er—"

"Welse!" half a dozen voices prompted.

"Miss Welse," he went on, an added respect marking his demeanor, "it grieves me to inform you that you are out of order. You had best sit down."

"I will not," she answered. "I rise to a question of privilege, and if I am not heard, I shall appeal to the meeting."

She swept the crowd with her eyes, and cries went up that she be given a fair show. The chairman yielded and motioned her to go on.

"Mr. Chairman and men: I do not know the business you have at present before you, but I do know that I have more important business to place before you. Just outside this cabin is a man probably dying from starvation. We have brought him from across the river. We should not have bothered you, but we were unable to make our own island. This man I speak of needs immediate attention."

"A couple of you nearest the door go out and look after him," the chairman ordered. "And you, Doc Holiday, go along and see what you can do."

"Ask for a recess," St. Vincent whispered.

Frona nodded her head. "And, Mr. Chairman, I make a motion for a recess until the man is cared for."

Cries of "No recess!" and "Go on with the business!" greeted the putting of it, and the motion was lost.

"Now, Gregory," with a smile and salutation as she took the stool beside him, "what is it?"

He gripped her hand tightly. "Don't believe them, Frona. They are trying to"—with a gulping swallow—"to kill me."

"Why? Do be calm. Tell me."

"Why, last night," he began hurriedly, but broke off to listen to the

Scandinavian previously sworn, who was speaking with ponderous slowness.

"I wake wide open quick," he was saying. "I coom to the door. I there hear one shot more."

He was interrupted by a warm-complexioned man, clad in faded mackinaws.

"What did you think?" he asked.

"Eh?" the witness queried, his face dark and troubled with perplexity.

"When you came to the door, what was your first thought?"

"A-w-w," the man sighed, his face clearing and infinite comprehension sounding in his voice. "I have no moccasins. I t'ink pretty damn cold." His satisfied expression changed to naive surprise when an outburst of laughter greeted his statement, but he went on stolidly. "One more shot I hear, and I run down the trail."

Then Corliss pressed in through the crowd to Frona, and she lost what the man was saying.

"What's up?" the engineer was asking. "Anything serious? Can I be of any use?"

"Yes, yes." She caught his hand gratefully. "Get over the back-channel somehow and tell my father to come. Tell him that Gregory St. Vincent is in trouble; that he is charged with— What are you charged with, Gregory?" she asked, turning to him.

"Murder."

"Murder?" from Corliss.

"Yes, yes. Say that he is charged with murder; that I am here; and that I need him. And tell him to bring me some clothes. And, Vance,"—with a pressure of the hand and swift upward look,—"don't take any . . . any big chances, but do try to make it."

"Oh, I'll make it all right." He tossed his head confidently and proceeded to elbow his way towards the door.

"Who is helping you in your defence?" she asked St. Vincent.

He shook his head. "No. They wanted to appoint some one,—a renegade lawyer from the States, Bill Brown,—but I declined him. He's taken the other side, now. It's lynch law, you know, and their minds are made up. They're bound to get me."

"I wish there were time to hear your side."

"But, Frona, I am innocent. I—"

"S-sh!" She laid her hand on his arm to hush him, and turned her attention to the witness.

"So the noospaper feller, he fight like anything; but Pierre and me, we pull him into the shack. He cry and stand in one place—"

"Who cried?" interrupted the prosecuting lawyer.

"Him. That feller there." The Scandinavian pointed directly at St. Vincent. "And I make a light. The slush-lamp I find spilt over most everything, but I have a candle in my pocket. It is good practice to carry a candle in the pocket," he affirmed gravely. "And Borg he lay on the floor dead. And the squaw say he did it, and then she die, too."

"Said who did it?"

Again his accusing finger singled out St. Vincent. "Him. That feller there."

"Did she?" Frona whispered.

"Yes," St. Vincent whispered back, "she did. But I cannot imagine what prompted her. She must have been out of her head."

The warm-faced man in the faded mackinaws then put the witness through a searching examination, which Frona followed closely, but which elicited little new.

"You have the right to cross-examine the witness," the chairman informed St. Vincent. "Any questions you want to ask?"

The correspondent shook his head.

"Go on," Frona urged.

"What's the use?" he asked, hopelessly. "I'm fore-doomed. The verdict was reached before the trial began."

"One moment, please." Frona's sharp command arrested the retiring witness. "You do not know of your own knowledge who committed this murder?"

The Scandinavian gazed at her with a bovine expression on his leaden features, as though waiting for her question to percolate to his understanding.

"You did not see who did it?" she asked again.

"Aw, yes. That feller there," accusative finger to the fore. "She say he did."

There was a general smile at this.

"But you did not see it?"

"I hear some shooting."

"But you did not see who did the shooting?"

"Aw, no; but she said—"

"That will do, thank you," she said sweetly, and the man retired.

The prosecution consulted its notes. "Pierre La Flitche!" was called out.

A slender, swart-skinned man, lithe of figure and graceful, stepped forward to the open space before the table. He was darkly handsome, with a quick, eloquent eye which roved frankly everywhere. It rested for a moment on Frona, open and honest in its admiration, and she smiled and half-nodded, for she liked him at first glance, and it seemed as though they had met of old time. He smiled pleasantly back, the smooth upper lip curling brightly and showing beautiful teeth, immaculately white.

In answer to the stereotyped preliminaries he stated that his name was that of his father's, a descendant of the *coureurs du bois*. His mother—with a shrug of the shoulders and flash of teeth—was a *breed*. He was born somewhere in the Barrens, on a hunting trip, he did not know where. Ah, *oui*, men called him an old-timer. He had come into the country in the days of Jack McQuestion, across the Rockies from the Great Slave.

On being told to go ahead with what he knew of the matter in hand, he deliberated a moment, as though casting about for the best departure.

"In the spring it is good to sleep with the open door," he began, his words sounding clear and flute-like and marked by haunting memories of the accents his forbears put into the tongue. "And so I sleep last night. But I sleep like the cat. The fall of the leaf, the breath of the wind, and my ears whisper to me, whisper, whisper, all the night long. So, the first shot," with a quick snap of the fingers, "and I am awake, just like that, and I am at the door."

St. Vincent leaned forward to Frona. "It was not the first shot."

She nodded, with her eyes still bent on La Flitche, who gallantly waited.

"Then two more shot," he went on, "quick, together, boom-boom, just like that. 'Borg's shack,' I say to myself, and run down the trail. I think Borg kill Bella, which was bad. Bella very fine girl," he confided with one of his irresistible smiles. "I like Bella. So I run. And John he run from his cabin like a fat cow, with great noise. 'What the matter?' he say; and I say, 'I don't know.' And then something come, wheugh! out of the dark, just like that, and knock John down, and knock me down. We grab everywhere all at once. It is a man. He is in undress. He fight. He cry, 'Oh! Oh! Oh!' just like that. We hold him tight, and bime-by pretty quick, he stop. Then we get up, and I say, 'Come along back.'"

"Who was the man?"

La Flitche turned partly, and rested his eyes on St. Vincent.

"Go on."

"So? The man he will not go back; but John and I say yes, and he go."

"Did he say anything?"

"I ask him what the matter; but he cry, he . . . he sob, *huh-tsch, huh-tsch,* just like that."

"Did you see anything peculiar about him?"

La Flitche's brows drew up interrogatively.

^Anything uncommon, out of the ordinary?"

"Ah, *oui*; blood on the hands." Disregarding the murmur in the room, he went on, his facile play of feature and gesture giving dramatic value to the recital. "John make a light, and Bella groan, like the hair-seal when you shoot him in the body, just like that when you shoot him in the body under the flipper. And Borg lay over in the corner. I look. He no breathe 'tall.

"Then Bella open her eyes, and I look in her eyes, and I know she know me, La Flitche. 'Who did it, Bella?' I ask. And she roll her head on the floor and whisper, so low, so slow, 'Him dead?' I know she mean Borg, and I say yes. Then she lift up on one elbow, and look about quick, in big hurry, and when she see Vincent she look no more, only she look at Vincent all the time. Then she point at him, just like that." Suiting the action to the word, La Flitche turned and thrust a wavering finger at the prisoner. "And she say, 'Him, him, him.' And I say, 'Bella, who did it?' And she say, 'Him, him, him. St. Vincha, him do it.' And then"—La Flitche's head felt limply forward on his chest, and came back naturally erect, as he finished, with a flash of teeth, "Dead."

The warm-faced man, Bill Brown, put the quarter-*breed* through the customary direct examination, which served to strengthen his testimony and to bring out the fact that a terrible struggle must have taken place in the killing of Borg. The heavy table was smashed, the stool and the bunk-board splintered, and the stove over-thrown. "Never did I see anything like it," La Flitche concluded his description of the wreck. "No, never."

Brown turned him over to Frona with a bow, which a smile of hers paid for in full. She did not deem it unwise to cultivate cordiality with the lawyer. What she was working for was time—time for her father to come, time to be closeted with St. Vincent and learn all the details of what really had occurred. So she put questions, questions, interminable questions, to La Flitche. Twice only did anything of moment crop up.

"You spoke of the first shot, Mr. La Flitche. Now, the walls of a log cabin are quite thick. Had your door been closed, do you think you could have heard that first shot?"

He shook his head, though his dark eyes told her he divined the point she was endeavoring to establish.

"And had the door of Borg's cabin been closed, would you have heard?"

Again he shook his head.

"Then, Mr. La Flitche, when you say the first shot, you do not mean necessarily the first shot fired, but rather the first shot you heard fired?"

He nodded, and though she had scored her point she could not see that it had any material bearing after all.

Again she worked up craftily to another and stronger climax, though she felt all the time that La Flitche fathomed her.

"You say it was very dark, Mr. La Flitche?"

"Ah, *oui*; quite dark."

"How dark? How did you know it was John you met?"

"John make much noise when he run. I know that kind of noise."

"Could you see him so as to know that it was he?"

"Ah, no."

"Then, Mr. La Flitche," she demanded, triumphantly, "will you please state how you knew there was blood on the hands of Mr. St. Vincent?"

His lip lifted in a dazzling smile, and he paused a moment. "How? I feel it warm on his hands. And my nose—ah, the smoke of the hunter camp long way off, the hole where the rabbit hide, the track of the moose which has gone before, does not my nose tell me?" He flung his head back, and with tense face, eyes closed, nostrils quivering and dilated, he simulated the quiescence of all the senses save one and the concentration of his whole being upon that one. Then his eyes fluttered partly open and he regarded her dreamily. "I smell the blood on his hands, the warm blood, the hot blood on his hands."

"And by gad he can do it!" some man exclaimed.

And so convinced was Frona that she glanced involuntarily at St. Vincent's hands, and saw there the rusty-brown stains on the cuffs of his flannel shirt.

As La Flitche left the stand, Bill Brown came over to her and shook hands. "No more than proper I should know the lawyer for the defence," he said, good-naturedly, running over his notes for the next witness.

"But don't you think it is rather unfair to me?" she asked, brightly. "I have not had time to prepare my case. I know nothing about it except what I have gleaned from your two witnesses. Don't you think, Mr. Brown," her voice rippling along in persuasive little notes, "don't you think it would be advisable to adjourn the meeting until to-morrow?"

"Hum," he deliberated, looking at his watch.

"Wouldn't be a bad idea. It's five o'clock, anyway, and the men ought to be cooking their suppers."

She thanked him, as some women can, without speech; yet, as he looked down into her face and eyes, he experienced a subtler and greater satisfaction than if she had spoken.

He stepped to his old position and addressed the room. "On consultation of the defence and the prosecution, and upon consideration of the lateness of the hour and the impossibility of finishing the trial within a reasonable limit, I—hum—I take the liberty of moving an adjournment until eight o'clock to-morrow morning."

"The ayes have it," the chairman proclaimed, coming down from his place and proceeding to build the fire, for he was a part-owner of the cabin and cook for his crowd.

CHAPTER XXVII

Frona turned to St. Vincent as the last of the crowd filed out. He clutched her hands spasmodically, like a drowning man.

"Do believe me, Frona. Promise me."

Her face flushed. "You are excited," she said, "or you would not say such things. Not that I blame you," she relented. "I hardly imagine the situation can be anything else but exciting."

"Yes, and well I know it," he answered, bitterly. "I am acting like a fool, and I can't help it. The strain has been terrible. And as though the horror of Borg's end were not enough, to be considered the murderer, and haled up for mob justice! Forgive me, Frona. I am beside myself. Of course, I know that you will believe me."

"Then tell me, Gregory."

"In the first place, the woman, Bella, lied. She must have been crazed to make that dying statement when I fought as I did for her and Borg. That is the only explanation—"

"Begin at the beginning," she interrupted. "Remember, I know nothing."

He settled himself more comfortably on the stool, and rolled a cigarette as he took up the history of the previous night.

"It must have been about one in the morning when I was awakened by the lighting of the slush-lamp. I thought it was Borg; wondered what he was prowling about for, and was on the verge of dropping off to sleep, when, though I do not know what prompted me, I opened my eyes. Two strange men were in the cabin. Both wore masks and fur caps with the flaps pulled down, so that I could see nothing of their faces save the glistening of the eyes through the eye-slits.

"I had no first thought, unless it was that danger threatened. I lay quietly for a second and deliberated. Borg had borrowed my pistol, and I was actually unarmed. My rifle was by the door. I decided to make a rush for it. But no sooner had I struck the floor than one of the men turned on me, at the same time firing his revolver. That was the first shot, and the one La Flitche did not hear. It was in the struggle afterwards that the door was burst open, which enabled him to hear the last three.

"Well; I was so close to the man, and my leap out of the bunk was so unexpected, that he missed me. The next moment we grappled and rolled on the floor. Of course, Borg was aroused, and the second man turned his attention to him and Bella. It was this second man who did the killing, for my man, naturally, had his hands full. You heard the testimony. From the way the cabin was wrecked, you can picture the struggle. We rolled and tossed about and fought till stools, table, shelves—everything was smashed.

"Oh, Frona, it was terrible! Borg fighting for life, Bella helping him, though wounded and groaning, and I unable to aid. But finally, in a very short while, I began to conquer the man with whom I was struggling. I had got him down on his back, pinioned his arms with my knees, and was slowly throttling him, when the other man finished his work and turned on me also. What could I do? Two to one, and winded! So I was thrown into the corner, and they made their escape. I confess that I must have been badly rattled by that time, for as soon as I caught my breath I took out after them, and without a weapon. Then I collided with La Flitche and John, and—and you know the rest. Only," he knit his brows in puzzlement, "only, I cannot understand why Bella should accuse me."

He looked at her appealingly, and, though she pressed his hand sympathetically, she remained silent, weighing pro and con what she had heard.

She shook her head slowly. "It's a bad case, and the thing is to convince them—"

"But, my God, Frona, I am innocent! I have not been a saint, perhaps, but my hands are clean from blood."

"But remember, Gregory," she said, gently, "I am not to judge you. Unhappily, it rests with the men of this miners' meeting, and the problem is: how are they to be convinced of your innocence? The two main points are against you,—Bella's dying words and the blood on your sleeve."

"The place was areek with blood," St. Vincent cried passionately, springing to his feet. "I tell you it was areek! How could I avoid floundering in it, fighting as I was for life? Can you not take my word—"

"There, there, Gregory. Sit down. You are truly beside yourself. If your case rested with me, you know you would go free and clean. But these men,—you know what mob rule is,—how are we to persuade them to let you go? Don't you see? You have no witnesses. A dying woman's words are more sacred than a living man's. Can you show cause for the woman to die with a lie on her lips? Had she any reason to hate you? Had you done her or her husband an injury?"

He shook his head.

"Certainly, to us the thing is inexplicable; but the miners need no explanation. To them it is obvious. It rests with us to disprove the obvious. Can we do it?"

The correspondent sank down despondently, with a collapsing of the chest and a drooping forward of the shoulders. "Then am I indeed lost."

"No, it's not so bad as that. You shall not be hanged. Trust me for that."

"But what can you do?" he asked, despairingly. "They have usurped the law, have made themselves the law."

"In the first place, the river has broken. That means everything. The Governor and the territorial judges may be expected in at any moment with a detachment of police at their backs. And they're certain to stop here. And, furthermore, we may be able to do something ourselves. The river is open, and if it comes to the worst, escape would be another way out; and escape is the last thing they would dream of."

"No, no; impossible. What are you and I against the many?"

"But there's my father and Baron Courbertin. Four determined people, acting together, may perform miracles, Gregory, dear. Trust me, it shall come out well."

She kissed him and ran her hand through his hair, but the worried look did not depart.

Jacob Welse crossed over the back-channel long before dark, and with him came Del, the baron, and Corliss. While Frona retired to change her clothes in one of the smaller cabins, which the masculine owners readily turned over to her, her father saw to the welfare of the mail-carrier. The despatches were of serious import, so serious that long after Jacob Welse had read and re-read them his face was dark and clouded; but he put the anxiety from him when he returned to Frona. St. Vincent, who was confined in an adjoining cabin, was permitted to see them.

"It looks bad," Jacob Welse said, on parting for the night. "But rest assured, St. Vincent, bad or not, you'll not be stretched up so long as I've a hand to play in the rumpus. I am certain you did not kill Borg, and there's my fist on it."

"A long day," Corliss remarked, as he walked back with Frona to her cabin.

"And a longer to-morrow," she answered, wearily. "And I'm so sleepy."

"You're a brave little woman, and I'm proud of you." It was ten o'clock, and he looked out through the dim twilight to the ghostly ice drifting steadily by. "And in this trouble," he went on, "depend upon me in any way."

"In any way?" she queried, with a catch in her voice.

"If I were a hero of the melodrama I'd say; 'To the death!' but as I'm not; I'll just repeat, in any way."

"You are good to me, Vance. I can never repay—"

"Tut! tut! I do not put myself on sale. Love is service, I believe."

She looked at him for a long time, but while her face betrayed soft wonder, at heart she was troubled, she knew not why, and the events of the day, and of all the days since she had known him, came fluttering through her mind.

"Do you believe in a white friendship?" she asked at last. "For I do hope that such a bond may hold us always. A bright, white friendship, a comradeship, as it were?" And as she asked, she was aware that the phrase did not quite express what she felt and would desire. And when he shook his head, she experienced a glad little inexplicable thrill.

"A comradeship?" he questioned. "When you know I love you?"

"Yes," she affirmed in a low voice.

"I am afraid, after all, that your knowledge of man is very limited. Believe me, we are not made of such clay. A comradeship? A coming in out of the cold to sit by your fire? Good. But a coming in when another man sits with you by your fire? No. Comradeship would demand that I delight in your delights, and yet, do you think for a moment that I could see you with another man's child in your arms, a child which might have been mine; with that other man looking out at me through the child's eyes, laughing at me through its mouth? I say, do you think I could delight in your delights? No, no; love cannot shackle itself with white friendships."

She put her hand on his arm.

"Do you think I am wrong?" he asked, bewildered by the strange look in her face.

She was sobbing quietly.

"You are tired and overwrought. So there, good-night. You must get to bed."

"No, don't go, not yet." And she arrested him. "No, no; I am foolish. As you say, I am tired. But listen, Vance. There is much to be done. We must plan to-morrow's work. Come inside. Father and Baron

Courbertin are together, and if the worst comes, we four must do big things."

"Spectacular," Jacob Welse commented, when Frona had briefly outlined the course of action and assigned them their parts. "But its very unexpectedness ought to carry it through."

"A *coup d'etat*!" was the Baron's verdict. "Magnificent! Ah! I feel warm all over at the thought. 'Hands up!' I cry, thus, and very fierce.

"And if they do not hold up their hands?" he appealed to Jacob Welse.

"Then shoot. Never bluff when you're behind a gun, Courbertin. It's held by good authorities to be unhealthy."

"And you are to take charge of La Bijou, Vance," Frona said. "Father thinks there will be little ice to-morrow if it doesn't jam to-night. All you've to do is to have the canoe by the bank just before the door. Of course, you won't know what is happening until St. Vincent comes running. Then in with him, and away you go—Dawson! So I'll say good-night and good-by now, for I may not have the opportunity in the morning."

"And keep the left-hand channel till you're past the bend," Jacob Welse counselled him; "then take the cut-offs to the right and follow the swiftest water. Now off with you and into your blankets. It's seventy miles to Dawson, and you'll have to make it at one clip."

CHAPTER XXVIII

Jacob Welse was given due respect when he arose at the convening of the miners' meeting and denounced the proceedings. While such meetings had performed a legitimate function in the past, he contended, when there was no law in the land, that time was now beyond recall; for law was now established, and it was just law. The Queen's government had shown itself fit to cope with the situation, and for them to usurp its powers was to step backward into the night out of which they had come. Further, no lighter word than "criminal" could characterize such conduct. And yet further, he promised them, in set, sober terms, if anything serious were the outcome, to take an active part in the prosecution of every one of them. At the conclusion of his speech he made a motion to hold the prisoner for the territorial court and to adjourn, but was voted down without discussion.

"Don't you see," St. Vincent said to Frona, "there is no hope?"

"But there is. Listen!" And she swiftly outlined the plot of the night before.

He followed her in a half-hearted way, too crushed to partake of her enthusiasm. "It's madness to attempt it," he objected, when she had done.

"And it looks very much like hanging not to attempt it," she answered a little spiritedly. "Surely you will make a fight?"

"Surely," he replied, hollowly.

The first witnesses were two Swedes, who told of the wash-tub incident, when Borg had given way to one of his fits of anger. Trivial as the incident was, in the light of subsequent events it at once became serious. It opened the way for the imagination into a vast familiar field. It was not so much what was said as what was left unsaid. Men born of women, the rudest of them, knew life well enough to be aware of its significance,—a vulgar common happening, capable of but one interpretation. Heads were wagged knowingly in the course of the testimony, and whispered comments went the rounds.

Half a dozen witnesses followed in rapid succession, all of whom had closely examined the scene of the crime and gone over the island carefully, and all of whom were agreed that there was not the slightest trace to be found of the two men mentioned by the prisoner in his preliminary statement.

To Frona's surprise, Del Bishop went upon the stand. She knew he disliked St. Vincent, but could not imagine any evidence he could possess which would bear upon the case.

Being sworn, and age and nationality ascertained, Bill Brown asked him his business.

"Pocket-miner," he challenged back, sweeping the assemblage with an aggressive glance.

Now, it happens that a very small class of men follow pocketing, and that a very large class of men, miners, too, disbelieve utterly in any such method or obtaining gold.

"Pocket-miner!" sneered a red-shirted, patriarchal-looking man, a man who had washed his first pan in the Californian diggings in the early fifties.

"Yep," Del affirmed.

"Now, look here, young feller," his interlocutor continued, "d'ye mean to tell me you ever struck it in such-fangled way?"

"Yep."

"Don't believe it," with a contemptuous shrug.

Del swallowed fast and raised his head with a jerk. "Mr. Chairman, I rise to make a statement. I won't interfere with the dignity of the court, but I just wish to simply and distinctly state that after the meeting's over I'm going to punch the head of every man that gets gay. Understand?"

"You're out of order," the chairman replied, rapping the table with the caulking-mallet.

"And your head, too," Del cried, turning upon him. "Damn poor order you preserve. Pocketing's got nothing to do with this here trial, and why don't you shut such fool questions out? I'll take care of you afterwards, you potwolloper!"

"You will, will you?" The chairman grew red in the face, dropped the mallet, and sprang to his feet.

Del stepped forward to meet him, but Bill Brown sprang in between and held them apart.

"Order, gentlemen, order," he begged. "This is no time for unseemly exhibitions. And remember there are ladies present."

The two men grunted and subsided, and Bill Brown asked, "Mr. Bishop, we understand that you are well acquainted with the prisoner. Will you please tell the court what you know of his general character?"

Del broadened into a smile. "Well, in the first place, he's an extremely quarrelsome disposition—"

"Hold! I won't have it!" The prisoner was on his feet, trembling with anger. "You shall not swear my life away in such fashion! To bring a madman, whom I have only met once in my life, to testify as to my character!"

The pocket-miner turned to him. "So you don't know me, eh, Gregory St. Vincent?"

"No," St. Vincent replied, coldly, "I do not know you, my man."

"Don't you man me!" Del shouted, hotly.

But St. Vincent ignored him, turning to the crowd.

"I never saw the fellow but once before, and then for a few brief moments in Dawson."

"You'll remember before I'm done," Del sneered; "so hold your hush and let me say my little say. I come into the country with him way back in '84."

St. Vincent regarded him with sudden interest.

"Yep, Mr. Gregory St. Vincent. I see you begin to recollect. I sported whiskers and my name was Brown, Joe Brown, in them days."

He grinned vindictively, and the correspondent seemed to lose all interest.

"Is it true, Gregory?" Frona whispered.

"I begin to recognize," he muttered, slowly. "I don't know . . . no, folly! The man must have died."

"You say in '84, Mr. Bishop?" Bill Brown prompted.

"Yep, in '84. He was a newspaper-man, bound round the world by way of

Alaska and Siberia. I'd run away from a whaler at Sitka,—that squares

it with Brown,—and I engaged with him for forty a month and found.

Well, he quarrelled with me—"

A snicker, beginning from nowhere in particular, but passing on from man to man and swelling in volume, greeted this statement. Even Frona and Del himself were forced to smile, and the only sober face was the prisoner's.

"But he quarrelled with Old Andy at Dyea, and with Chief George of the Chilcoots, and the Factor at Pelly, and so on down the line. He got us into no end of trouble, and 'specially woman-trouble. He was always monkeying around—"

"Mr. Chairman, I object." Frona stood up, her face quite calm and blood under control. "There is no necessity for bringing in the amours of Mr. St. Vincent. They have no bearing whatsoever upon the case; and, further, none of the men of this meeting are clean enough to be prompted by the right motive in conducting such an inquiry. So I demand that the prosecution at least confine itself to relevant testimony."

Bill Brown came up smugly complacent and smiling. "Mr. Chairman, we willingly accede to the request made by the defence. Whatever we have brought out has been relevant and material. Whatever we intend to bring out shall be relevant and material. Mr. Bishop is our star witness, and his testimony is to the point. It must be taken into consideration that we nave no direct evidence as to the murder of John Borg. We can bring no eye-witnesses into court. Whatever we have is circumstantial. It is incumbent upon us to show cause. To show cause it is necessary to go into the character of the accused. This we intend to do. We intend to show his adulterous and lustful nature, which has culminated in a dastardly deed and jeopardized his neck. We intend to show that the truth is not in him; that he is a liar beyond price; that no word he may speak upon the stand need be accepted by a jury of his peers. We intend to show all this, and to weave it together, thread by thread, till we have a rope long enough and strong enough to hang him with before the day is done. So I respectfully submit, Mr. Chairman, that the witness be allowed to proceed."

The chairman decided against Frona, and her appeal to the meeting was voted down. Bill Brown nodded to Del to resume.

"As I was saying, he got us into no end of trouble. Now, I've been mixed up with water all my life,—never can get away from it, it seems,—and the more I'm mixed the less I know about it. St. Vincent knew this, too, and him a clever hand at the paddle; yet he left me to run the Box Canyon alone while he walked around. Result: I was turned over, lost half the outfit and all the tobacco, and then he put the blame on me besides. Right after that he got tangled up with the Lake Le Barge Sticks, and both of us came near croaking."

"And why was that?" Bill Brown interjected.

"All along of a pretty squaw that looked too kindly at him. After we got clear, I lectured him on women in general and squaws in particular, and he promised to behave. Then we had a hot time with the Little Salmons. He was cuter this time, and I didn't know for keeps, but I guessed. He said it was the medicine man who got horstile; but nothing'll stir up a medicine man quicker'n women, and the facts pointed that way. When I talked it over with him in a fatherly way he got wrathy, and I had to take him out on the bank and give him a threshing. Then he got sulky, and didn't brighten up till we ran into the mouth of the Reindeer River, where a camp of Siwashes were fishing salmon. But he had it in for me all the time, only I didn't know it,—was ready any time to give me the double cross.

"Now, there's no denying he's got a taking way with women. All he has to do is to whistle 'em up like dogs. Most remarkable faculty, that. There was the wickedest, prettiest squaw among the Reindeers. Never saw her beat, excepting Bella. Well, I guess he whistled her up, for he delayed in the camp longer than was necessary. Being partial to women—"

"That will do, Mr. Bishop," interrupted the chairman, who, from profitless watching of Frona's immobile face, had turned to her hand, the nervous twitching and clinching of which revealed what her face had hidden. "That will do, Mr. Bishop. I think we have had enough of squaws."

"Pray do not temper the testimony," Frona chirruped, sweetly. "It seems very important."

"Do you know what I am going to say next?" Del demanded hotly of the chairman. "You don't, eh? Then shut up. I'm running this particular sideshow."

Bill Brown sprang in to avert hostilities, but the chairman restrained himself, and Bishop went on.

"I'd been done with the whole shooting-match, squaws and all, if you hadn't broke me off. Well, as I said, he had it in for me, and the first thing I didn't know, he'd hit me on the head with a rifle-stock, bundled the squaw into the canoe, and pulled out. You all know what the Yukon country was in '84. And there I was, without an outfit, left alone, a thousand miles from anywhere. I got out all right, though there's no need of telling how, and so did he. You've all heard of his adventures in Siberia. Well," with an impressive pause, "I happen to know a thing or two myself."

He shoved a hand into the big pocket of his mackinaw jacket and pulled out a dingy leather-bound volume of venerable appearance.

"I got this from Pete Whipple's old woman,—Whipple of Eldorado. It concerns her grand-uncle or great-grand-uncle, I don't know which; and if there's anybody here can read Russian, why, it'll go into the details of that Siberian trip. But as there's no one here that can—"

"Courbertin! He can read it!" some one called in the crowd.

A way was made for the Frenchman forthwith, and he was pushed and shoved, protestingly, to the front.

"Savve the lingo?" Del demanded.

"Yes; but so poorly, so miserable," Courbertin demurred. "It is a long time. I forget."

"Go ahead. We won't criticise."

"No, but—"

"Go ahead!" the chairman commanded.

Del thrust the book into his hands, opened at the yellow title-page. "I've been itching to get my paws on some buck like you for months and months," he assured him, gleefully. "And now I've got you, you can't shake me, Charley. So fire away."

Courbertin began hesitatingly: "*The Journal of Father Yakontsk, Comprising an Account in Brief of his Life in the Benedictine Monastery at Obidorsky, and in Full of his Marvellous Adventures in East Siberia among the Deer Men.*"

The baron looked up for instructions.

"Tell us when it was printed," Del ordered him.

"In Warsaw, 1807."

The pocket-miner turned triumphantly to the room. "Did you hear that?"

Just keep track of it. 1807, remember!"

The baron took up the opening paragraph. "*'It was because of Tamerlane,'*" he commenced, unconsciously putting his translation into a construction with which he was already familiar.

At his first words Frona turned white, and she remained white throughout the reading. Once she stole a glance at her father, and was glad that he was looking straight before him, for she did not feel able to meet his gaze just them. On the other hand, though she knew St. Vincent was eying her narrowly, she took no notice of him, and all he could see was a white face devoid of expression.

"'*When Tamerlane swept with fire and sword over Eastern Asia*,'" Courbertin read slowly, "*states were disrupted, cities overthrown, and tribes scattered like—like star-dust. A vast people was hurled broadcast over the land. Fleeing before the conquerors,'—no, no,—'before the mad lust of the conquerors, these refugees swung far into Siberia, circling, circling to the north and east and fringing the rim of the polar basin with a spray of Mongol tribes.*'"

"Skip a few pages," Bill Brown advised, "and read here and there. We haven't got all night."

Courbertin complied. "'*The coast people are Eskimo stock, merry of nature and not offensive. They call themselves the Oukilion, or the Sea Men. From them I bought dogs and food. But they are subject to the Chow Chuen, who live in the interior and are known as the Deer Men. The Chow Chuen are a fierce and savage race. When I left the coast they fell upon me, took from me my goods, and made me a slave.*'" He ran over a few pages. "*'I worked my way to a seat among the head men, but I was no nearer my freedom. My wisdom was of too great value to them for me to depart... Old Pi-Une was a great chief, and it was decreed that I should marry his daughter Ilswunga. Ilswunga was a filthy creature. She would not bathe, and her ways were not good... I did marry Ilswunga, but she was a wife to me only in name. Then did she complain to her father, the old Pi-Une, and he was very wroth. And dissension was sown among the tribes; but in the end I became mightier than ever, what of my cunning and resource; and Ilswunga made no more complaint, for I taught her games with cards which she might play by herself, and other things.*'"

"Is that enough?" Courbertin asked.

"Yes, that will do," Bill Brown answered. "But one moment. Please state again the date of publication."

"1807, in Warsaw."

"Hold on, baron," Del Bishop spoke up. "Now that you're on the stand, I've got a question or so to slap into you." He turned to the court-room. "Gentlemen, you've all heard somewhat of the prisoner's experiences in Siberia. You've caught on to the remarkable sameness between them and those published by Father Yakontsk nearly a hundred years ago. And you have concluded that there's been some wholesale cribbing somewhere. I propose to show you that it's more than cribbing. The prisoner gave me the shake on the Reindeer River in '88. Fall of '88 he was at St. Michael's on his way to Siberia. '89 and '90 he was, by his talk, cutting up antics in Siberia. '91 he come back to the world, working the conquering-hero graft in 'Frisco. Now let's see if the Frenchman can make us wise."

"You were in Japan?" he asked.

Courbertin, who had followed the dates, made a quick calculation, and could but illy conceal his surprise. He looked appealingly to Frona, but she did not help him. "Yes," he said, finally.

"And you met the prisoner there?"

"Yes."

"What year was it?"

There was a general craning forward to catch the answer.

"1889," and it came unwillingly.

"Now, how can that be, baron?" Del asked in a wheedling tone. "The prisoner was in Siberia at that time."

Courbertin shrugged his shoulders that it was no concern of his, and came off the stand. An impromptu recess was taken by the court-room for several minutes, wherein there was much whispering and shaking of heads.

"It is all a lie." St. Vincent leaned close to Frona's ear, but she did not hear.

"Appearances are against me, but I can explain it all."

But she did not move a muscle, and he was called to the stand by the chairman. She turned to her father, and the tears rushed up into her eyes when he rested his hand on hers.

"Do you care to pull out?" he asked after a momentary hesitation.

She shook her head, and St. Vincent began to speak. It was the same story he had told her, though told now a little more fully, and in nowise did it conflict with the evidence of La Flitche and John. He acknowledged the wash-tub incident, caused, he explained, by an act of simple courtesy on his part and by John Borg's unreasoning anger. He acknowledged that Bella had been killed by his own pistol, but stated that the pistol had been borrowed by Borg several days previously and not returned. Concerning Bella's accusation he could say nothing. He could not see why she should die with a lie on her lips. He had never in the slightest way incurred her displeasure, so even revenge could not be advanced. It was inexplicable. As for the testimony of Bishop, he did not care to discuss it. It was a tissue of falsehood cunningly interwoven with truth. It was true the man had gone into Alaska with him in 1888, but his version of the things which happened there was maliciously untrue. Regarding the baron, there was a slight mistake in the dates, that was all.

In questioning him. Bill Brown brought out one little surprise. From the prisoner's story, he had made a hard fight against the two mysterious men. "If," Brown asked, "such were the case, how can you explain away the fact that you came out of the struggle unmarked? On examination of the body of John Borg, many bruises and contusions were noticeable. How is it, if you put up such a stiff fight, that you escaped being battered?"

St. Vincent did not know, though he confessed to feeling stiff and sore all over. And it did not matter, anyway. He had killed neither Borg nor his wife, that much he did know.

Frona prefaced her argument to the meeting with a pithy discourse on the sacredness of human life, the weaknesses and dangers of circumstantial evidence, and the rights of the accused wherever doubt arose. Then she plunged into the evidence, stripping off the superfluous and striving to confine herself to facts. In the first place, she denied that a motive for the deed had been shown. As it was, the introduction of such evidence was an insult to their intelligence, and she had sufficient faith in their manhood and perspicacity to know that such puerility would not sway them in the verdict they were to give.

And, on the other hand, in dealing with the particular points at issue, she denied that any intimacy had been shown to have existed between Bella and St. Vincent; and she denied, further, that it had been shown that any intimacy had been attempted on the part of St. Vincent. Viewed honestly, the wash-tub incident—the only evidence brought forward—was a laughable little affair, portraying how the simple courtesy of a gentleman might be misunderstood by a mad boor of a husband. She left it to their common sense; they were not fools.

They had striven to prove the prisoner bad-tempered. She did not need to prove anything of the sort concerning John Borg. They all knew his terrible fits of anger; they all knew that his temper was proverbial in the community; that it had prevented him having friends and had made him many enemies. Was it not very probable, therefore, that the masked men were two such enemies? As to what particular motive actuated these two men, she could not say; but it rested with them, the judges, to know whether in all Alaska there were or were not two men whom John Borg could have given cause sufficient for them to take his life.

Witness had testified that no traces had been found of these two men; but the witness had not testified that no traces had been found of St. Vincent, Pierre La Flitche, or John the Swede. And there was no need for them so to testify. Everybody knew that no foot-marks were left when St. Vincent ran up the trail, and when he came back with La Flitche and the other man. Everybody knew the condition of the trail, that it was a hard-packed groove in the ground, on which a soft moccasin could leave no impression; and that had the ice not gone down the river, no traces would have been left by the murderers in passing from and to the mainland.

At this juncture La Flitche nodded his head in approbation, and she went on.

> Capital had been made out of the blood on St. Vincent's hands. If they chose to examine the moccasins at that moment on the feet of Mr. La Flitche, they would also find blood. That did not argue that Mr. La Flitche had been a party to the shedding of the blood.

Mr. Brown had drawn attention to the fact that the prisoner had not been bruised or marked in the savage encounter which had taken place. She thanked him for having done so. John Borg's body showed that it had been roughly used. He was a larger, stronger, heavier man than St. Vincent. If, as charged, St. Vincent had committed the murder, and necessarily, therefore, engaged in a struggle severe enough to bruise John Borg, how was it that he had come out unharmed? That was a point worthy of consideration.

Another one was, why did he run down the trail? It was inconceivable, if he had committed the murder, that he should, without dressing or preparation for escape, run towards the other cabins. It was, however, easily conceivable that he should take up the pursuit of the real murderers, and in the darkness—exhausted, breathless, and certainly somewhat excited—run blindly down the trail.

Her summing up was a strong piece of synthesis; and when she had done, the meeting applauded her roundly. But she was angry and hurt, for she knew the demonstration was for her sex rather than for her cause and the work she had done.

Bill Brown, somewhat of a shyster, and his ear ever cocked to the crowd, was not above taking advantage when opportunity offered, and when it did not offer, to dogmatize artfully. In this his native humor was a strong factor, and when he had finished with the mysterious masked men they were as exploded sun-myths,—which phrase he promptly applied to them.

They could not have got off the island. The condition of the ice for the three or four hours preceding the break-up would not have permitted it. The prisoner had implicated none of the residents of the island, while every one of them, with the exception of the prisoner, had been accounted for elsewhere. Possibly the prisoner was excited when he ran down the trail into the arms of La Flitche and John the Swede. One should have thought, however, that he had grown used to such things in Siberia. But that was immaterial; the facts were that he was undoubtedly in an abnormal state of excitement, that he was hysterically excited, and that a murderer under such circumstances would take little account of where he ran. Such things had happened before. Many a man had butted into his own retribution.

In the matter of the relations of Borg, Bella, and St. Vincent, he made a strong appeal to the instinctive prejudices of his listeners, and for the time being abandoned matter-of-fact reasoning for all-potent sentimental platitudes. He granted that circumstantial evidence never proved anything absolutely. It was not necessary it should. Beyond the shadow of a reasonable doubt was all that was required. That this had been done, he went on to review the testimony.

"And, finally," he said, "you can't get around Bella's last words. We know nothing of our own direct knowledge. We've been feeling around in the dark, clutching at little things, and trying to figure it all out. But, gentlemen," he paused to search the faces of his listeners, "Bella knew the truth. Hers is no circumstantial evidence. With quick, anguished breath, and life-blood ebbing from her, and eyeballs glazing, she spoke the truth. With dark night coming on, and the death-rattle in her throat, she raised herself weakly and pointed a shaking finger at the accused, thus, and she said, 'Him, him, him. St. Vincha, him do it.'"

With Bill Brown's finger still boring into him, St. Vincent struggled to his feet. His face looked old and gray, and he looked about him speechlessly. "Funk! Funk!" was whispered back and forth, and not so softly but what he heard. He moistened his lips repeatedly, and his tongue fought for articulation. "It is as I have said," he succeeded, finally. "I did not do it. Before God, I did not do it!" He stared fixedly at John the Swede, waiting the while on his laggard thought. "I . . . I did not do it . . . I did not . . . I . . . I did not."

He seemed to have become lost in some supreme meditation wherein John the Swede figured largely, and as Frona caught him by the hand and pulled him gently down, some man cried out, "Secret ballot!"

But Bill Brown was on his feet at once. "No! I say no! An open ballot! We are men, and as men are not afraid to put ourselves on record."

A chorus of approval greeted him, and the open ballot began. Man after man, called upon by name, spoke the one word, "Guilty."

Baron Courbertin came forward and whispered to Frona. She nodded her head and smiled, and he edged his way back, taking up a position by the door. He voted "Not guilty" when his turn came, as did Frona and Jacob Welse. Pierre La Flitche wavered a moment, looking keenly at Frona and St. Vincent, then spoke up, clear and flute-like, "Guilty."

As the chairman arose, Jacob Welse casually walked over to the opposite side of the table and stood with his back to the stove. Courbertin, who had missed nothing, pulled a pickle-keg out from the wall and stepped upon it.

The chairman cleared his throat and rapped for order. "Gentlemen," he announced, "the prisoner—"

"Hands up!" Jacob Welse commanded peremptorily, and a fraction of a second after him came the shrill "Hands up, gentlemen!" of Courbertin.

Front and rear they commanded the crowd with their revolvers. Every hand was in the air, the chairman's having gone up still grasping the mallet. There was no disturbance. Each stood or sat in the same posture as when the command went forth. Their eyes, playing here and there among the central figures, always returned to Jacob Welse.

St. Vincent sat as one dumfounded. Frona thrust a revolver into his hand, but his limp fingers refused to close on it.

"Come, Gregory," she entreated. "Quick! Corliss is waiting with the canoe. Come!"

She shook him, and he managed to grip the weapon. Then she pulled and tugged, as when awakening a heavy sleeper, till he was on his feet. But his face was livid, his eyes like a somnambulist's, and he was afflicted as with a palsy. Still holding him, she took a step backward for him to come on. He ventured it with a shaking knee. There was no sound save the heavy breathing of many men. A man coughed slightly and cleared his throat. It was disquieting, and all eyes centred upon him rebukingly. The man became embarrassed, and shifted his weight uneasily to the other leg. Then the heavy breathing settled down again.

St. Vincent took another step, but his fingers relaxed and the revolver fell with a loud noise to the floor. He made no effort to recover it. Frona stooped hurriedly, but Pierre La Flitche had set his foot upon it. She looked up and saw his hands above his head and his eyes fixed absently on Jacob Welse. She pushed at his leg, and the muscles were tense and hard, giving the lie to the indifference on his face. St. Vincent looked down helplessly, as though he could not understand.

But this delay drew the attention of Jacob Welse, and, as he tried to make out the cause, the chairman found his chance. Without crooking, his right arm swept out and down, the heavy caulking-mallet leaping from his hand. It spanned the short distance and smote Jacob Welse below the ear. His revolver went off as he fell, and John the Swede grunted and clapped a hand to his thigh.

Simultaneous with this the baron was overcome. Del Bishop, with hands still above his head and eyes fixed innocently before him, had simply kicked the pickle-keg out from under the Frenchman and brought him to the floor. His bullet, however, sped harmlessly through the roof. La Flitche seized Frona in his arms. St. Vincent, suddenly awakening, sprang for the door, but was tripped up by the *breed*'s ready foot.

The chairman pounded the table with his fist and concluded his broken sentence, "Gentlemen, the prisoner is found guilty as charged."

CHAPTER XXIX

Frona had gone at once to her father's side, but he was already recovering. Courbertin was brought forward with a scratched face, sprained wrist, and an insubordinate tongue. To prevent discussion and to save time, Bill Brown claimed the floor.

"Mr. Chairman, while we condemn the attempt on the part of Jacob Welse, Frona Welse, and Baron Courbertin to rescue the prisoner and thwart justice, we cannot, under the circumstances, but sympathize with them. There is no need that I should go further into this matter. You all know, and doubtless, under a like situation, would have done the same. And so, in order that we may expeditiously finish the business, I make a motion to disarm the three prisoners and let them go."

The motion was carried, and the two men searched for weapons. Frona was saved this by giving her word that she was no longer armed. The meeting then resolved itself into a hanging committee, and began to file out of the cabin.

"Sorry I had to do it," the chairman said, half-apologetically, half-defiantly.

Jacob Welse smiled. "You took your chance," he answered, "and I can't blame you. I only wish I'd got you, though."

Excited voices arose from across the cabin. "Here, you! Leggo!" "Step on his fingers, Tim!" "Break that grip!" "Ouch! Ow!" "Pry his mouth open!"

Frona saw a knot of struggling men about St. Vincent, and ran over. He had thrown himself down on the floor and, tooth and nail, was fighting like a madman. Tim Dugan, a stalwart Celt, had come to close quarters with him, and St. Vincent's teeth were sunk in the man's arm.

"Smash 'm, Tim! Smash 'm!"

"How can I, ye fule? Get a pry on his mouth, will ye?"

"One moment, please." The men made way for her, drawing back and leaving St. Vincent and Tim.

Frona knelt down by him. "Leave go, Gregory. Do leave go."

He looked up at her, and his eyes did not seem human. He breathed stertorously, and in his throat were the queer little gasping noises of one overwrought.

"It is I, Gregory." She brushed her hand soothingly across his brow.

"Don't you understand? It is I, Frona. Do leave go."

His whole body slowly relaxed, and a peaceful expression grew upon his face. His jaw dropped, and the man's arm was withdrawn.

"Now listen, Gregory. Though you are to die—"

"But I cannot! I cannot!" he groaned. "You said that I could trust to you, that all would come well."

She thought of the chance which had been given, but said nothing.

"Oh, Frona! Frona!" He sobbed and buried his face in her lap.

"At least you can be a man. It is all that remains."

"Come on!" Tim Dugan commanded. "Sorry to bother ye, miss, but we've got to fetch 'm along. Drag 'm out, you fellys! Catch 'm by the legs, Blackey, and you, too, Johnson."

St. Vincent's body stiffened at the words, the rational gleam went out of his eyes, and his fingers closed spasmodically on Frona's. She looked entreaty at the men, and they hesitated.

"Give me a minute with him," she begged, "just a minute."

"He ain't worth it," Dugan sneered, after they had drawn apart. "Look at 'm."

"It's a damned shame," corroborated Blackey, squinting sidewise at Frona whispering in St. Vincent's ear, the while her hand wandered caressingly through his hair.

What she said they did not hear, but she got him on his feet and led him forward. He walked as a dead man might walk, and when he entered the open air gazed forth wonderingly upon the muddy sweep of the Yukon. The crowd had formed by the bank, about a pine tree. A boy, engaged in running a rope over one of the branches, finished his task and slid down the trunk to the ground. He looked quickly at the palms of his hands and blew upon them, and a laugh went up. A couple of wolf-dogs, on the outskirts, bristled up to each other and bared their fangs. Men encouraged them. They closed in and rolled over, but were kicked aside to make room for St. Vincent.

Corliss came up the bank to Frona. "What's up?" he whispered. "Is it off?"

She tried to speak, but swallowed and nodded her head.

"This way, Gregory." She touched his arm and guided him to the box beneath the rope.

Corliss, keeping step with them, looked over the crowd speculatively and felt into his jacket-pocket. "Can I do anything?" he asked, gnawing his under lip impatiently. "Whatever you say goes, Frona. I can stand them off."

She looked at him, aware of pleasure in the sight. She knew he would dare it, but she knew also that it would be unfair. St. Vincent had had his chance, and it was not right that further sacrifice should be made. "No, Vance. It is too late. Nothing can be done."

"At least let me try," he persisted.

"No; it is not our fault that our plan failed, and . . . and . . ." Her eyes filled. "Please do not ask it of me."

"Then let me take you away. You cannot remain here."

"I must," she answered, simply, and turned to St. Vincent, who seemed dreaming.

Blackey was tying the hangman's knot in the rope's end, preparatory to slipping the noose over St. Vincent's head.

"Kiss me, Gregory," she said, her hand on his arm.

He started at the touch, and saw all eager eyes centred upon him, and the yellow noose, just shaped, in the hands of the hangman. He threw up his arms, as though to ward it off, and cried loudly, "No! no! Let me confess! Let me tell the truth, then you'll believe me!"

Bill Brown and the chairman shoved Blackey back, and the crowd gathered in. Cries and protestations rose from its midst. "No, you don't," a boy's shrill voice made itself heard. "I'm not going to go. I climbed the tree and made the rope fast, and I've got a right to stay." "You're only a kid," replied a man's voice, "and it ain't good for you." "I don't care, and I'm not a kid. I'm—I'm used to such things. And, anyway, I climbed the tree. Look at my hands." "Of course he can stay," other voices took up the trouble. "Leave him alone, Curley." "You ain't the whole thing." A laugh greeted this, and things quieted down.

"Silence!" the chairman called, and then to St. Vincent, "Go ahead, you, and don't take all day about it."

"Give us a chance to hear!" the crowd broke out again. "Put 'm on the box! Put 'm on the box!"

St. Vincent was helped up, and began with eager volubility.

"I didn't do it, but I saw it done. There weren't two men—only one.

He did it, and Bella helped him."

A wave of laughter drowned him out.

"Not so fast," Bill Brown cautioned him. "Kindly explain how Bella helped this man kill herself. Begin at the beginning."

"That night, before he turned in, Borg set his burglar alarm—"

"Burglar alarm?"

"That's what I called it,—a tin bread-pan attached to the latch so the door couldn't open without tumbling it down. He set it every night, as though he were afraid of what might happen,—the very thing which did happen, for that matter. On the night of the murder I awoke with the feeling that some one was moving around. The slush-lamp was burning low, and I saw Bella at the door. Borg was snoring; I could hear him plainly. Bella was taking down the bread-pan, and she exercised great care about it. Then she opened the door, and an Indian came in softly. He had no mask, and I should know him if ever I see him again, for a scar ran along the forehead and down over one eye."

"I suppose you sprang out of bed and gave the alarm?"

"No, I didn't," St. Vincent answered, with a defiant toss of the head, as though he might as well get the worst over with. "I just lay there and waited."

"What did you think?"

"That Bella was in collusion with the Indian, and that Borg was to be murdered. It came to me at once."

"And you did nothing?"

"Nothing." His voice sank, and his eyes dropped to Frona, leaning against the box beneath him and steadying it. She did not seem to be affected. "Bella came over to me, but I closed my eyes and breathed regularly. She held the slush-lamp to me, but I played sleep naturally enough to fool her. Then I heard a snort of sudden awakening and alarm, and a cry, and I looked out. The Indian was hacking at Borg with a knife, and Borg was warding off with his arms and trying to grapple him. When they did grapple, Bella crept up from behind and threw her arm in a strangle-hold about her husband's neck. She put her knee into the small of his back, and bent him backward and, with the Indian helping, threw him to the floor."

"And what did you do?"

"I watched."

"Had you a revolver?"

"Yes."

"The one you previously said John Borg had borrowed?"

"Yes; but I watched."

"Did John Borg call for help?"

"Yes."

"Can you give his words?"

"He called, 'St. Vincent! Oh, St. Vincent! Oh, my God! Oh, St. Vincent, help me!'" He shuddered at the recollection, and added, "It was terrible."

"I should say so," Brown grunted. "And you?"

"I watched," was the dogged reply, while a groan went up from the crowd. "Borg shook clear of them, however, and got on his legs. He hurled Bella across the cabin with a back-sweep of the arm and turned upon the Indian. Then they fought. The Indian had dropped the knife, and the sound of Borg's blows was sickening. I thought he would surely beat the Indian to death. That was when the furniture was smashed. They rolled and snarled and struggled like wild beasts. I wondered the Indian's chest did not cave in under some of Borg's blows. But Bella got the knife and stabbed her husband repeatedly about the body. The Indian had clinched with him, and his arms were not free; so he kicked out at her sideways. He must have broken her legs, for she cried out and fell down, and though she tried, she never stood up again. Then he went down, with the Indian under him, across the stove."

"Did he call any more for help?"

"He begged me to come to him."

"And?"

"I watched. He managed to get clear of the Indian and staggered over to me. He was streaming blood, and I could see he was very weak. 'Give me your gun,' he said; 'quick, give me it.' He felt around blindly. Then his mind seemed to clear a bit, and he reached across me to the holster hanging on the wall and took the pistol. The Indian came at him with the knife again, but he did not try to defend himself. Instead, he went on towards Bella, with the Indian still hanging to him and hacking at him. The Indian seemed to bother and irritate him, and he shoved him away. He knelt down and turned Bella's face up to the light; but his own face was covered with blood and he could not see. So he stopped long enough to brush the blood from his eyes. He appeared to look in order to make sure. Then he put the revolver to her breast and fired.

"The Indian went wild at this, and rushed at him with the knife, at the same time knocking the pistol out of his hand. It was then the shelf with the slush-lamp was knocked down. They continued to fight in the darkness, and there were more shots fired, though I do not know by whom. I crawled out of the bunk, but they struck against me in their struggles, and I fell over Bella. That's when the blood got on my hands. As I ran out the door, more shots were fired. Then I met La Flitche and John, and . . . and you know the rest. This is the truth I have told you, I swear it!"

He looked down at Frona. She was steadying the box, and her face was composed. He looked out over the crowd and saw unbelief. Many were laughing.

"Why did you not tell this story at first?" Bill Brown demanded.

"Because . . . because . . ."

"Well?"

"Because I might have helped."

There was more laughter at this, and Bill Brown turned away from him. "Gentlemen, you have heard this pipe dream. It is a wilder fairy story than his first. At the beginning of the trial we promised to show that the truth was not in him. That we succeeded, your verdict is ample testimony. But that he should likewise succeed, and more brilliantly, we did not expect. That he has, you cannot doubt. What do you think of him? Lie upon lie he has given us; he has been proven a chronic liar; are you to believe this last and fearfully impossible lie? Gentlemen, I can only ask that you reaffirm your judgment. And to those who may doubt his mendacity,—surely there are but few,—let me state, that if his story is true; if he broke salt with this man, John Borg, and lay in his blankets while murder was done; if he did hear, unmoved, the voice of the man calling to him for help; if he did lie there and watch that carnival of butchery without his manhood prompting him,—let me state, gentlemen, I say, let me state that he is none the less deserveful of hanging. We cannot make a mistake. What shall it be?"

"Death!" "String him up!" "Stretch 'm!" were the cries.

But the crowd suddenly turned its attention to the river, and even Blackey refrained from his official task. A large raft, worked by a sweep at either end, was slipping past the tail of Split-up Island, close to the shore. When it was at their feet, its nose was slewed into the bank, and while its free end swung into the stream to make the consequent circle, a snubbing-rope was flung ashore and several turns taken about the tree under which St. Vincent stood. A cargo of moose-meat, red and raw, cut into quarters, peeped from beneath a cool covering of spruce boughs. And because of this, the two men on the raft looked up to those on the bank with pride in their eyes.

"Tryin' to make Dawson with it," one of them explained, "and the sun's all-fired hot."

"Nope," said his comrade, in reply to a query, "don't care to stop and trade. It's worth a dollar and a half a pound down below, and we're hustlin' to get there. But we've got some pieces of a man we want to leave with you." He turned and pointed to a loose heap of blankets which slightly disclosed the form of a man beneath. "We gathered him in this mornin', 'bout thirty mile up the Stewart, I should judge."

"Stands in need of doctorin'," the other man spoke up, "and the meat's spoilin', and we ain't got time for nothin'." "Beggar don't have anythin' to say. Don't savve the burro." "Looks as he might have been mixin' things with a grizzly or somethin',—all battered and gouged. Injured internally, from the looks of it. Where'll you have him?"

Frona, standing by St. Vincent, saw the injured man borne over the crest of the bank and through the crowd. A bronzed hand drooped down and a bronzed face showed from out the blankets. The bearers halted near them while a decision could be reached as to where he should be carried. Frona felt a sudden fierce grip on her arm.

"Look! look!" St. Vincent was leaning forward and pointing wildly at the injured man. "Look! That scar!"

The Indian opened his eyes and a grin of recognition distorted his face.

"It is he! It is he!" St. Vincent, trembling with eagerness, turned upon the crowd. "I call you all to witness! That is the man who killed John Borg!"

No laughter greeted this, for there was a terrible earnestness in his manner. Bill Brown and the chairman tried to make the Indian talk, but could not. A miner from British Columbia was pressed into service, but his Chinook made no impression. Then La Flitche was called. The handsome *breed* bent over the man and talked in gutturals which only his mother's heredity made possible. It sounded all one, yet it was apparent that he was trying many tongues. But no response did he draw, and he paused disheartened. As though with sudden recollection, he made another attempt. At once a gleam of intelligence shot across the Indian's face, and his larynx vibrated to similar sounds.

"It is the Stick talk of the Upper White," La Flitche stopped long enough to explain.

Then, with knit brows and stumbling moments when he sought dim-remembered words, he plied the man with questions. To the rest it was like a pantomime,—the meaningless grunts and waving arms and facial expressions of puzzlement, surprise, and understanding. At times a passion wrote itself on the face of the Indian, and a sympathy on the face of La Flitche. Again, by look and gesture, St. Vincent was referred to, and once a sober, mirthless laugh shaped the mouths of them.

"So? It is good," La Flitche said, when the Indian's head dropped back. "This man make true talk. He come from White River, way up. He cannot understand. He surprised very much, so many white men. He never think so many white men in the world. He die soon. His name Gow.

"Long time ago, three year, this man John Borg go to this man Gow's country. He hunt, he bring plenty meat to the camp, wherefore White River Sticks like him. Gow have one squaw, Pisk-ku. Bime-by John Borg make preparation to go 'way. He go to Gow, and he say, 'Give me your squaw. We trade. For her I give you many things.' But Gow say no. Pisk-ku good squaw. No woman sew moccasin like she. She tan moose-skin the best, and make the softest leather. He like Pisk-ku. Then John Borg say he don't care; he want Pisk-ku. Then they have a *skookum* big fight, and Pisk-ku go 'way with John Borg. She no want to go 'way, but she go anyway. Borg call her 'Bella,' and give her plenty good things, but she like Gow all the time." La Flitche pointed to the scar which ran down the forehead and past the eye of the Indian. "John Borg he do that."

"Long time Gow pretty near die. Then he get well, but his head sick. He don't know nobody. Don't know his father, his mother, or anything. Just like a little baby. Just like that. Then one day, quick, click! something snap, and his head get well all at once. He know his father and mother, he remember Pisk-ku, he remember everything. His father say John Borg go down river. Then Gow go down river. Spring-time, ice very bad. He very much afraid, so many white men, and when he come to this place he travel by night. Nobody see him 'tall, but he see everybody. He like a cat, see in the dark. Somehow, he come straight to John Borg's cabin. He do not know how this was, except that the work he had to do was good work."

St. Vincent pressed Frona's hand, but she shook her fingers clear and withdrew a step.

"He see Pisk-ku feed the dogs, and he have talk with her. That night he come and she open the door. Then you know that which was done. St. Vincent do nothing, Borg kill Bella. Gow kill Borg. Borg kill Gow, for Gow die pretty quick. Borg have strong arm. Gow sick inside, all smashed up. Gow no care; Pisk-ku dead.

"After that he go 'cross ice to the land. I tell him all you people say it cannot be; no man can cross the ice at that time. He laugh, and say that it is, and what is, must be. Anyway, he have very hard time, but he get 'cross all right. He very sick inside. Bime-by he cannot walk; he crawl. Long time he come to Stewart River. Can go no more, so he lay down to die. Two white men find him and bring him to this place. He don't care. He die anyway."

La Flitche finished abruptly, but nobody spoke. Then he added, "I think Gow damn good man."

Frona came up to Jacob Welse. "Take me away, father," she said. "I am so tired."

CHAPTER XXX

Next morning, Jacob Welse, for all of the Company and his millions in mines, chopped up the day's supply of firewood, lighted a cigar, and went down the island in search of Baron Courbertin. Frona finished the breakfast dishes, hung out the robes to air, and fed the dogs. Then she took a worn Wordsworth from her clothes-bag, and, out by the bank, settled herself comfortably in a seat formed by two uprooted pines. But she did no more than open the book; for her eyes strayed out and over the Yukon to the eddy below the bluffs, and the bend above, and the tail of the spit which lay in the midst of the river. The rescue and the race were still fresh with her, though there were strange lapses, here and there, of which she remembered little. The struggle by the fissure was immeasurable; she knew not how long it lasted; and the race down Split-up to Roubeau Island was a thing of which her reason convinced her, but of which she recollected nothing.

The whim seized her, and she followed Corliss through the three days' events, but she tacitly avoided the figure of another man whom she would not name. Something terrible was connected therewith, she knew, which must be faced sooner or later; but she preferred to put that moment away from her. She was stiff and sore of mind as well as of body, and will and action were for the time being distasteful. It was more pleasant, even, to dwell on Tommy, on Tommy of the bitter tongue and craven heart; and she made a note that the wife and children in Toronto should not be forgotten when the Northland paid its dividends to the Welse.

The crackle of a foot on a dead willow-twig roused her, and her eyes met St. Vincent's.

"You have not congratulated me upon my escape," he began, breezily. "But you must have been dead-tired last night. I know I was. And you had that hard pull on the river besides."

He watched her furtively, trying to catch some cue as to her attitude and mood.

"You're a heroine, that's what you are, Frona," he began again, with exuberance. "And not only did you save the mail-man, but by the delay you wrought in the trial you saved me. If one more witness had gone on the stand that first day, I should have been duly hanged before Gow put in an appearance. Fine chap, Gow. Too bad he's going to die."

"I am glad that I could be of help," she replied, wondering the while what she could say.

"And of course I am to be congratulated—"

"Your trial is hardly a thing for congratulation," she spoke up quickly, looking him straight in the eyes for the moment. "I am glad that it came out as it did, but surely you cannot expect me to congratulate you."

"O-o-o," with long-drawn inflection. "So that's where it pinches." He smiled good-humoredly, and moved as though to sit down, but she made no room for him, and he remained standing. "I can certainly explain. If there have been women—"

Frona had been clinching her hand nervously, but at the word burst out in laughter.

"Women?" she queried. "Women?" she repeated. "Do not be ridiculous, Gregory."

"After the way you stood by me through the trial," he began, reproachfully, "I thought—"

"Oh, you do not understand," she said, hopelessly. "You do not understand. Look at me, Gregory, and see if I can make you understand. Your presence is painful to me. Your kisses hurt me. The memory of them still burns my cheek, and my lips feel unclean. And why? Because of women, which you may explain away? How little do you understand! But shall I tell you?"

Voices of men came to her from down the river-bank, and the splashing of water. She glanced quickly and saw Del Bishop guiding a poling-boat against the current, and Corliss on the bank, bending to the tow-rope.

"Shall I tell you why, Gregory St. Vincent?" she said again. "Tell you why your kisses have cheapened me? Because you broke the faith of food and blanket. Because you broke salt with a man, and then watched that man fight unequally for life without lifting your hand. Why, I had rather you had died in defending him; the memory of you would have been good. Yes, I had rather you had killed him yourself. At least, it would have shown there was blood in your body."

"So this is what you would call love?" he began, scornfully, his fretting, fuming devil beginning to rouse. "A fair-weather love, truly. But, Lord, how we men learn!"

"I had thought you were well lessoned," she retorted; "what of the other women?"

"But what do you intend to do?" he demanded, taking no notice. "I am not an easy man to cross. You cannot throw me over with impunity. I shall not stand for it, I warn you. You have dared do things in this country which would blacken you were they known. I have ears. I have not been asleep. You will find it no child's play to explain away things which you may declare most innocent."

She looked at him with a smile which carried pity in its cold mirth, and it goaded him.

"I am down, a thing to make a jest upon, a thing to pity, but I promise you that I can drag you with me. My kisses have cheapened you, eh? Then how must you have felt at Happy Camp on the Dyea Trail?"

As though in answer, Corliss swung down upon them with the tow-rope.

Frona beckoned a greeting to him. "Vance," she said, "the mail-carrier has brought important news to father, so important that he must go outside. He starts this afternoon with Baron Courbertin in La Bijou. Will you take me down to Dawson? I should like to go at once, to-day."

"He . . . he suggested you," she added shyly, indicating St. Vincent.

LOVE OF LIFE, AND OTHER STORIES

LOVE OF LIFE

"This out of all will remain—

They have lived and have tossed:

So much of the game will be gain,

Though the gold of the dice has been lost."

They limped painfully down the bank, and once the foremost of the two men staggered among the rough-strewn rocks. They were tired and weak, and their faces had the drawn expression of patience which comes of hardship long endured. They were heavily burdened with blanket packs which were strapped to their shoulders. Head-straps, passing across the forehead, helped support these packs. Each man carried a rifle. They walked in a stooped posture, the shoulders well forward, the head still farther forward, the eyes bent upon the ground.

"I wish we had just about two of them cartridges that's layin' in that cache of ourn," said the second man.

His voice was utterly and drearily expressionless. He spoke without enthusiasm; and the first man, limping into the milky stream that foamed over the rocks, vouchsafed no reply.

The other man followed at his heels. They did not remove their footgear, though the water was icy cold—so cold that their ankles ached and their feet went numb. In places the water dashed against their knees, and both men staggered for footing.

The man who followed slipped on a smooth boulder, nearly fell, but recovered himself with a violent effort, at the same time uttering a sharp exclamation of pain. He seemed faint and dizzy and put out his free hand while he reeled, as though seeking support against the air. When he had steadied himself he stepped forward, but reeled again and nearly fell. Then he stood still and looked at the other man, who had never turned his head.

The man stood still for fully a minute, as though debating with himself. Then he called out:

"I say, Bill, I've sprained my ankle."

Bill staggered on through the milky water. He did not look around. The man watched him go, and though his face was expressionless as ever, his eyes were like the eyes of a wounded deer.

The other man limped up the farther bank and continued straight on without looking back. The man in the stream watched him. His lips trembled a little, so that the rough thatch of brown hair which covered them was visibly agitated. His tongue even strayed out to moisten them.

"Bill!" he cried out.

It was the pleading cry of a strong man in distress, but Bill's head did not turn. The man watched him go, limping grotesquely and lurching forward with stammering gait up the slow slope toward the soft sky-line of the low-lying hill. He watched him go till he passed over the crest and disappeared. Then he turned his gaze and slowly took in the circle of the world that remained to him now that Bill was gone.

Near the horizon the sun was smouldering dimly, almost obscured by formless mists and vapors, which gave an impression of mass and density without outline or tangibility. The man pulled out his watch, the while resting his weight on one leg. It was four o'clock, and as the season was near the last of July or first of August,—he did not know the precise date within a week or two,—he knew that the sun roughly marked the northwest. He looked to the south and knew that somewhere beyond those bleak hills lay the Great Bear Lake; also, he knew that in that direction the Arctic Circle cut its forbidding way across the Canadian Barrens. This stream in which he stood was a feeder to the Coppermine River, which in turn flowed north and emptied into Coronation Gulf and the Arctic Ocean. He had never been there, but he had seen it, once, on a Hudson Bay Company chart.

Again his gaze completed the circle of the world about him. It was not a heartening spectacle. Everywhere was soft sky-line. The hills were all low-lying. There were no trees, no shrubs, no grasses—naught but a tremendous and terrible desolation that sent fear swiftly dawning into his eyes.

"Bill!" he whispered, once and twice; "Bill!"

He cowered in the midst of the milky water, as though the vastness were pressing in upon him with overwhelming force, brutally crushing him with its complacent awfulness. He began to shake as with an ague-fit, till the gun fell from his hand with a splash. This served to rouse him. He fought with his fear and pulled himself together, groping in the water and recovering the weapon. He hitched his pack farther over on his left shoulder, so as to take a portion of its weight from off the injured ankle. Then he proceeded, slowly and carefully, wincing with pain, to the bank.

He did not stop. With a desperation that was madness, unmindful of the pain, he hurried up the slope to the crest of the hill over which his comrade had disappeared—more grotesque and comical by far than that limping, jerking comrade. But at the crest he saw a shallow valley, empty of life. He fought with his fear again, overcame it, hitched the pack still farther over on his left shoulder, and lurched on down the slope.

The bottom of the valley was soggy with water, which the thick moss held, spongelike, close to the surface. This water squirted out from under his feet at every step, and each time he lifted a foot the action culminated in a sucking sound as the wet moss reluctantly released its grip. He picked his way from muskeg to muskeg, and followed the other man's footsteps along and across the rocky ledges which thrust like islets through the sea of moss.

Though alone, he was not lost. Farther on he knew he would come to where dead spruce and fir, very small and weazened, bordered the shore of a little lake, the *titchin-nichilie*, in the tongue of the country, the "land of little sticks." And into that lake flowed a small stream, the water of which was not milky. There was rush-grass on that stream—this he remembered well—but no timber, and he would follow it till its first trickle ceased at a divide. He would cross this divide to the first trickle of another stream, flowing to the west, which he would follow until it emptied into the river Dease, and here he would find a cache under an upturned canoe and piled over with many rocks. And in this cache would be ammunition for his empty gun, fish-hooks and lines, a small net—all the utilities for the killing and snaring of food. Also, he would find flour,—not much,—a piece of bacon, and some beans.

Bill would be waiting for him there, and they would paddle away south down the Dease to the Great Bear Lake. And south across the lake they would go, ever south, till they gained the Mackenzie. And south, still south, they would go, while the winter raced vainly after them, and the ice formed in the eddies, and the days grew chill and crisp, south to some warm Hudson Bay Company post, where timber grew tall and generous and there was grub without end.

These were the thoughts of the man as he strove onward. But hard as he strove with his body, he strove equally hard with his mind, trying to think that Bill had not deserted him, that Bill would surely wait for him at the cache. He was compelled to think this thought, or else there would not be any use to strive, and he would have lain down and died. And as the dim ball of the sun sank slowly into the northwest he covered every inch—and many times—of his and Bill's flight south before the downcoming winter. And he conned the grub of the cache and the grub of the Hudson Bay Company post over and over again. He had not eaten for two days; for a far longer time he had not had all he wanted to eat. Often he stooped and picked pale muskeg berries, put them into his mouth, and chewed and swallowed them. A muskeg berry is a bit of seed enclosed in a bit of water. In the mouth the water melts away and the seed chews sharp and bitter. The man knew there was no nourishment in the berries, but he chewed them patiently with a hope greater than knowledge and defying experience.

At nine o'clock he stubbed his toe on a rocky ledge, and from sheer weariness and weakness staggered and fell. He lay for some time, without movement, on his side. Then he slipped out of the pack-straps and clumsily dragged himself into a sitting posture. It was not yet dark, and in the lingering twilight he groped about among the rocks for shreds of dry moss. When he had gathered a heap he built a fire,—a smouldering, smudgy fire,—and put a tin pot of water on to boil.

He unwrapped his pack and the first thing he did was to count his matches. There were sixty-seven. He counted them three times to make sure. He divided them into several portions, wrapping them in oil paper, disposing of one bunch in his empty tobacco pouch, of another bunch in the inside band of his battered hat, of a third bunch under his shirt on the chest. This accomplished, a panic came upon him, and he unwrapped them all and counted them again. There were still sixty-seven.

He dried his wet foot-gear by the fire. The moccasins were in soggy shreds. The blanket socks were worn through in places, and his feet were raw and bleeding. His ankle was throbbing, and he gave it an examination. It had swollen to the size of his knee. He tore a long strip from one of his two blankets and bound the ankle tightly. He tore other strips and bound them about his feet to serve for both moccasins and socks. Then he drank the pot of water, steaming hot, wound his watch, and crawled between his blankets.

He slept like a dead man. The brief darkness around midnight came and went. The sun arose in the northeast—at least the day dawned in that quarter, for the sun was hidden by gray clouds.

At six o'clock he awoke, quietly lying on his back. He gazed straight up into the gray sky and knew that he was hungry. As he rolled over on his elbow he was startled by a loud snort, and saw a bull caribou regarding him with alert curiosity. The animal was not mere than fifty feet away, and instantly into the man's mind leaped the vision and the savor of a caribou steak sizzling and frying over a fire. Mechanically he reached for the empty gun, drew a bead, and pulled the trigger. The bull snorted and leaped away, his hoofs rattling and clattering as he fled across the ledges.

The man cursed and flung the empty gun from him. He groaned aloud as he started to drag himself to his feet. It was a slow and arduous task.

His joints were like rusty hinges. They worked harshly in their sockets, with much friction, and each bending or unbending was accomplished only through a sheer exertion of will. When he finally gained his feet, another minute or so was consumed in straightening up, so that he could stand erect as a man should stand.

He crawled up a small knoll and surveyed the prospect. There were no trees, no bushes, nothing but a gray sea of moss scarcely diversified by gray rocks, gray lakelets, and gray streamlets. The sky was gray. There was no sun nor hint of sun. He had no idea of north, and he had forgotten the way he had come to this spot the night before. But he was not lost. He knew that. Soon he would come to the land of the little sticks. He felt that it lay off to the left somewhere, not far—possibly just over the next low hill.

He went back to put his pack into shape for travelling. He assured himself of the existence of his three separate parcels of matches, though he did not stop to count them. But he did linger, debating, over a squat moose-hide sack. It was not large. He could hide it under his two hands. He knew that it weighed fifteen pounds,—as much as all the rest of the pack,—and it worried him. He finally set it to one side and proceeded to roll the pack. He paused to gaze at the squat moose-hide sack. He picked it up hastily with a defiant glance about him, as though the desolation were trying to rob him of it; and when he rose to his feet to stagger on into the day, it was included in the pack on his back.

He bore away to the left, stopping now and again to eat muskeg berries. His ankle had stiffened, his limp was more pronounced, but the pain of it was as nothing compared with the pain of his stomach. The hunger pangs were sharp. They gnawed and gnawed until he could not keep his mind steady on the course he must pursue to gain the land of little sticks. The muskeg berries did not allay this gnawing, while they made his tongue and the roof of his mouth sore with their irritating bite.

He came upon a valley where rock ptarmigan rose on whirring wings from the ledges and muskegs. Ker—ker—ker was the cry they made. He threw stones at them, but could not hit them. He placed his pack on the ground and stalked them as a cat stalks a sparrow. The sharp rocks cut through his pants' legs till his knees left a trail of blood; but the hurt was lost in the hurt of his hunger. He squirmed over the wet moss, saturating his clothes and chilling his body; but he was not aware of it, so great was his fever for food. And always the ptarmigan rose, whirring, before him, till their ker—ker—ker became a mock to him, and he cursed them and cried aloud at them with their own cry.

Once he crawled upon one that must have been asleep. He did not see it till it shot up in his face from its rocky nook. He made a clutch as startled as was the rise of the ptarmigan, and there remained in his hand three tail-feathers. As he watched its flight he hated it, as though it had done him some terrible wrong. Then he returned and shouldered his pack.

As the day wore along he came into valleys or swales where the game was more plentiful. A band of caribou passed by, twenty and odd animals, tantalizingly within rifle range. He felt a wild desire to run after them, a certitude that he could run them down. A black fox came toward him, carrying a ptarmigan in his mouth. The man shouted. It was a fearful cry, but the fox, leaping away in fright, did not drop the ptarmigan.

Late in the afternoon he followed a stream, milky with lime, which ran through sparse patches of rush-grass. Grasping these rushes firmly near the root, he pulled up what resembled a young onion-sprout no larger than a shingle-nail. It was tender, and his teeth sank into it with a crunch that promised deliciously of food. But its fibers were tough. It was composed of stringy filaments saturated with water, like the berries, and devoid of nourishment. He threw off his pack and went into the rush-grass on hands and knees, crunching and munching, like some bovine creature.

He was very weary and often wished to rest—to lie down and sleep; but he was continually driven on—not so much by his desire to gain the land of little sticks as by his hunger. He searched little ponds for frogs and dug up the earth with his nails for worms, though he knew in spite that neither frogs nor worms existed so far north.

He looked into every pool of water vainly, until, as the long twilight came on, he discovered a solitary fish, the size of a minnow, in such a pool. He plunged his arm in up to the shoulder, but it eluded him. He reached for it with both hands and stirred up the milky mud at the bottom. In his excitement he fell in, wetting himself to the waist. Then the water was too muddy to admit of his seeing the fish, and he was compelled to wait until the sediment had settled.

The pursuit was renewed, till the water was again muddied. But he could not wait. He unstrapped the tin bucket and began to bale the pool. He baled wildly at first, splashing himself and flinging the water so short a distance that it ran back into the pool. He worked more carefully, striving to be cool, though his heart was pounding against his chest and his hands were trembling. At the end of half an hour the pool was nearly dry. Not a cupful of water remained. And there was no fish. He found a hidden crevice among the stones through which it had escaped to the adjoining and larger pool—a pool which he could not empty in a night and a day. Had he known of the crevice, he could have closed it with a rock at the beginning and the fish would have been his.

Thus he thought, and crumpled up and sank down upon the wet earth. At first he cried softly to himself, then he cried loudly to the pitiless desolation that ringed him around; and for a long time after he was shaken by great dry sobs.

He built a fire and warmed himself by drinking quarts of hot water, and made camp on a rocky ledge in the same fashion he had the night before. The last thing he did was to see that his matches were dry and to wind his watch. The blankets were wet and clammy. His ankle pulsed with pain. But he knew only that he was hungry, and through his restless sleep he dreamed of feasts and banquets and of food served and spread in all imaginable ways.

He awoke chilled and sick. There was no sun. The gray of earth and sky had become deeper, more profound. A raw wind was blowing, and the first flurries of snow were whitening the hilltops. The air about him thickened and grew white while he made a fire and boiled more water. It was wet snow, half rain, and the flakes were large and soggy. At first they melted as soon as they came in contact with the earth, but ever more fell, covering the ground, putting out the fire, spoiling his supply of moss-fuel.

This was a signal for him to strap on his pack and stumble onward, he knew not where. He was not concerned with the land of little sticks, nor with Bill and the cache under the upturned canoe by the river Dease. He was mastered by the verb "to eat." He was hunger-mad. He took no heed of the course he pursued, so long as that course led him through the swale bottoms. He felt his way through the wet snow to the watery muskeg berries, and went by feel as he pulled up the rush-grass by the roots. But it was tasteless stuff and did not satisfy. He found a weed that tasted sour and he ate all he could find of it, which was not much, for it was a creeping growth, easily hidden under the several inches of snow.

He had no fire that night, nor hot water, and crawled under his blanket to sleep the broken hunger-sleep. The snow turned into a cold rain. He awakened many times to feel it falling on his upturned face. Day came—a gray day and no sun. It had ceased raining. The keenness of his hunger had departed. Sensibility, as far as concerned the yearning for food, had been exhausted. There was a dull, heavy ache in his stomach, but it did not bother him so much. He was more rational, and once more he was chiefly interested in the land of little sticks and the cache by the river Dease.

He ripped the remnant of one of his blankets into strips and bound his bleeding feet. Also, he recinched the injured ankle and prepared himself for a day of travel. When he came to his pack, he paused long over the squat moose-hide sack, but in the end it went with him.

The snow had melted under the rain, and only the hilltops showed white. The sun came out, and he succeeded in locating the points of the compass, though he knew now that he was lost. Perhaps, in his previous days' wanderings, he had edged away too far to the left. He now bore off to the right to counteract the possible deviation from his true course.

Though the hunger pangs were no longer so exquisite, he realized that he was weak. He was compelled to pause for frequent rests, when he attacked the muskeg berries and rush-grass patches. His tongue felt dry and large, as though covered with a fine hairy growth, and it tasted bitter in his mouth. His heart gave him a great deal of trouble. When he had travelled a few minutes it would begin a remorseless thump, thump, thump, and then leap up and away in a painful flutter of beats that choked him and made him go faint and dizzy.

In the middle of the day he found two minnows in a large pool. It was impossible to bale it, but he was calmer now and managed to catch them in his tin bucket. They were no longer than his little finger, but he was not particularly hungry. The dull ache in his stomach had been growing duller and fainter. It seemed almost that his stomach was dozing. He ate the fish raw, masticating with painstaking care, for the eating was an act of pure reason. While he had no desire to eat, he knew that he must eat to live.

In the evening he caught three more minnows, eating two and saving the third for breakfast. The sun had dried stray shreds of moss, and he was able to warm himself with hot water. He had not covered more than ten miles that day; and the next day, travelling whenever his heart permitted him, he covered no more than five miles. But his stomach did not give him the slightest uneasiness. It had gone to sleep. He was in a strange country, too, and the caribou were growing more plentiful, also the wolves. Often their yelps drifted across the desolation, and once he saw three of them slinking away before his path.

Another night; and in the morning, being more rational, he untied the leather string that fastened the squat moose-hide sack. From its open mouth poured a yellow stream of coarse gold-dust and nuggets. He roughly divided the gold in halves, caching one half on a prominent ledge, wrapped in a piece of blanket, and returning the other half to the sack. He also began to use strips of the one remaining blanket for his feet. He still clung to his gun, for there were cartridges in that cache by the river Dease.

This was a day of fog, and this day hunger awoke in him again. He was very weak and was afflicted with a giddiness which at times blinded him. It was no uncommon thing now for him to stumble and fall; and stumbling once, he fell squarely into a ptarmigan nest. There were four newly hatched chicks, a day old—little specks of pulsating life no more than a mouthful; and he ate them ravenously, thrusting them alive into his mouth and crunching them like egg-shells between his teeth. The mother ptarmigan beat about him with great outcry. He used his gun as a club with which to knock her over, but she dodged out of reach. He threw stones at her and with one chance shot broke a wing. Then she fluttered away, running, trailing the broken wing, with him in pursuit.

The little chicks had no more than whetted his appetite. He hopped and bobbed clumsily along on his injured ankle, throwing stones and screaming hoarsely at times; at other times hopping and bobbing silently along, picking himself up grimly and patiently when he fell, or rubbing his eyes with his hand when the giddiness threatened to overpower him.

The chase led him across swampy ground in the bottom of the valley, and he came upon footprints in the soggy moss. They were not his own—he could see that. They must be Bill's. But he could not stop, for the mother ptarmigan was running on. He would catch her first, then he would return and investigate.

He exhausted the mother ptarmigan; but he exhausted himself. She lay panting on her side. He lay panting on his side, a dozen feet away, unable to crawl to her. And as he recovered she recovered, fluttering out of reach as his hungry hand went out to her. The chase was resumed. Night settled down and she escaped. He stumbled from weakness and pitched head foremost on his face, cutting his cheek, his pack upon his back. He did not move for a long while; then he rolled over on his side, wound his watch, and lay there until morning.

Another day of fog. Half of his last blanket had gone into foot-wrappings. He failed to pick up Bill's trail. It did not matter. His hunger was driving him too compellingly—only—only he wondered if Bill, too, were lost. By midday the irk of his pack became too oppressive. Again he divided the gold, this time merely spilling half of it on the ground. In the afternoon he threw the rest of it away, there remaining to him only the half-blanket, the tin bucket, and the rifle.

An hallucination began to trouble him. He felt confident that one cartridge remained to him. It was in the chamber of the rifle and he had overlooked it. On the other hand, he knew all the time that the chamber was empty. But the hallucination persisted. He fought it off for hours, then threw his rifle open and was confronted with emptiness. The disappointment was as bitter as though he had really expected to find the cartridge.

He plodded on for half an hour, when the hallucination arose again. Again he fought it, and still it persisted, till for very relief he opened his rifle to unconvince himself. At times his mind wandered farther afield, and he plodded on, a mere automaton, strange conceits and whimsicalities gnawing at his brain like worms. But these excursions out of the real were of brief duration, for ever the pangs of the hunger-bite called him back. He was jerked back abruptly once from such an excursion by a sight that caused him nearly to faint. He reeled and swayed, doddering like a drunken man to keep from falling. Before him stood a horse. A horse! He could not believe his eyes. A thick mist was in them, intershot with sparkling points of light. He rubbed his eyes savagely to clear his vision, and beheld, not a horse, but a great brown bear. The animal was studying him with bellicose curiosity.

The man had brought his gun halfway to his shoulder before he realized. He lowered it and drew his hunting-knife from its beaded sheath at his hip. Before him was meat and life. He ran his thumb along the edge of his knife. It was sharp. The point was sharp. He would fling himself upon the bear and kill it. But his heart began its warning thump, thump, thump. Then followed the wild upward leap and tattoo of flutters, the pressing as of an iron band about his forehead, the creeping of the dizziness into his brain.

His desperate courage was evicted by a great surge of fear. In his weakness, what if the animal attacked him? He drew himself up to his most imposing stature, gripping the knife and staring hard at the bear. The bear advanced clumsily a couple of steps, reared up, and gave vent to a tentative growl. If the man ran, he would run after him; but the man did not run. He was animated now with the courage of fear. He, too, growled, savagely, terribly, voicing the fear that is to life germane and that lies twisted about life's deepest roots.

The bear edged away to one side, growling menacingly, himself appalled by this mysterious creature that appeared upright and unafraid. But the man did not move. He stood like a statue till the danger was past, when he yielded to a fit of trembling and sank down into the wet moss.

He pulled himself together and went on, afraid now in a new way. It was not the fear that he should die passively from lack of food, but that he should be destroyed violently before starvation had exhausted the last particle of the endeavor in him that made toward surviving. There were the wolves. Back and forth across the desolation drifted their howls, weaving the very air into a fabric of menace that was so tangible that he found himself, arms in the air, pressing it back from him as it might be the walls of a wind-blown tent.

Now and again the wolves, in packs of two and three, crossed his path. But they sheered clear of him. They were not in sufficient numbers, and besides they were hunting the caribou, which did not battle, while this strange creature that walked erect might scratch and bite.

In the late afternoon he came upon scattered bones where the wolves had made a kill. The debris had been a caribou calf an hour before, squawking and running and very much alive. He contemplated the bones, clean-picked and polished, pink with the cell-life in them which had not yet died. Could it possibly be that he might be that ere the day was done! Such was life, eh? A vain and fleeting thing. It was only life that pained. There was no hurt in death. To die was to sleep. It meant cessation, rest. Then why was he not content to die?

But he did not moralize long. He was squatting in the moss, a bone in his mouth, sucking at the shreds of life that still dyed it faintly pink. The sweet meaty taste, thin and elusive almost as a memory, maddened him. He closed his jaws on the bones and crunched. Sometimes it was the bone that broke, sometimes his teeth. Then he crushed the bones between rocks, pounded them to a pulp, and swallowed them. He pounded his fingers, too, in his haste, and yet found a moment in which to feel surprise at the fact that his fingers did not hurt much when caught under the descending rock.

Came frightful days of snow and rain. He did not know when he made camp, when he broke camp. He travelled in the night as much as in the day. He rested wherever he fell, crawled on whenever the dying life in him flickered up and burned less dimly. He, as a man, no longer strove. It was the life in him, unwilling to die, that drove him on. He did not suffer. His nerves had become blunted, numb, while his mind was filled with weird visions and delicious dreams.

But ever he sucked and chewed on the crushed bones of the caribou calf, the least remnants of which he had gathered up and carried with him. He crossed no more hills or divides, but automatically followed a large stream which flowed through a wide and shallow valley. He did not see this stream nor this valley. He saw nothing save visions. Soul and body walked or crawled side by side, yet apart, so slender was the thread that bound them.

He awoke in his right mind, lying on his back on a rocky ledge. The sun was shining bright and warm. Afar off he heard the squawking of caribou calves. He was aware of vague memories of rain and wind and snow, but whether he had been beaten by the storm for two days or two weeks he did not know.

For some time he lay without movement, the genial sunshine pouring upon him and saturating his miserable body with its warmth. A fine day, he thought. Perhaps he could manage to locate himself. By a painful effort he rolled over on his side. Below him flowed a wide and sluggish river. Its unfamiliarity puzzled him. Slowly he followed it with his eyes, winding in wide sweeps among the bleak, bare hills, bleaker and barer and lower-lying than any hills he had yet encountered. Slowly, deliberately, without excitement or more than the most casual interest, he followed the course of the strange stream toward the sky-line and saw it emptying into a bright and shining sea. He was still unexcited. Most unusual, he thought, a vision or a mirage—more likely a vision, a trick of his disordered mind. He was confirmed in this by sight of a ship lying at anchor in the midst of the shining sea. He closed his eyes for a while, then opened them. Strange how the vision persisted! Yet not strange. He knew there were no seas or ships in the heart of the barren lands, just as he had known there was no cartridge in the empty rifle.

He heard a snuffle behind him—a half-choking gasp or cough. Very slowly, because of his exceeding weakness and stiffness, he rolled over on his other side. He could see nothing near at hand, but he waited patiently. Again came the snuffle and cough, and outlined between two jagged rocks not a score of feet away he made out the gray head of a wolf. The sharp ears were not pricked so sharply as he had seen them on other wolves; the eyes were bleared and bloodshot, the head seemed to droop limply and forlornly. The animal blinked continually in the sunshine. It seemed sick. As he looked it snuffled and coughed again.

This, at least, was real, he thought, and turned on the other side so that he might see the reality of the world which had been veiled from him before by the vision. But the sea still shone in the distance and the ship was plainly discernible. Was it reality, after all? He closed his eyes for a long while and thought, and then it came to him. He had been making north by east, away from the Dease Divide and into the Coppermine Valley. This wide and sluggish river was the Coppermine. That shining sea was the Arctic Ocean. That ship was a whaler, strayed east, far east, from the mouth of the Mackenzie, and it was lying at anchor in Coronation Gulf. He remembered the Hudson Bay Company chart he had seen long ago, and it was all clear and reasonable to him.

He sat up and turned his attention to immediate affairs. He had worn through the blanket-wrappings, and his feet were shapeless lumps of raw meat. His last blanket was gone. Rifle and knife were both missing. He had lost his hat somewhere, with the bunch of matches in the band, but the matches against his chest were safe and dry inside the tobacco pouch and oil paper. He looked at his watch. It marked eleven o'clock and was still running. Evidently he had kept it wound.

He was calm and collected. Though extremely weak, he had no sensation of pain. He was not hungry. The thought of food was not even pleasant to him, and whatever he did was done by his reason alone. He ripped off his pants' legs to the knees and bound them about his feet. Somehow he had succeeded in retaining the tin bucket. He would have some hot water before he began what he foresaw was to be a terrible journey to the ship.

His movements were slow. He shook as with a palsy. When he started to collect dry moss, he found he could not rise to his feet. He tried again and again, then contented himself with crawling about on hands and knees. Once he crawled near to the sick wolf. The animal dragged itself reluctantly out of his way, licking its chops with a tongue which seemed hardly to have the strength to curl. The man noticed that the tongue was not the customary healthy red. It was a yellowish brown and seemed coated with a rough and half-dry mucus.

After he had drunk a quart of hot water the man found he was able to stand, and even to walk as well as a dying man might be supposed to walk. Every minute or so he was compelled to rest. His steps were feeble and uncertain, just as the wolf's that trailed him were feeble and uncertain; and that night, when the shining sea was blotted out by blackness, he knew he was nearer to it by no more than four miles.

Throughout the night he heard the cough of the sick wolf, and now and then the squawking of the caribou calves. There was life all around him, but it was strong life, very much alive and well, and he knew the sick wolf clung to the sick man's trail in the hope that the man would die first. In the morning, on opening his eyes, he beheld it regarding him with a wistful and hungry stare. It stood crouched, with tail between its legs, like a miserable and woe-begone dog. It shivered in the chill morning wind, and grinned dispiritedly when the man spoke to it in a voice that achieved no more than a hoarse whisper.

The sun rose brightly, and all morning the man tottered and fell toward the ship on the shining sea. The weather was perfect. It was the brief Indian Summer of the high latitudes. It might last a week. To-morrow or next day it might be gone.

In the afternoon the man came upon a trail. It was of another man, who did not walk, but who dragged himself on all fours. The man thought it might be Bill, but he thought in a dull, uninterested way. He had no curiosity. In fact, sensation and emotion had left him. He was no longer susceptible to pain. Stomach and nerves had gone to sleep. Yet the life that was in him drove him on. He was very weary, but it refused to die. It was because it refused to die that he still ate muskeg berries and minnows, drank his hot water, and kept a wary eye on the sick wolf.

He followed the trail of the other man who dragged himself along, and soon came to the end of it—a few fresh-picked bones where the soggy moss was marked by the foot-pads of many wolves. He saw a squat moose-hide sack, mate to his own, which had been torn by sharp teeth. He picked it up, though its weight was almost too much for his feeble fingers. Bill had carried it to the last. Ha! ha! He would have the laugh on Bill. He would survive and carry it to the ship in the shining sea. His mirth was hoarse and ghastly, like a raven's croak, and the sick wolf joined him, howling lugubriously. The man ceased suddenly. How could he have the laugh on Bill if that were Bill; if those bones, so pinky-white and clean, were Bill?

He turned away. Well, Bill had deserted him; but he would not take the gold, nor would he suck Bill's bones. Bill would have, though, had it been the other way around, he mused as he staggered on.

He came to a pool of water. Stooping over in quest of minnows, he jerked his head back as though he had been stung. He had caught sight of his reflected face. So horrible was it that sensibility awoke long enough to be shocked. There were three minnows in the pool, which was too large to drain; and after several ineffectual attempts to catch them in the tin bucket he forbore. He was afraid, because of his great weakness, that he might fall in and drown. It was for this reason that he did not trust himself to the river astride one of the many drift-logs which lined its sand-spits.

That day he decreased the distance between him and the ship by three miles; the next day by two—for he was crawling now as Bill had crawled; and the end of the fifth day found the ship still seven miles away and him unable to make even a mile a day. Still the Indian Summer held on, and he continued to crawl and faint, turn and turn about; and ever the sick wolf coughed and wheezed at his heels. His knees had become raw meat like his feet, and though he padded them with the shirt from his back it was a red track he left behind him on the moss and stones. Once, glancing back, he saw the wolf licking hungrily his bleeding trail, and he saw sharply what his own end might be—unless—unless he could get the wolf. Then began as grim a tragedy of existence as was ever played—a sick man that crawled, a sick wolf that limped, two creatures dragging their dying carcasses across the desolation and hunting each other's lives.

Had it been a well wolf, it would not have mattered so much to the man; but the thought of going to feed the maw of that loathsome and all but dead thing was repugnant to him. He was finicky. His mind had begun to wander again, and to be perplexed by hallucinations, while his lucid intervals grew rarer and shorter.

He was awakened once from a faint by a wheeze close in his ear. The wolf leaped lamely back, losing its footing and falling in its weakness. It was ludicrous, but he was not amused. Nor was he even afraid. He was too far gone for that. But his mind was for the moment clear, and he lay and considered. The ship was no more than four miles away. He could see it quite distinctly when he rubbed the mists out of his eyes, and he could see the white sail of a small boat cutting the water of the shining sea. But he could never crawl those four miles. He knew that, and was very calm in the knowledge. He knew that he could not crawl half a mile. And yet he wanted to live. It was unreasonable that he should die after all he had undergone. Fate asked too much of him. And, dying, he declined to die. It was stark madness, perhaps, but in the very grip of Death he defied Death and refused to die.

He closed his eyes and composed himself with infinite precaution. He steeled himself to keep above the suffocating languor that lapped like a rising tide through all the wells of his being. It was very like a sea, this deadly languor, that rose and rose and drowned his consciousness bit by bit. Sometimes he was all but submerged, swimming through oblivion with a faltering stroke; and again, by some strange alchemy of soul, he would find another shred of will and strike out more strongly.

Without movement he lay on his back, and he could hear, slowly drawing near and nearer, the wheezing intake and output of the sick wolf's breath. It drew closer, ever closer, through an infinitude of time, and he did not move. It was at his ear. The harsh dry tongue grated like sandpaper against his cheek. His hands shot out—or at least he willed them to shoot out. The fingers were curved like talons, but they closed on empty air. Swiftness and certitude require strength, and the man had not this strength.

The patience of the wolf was terrible. The man's patience was no less terrible. For half a day he lay motionless, fighting off unconsciousness and waiting for the thing that was to feed upon him and upon which he wished to feed. Sometimes the languid sea rose over him and he dreamed long dreams; but ever through it all, waking and dreaming, he waited for the wheezing breath and the harsh caress of the tongue.

He did not hear the breath, and he slipped slowly from some dream to the feel of the tongue along his hand. He waited. The fangs pressed softly; the pressure increased; the wolf was exerting its last strength in an effort to sink teeth in the food for which it had waited so long. But the man had waited long, and the lacerated hand closed on the jaw. Slowly, while the wolf struggled feebly and the hand clutched feebly, the other hand crept across to a grip. Five minutes later the whole weight of the man's body was on top of the wolf. The hands had not sufficient strength to choke the wolf, but the face of the man was pressed close to the throat of the wolf and the mouth of the man was full of hair. At the end of half an hour the man was aware of a warm trickle in his throat. It was not pleasant. It was like molten lead being forced into his stomach, and it was forced by his will alone. Later the man rolled over on his back and slept.

* * * * *

There were some members of a scientific expedition on the whale-ship *Bedford*. From the deck they remarked a strange object on the shore. It was moving down the beach toward the water. They were unable to classify it, and, being scientific men, they climbed into the whale-boat alongside and went ashore to see. And they saw something that was alive but which could hardly be called a man. It was blind, unconscious. It squirmed along the ground like some monstrous worm. Most of its efforts were ineffectual, but it was persistent, and it writhed and twisted and went ahead perhaps a score of feet an hour.

* * * * *

Three weeks afterward the man lay in a bunk on the whale-ship *Bedford*, and with tears streaming down his wasted cheeks told who he was and what he had undergone. He also babbled incoherently of his mother, of sunny Southern California, and a home among the orange groves and flowers.

The days were not many after that when he sat at table with the scientific men and ship's officers. He gloated over the spectacle of so much food, watching it anxiously as it went into the mouths of others. With the disappearance of each mouthful an expression of deep regret came into his eyes. He was quite sane, yet he hated those men at mealtime. He was haunted by a fear that the food would not last. He inquired of the cook, the cabin-boy, the captain, concerning the food stores. They reassured him countless times; but he could not believe them, and pried cunningly about the lazarette to see with his own eyes.

It was noticed that the man was getting fat. He grew stouter with each day. The scientific men shook their heads and theorized. They limited the man at his meals, but still his girth increased and he swelled prodigiously under his shirt.

The sailors grinned. They knew. And when the scientific men set a watch on the man, they knew too. They saw him slouch for'ard after breakfast, and, like a mendicant, with outstretched palm, accost a sailor. The sailor grinned and passed him a fragment of sea biscuit. He clutched it avariciously, looked at it as a miser looks at gold, and thrust it into his shirt bosom. Similar were the donations from other grinning sailors.

The scientific men were discreet. They let him alone. But they privily examined his bunk. It was lined with hardtack; the mattress was stuffed with hardtack; every nook and cranny was filled with hardtack. Yet he was sane. He was taking precautions against another possible famine—that was all. He would recover from it, the scientific men said; and he did, ere the *Bedford*'s anchor rumbled down in San Francisco Bay.

A DAY'S LODGING

It was the gosh-dangdest stampede I ever seen. A thousand dog-teams hittin' the ice. You couldn't see 'm fer smoke. Two white men an' a Swede froze to death that night, an' there was a dozen busted their lungs. But didn't I see with my own eyes the bottom of the water-hole? It was yellow with gold like a mustard-plaster. That's why I staked the Yukon for a minin' claim. That's what made the stampede. An' then there was nothin' to it. That's what I said—NOTHIN' to it. An' I ain't got over guessin' yet.—Narrative of Shorty.

John Messner clung with mittened hand to the bucking gee-pole and held the sled in the trail. With the other mittened hand he rubbed his cheeks and nose. He rubbed his cheeks and nose every little while. In point of fact, he rarely ceased from rubbing them, and sometimes, as their numbness increased, he rubbed fiercely. His forehead was covered by the visor of his fur cap, the flaps of which went over his ears. The rest of his face was protected by a thick beard, golden-brown under its coating of frost.

Behind him churned a heavily loaded Yukon sled, and before him toiled a string of five dogs. The rope by which they dragged the sled rubbed against the side of Messner's leg. When the dogs swung on a bend in the trail, he stepped over the rope. There were many bends, and he was compelled to step over it often. Sometimes he tripped on the rope, or stumbled, and at all times he was awkward, betraying a weariness so great that the sled now and again ran upon his heels.

When he came to a straight piece of trail, where the sled could get along for a moment without guidance, he let go the gee-pole and batted his right hand sharply upon the hard wood. He found it difficult to keep up the circulation in that hand. But while he pounded the one hand, he never ceased from rubbing his nose and cheeks with the other.

"It's too cold to travel, anyway," he said. He spoke aloud, after the manner of men who are much by themselves. "Only a fool would travel at such a temperature. If it isn't eighty below, it's because it's seventy-nine."

He pulled out his watch, and after some fumbling got it back into the breast pocket of his thick woollen jacket. Then he surveyed the heavens and ran his eye along the white sky-line to the south.

"Twelve o'clock," he mumbled, "A clear sky, and no sun."

He plodded on silently for ten minutes, and then, as though there had been no lapse in his speech, he added:

"And no ground covered, and it's too cold to travel."

Suddenly he yelled "Whoa!" at the dogs, and stopped. He seemed in a wild panic over his right hand, and proceeded to hammer it furiously against the gee-pole.

"You—poor—devils!" he addressed the dogs, which had dropped down heavily on the ice to rest. His was a broken, jerky utterance, caused by the violence with which he hammered his numb hand upon the wood. "What have you done anyway that a two-legged other animal should come along, break you to harness, curb all your natural proclivities, and make slave-beasts out of you?"

He rubbed his nose, not reflectively, but savagely, in order to drive the blood into it, and urged the dogs to their work again. He travelled on the frozen surface of a great river. Behind him it stretched away in a mighty curve of many miles, losing itself in a fantastic jumble of mountains, snow-covered and silent. Ahead of him the river split into many channels to accommodate the freight of islands it carried on its breast. These islands were silent and white. No animals nor humming insects broke the silence. No birds flew in the chill air. There was no sound of man, no mark of the handiwork of man. The world slept, and it was like the sleep of death.

John Messner seemed succumbing to the apathy of it all. The frost was benumbing his spirit. He plodded on with bowed head, unobservant, mechanically rubbing nose and cheeks, and batting his steering hand against the gee-pole in the straight trail-stretches.

But the dogs were observant, and suddenly they stopped, turning their heads and looking back at their master out of eyes that were wistful and questioning. Their eyelashes were frosted white, as were their muzzles, and they had all the seeming of decrepit old age, what of the frost-rime and exhaustion.

The man was about to urge them on, when he checked himself, roused up with an effort, and looked around. The dogs had stopped beside a water-hole, not a fissure, but a hole man-made, chopped laboriously with an axe through three and a half feet of ice. A thick skin of new ice showed that it had not been used for some time. Messner glanced about him. The dogs were already pointing the way, each wistful and hoary muzzle turned toward the dim snow-path that left the main river trail and climbed the bank of the island.

"All right, you sore-footed brutes," he said. "I'll investigate. You're not a bit more anxious to quit than I am."

He climbed the bank and disappeared. The dogs did not lie down, but on their feet eagerly waited his return. He came back to them, took a hauling-rope from the front of the sled, and put it around his shoulders. Then he *gee'd* the dogs to the right and put them at the bank on the run. It was a stiff pull, but their weariness fell from them as they crouched low to the snow, whining with eagerness and gladness as they struggled upward to the last ounce of effort in their bodies. When a dog slipped or faltered, the one behind nipped his hind quarters. The man shouted encouragement and threats, and threw all his weight on the hauling-rope.

They cleared the bank with a rush, swung to the left, and dashed up to a small log cabin. It was a deserted cabin of a single room, eight feet by ten on the inside. Messner unharnessed the animals, unloaded his sled and took possession. The last chance wayfarer had left a supply of firewood. Messner set up his light sheet-iron stove and starred a fire. He put five sun-cured salmon into the oven to thaw out for the dogs, and from the water-hole filled his coffee-pot and cooking-pail.

While waiting for the water to boil, he held his face over the stove. The moisture from his breath had collected on his beard and frozen into a great mass of ice, and this he proceeded to thaw out. As it melted and dropped upon the stove it sizzled and rose about him in steam. He helped the process with his fingers, working loose small ice-chunks that fell rattling to the floor.

A wild outcry from the dogs without did not take him from his task. He heard the wolfish snarling and yelping of strange dogs and the sound of voices. A knock came on the door.

"Come in," Messner called, in a voice muffled because at the moment he was sucking loose a fragment of ice from its anchorage on his upper lip.

The door opened, and, gazing out of his cloud of steam, he saw a man and a woman pausing on the threshold.

"Come in," he said peremptorily, "and shut the door!"

Peering through the steam, he could make out but little of their personal appearance. The nose and cheek strap worn by the woman and the trail-wrappings about her head allowed only a pair of black eyes to be seen. The man was dark-eyed and smooth-shaven all except his mustache, which was so iced up as to hide his mouth.

"We just wanted to know if there is any other cabin around here," he said, at the same time glancing over the unfurnished state of the room. "We thought this cabin was empty."

"It isn't my cabin," Messner answered. "I just found it a few minutes ago. Come right in and camp. Plenty of room, and you won't need your stove. There's room for all."

At the sound of his voice the woman peered at him with quick curiousness.

"Get your things off," her companion said to her. "I'll unhitch and get the water so we can start cooking."

Messner took the thawed salmon outside and fed his dogs. He had to guard them against the second team of dogs, and when he had reëntered the cabin the other man had unpacked the sled and fetched water. Messner's pot was boiling. He threw in the coffee, settled it with half a cup of cold water, and took the pot from the stove. He thawed some sour-dough biscuits in the oven, at the same time heating a pot of beans he had boiled the night before and that had ridden frozen on the sled all morning.

Removing his utensils from the stove, so as to give the newcomers a chance to cook, he proceeded to take his meal from the top of his grub-box, himself sitting on his bed-roll. Between mouthfuls he talked trail and dogs with the man, who, with head over the stove, was thawing the ice from his mustache. There were two bunks in the cabin, and into one of them, when he had cleared his lip, the stranger tossed his bed-roll.

"We'll sleep here," he said, "unless you prefer this bunk. You're the first comer and you have first choice, you know."

"That's all right," Messner answered. "One bunk's just as good as the other."

He spread his own bedding in the second bunk, and sat down on the edge. The stranger thrust a physician's small travelling case under his blankets at one end to serve for a pillow.

"Doctor?" Messner asked.

"Yes," came the answer, "but I assure you I didn't come into the Klondike to practise."

The woman busied herself with cooking, while the man sliced bacon and fired the stove. The light in the cabin was dim, filtering through in a small window made of onion-skin writing paper and oiled with bacon grease, so that John Messner could not make out very well what the woman looked like. Not that he tried. He seemed to have no interest in her. But she glanced curiously from time to time into the dark corner where he sat.

"Oh, it's a great life," the doctor proclaimed enthusiastically, pausing from sharpening his knife on the stovepipe. "What I like about it is the struggle, the endeavor with one's own hands, the primitiveness of it, the realness."

"The temperature is real enough," Messner laughed.

"Do you know how cold it actually is?" the doctor demanded.

The other shook his head.

"Well, I'll tell you. Seventy-four below zero by spirit thermometer on the sled."

"That's one hundred and six below freezing point—too cold for travelling, eh?"

"Practically suicide," was the doctor's verdict. "One exerts himself. He breathes heavily, taking into his lungs the frost itself. It chills his lungs, freezes the edges of the tissues. He gets a dry, hacking cough as the dead tissue sloughs away, and dies the following summer of pneumonia, wondering what it's all about. I'll stay in this cabin for a week, unless the thermometer rises at least to fifty below."

"I say, Tess," he said, the next moment, "don't you think that coffee's boiled long enough!"

At the sound of the woman's name, John Messner became suddenly alert. He looked at her quickly, while across his face shot a haunting expression, the ghost of some buried misery achieving swift resurrection. But the next moment, and by an effort of will, the ghost was laid again. His face was as placid as before, though he was still alert, dissatisfied with what the feeble light had shown him of the woman's face.

Automatically, her first act had been to set the coffee-pot back. It was not until she had done this that she glanced at Messner. But already he had composed himself. She saw only a man sitting on the edge of the bunk and incuriously studying the toes of his moccasins. But, as she turned casually to go about her cooking, he shot another swift look at her, and she, glancing as swiftly back, caught his look. He shifted on past her to the doctor, though the slightest smile curled his lip in appreciation of the way she had trapped him.

She drew a candle from the grub-box and lighted it. One look at her illuminated face was enough for Messner. In the small cabin the widest limit was only a matter of several steps, and the next moment she was alongside of him. She deliberately held the candle close to his face and stared at him out of eyes wide with fear and recognition. He smiled quietly back at her.

"What are you looking for, Tess?" the doctor called.

"Hairpins," she replied, passing on and rummaging in a clothes-bag on the bunk.

They served their meal on their grub-box, sitting on Messner's grub-box and facing him. He had stretched out on his bunk to rest, lying on his side, his head on his arm. In the close quarters it was as though the three were together at table.

"What part of the States do you come from?" Messner asked.

"San Francisco," answered the doctor. "I've been in here two years, though."

"I hail from California myself," was Messner's announcement.

The woman looked at him appealingly, but he smiled and went on:

"Berkeley, you know."

The other man was becoming interested.

"U. C.?" he asked.

"Yes, Class of '86."

"I meant faculty," the doctor explained. "You remind me of the type."

"Sorry to hear you say so," Messner smiled back. "I'd prefer being taken for a prospector or a dog-musher."

"I don't think he looks any more like a professor than you do a doctor," the woman broke in.

"Thank you," said Messner. Then, turning to her companion, "By the way, Doctor, what is your name, if I may ask?"

"Haythorne, if you'll take my word for it. I gave up cards with civilization."

"And Mrs. Haythorne," Messner smiled and bowed.

She flashed a look at him that was more anger than appeal.

Haythorne was about to ask the other's name. His mouth had opened to form the question when Messner cut him off.

"Come to think of it, Doctor, you may possibly be able to satisfy my curiosity. There was a sort of scandal in faculty circles some two or three years ago. The wife of one of the English professors—er, if you will pardon me, Mrs. Haythorne—disappeared with some San Francisco doctor, I understood, though his name does not just now come to my lips. Do you remember the incident?"

Haythorne nodded his head. "Made quite a stir at the time. His name was Womble—Graham Womble. He had a magnificent practice. I knew him somewhat."

"Well, what I was trying to get at was what had become of them. I was wondering if you had heard. They left no trace, hide nor hair."

"He covered his tracks cunningly." Haythorne cleared his throat. "There was rumor that they went to the South Seas—were lost on a trading schooner in a typhoon, or something like that."

"I never heard that," Messner said. "You remember the case, Mrs. Haythorne?"

"Perfectly," she answered, in a voice the control of which was in amazing contrast to the anger that blazed in the face she turned aside so that Haythorne might not see.

The latter was again on the verge of asking his name, when Messner remarked:

"This Dr. Womble, I've heard he was very handsome, and—er—quite a success, so to say, with the ladies."

"Well, if he was, he finished himself off by that affair," Haythorne grumbled.

"And the woman was a termagant—at least so I've been told. It was generally accepted in Berkeley that she made life—er—not exactly paradise for her husband."

"I never heard that," Haythorne rejoined. "In San Francisco the talk was all the other way."

"Woman sort of a martyr, eh?—crucified on the cross of matrimony?"

The doctor nodded. Messner's gray eyes were mildly curious as he went on:

"That was to be expected—two sides to the shield. Living in Berkeley I only got the one side. She was a great deal in San Francisco, it seems."

"Some coffee, please," Haythorne said.

The woman refilled his mug, at the same time breaking into light laughter.

"You're gossiping like a pair of beldames," she chided them.

"It's so interesting," Messner smiled at her, then returned to the doctor. "The husband seems then to have had a not very savory reputation in San Francisco?"

"On the contrary, he was a moral prig," Haythorne blurted out, with apparently undue warmth. "He was a little scholastic shrimp without a drop of red blood in his body."

"Did you know him?"

"Never laid eyes on him. I never knocked about in university circles."

"One side of the shield again," Messner said, with an air of weighing the matter judicially. "While he did not amount to much, it is true—that is, physically—I'd hardly say he was as bad as all that. He did take an active interest in student athletics. And he had some talent. He once wrote a Nativity play that brought him quite a bit of local appreciation. I have heard, also, that he was slated for the head of the English department, only the affair happened and he resigned and went away. It quite broke his career, or so it seemed. At any rate, on our side the shield, it was considered a knock-out blow to him. It was thought he cared a great deal for his wife."

Haythorne, finishing his mug of coffee, grunted uninterestedly and lighted his pipe.

"It was fortunate they had no children," Messner continued.

But Haythorne, with a glance at the stove, pulled on his cap and mittens.

"I'm going out to get some wood," he said. "Then I can take off my moccasins and be comfortable."

The door slammed behind him. For a long minute there was silence. The man continued in the same position on the bed. The woman sat on the grub-box, facing him.

"What are you going to do?" she asked abruptly.

Messner looked at her with lazy indecision. "What do you think I ought to do? Nothing scenic, I hope. You see I am stiff and trail-sore, and this bunk is so restful."

She gnawed her lower lip and fumed dumbly.

"But—" she began vehemently, then clenched her hands and stopped.

"I hope you don't want me to kill Mr.—er—Haythorne," he said gently, almost pleadingly. "It would be most distressing, and, I assure you, really it is unnecessary."

"But you must do something," she cried.

"On the contrary, it is quite conceivable that I do not have to do anything."

"You would stay here?"

He nodded.

She glanced desperately around the cabin and at the bed unrolled on the other bunk. "Night is coming on. You can't stop here. You can't! I tell you, you simply can't!"

"Of course I can. I might remind you that I found this cabin first and that you are my guests."

Again her eyes travelled around the room, and the terror in them leaped up at sight of the other bunk.

"Then we'll have to go," she announced decisively.

"Impossible. You have a dry, hacking cough—the sort Mr.—er—Haythorne so aptly described. You've already slightly chilled your lungs. Besides, he is a physician and knows. He would never permit it."

"Then what are you going to do?" she demanded again, with a tense, quiet utterance that boded an outbreak.

Messner regarded her in a way that was almost paternal, what of the profundity of pity and patience with which he contrived to suffuse it.

"My dear Theresa, as I told you before, I don't know. I really haven't thought about it."

"Oh! You drive me mad!" She sprang to her feet, wringing her hands in impotent wrath. "You never used to be this way."

"I used to be all softness and gentleness," he nodded concurrence. "Was that why you left me?"

"You are so different, so dreadfully calm. You frighten me. I feel you have something terrible planned all the while. But whatever you do, don't do anything rash. Don't get excited—"

"I don't get excited any more," he interrupted. "Not since you went away."

"You have improved—remarkably," she retorted.

He smiled acknowledgment. "While I am thinking about what I shall do, I'll tell you what you will have to do—tell Mr.—er—Haythorne who I am. It may make our stay in this cabin more—may I say, sociable?"

"Why have you followed me into this frightful country?" she asked irrelevantly.

"Don't think I came here looking for you, Theresa. Your vanity shall not be tickled by any such misapprehension. Our meeting is wholly fortuitous. I broke with the life academic and I had to go somewhere. To be honest, I came into the Klondike because I thought it the place you were least liable to be in."

There was a fumbling at the latch, then the door swung in and Haythorne entered with an armful of firewood. At the first warning, Theresa began casually to clear away the dishes. Haythorne went out again after more wood.

"Why didn't you introduce us?" Messner queried.

"I'll tell him," she replied, with a toss of her head. "Don't think I'm afraid."

"I never knew you to be afraid, very much, of anything."

"And I'm not afraid of confession, either," she said, with softening face and voice.

"In your case, I fear, confession is exploitation by indirection, profit-making by ruse, self-aggrandizement at the expense of God."

"Don't be literary," she pouted, with growing tenderness. "I never did like epigrammatic discussion. Besides, I'm not afraid to ask you to forgive me."

"There is nothing to forgive, Theresa. I really should thank you. True, at first I suffered; and then, with all the graciousness of spring, it dawned upon me that I was happy, very happy. It was a most amazing discovery."

"But what if I should return to you?" she asked.

"I should" (he looked at her whimsically), "be greatly perturbed."

"I am your wife. You know you have never got a divorce."

"I see," he meditated. "I have been careless. It will be one of the first things I attend to."

She came over to his side, resting her hand on his arm. "You don't want me, John?" Her voice was soft and caressing, her hand rested like a lure. "If I told you I had made a mistake? If I told you that I was very unhappy?—and I am. And I did make a mistake."

Fear began to grow on Messner. He felt himself wilting under the lightly laid hand. The situation was slipping away from him, all his beautiful calmness was going. She looked at him with melting eyes, and he, too, seemed all dew and melting. He felt himself on the edge of an abyss, powerless to withstand the force that was drawing him over.

"I am coming back to you, John. I am coming back to-day . . . now."

As in a nightmare, he strove under the hand. While she talked, he seemed to hear, rippling softly, the song of the Lorelei. It was as though, somewhere, a piano were playing and the actual notes were impinging on his ear-drums.

Suddenly he sprang to his feet, thrust her from him as her arms attempted to clasp him, and retreated backward to the door. He was in a panic.

"I'll do something desperate!" he cried.

"I warned you not to get excited." She laughed mockingly, and went about washing the dishes. "Nobody wants you. I was just playing with you. I am happier where I am."

But Messner did not believe. He remembered her facility in changing front. She had changed front now. It was exploitation by indirection. She was not happy with the other man. She had discovered her mistake. The flame of his ego flared up at the thought. She wanted to come back to him, which was the one thing he did not want. Unwittingly, his hand rattled the door-latch.

"Don't run away," she laughed. "I won't bite you."

"I am not running away," he replied with child-like defiance, at the same time pulling on his mittens. "I'm only going to get some water."

He gathered the empty pails and cooking pots together and opened the door. He looked back at her.

"Don't forget you're to tell Mr.—er—Haythorne who I am."

Messner broke the skin that had formed on the water-hole within the hour, and filled his pails. But he did not return immediately to the cabin. Leaving the pails standing in the trail, he walked up and down, rapidly, to keep from freezing, for the frost bit into the flesh like fire. His beard was white with his frozen breath when the perplexed and frowning brows relaxed and decision came into his face. He had made up his mind to his course of action, and his frigid lips and cheeks crackled into a chuckle over it. The pails were already skinned over with young ice when he picked them up and made for the cabin.

When he entered he found the other man waiting, standing near the stove, a certain stiff awkwardness and indecision in his manner. Messner set down his water-pails.

"Glad to meet you, Graham Womble," he said in conventional tones, as though acknowledging an introduction.

Messner did not offer his hand. Womble stirred uneasily, feeling for the other the hatred one is prone to feel for one he has wronged.

"And so you're the chap," Messner said in marvelling accents. "Well, well. You see, I really am glad to meet you. I have been—er—curious to know what Theresa found in you—where, I may say, the attraction lay. Well, well."

And he looked the other up and down as a man would look a horse up and down.

"I know how you must feel about me," Womble began.

"Don't mention it," Messner broke in with exaggerated cordiality of voice and manner. "Never mind that. What I want to know is how do you find her? Up to expectations? Has she worn well? Life been all a happy dream ever since?"

"Don't be silly," Theresa interjected.

"I can't help being natural," Messner complained.

"You can be expedient at the same time, and practical," Womble said sharply. "What we want to know is what are you going to do?"

Messner made a well-feigned gesture of helplessness. "I really don't know. It is one of those impossible situations against which there can be no provision."

"All three of us cannot remain the night in this cabin."

Messner nodded affirmation.

"Then somebody must get out."

"That also is incontrovertible," Messner agreed. "When three bodies cannot occupy the same space at the same time, one must get out."

"And you're that one," Womble announced grimly. "It's a ten-mile pull to the next camp, but you can make it all right."

"And that's the first flaw in your reasoning," the other objected. "Why, necessarily, should I be the one to get out? I found this cabin first."

"But Tess can't get out," Womble explained. "Her lungs are already slightly chilled."

"I agree with you. She can't venture ten miles of frost. By all means she must remain."

"Then it is as I said," Womble announced with finality.

Messner cleared his throat. "Your lungs are all right, aren't they?"

"Yes, but what of it?"

Again the other cleared his throat and spoke with painstaking and judicial slowness. "Why, I may say, nothing of it, except, ah, according to your own reasoning, there is nothing to prevent your getting out, hitting the frost, so to speak, for a matter of ten miles. You can make it all right."

Womble looked with quick suspicion at Theresa and caught in her eyes a glint of pleased surprise.

"Well?" he demanded of her.

She hesitated, and a surge of anger darkened his face. He turned upon Messner.

"Enough of this. You can't stop here."

"Yes, I can."

"I won't let you." Womble squared his shoulders. "I'm running things."

"I'll stay anyway," the other persisted.

"I'll put you out."

"I'll come back."

Womble stopped a moment to steady his voice and control himself. Then he spoke slowly, in a low, tense voice.

"Look here, Messner, if you refuse to get out, I'll thrash you. This isn't California. I'll beat you to a jelly with my two fists."

Messner shrugged his shoulders. "If you do, I'll call a miners' meeting and see you strung up to the nearest tree. As you said, this is not California. They're a simple folk, these miners, and all I'll have to do will be to show them the marks of the beating, tell them the truth about you, and present my claim for my wife."

The woman attempted to speak, but Womble turned upon her fiercely.

"You keep out of this," he cried.

In marked contrast was Messner's "Please don't intrude, Theresa."

What of her anger and pent feelings, her lungs were irritated into the dry, hacking cough, and with blood-suffused face and one hand clenched against her chest, she waited for the paroxysm to pass.

Womble looked gloomily at her, noting her cough.

"Something must be done," he said. "Yet her lungs can't stand the exposure. She can't travel till the temperature rises. And I'm not going to give her up."

Messner hemmed, cleared his throat, and hemmed again, semi-apologetically, and said, "I need some money."

Contempt showed instantly in Womble's face. At last, beneath him in vileness, had the other sunk himself.

"You've got a fat sack of dust," Messner went on. "I saw you unload it from the sled."

"How much do you want?" Womble demanded, with a contempt in his voice equal to that in his face.

"I made an estimate of the sack, and I—ah—should say it weighed about twenty pounds. What do you say we call it four thousand?"

"But it's all I've got, man!" Womble cried out.

"You've got her," the other said soothingly. "She must be worth it. Think what I'm giving up. Surely it is a reasonable price."

"All right." Womble rushed across the floor to the gold-sack. "Can't put this deal through too quick for me, you—you little worm!"

"Now, there you err," was the smiling rejoinder. "As a matter of ethics isn't the man who gives a bribe as bad as the man who takes a bribe? The receiver is as bad as the thief, you know; and you needn't console yourself with any fictitious moral superiority concerning this little deal."

"To hell with your ethics!" the other burst out. "Come here and watch the weighing of this dust. I might cheat you."

And the woman, leaning against the bunk, raging and impotent, watched herself weighed out in yellow dust and nuggets in the scales erected on the grub-box. The scales were small, making necessary many weighings, and Messner with precise care verified each weighing.

"There's too much silver in it," he remarked as he tied up the gold-sack. "I don't think it will run quite sixteen to the ounce. You got a trifle the better of me, Womble."

He handled the sack lovingly, and with due appreciation of its preciousness carried it out to his sled.

Returning, he gathered his pots and pans together, packed his grub-box, and rolled up his bed. When the sled was lashed and the complaining dogs harnessed, he returned into the cabin for his mittens.

"Good-by, Tess," he said, standing at the open door.

She turned on him, struggling for speech but too frantic to word the passion that burned in her.

"Good-by, Tess," he repeated gently.

"Beast!" she managed to articulate.

She turned and tottered to the bunk, flinging herself face down upon it, sobbing: "You beasts! You beasts!"

John Messner closed the door softly behind him, and, as he started the dogs, looked back at the cabin with a great relief in his face. At the bottom of the bank, beside the water-hole, he halted the sled. He worked the sack of gold out between the lashings and carried it to the water-hole. Already a new skin of ice had formed. This he broke with his fist. Untying the knotted mouth with his teeth, he emptied the contents of the sack into the water. The river was shallow at that point, and two feet beneath the surface he could see the bottom dull-yellow in the fading light. At the sight of it, he spat into the hole.

He started the dogs along the Yukon trail. Whining spiritlessly, they were reluctant to work. Clinging to the gee-pole with his right band and with his left rubbing cheeks and nose, he stumbled over the rope as the dogs swung on a bend.

"Mush-on, you poor, sore-footed brutes!" he cried. "That's it, mush-on!"

THE WHITE MAN'S WAY

"To cook by your fire and to sleep under your roof for the night," I had announced on entering old Ebbits's cabin; and he had looked at me blear-eyed and vacuous, while Zilla had favored me with a sour face and a contemptuous grunt. Zilla was his wife, and no more bitter-tongued, implacable old squaw dwelt on the Yukon. Nor would I have stopped there had my dogs been less tired or had the rest of the village been inhabited. But this cabin alone had I found occupied, and in this cabin, perforce, I took my shelter.

Old Ebbits now and again pulled his tangled wits together, and hints and sparkles of intelligence came and went in his eyes. Several times during the preparation of my supper he even essayed hospitable inquiries about my health, the condition and number of my dogs, and the distance I had travelled that day. And each time Zilla had looked sourer than ever and grunted more contemptuously.

Yet I confess that there was no particular call for cheerfulness on their part. There they crouched by the fire, the pair of them, at the end of their days, old and withered and helpless, racked by rheumatism, bitten by hunger, and tantalized by the frying-odors of my abundance of meat. They rocked back and forth in a slow and hopeless way, and regularly, once every five minutes, Ebbits emitted a low groan. It was not so much a groan of pain, as of pain-weariness. He was oppressed by the weight and the torment of this thing called life, and still more was he oppressed by the fear of death. His was that eternal tragedy of the aged, with whom the joy of life has departed and the instinct for death has not come.

When my moose-meat spluttered rowdily in the frying-pan, I noticed old Ebbits's nostrils twitch and distend as he caught the food-scent. He ceased rocking for a space and forgot to groan, while a look of intelligence seemed to come into his face.

Zilla, on the other hand, rocked more rapidly, and for the first time, in sharp little yelps, voiced her pain. It came to me that their behavior was like that of hungry dogs, and in the fitness of things I should not have been astonished had Zilla suddenly developed a tail and thumped it on the floor in right doggish fashion. Ebbits drooled a little and stopped his rocking very frequently to lean forward and thrust his tremulous nose nearer to the source of gustatory excitement.

When I passed them each a plate of the fried meat, they ate greedily, making loud mouth-noises—champings of worn teeth and sucking intakes of the breath, accompanied by a continuous spluttering and mumbling. After that, when I gave them each a mug of scalding tea, the noises ceased. Easement and content came into their faces. Zilla relaxed her sour mouth long enough to sigh her satisfaction. Neither rocked any more, and they seemed to have fallen into placid meditation. Then a dampness came into Ebbits's eyes, and I knew that the sorrow of self-pity was his. The search required to find their pipes told plainly that they had been without tobacco a long time, and the old man's eagerness for the narcotic rendered him helpless, so that I was compelled to light his pipe for him.

"Why are you all alone in the village?" I asked. "Is everybody dead? Has there been a great sickness? Are you alone left of the living?"

Old Ebbits shook his head, saying: "Nay, there has been no great sickness. The village has gone away to hunt meat. We be too old, our legs are not strong, nor can our backs carry the burdens of camp and trail. Wherefore we remain here and wonder when the young men will return with meat."

"What if the young men do return with meat?" Zilla demanded harshly.

"They may return with much meat," he quavered hopefully.

"Even so, with much meat," she continued, more harshly than before. "But of what worth to you and me? A few bones to gnaw in our toothless old age. But the back-fat, the kidneys, and the tongues—these shall go into other mouths than thine and mine, old man."

Ebbits nodded his head and wept silently.

323

"There be no one to hunt meat for us," she cried, turning fiercely upon me.

There was accusation in her manner, and I shrugged my shoulders in token that I was not guilty of the unknown crime imputed to me.

"Know, O White Man, that it is because of thy kind, because of all white men, that my man and I have no meat in our old age and sit without tobacco in the cold."

"Nay," Ebbits said gravely, with a stricter sense of justice. "Wrong has been done us, it be true; but the white men did not mean the wrong."

"Where be Moklan?" she demanded. "Where be thy strong son, Moklan, and the fish he was ever willing to bring that you might eat?"

The old man shook his head.

"And where be Bidarshik, thy strong son? Ever was he a mighty hunter, and ever did he bring thee the good back-fat and the sweet dried tongues of the moose and the caribou. I see no back-fat and no sweet dried tongues. Your stomach is full with emptiness through the days, and it is for a man of a very miserable and lying people to give you to eat."

"Nay," old Ebbits interposed in kindliness, "the white man's is not a lying people. The white man speaks true. Always does the white man speak true." He paused, casting about him for words wherewith to temper the severity of what he was about to say. "But the white man speaks true in different ways. To-day he speaks true one way, to-morrow he speaks true another way, and there is no understanding him nor his way."

"To-day speak true one way, to-morrow speak true another way, which is to lie," was Zilla's dictum.

"There is no understanding the white man," Ebbits went on doggedly.

The meat, and the tea, and the tobacco seemed to have brought him back to life, and he gripped tighter hold of the idea behind his age-bleared eyes. He straightened up somewhat. His voice lost its querulous and whimpering note, and became strong and positive. He turned upon me with dignity, and addressed me as equal addresses equal.

"The white man's eyes are not shut," he began. "The white man sees all things, and thinks greatly, and is very wise. But the white man of one day is not the white man of next day, and there is no understanding him. He does not do things always in the same way. And what way his next way is to be, one cannot know. Always does the Indian do the one thing in the one way. Always does the moose come down from the high mountains when the winter is here. Always does the salmon come in the spring when the ice has gone out of the river. Always does everything do all things in the same way, and the Indian knows and understands. But the white man does not do all things in the same way, and the Indian does not know nor understand.

"Tobacco be very good. It be food to the hungry man. It makes the strong man stronger, and the angry man to forget that he is angry. Also is tobacco of value. It is of very great value. The Indian gives one large salmon for one leaf of tobacco, and he chews the tobacco for a long time. It is the juice of the tobacco that is good. When it runs down his throat it makes him feel good inside. But the white man! When his mouth is full with the juice, what does he do? That juice, that juice of great value, he spits it out in the snow and it is lost. Does the white man like tobacco? I do not know. But if he likes tobacco, why does he spit out its value and lose it in the snow? It is a great foolishness and without understanding."

He ceased, puffed at the pipe, found that it was out, and passed it over to Zilla, who took the sneer at the white man off her lips in order to pucker them about the pipe-stem. Ebbits seemed sinking back into his senility with the tale untold, and I demanded:

"What of thy sons, Moklan and Bidarshik? And why is it that you and your old woman are without meat at the end of your years?"

He roused himself as from sleep, and straightened up with an effort.

"It is not good to steal," he said. "When the dog takes your meat you beat the dog with a club. Such is the law. It is the law the man gave to the dog, and the dog must live to the law, else will it suffer the pain of the club. When man takes your meat, or your canoe, or your wife, you kill that man. That is the law, and it is a good law. It is not good to steal, wherefore it is the law that the man who steals must die. Whoso breaks the law must suffer hurt. It is a great hurt to die."

"But if you kill the man, why do you not kill the dog?" I asked.

Old Ebbits looked at me in childlike wonder, while Zilla sneered openly at the absurdity of my question.

"It is the way of the white man," Ebbits mumbled with an air of resignation.

"It is the foolishness of the white man," snapped Zilla.

"Then let old Ebbits teach the white man wisdom," I said softly.

"The dog is not killed, because it must pull the sled of the man. No man pulls another man's sled, wherefore the man is killed."

"Oh," I murmured.

"That is the law," old Ebbits went on. "Now listen, O White Man, and I will tell you of a great foolishness. There is an Indian. His name is Mobits. From white man he steals two pounds of flour. What does the white man do? Does he beat Mobits? No. Does he kill Mobits? No. What does he do to Mobits? I will tell you, O White Man. He has a house. He puts Mobits in that house. The roof is good. The walls are thick. He makes a fire that Mobits may be warm. He gives Mobits plenty grub to eat. It is good grub. Never in his all days does Mobits eat so good grub. There is bacon, and bread, and beans without end. Mobits have very good time.

"There is a big lock on door so that Mobits does not run away. This also is a great foolishness. Mobits will not run away. All the time is there plenty grub in that place, and warm blankets, and a big fire. Very foolish to run away. Mobits is not foolish. Three months Mobits stop in that place. He steal two pounds of flour. For that, white man take plenty good care of him. Mobits eat many pounds of flour, many pounds of sugar, of bacon, of beans without end. Also, Mobits drink much tea. After three months white man open door and tell Mobits he must go. Mobits does not want to go. He is like dog that is fed long time in one place. He want to stay in that place, and the white man must drive Mobits away. So Mobits come back to this village, and he is very fat. That is the white man's way, and there is no understanding it. It is a foolishness, a great foolishness."

"But thy sons?" I insisted. "Thy very strong sons and thine old-age hunger?"

"There was Moklan," Ebbits began.

"A strong man," interrupted the mother. "He could dip paddle all of a day and night and never stop for the need of rest. He was wise in the way of the salmon and in the way of the water. He was very wise."

"There was Moklan," Ebbits repeated, ignoring the interruption. "In the spring, he went down the Yukon with the young men to trade at Cambell Fort. There is a post there, filled with the goods of the white man, and a trader whose name is Jones. Likewise is there a white man's medicine man, what you call missionary. Also is there bad water at Cambell Fort, where the Yukon goes slim like a maiden, and the water is fast, and the currents rush this way and that and come together, and there are whirls and sucks, and always are the currents changing and the face of the water changing, so at any two times it is never the same. Moklan is my son, wherefore he is brave man—"

"Was not my father brave man?" Zilla demanded.

"Thy father was brave man," Ebbits acknowledged, with the air of one who will keep peace in the house at any cost. "Moklan is thy son and mine, wherefore he is brave. Mayhap, because of thy very brave father, Moklan is too brave. It is like when too much water is put in the pot it spills over. So too much bravery is put into Moklan, and the bravery spills over.

"The young men are much afraid of the bad water at Cambell Fort. But Moklan is not afraid. He laughs strong, Ho! ho! and he goes forth into the bad water. But where the currents come together the canoe is turned over. A whirl takes Moklan by the legs, and he goes around and around, and down and down, and is seen no more."

"Ai! ai!" wailed Zilla. "Crafty and wise was he, and my first-born!"

"I am the father of Moklan," Ebbits said, having patiently given the woman space for her noise. "I get into canoe and journey down to Cambell Fort to collect the debt!"

"Debt!" interrupted. "What debt?"

"The debt of Jones, who is chief trader," came the answer. "Such is the law of travel in a strange country."

I shook my head in token of my ignorance, and Ebbits looked compassion at me, while Zilla snorted her customary contempt.

"Look you, O White Man," he said. "In thy camp is a dog that bites. When the dog bites a man, you give that man a present because you are sorry and because it is thy dog. You make payment. Is it not so? Also, if you have in thy country bad hunting, or bad water, you must make payment. It is just. It is the law. Did not my father's brother go over into the Tanana Country and get killed by a bear? And did not the Tanana tribe pay my father many blankets and fine furs? It was just. It was bad hunting, and the Tanana people made payment for the bad hunting.

"So I, Ebbits, journeyed down to Cambell Fort to collect the debt. Jones, who is chief trader, looked at me, and he laughed. He made great laughter, and would not give payment. I went to the medicine-man, what you call missionary, and had large talk about the bad water and the payment that should be mine. And the missionary made talk about other things. He talk about where Moklan has gone, now he is dead. There be large fires in that place, and if missionary make true talk, I know that Moklan will be cold no more. Also the missionary talk about where I shall go when I am dead. And he say bad things. He say that I am blind. Which is a lie. He say that I am in great darkness. Which is a lie. And I say that the day come and the night come for everybody just the same, and that in my village it is no more dark than at Cambell Fort. Also, I say that darkness and light and where we go when we die be different things from the matter of payment of just debt for bad water. Then the missionary make large anger, and call me bad names of darkness, and tell me to go away. And so I come back from Cambell Fort, and no payment has been made, and Moklan is dead, and in my old age I am without fish and meat."

"Because of the white man," said Zilla.

"Because of the white man," Ebbits concurred. "And other things because of the white man. There was Bidarshik. One way did the white man deal with him; and yet another way for the same thing did the white man deal with Yamikan. And first must I tell you of Yamikan, who was a young man of this village and who chanced to kill a white man. It is not good to kill a man of another people. Always is there great trouble. It was not the fault of Yamikan that he killed the white man. Yamikan spoke always soft words and ran away from wrath as a dog from a stick. But this white man drank much whiskey, and in the night-time came to Yamikan's house and made much fight. Yamikan cannot run away, and the white man tries to kill him. Yamikan does not like to die, so he kills the white man.

"Then is all the village in great trouble. We are much afraid that we must make large payment to the white man's people, and we hide our blankets, and our furs, and all our wealth, so that it will seem that we are poor people and can make only small payment. After long time white men come. They are soldier white men, and they take Yamikan away with them. His mother make great noise and throw ashes in her hair, for she knows Yamikan is dead. And all the village knows that Yamikan is dead, and is glad that no payment is asked.

"That is in the spring when the ice has gone out of the river. One year go by, two years go by. It is spring-time again, and the ice has gone out of the river. And then Yamikan, who is dead, comes back to us, and he is not dead, but very fat, and we know that he has slept warm and had plenty grub to eat. He has much fine clothes and is all the same white man, and he has gathered large wisdom so that he is very quick head man in the village.

"And he has strange things to tell of the way of the white man, for he has seen much of the white man and done a great travel into the white man's country. First place, soldier white men take him down the river long way.

All the way do they take him down the river to the end, where it runs into a lake which is larger than all the land and large as the sky. I do not know the Yukon is so big river, but Yamikan has seen with his own eyes. I do not think there is a lake larger than all the land and large as the sky, but Yamikan has seen. Also, he has told me that the waters of this lake be salt, which is a strange thing and beyond understanding.

"But the White Man knows all these marvels for himself, so I shall not weary him with the telling of them. Only will I tell him what happened to Yamikan. The white man give Yamikan much fine grub. All the time does Yamikan eat, and all the time is there plenty more grub. The white man lives under the sun, so said Yamikan, where there be much warmth, and animals have only hair and no fur, and the green things grow large and strong and become flour, and beans, and potatoes. And under the sun there is never famine. Always is there plenty grub. I do not know. Yamikan has said.

"And here is a strange thing that befell Yamikan. Never did the white man hurt him. Only did they give him warm bed at night and plenty fine grub. They take him across the salt lake which is big as the sky. He is on white man's fire-boat, what you call steamboat, only he is on boat maybe twenty times bigger than steamboat on Yukon. Also, it is made of iron, this boat, and yet does it not sink. This I do not understand, but Yamikan has said, 'I have journeyed far on the iron boat; behold! I am still alive.' It is a white man's soldier-boat with many soldier men upon it.

"After many sleeps of travel, a long, long time, Yamikan comes to a land where there is no snow. I cannot believe this. It is not in the nature of things that when winter comes there shall be no snow. But Yamikan has seen. Also have I asked the white men, and they have said yes, there is no snow in that country. But I cannot believe, and now I ask you if snow never come in that country. Also, I would hear the name of that country. I have heard the name before, but I would hear it again, if it be the same—thus will I know if I have heard lies or true talk."

Old Ebbits regarded me with a wistful face. He would have the truth at any cost, though it was his desire to retain his faith in the marvel he had never seen.

"Yes," I answered, "it is true talk that you have heard. There is no snow in that country, and its name is California."

"Cal-ee-forn-ee-yeh," he mumbled twice and thrice, listening intently to the sound of the syllables as they fell from his lips. He nodded his head in confirmation. "Yes, it is the same country of which Yamikan made talk."

I recognized the adventure of Yamikan as one likely to occur in the early days when Alaska first passed into the possession of the United States. Such a murder case, occurring before the instalment of territorial law and officials, might well have been taken down to the United States for trial before a Federal court.

"When Yamikan is in this country where there is no snow," old Ebbits continued, "he is taken to large house where many men make much talk. Long time men talk. Also many questions do they ask Yamikan. By and by they tell Yamikan he have no more trouble. Yamikan does not understand, for never has he had any trouble. All the time have they given him warm place to sleep and plenty grub.

"But after that they give him much better grub, and they give him money, and they take him many places in white man's country, and he see many strange things which are beyond the understanding of Ebbits, who is an old man and has not journeyed far. After two years, Yamikan comes back to this village, and he is head man, and very wise until he dies.

"But before he dies, many times does he sit by my fire and make talk of the strange things he has seen. And Bidarshik, who is my son, sits by the fire and listens; and his eyes are very wide and large because of the things he hears. One night, after Yamikan has gone home, Bidarshik stands up, so, very tall, and he strikes his chest with his fist, and says, 'When I am a man, I shall journey in far places, even to the land where there is no snow, and see things for myself.'"

"Always did Bidarshik journey in far places," Zilla interrupted proudly.

"It be true," Ebbits assented gravely. "And always did he return to sit by the fire and hunger for yet other and unknown far places."

"And always did he remember the salt lake as big as the sky and the country under the sun where there is no snow," quoth Zilla.

"And always did he say, 'When I have the full strength of a man, I will go and see for myself if the talk of Yamikan be true talk,'" said Ebbits.

"But there was no way to go to the white man's country," said Zilla.

"Did he not go down to the salt lake that is big as the sky?" Ebbits demanded.

"And there was no way for him across the salt lake," said Zilla.

"Save in the white man's fire-boat which is of iron and is bigger than twenty steamboats on the Yukon," said Ebbits. He scowled at Zilla, whose withered lips were again writhing into speech, and compelled her to silence. "But the white man would not let him cross the salt lake in the fire-boat, and he returned to sit by the fire and hunger for the country under the sun where there is no snow.'"

"Yet on the salt lake had he seen the fire-boat of iron that did not sink," cried out Zilla the irrepressible.

"Ay," said Ebbits, "and he saw that Yamikan had made true talk of the things he had seen. But there was no way for Bidarshik to journey to the white man's land under the sun, and he grew sick and weary like an old man and moved not away from the fire. No longer did he go forth to kill meat—"

"And no longer did he eat the meat placed before him," Zilla broke in. "He would shake his head and say, 'Only do I care to eat the grub of the white man and grow fat after the manner of Yamikan.'"

"And he did not eat the meat," Ebbits went on. "And the sickness of Bidarshik grew into a great sickness until I thought he would die. It was not a sickness of the body, but of the head. It was a sickness of desire. I, Ebbits, who am his father, make a great think. I have no more sons and I do not want Bidarshik to die. It is a head-sickness, and there is but one way to make it well. Bidarshik must journey across the lake as large as the sky to the land where there is no snow, else will he die. I make a very great think, and then I see the way for Bidarshik to go.

"So, one night when he sits by the fire, very sick, his head hanging down, I say, 'My son, I have learned the way for you to go to the white man's land.' He looks at me, and his face is glad. 'Go,' I say, 'even as Yamikan went.' But Bidarshik is sick and does not understand. 'Go forth,' I say, 'and find a white man, and, even as Yamikan, do you kill that white man. Then will the soldier white men come and get you, and even as they took Yamikan will they take you across the salt lake to the white man's land. And then, even as Yamikan, will you return very fat, your eyes full of the things you have seen, your head filled with wisdom.'

"And Bidarshik stands up very quick, and his hand is reaching out for his gun. 'Where do you go?' I ask. 'To kill the white man,' he says. And I see that my words have been good in the ears of Bidarshik and that he will grow well again. Also do I know that my words have been wise.

"There is a white man come to this village. He does not seek after gold in the ground, nor after furs in the forest. All the time does he seek after bugs and flies. He does not eat the bugs and flies, then why does he seek after them? I do not know. Only do I know that he is a funny white man. Also does he seek after the eggs of birds. He does not eat the eggs. All that is inside he takes out, and only does he keep the shell. Eggshell is not good to eat. Nor does he eat the eggshells, but puts them away in soft boxes where they will not break. He catch many small birds. But he does not eat the birds. He takes only the skins and puts them away in boxes. Also does he like bones. Bones are not good to eat. And this strange white man likes best the bones of long time ago which he digs out of the ground.

"But he is not a fierce white man, and I know he will die very easy; so I say to Bidarshik, 'My son, there is the white man for you to kill.' And Bidarshik says that my words be wise. So he goes to a place he knows where are many bones in the ground. He digs up very many of these bones and brings them to the strange white man's camp. The white man is made very glad. His face shines like the sun, and he smiles with much gladness as he looks at the bones. He bends his head over, so, to look well at the bones, and then Bidarshik strikes him hard on the head, with axe, once, so, and the strange white man kicks and is dead.

"'Now,' I say to Bidarshik, 'will the white soldier men come and take you away to the land under the sun, where you will eat much and grow fat.' Bidarshik is happy. Already has his sickness gone from him, and he sits by the fire and waits for the coming of the white soldier men.

"How was I to know the way of the white man is never twice the same?" the old man demanded, whirling upon me fiercely. "How was I to know that what the white man does yesterday he will not do to-day, and that what he does to-day he will not do to-morrow?" Ebbits shook his head sadly. "There is no understanding the white man. Yesterday he takes Yamikan to the land under the sun and makes him fat with much grub. To-day he takes Bidarshik and—what does he do with Bidarshik? Let me tell you what he does with Bidarshik.

"I, Ebbits, his father, will tell you. He takes Bidarshik to Cambell Fort, and he ties a rope around his neck, so, and, when his feet are no more on the ground, he dies."

"Ai! ai!" wailed Zilla. "And never does he cross the lake large as the sky, nor see the land under the sun where there is no snow."

"Wherefore," old Ebbits said with grave dignity, "there be no one to hunt meat for me in my old age, and I sit hungry by my fire and tell my story to the White Man who has given me grub, and strong tea, and tobacco for my pipe."

"Because of the lying and very miserable white people," Zilla proclaimed shrilly.

"Nay," answered the old man with gentle positiveness. "Because of the way of the white man, which is without understanding and never twice the same."

THE STORY OF KEESH

Keesh lived long ago on the rim of the polar sea, was head man of his village through many and prosperous years, and died full of honors with his name on the lips of men. So long ago did he live that only the old men remember his name, his name and the tale, which they got from the old men before them, and which the old men to come will tell to their children and their children's children down to the end of time. And the winter darkness, when the north gales make their long sweep across the ice-pack, and the air is filled with flying white, and no man may venture forth, is the chosen time for the telling of how Keesh, from the poorest *igloo* in the village, rose to power and place over them all.

He was a bright boy, so the tale runs, healthy and strong, and he had seen thirteen suns, in their way of reckoning time. For each winter the sun leaves the land in darkness, and the next year a new sun returns so that they may be warm again and look upon one another's faces. The father of Keesh had been a very brave man, but he had met his death in a time of famine, when he sought to save the lives of his people by taking the life of a great polar bear. In his eagerness he came to close grapples with the bear, and his bones were crushed; but the bear had much meat on him and the people were saved. Keesh was his only son, and after that Keesh lived alone with his mother. But the people are prone to forget, and they forgot the deed of his father; and he being but a boy, and his mother only a woman, they, too, were swiftly forgotten, and ere long came to live in the meanest of all the *igloo*s.

It was at a council, one night, in the big *igloo* of Klosh-Kwan, the chief, that Keesh showed the blood that ran in his veins and the manhood that stiffened his back. With the dignity of an elder, he rose to his feet, and waited for silence amid the babble of voices.

"It is true that meat be apportioned me and mine," he said. "But it is ofttimes old and tough, this meat, and, moreover, it has an unusual quantity of bones."

The hunters, grizzled and gray, and lusty and young, were aghast. The like had never been known before. A child, that talked like a grown man, and said harsh things to their very faces!

But steadily and with seriousness, Keesh went on. "For that I know my father, Bok, was a great hunter, I speak these words. It is said that Bok brought home more meat than any of the two best hunters, that with his own hands he attended to the division of it, that with his own eyes he saw to it that the least old woman and the last old man received fair share."

"Na! Na!" the men cried. "Put the child out!" "Send him off to bed!" "He is no man that he should talk to men and graybeards!"

He waited calmly till the uproar died down.

"Thou hast a wife, Ugh-Gluk," he said, "and for her dost thou speak. And thou, too, Massuk, a mother also, and for them dost thou speak. My mother has no one, save me; wherefore I speak. As I say, though Bok be dead because he hunted over-keenly, it is just that I, who am his son, and that Ikeega, who is my mother and was his wife, should have meat in plenty so long as there be meat in plenty in the tribe. I, Keesh, the son of Bok, have spoken."

He sat down, his ears keenly alert to the flood of protest and indignation his words had created.

"That a boy should speak in council!" old Ugh-Gluk was mumbling.

"Shall the babes in arms tell us men the things we shall do?" Massuk demanded in a loud voice. "Am I a man that I should be made a mock by every child that cries for meat?"

The anger boiled a white heat. They ordered him to bed, threatened that he should have no meat at all, and promised him sore beatings for his presumption. Keesh's eyes began to flash, and the blood to pound darkly under his skin. In the midst of the abuse he sprang to his feet.

"Hear me, ye men!" he cried. "Never shall I speak in the council again, never again till the men come to me and say, 'It is well, Keesh, that thou shouldst speak, it is well and it is our wish.' Take this now, ye men, for my last word. Bok, my father, was a great hunter. I, too, his son, shall go and hunt the meat that I eat. And be it known, now, that the division of that which I kill shall be fair. And no widow nor weak one shall cry in the night because there is no meat, when the strong men are groaning in great pain for that they have eaten overmuch. And in the days to come there shall be shame upon the strong men who have eaten overmuch. I, Keesh, have said it!"

Jeers and scornful laughter followed him out of the *igloo*, but his jaw was set and he went his way, looking neither to right nor left.

The next day he went forth along the shore-line where the ice and the land met together. Those who saw him go noted that he carried his bow, with a goodly supply of bone-barbed arrows, and that across his shoulder was his father's big hunting-spear. And there was laughter, and much talk, at the event. It was an unprecedented occurrence. Never did boys of his tender age go forth to hunt, much less to hunt alone. Also were there shaking of heads and prophetic mutterings, and the women looked pityingly at Ikeega, and her face was grave and sad.

"He will be back ere long," they said cheeringly.

"Let him go; it will teach him a lesson," the hunters said. "And he will come back shortly, and he will be meek and soft of speech in the days to follow."

But a day passed, and a second, and on the third a wild gale blew, and there was no Keesh. Ikeega tore her hair and put soot of the seal-oil on her face in token of her grief; and the women assailed the men with bitter words in that they had mistreated the boy and sent him to his death; and the men made no answer, preparing to go in search of the body when the storm abated.

Early next morning, however, Keesh strode into the village. But he came not shamefacedly. Across his shoulders he bore a burden of fresh-killed meat. And there was importance in his step and arrogance in his speech.

"Go, ye men, with the dogs and sledges, and take my trail for the better part of a day's travel," he said. "There is much meat on the ice—a she-bear and two half-grown cubs."

Ikeega was overcome with joy, but he received her demonstrations in manlike fashion, saying: "Come, Ikeega, let us eat. And after that I shall sleep, for I am weary."

And he passed into their *igloo* and ate profoundly, and after that slept for twenty running hours.

There was much doubt at first, much doubt and discussion. The killing of a polar bear is very dangerous, but thrice dangerous is it, and three times thrice, to kill a mother bear with her cubs. The men could not bring themselves to believe that the boy Keesh, single-handed, had accomplished so great a marvel. But the women spoke of the fresh-killed meat he had brought on his back, and this was an overwhelming argument against their unbelief. So they finally departed, grumbling greatly that in all probability, if the thing were so, he had neglected to cut up the carcasses. Now in the north it is very necessary that this should be done as soon as a kill is made. If not, the meat freezes so solidly as to turn the edge of the sharpest knife, and a three-hundred-pound bear, frozen stiff, is no easy thing to put upon a sled and haul over the rough ice. But arrived at the spot, they found not only the kill, which they had doubted, but that Keesh had quartered the beasts in true hunter fashion, and removed the entrails.

Thus began the mystery of Keesh, a mystery that deepened and deepened with the passing of the days. His very next trip he killed a young bear, nearly full-grown, and on the trip following, a large male bear and his mate. He was ordinarily gone from three to four days, though it was nothing unusual for him to stay away a week at a time on the ice-field. Always he declined company on these expeditions, and the people marvelled. "How does he do it?" they demanded of one another. "Never does he take a dog with him, and dogs are of such great help, too."

"Why dost thou hunt only bear?" Klosh-Kwan once ventured to ask him.

And Keesh made fitting answer. "It is well known that there is more meat on the bear," he said.

But there was also talk of witchcraft in the village. "He hunts with evil spirits," some of the people contended, "wherefore his hunting is rewarded. How else can it be, save that he hunts with evil spirits?"

"Mayhap they be not evil, but good, these spirits," others said. "It is known that his father was a mighty hunter. May not his father hunt with him so that he may attain excellence and patience and understanding? Who knows?"

None the less, his success continued, and the less skilful hunters were often kept busy hauling in his meat. And in the division of it he was just. As his father had done before him, he saw to it that the least old woman and the last old man received a fair portion, keeping no more for himself than his needs required. And because of this, and of his merit as a hunter, he was looked upon with respect, and even awe; and there was talk of making him chief after old Klosh-Kwan. Because of the things he had done, they looked for him to appear again in the council, but he never came, and they were ashamed to ask.

"I am minded to build me an *igloo*," he said one day to Klosh-Kwan and a number of the hunters. "It shall be a large *igloo*, wherein Ikeega and I can dwell in comfort."

"Ay," they nodded gravely.

"But I have no time. My business is hunting, and it takes all my time. So it is but just that the men and women of the village who eat my meat should build me my *igloo*."

And the *igloo* was built accordingly, on a generous scale which exceeded even the dwelling of Klosh-Kwan. Keesh and his mother moved into it, and it was the first prosperity she had enjoyed since the death of Bok. Nor was material prosperity alone hers, for, because of her wonderful son and the position he had given her, she came to be looked upon as the first woman in all the village; and the women were given to visiting her, to asking her advice, and to quoting her wisdom when arguments arose among themselves or with the men.

But it was the mystery of Keesh's marvellous hunting that took chief place in all their minds. And one day Ugh-Gluk taxed him with witchcraft to his face.

"It is charged," Ugh-Gluk said ominously, "that thou dealest with evil spirits, wherefore thy hunting is rewarded."

"Is not the meat good?" Keesh made answer. "Has one in the village yet to fall sick from the eating of it? How dost thou know that witchcraft be concerned? Or dost thou guess, in the dark, merely because of the envy that consumes thee?"

And Ugh-Gluk withdrew discomfited, the women laughing at him as he walked away. But in the council one night, after long deliberation, it was determined to put spies on his track when he went forth to hunt, so that his methods might be learned. So, on his next trip, Bim and Bawn, two young men, and of hunters the craftiest, followed after him, taking care not to be seen. After five days they returned, their eyes bulging and their tongues a-tremble to tell what they had seen. The council was hastily called in Klosh-Kwan's dwelling, and Bim took up the tale.

"Brothers! As commanded, we journeyed on the trail of Keesh, and cunningly we journeyed, so that he might not know. And midway of the first day he picked up with a great he-bear. It was a very great bear."

"None greater," Bawn corroborated, and went on himself. "Yet was the bear not inclined to fight, for he turned away and made off slowly over the ice. This we saw from the rocks of the shore, and the bear came toward us, and after him came Keesh, very much unafraid. And he shouted harsh words after the bear, and waved his arms about, and made much noise. Then did the bear grow angry, and rise up on his hind legs, and growl. But Keesh walked right up to the bear."

"Ay," Bim continued the story. "Right up to the bear Keesh walked. And the bear took after him, and Keesh ran away. But as he ran he dropped a little round ball on the ice. And the bear stopped and smelled of it, then swallowed it up. And Keesh continued to run away and drop little round balls, and the bear continued to swallow them up."

Exclamations and cries of doubt were being made, and Ugh-Gluk expressed open unbelief.

"With our own eyes we saw it," Bim affirmed.

And Bawn—"Ay, with our own eyes. And this continued until the bear stood suddenly upright and cried aloud in pain, and thrashed his fore paws madly about. And Keesh continued to make off over the ice to a safe distance. But the bear gave him no notice, being occupied with the misfortune the little round balls had wrought within him."

"Ay, within him," Bim interrupted. "For he did claw at himself, and leap about over the ice like a playful puppy, save from the way he growled and squealed it was plain it was not play but pain. Never did I see such a sight!"

"Nay, never was such a sight seen," Bawn took up the strain. "And furthermore, it was such a large bear."

"Witchcraft," Ugh-Gluk suggested.

"I know not," Bawn replied. "I tell only of what my eyes beheld. And after a while the bear grew weak and tired, for he was very heavy and he had jumped about with exceeding violence, and he went off along the shore-ice, shaking his head slowly from side to side and sitting down ever and again to squeal and cry. And Keesh followed after the bear, and we followed after Keesh, and for that day and three days more we followed. The bear grew weak, and never ceased crying from his pain."

"It was a charm!" Ugh-Gluk exclaimed. "Surely it was a charm!"

"It may well be."

And Bim relieved Bawn. "The bear wandered, now this way and now that, doubling back and forth and crossing his trail in circles, so that at the end he was near where Keesh had first come upon him. By this time he was quite sick, the bear, and could crawl no farther, so Keesh came up close and speared him to death."

"And then?" Klosh-Kwan demanded.

"Then we left Keesh skinning the bear, and came running that the news of the killing might be told."

And in the afternoon of that day the women hauled in the meat of the bear while the men sat in council assembled. When Keesh arrived a messenger was sent to him, bidding him come to the council. But he sent reply, saying that he was hungry and tired; also that his *igloo* was large and comfortable and could hold many men.

And curiosity was so strong on the men that the whole council, Klosh-Kwan to the fore, rose up and went to the *igloo* of Keesh. He was eating, but he received them with respect and seated them according to their rank. Ikeega was proud and embarrassed by turns, but Keesh was quite composed.

Klosh-Kwan recited the information brought by Bim and Bawn, and at its close said in a stern voice: "So explanation is wanted, O Keesh, of thy manner of hunting. Is there witchcraft in it?"

Keesh looked up and smiled. "Nay, O Klosh-Kwan. It is not for a boy to know aught of witches, and of witches I know nothing. I have but devised a means whereby I may kill the ice-bear with ease, that is all. It be headcraft, not witchcraft."

"And may any man?"

"Any man."

There was a long silence. The men looked in one another's faces, and Keesh went on eating.

"And . . . and . . . and wilt thou tell us, O Keesh?" Klosh-Kwan finally asked in a tremulous voice.

"Yea, I will tell thee." Keesh finished sucking a marrow-bone and rose to his feet. "It is quite simple. Behold!"

He picked up a thin strip of whalebone and showed it to them. The ends were sharp as needle-points. The strip he coiled carefully, till it disappeared in his hand. Then, suddenly releasing it, it sprang straight again. He picked up a piece of blubber.

"So," he said, "one takes a small chunk of blubber, thus, and thus makes it hollow. Then into the hollow goes the whalebone, so, tightly coiled, and another piece of blubber is fitted over the whale-bone. After that it is put outside where it freezes into a little round ball. The bear swallows the little round ball, the blubber melts, the whalebone with its sharp ends stands out straight, the bear gets sick, and when the bear is very sick, why, you kill him with a spear. It is quite simple."

And Ugh-Gluk said "Oh!" and Klosh-Kwan said "Ah!" And each said something after his own manner, and all understood.

And this is the story of Keesh, who lived long ago on the rim of the polar sea. Because he exercised headcraft and not witchcraft, he rose from the meanest *igloo* to be head man of his village, and through all the years that he lived, it is related, his tribe was prosperous, and neither widow nor weak one cried aloud in the night because there was no meat.

THE UNEXPECTED

It is a simple matter to see the obvious, to do the expected. The tendency of the individual life is to be static rather than dynamic, and this tendency is made into a propulsion by civilization, where the obvious only is seen, and the unexpected rarely happens. When the unexpected does happen, however, and when it is of sufficiently grave import, the unfit perish. They do not see what is not obvious, are unable to do the unexpected, are incapable of adjusting their well-grooved lives to other and strange grooves. In short, when they come to the end of their own groove, they die.

On the other hand, there are those that make toward survival, the fit individuals who escape from the rule of the obvious and the expected and adjust their lives to no matter what strange grooves they may stray into, or into which they may be forced. Such an individual was Edith Whittlesey. She was born in a rural district of England, where life proceeds by rule of thumb and the unexpected is so very unexpected that when it happens it is looked upon as an immorality. She went into service early, and while yet a young woman, by rule-of-thumb progression, she became a lady's maid.

The effect of civilization is to impose human law upon environment until it becomes machine-like in its regularity. The objectionable is eliminated, the inevitable is foreseen. One is not even made wet by the rain nor cold by the frost; while death, instead of stalking about grewsome and accidental, becomes a prearranged pageant, moving along a well-oiled groove to the family vault, where the hinges are kept from rusting and the dust from the air is swept continually away.

Such was the environment of Edith Whittlesey. Nothing happened. It could scarcely be called a happening, when, at the age of twenty-five, she accompanied her mistress on a bit of travel to the United States. The groove merely changed its direction. It was still the same groove and well oiled. It was a groove that bridged the Atlantic with uneventfulness, so that the ship was not a ship in the midst of the sea, but a capacious, many-corridored hotel that moved swiftly and placidly, crushing the waves into submission with its colossal bulk until the sea was a mill-pond, monotonous with quietude. And at the other side the groove continued on over the land—a well-disposed, respectable groove that supplied hotels at every stopping-place, and hotels on wheels between the stopping-places.

In Chicago, while her mistress saw one side of social life, Edith Whittlesey saw another side; and when she left her lady's service and became Edith Nelson, she betrayed, perhaps faintly, her ability to grapple with the unexpected and to master it. Hans Nelson, immigrant, Swede by birth and carpenter by occupation, had in him that Teutonic unrest that drives the race ever westward on its great adventure. He was a large-muscled, stolid sort of a man, in whom little imagination was coupled with immense initiative, and who possessed, withal, loyalty and affection as sturdy as his own strength.

"When I have worked hard and saved me some money, I will go to Colorado," he had told Edith on the day after their wedding. A year later they were in Colorado, where Hans Nelson saw his first mining and caught the mining-fever himself. His prospecting led him through the Dakotas, Idaho, and eastern Oregon, and on into the mountains of British Columbia. In camp and on trail, Edith Nelson was always with him, sharing his luck, his hardship, and his toil. The short step of the house-reared woman she exchanged for the long stride of the mountaineer. She learned to look upon danger clear-eyed and with understanding, losing forever that panic fear which is bred of ignorance and which afflicts the city-reared, making them as silly as silly horses, so that they await fate in frozen horror instead of grappling with it, or stampede in blind self-destroying terror which clutters the way with their crushed carcasses.

Edith Nelson met the unexpected at every turn of the trail, and she trained her vision so that she saw in the landscape, not the obvious, but the concealed. She, who had never cooked in her life, learned to make bread without the mediation of hops, yeast, or baking-powder, and to bake bread, top and bottom, in a frying-pan before an open fire. And when the last cup of flour was gone and the last rind of bacon, she was able to rise to the occasion, and of moccasins and the softer-tanned bits of leather in the outfit to make a grub-stake substitute that somehow held a man's soul in his body and enabled him to stagger on. She learned to pack a horse as well as a man,—a task to break the heart and the pride of any city-dweller, and she knew how to throw the hitch best suited for any particular kind of pack. Also, she could build a fire of wet wood in a downpour of rain and not lose her temper. In short, in all its guises she mastered the unexpected. But the Great Unexpected was yet to come into her life and put its test upon her.

The gold-seeking tide was flooding northward into Alaska, and it was inevitable that Hans Nelson and his wife should be caught up by the stream and swept toward the Klondike. The fall of 1897 found them at Dyea, but without the money to carry an outfit across Chilcoot Pass and float it down to Dawson. So Hans Nelson worked at his trade that winter and helped rear the mushroom outfitting-town of Skaguay.

He was on the edge of things, and throughout the winter he heard all Alaska calling to him. Latuya Bay called loudest, so that the summer of 1898 found him and his wife threading the mazes of the broken coast-line in seventy-foot Siwash canoes. With them were Indians, also three other men. The Indians landed them and their supplies in a lonely bight of land a hundred miles or so beyond Latuya Bay, and returned to Skaguay; but the three other men remained, for they were members of the organized party. Each had put an equal share of capital into the outfitting, and the profits were to be divided equally. In that Edith Nelson undertook to cook for the outfit, a man's share was to be her portion.

First, spruce trees were cut down and a three-room cabin constructed. To keep this cabin was Edith Nelson's task. The task of the men was to search for gold, which they did; and to find gold, which they likewise did. It was not a startling find, merely a low-pay placer where long hours of severe toil earned each man between fifteen and twenty dollars a day. The brief Alaskan summer protracted itself beyond its usual length, and they took advantage of the opportunity, delaying their return to Skaguay to the last moment. And then it was too late. Arrangements had been made to accompany the several dozen local Indians on their fall trading trip down the coast. The Siwashes had waited on the white people until the eleventh hour, and then departed.

There was no course left the party but to wait for chance transportation. In the meantime the claim was cleaned up and firewood stocked in.

The Indian summer had dreamed on and on, and then, suddenly, with the sharpness of bugles, winter came. It came in a single night, and the miners awoke to howling wind, driving snow, and freezing water. Storm followed storm, and between the storms there was the silence, broken only by the boom of the surf on the desolate shore, where the salt spray rimmed the beach with frozen white.

All went well in the cabin. Their gold-dust had weighed up something like eight thousand dollars, and they could not but be contented. The men made snowshoes, hunted fresh meat for the larder, and in the long evenings played endless games of whist and pedro. Now that the mining had ceased, Edith Nelson turned over the fire-building and the dish-washing to the men, while she darned their socks and mended their clothes.

There was no grumbling, no bickering, nor petty quarrelling in the little cabin, and they often congratulated one another on the general happiness of the party. Hans Nelson was stolid and easy-going, while Edith had long before won his unbounded admiration by her capacity for getting on with people. Harkey, a long, lank Texan, was unusually friendly for one with a saturnine disposition, and, as long as his theory that gold grew was not challenged, was quite companionable. The fourth member of the party, Michael Dennin, contributed his Irish wit to the gayety of the cabin. He was a large, powerful man, prone to sudden rushes of anger over little things, and of unfailing good-humor under the stress and strain of big things. The fifth and last member, Dutchy, was the willing butt of the party. He even went out of his way to raise a laugh at his own expense in order to keep things cheerful. His deliberate aim in life seemed to be that of a maker of laughter. No serious quarrel had ever vexed the serenity of the party; and, now that each had sixteen hundred dollars to show for a short summer's work, there reigned the well-fed, contented spirit of prosperity.

And then the unexpected happened. They had just sat down to the breakfast table. Though it was already eight o'clock (late breakfasts had followed naturally upon cessation of the steady work at mining) a candle in the neck of a bottle lighted the meal. Edith and Hans sat at each end of the table. On one side, with their backs to the door, sat Harkey and Dutchy. The place on the other side was vacant. Dennin had not yet come in.

Hans Nelson looked at the empty chair, shook his head slowly, and, with a ponderous attempt at humor, said: "Always is he first at the grub. It is very strange. Maybe he is sick."

"Where is Michael?" Edith asked.

"Got up a little ahead of us and went outside," Harkey answered.

Dutchy's face beamed mischievously. He pretended knowledge of Dennin's absence, and affected a mysterious air, while they clamored for information. Edith, after a peep into the men's bunk-room, returned to the table. Hans looked at her, and she shook her head.

"He was never late at meal-time before," she remarked.

"I cannot understand," said Hans. "Always has he the great appetite like the horse."

"It is too bad," Dutchy said, with a sad shake of his head.

They were beginning to make merry over their comrade's absence.

"It is a great pity!" Dutchy volunteered.

"What?" they demanded in chorus.

"Poor Michael," was the mournful reply.

"Well, what's wrong with Michael?" Harkey asked.

"He is not hungry no more," wailed Dutchy. "He has lost der appetite. He do not like der grub."

"Not from the way he pitches into it up to his ears," remarked Harkey.

"He does dot shust to be politeful to Mrs. Nelson," was Dutchy's quick retort. "I know, I know, and it is too pad. Why is he not here? Pecause he haf gone out. Why haf he gone out? For der defelopment of der appetite. How does he defelop der appetite? He walks barefoots in der snow. Ach! don't I know? It is der way der rich peoples chases after der appetite when it is no more and is running away. Michael haf sixteen hundred dollars. He is rich peoples. He haf no appetite. Derefore, pecause, he is chasing der appetite. Shust you open der door und you will see his barefoots in der snow. No, you will not see der appetite. Dot is shust his trouble. When he sees der appetite he will catch it und come to preak-fast."

They burst into loud laughter at Dutchy's nonsense. The sound had scarcely died away when the door opened and Dennin came in. All turned to look at him. He was carrying a shot-gun. Even as they looked, he lifted it to his shoulder and fired twice. At the first shot Dutchy sank upon the table, overturning his mug of coffee, his yellow mop of hair dabbling in his plate of mush. His forehead, which pressed upon the near edge of the plate, tilted the plate up against his hair at an angle of forty-five degrees. Harkey was in the air, in his spring to his feet, at the second shot, and he pitched face down upon the floor, his "My God!" gurgling and dying in his throat.

It was the unexpected. Hans and Edith were stunned. They sat at the table with bodies tense, their eyes fixed in a fascinated gaze upon the murderer. Dimly they saw him through the smoke of the powder, and in the silence nothing was to be heard save the drip-drip of Dutchy's spilled coffee on the floor. Dennin threw open the breech of the shot-gun, ejecting the empty shells. Holding the gun with one hand, he reached with the other into his pocket for fresh shells.

He was thrusting the shells into the gun when Edith Nelson was aroused to action. It was patent that he intended to kill Hans and her. For a space of possibly three seconds of time she had been dazed and paralysed by the horrible and inconceivable form in which the unexpected had made its appearance. Then she rose to it and grappled with it. She grappled with it concretely, making a cat-like leap for the murderer and gripping his neck-cloth with both her hands. The impact of her body sent him stumbling backward several steps. He tried to shake her loose and still retain his hold on the gun. This was awkward, for her firm-fleshed body had become a cat's.

She threw herself to one side, and with her grip at his throat nearly jerked him to the floor. He straightened himself and whirled swiftly. Still faithful to her hold, her body followed the circle of his whirl so that her feet left the floor, and she swung through the air fastened to his throat by her hands. The whirl culminated in a collision with a chair, and the man and woman crashed to the floor in a wild struggling fall that extended itself across half the length of the room.

Hans Nelson was half a second behind his wife in rising to the unexpected. His nerve processed and mental processes were slower than hers. His was the grosser organism, and it had taken him half a second longer to perceive, and determine, and proceed to do. She had already flown at Dennin and gripped his throat, when Hans sprang to his feet. But her coolness was not his. He was in a blind fury, a Berserker rage. At the instant he sprang from his chair his mouth opened and there issued forth a sound that was half roar, half bellow. The whirl of the two bodies had already started, and still roaring, or bellowing, he pursued this whirl down the room, overtaking it when it fell to the floor.

Hans hurled himself upon the prostrate man, striking madly with his fists. They were sledge-like blows, and when Edith felt Dennin's body relax she loosed her grip and rolled clear. She lay on the floor, panting and watching. The fury of blows continued to rain down. Dennin did not seem to mind the blows. He did not even move. Then it dawned upon her that he was unconscious. She cried out to Hans to stop. She cried out again. But he paid no heed to her voice. She caught him by the arm, but her clinging to it merely impeded his effort.

It was no reasoned impulse that stirred her to do what she then did. Nor was it a sense of pity, nor obedience to the "Thou shalt not" of religion. Rather was it some sense of law, an ethic of her race and early environment, that compelled her to interpose her body between her husband and the helpless murderer. It was not until Hans knew he was striking his wife that he ceased. He allowed himself to be shoved away by her in much the same way that a ferocious but obedient dog allows itself to be shoved away by its master. The analogy went even farther. Deep in his throat, in an animal-like way, Hans's rage still rumbled, and several times he made as though to spring back upon his prey and was only prevented by the woman's swiftly interposed body.

Back and farther back Edith shoved her husband. She had never seen him in such a condition, and she was more frightened of him than she had been of Dennin in the thick of the struggle. She could not believe that this raging beast was her Hans, and with a shock she became suddenly aware of a shrinking, instinctive fear that he might snap her hand in his teeth like any wild animal. For some seconds, unwilling to hurt her, yet dogged in his desire to return to the attack, Hans dodged back and forth. But she resolutely dodged with him, until the first glimmerings of reason returned and he gave over.

Both crawled to their feet. Hans staggered back against the wall, where he leaned, his face working, in his throat the deep and continuous rumble that died away with the seconds and at last ceased. The time for the reaction had come. Edith stood in the middle of the floor, wringing her hands, panting and gasping, her whole body trembling violently.

Hans looked at nothing, but Edith's eyes wandered wildly from detail to detail of what had taken place. Dennin lay without movement. The overturned chair, hurled onward in the mad whirl, lay near him. Partly under him lay the shot-gun, still broken open at the breech. Spilling out of his right hand were the two cartridges which he had failed to put into the gun and which he had clutched until consciousness left him. Harkey lay on the floor, face downward, where he had fallen; while Dutchy rested forward on the table, his yellow mop of hair buried in his mush-plate, the plate itself still tilted at an angle of forty-five degrees. This tilted plate fascinated her. Why did it not fall down? It was ridiculous. It was not in the nature of things for a mush-plate to up-end itself on the table, even if a man or so had been killed.

She glanced back at Dennin, but her eyes returned to the tilted plate. It was so ridiculous! She felt a hysterical impulse to laugh. Then she noticed the silence, and forgot the plate in a desire for something to happen. The monotonous drip of the coffee from the table to the floor merely emphasized the silence. Why did not Hans do something? say something? She looked at him and was about to speak, when she discovered that her tongue refused its wonted duty. There was a peculiar ache in her throat, and her mouth was dry and furry. She could only look at Hans, who, in turn, looked at her.

Suddenly the silence was broken by a sharp, metallic clang. She screamed, jerking her eyes back to the table. The plate had fallen down. Hans sighed as though awakening from sleep. The clang of the plate had aroused them to life in a new world. The cabin epitomized the new world in which they must thenceforth live and move. The old cabin was gone forever. The horizon of life was totally new and unfamiliar. The unexpected had swept its wizardry over the face of things, changing the perspective, juggling values, and shuffling the real and the unreal into perplexing confusion.

"My God, Hans!" was Edith's first speech.

He did not answer, but stared at her with horror. Slowly his eyes wandered over the room, for the first time taking in its details. Then he put on his cap and started for the door.

"Where are you going?" Edith demanded, in an agony of apprehension.

His hand was on the door-knob, and he half turned as he answered, "To dig some graves."

"Don't leave me, Hans, with—" her eyes swept the room—"with this."

"The graves must be dug sometime," he said.

"But you do not know how many," she objected desperately. She noted his indecision, and added, "Besides, I'll go with you and help."

Hans stepped back to the table and mechanically snuffed the candle. Then between them they made the examination. Both Harkey and Dutchy were dead—frightfully dead, because of the close range of the shot-gun. Hans refused to go near Dennin, and Edith was forced to conduct this portion of the investigation by herself.

"He isn't dead," she called to Hans.

He walked over and looked down at the murderer.

"What did you say?" Edith demanded, having caught the rumble of inarticulate speech in her husband's throat.

"I said it was a damn shame that he isn't dead," came the reply.

Edith was bending over the body.

"Leave him alone," Hans commanded harshly, in a strange voice.

She looked at him in sudden alarm. He had picked up the shot-gun dropped by Dennin and was thrusting in the shells.

"What are you going to do?" she cried, rising swiftly from her bending position.

Hans did not answer, but she saw the shot-gun going to his shoulder. She grasped the muzzle with her hand and threw it up.

"Leave me alone!" he cried hoarsely.

He tried to jerk the weapon away from her, but she came in closer and clung to him.

"Hans! Hans! Wake up!" she cried. "Don't be crazy!"

"He killed Dutchy and Harkey!" was her husband's reply; "and I am going to kill him."

"But that is wrong," she objected. "There is the law."

He sneered his incredulity of the law's potency in such a region, but he merely iterated, dispassionately, doggedly, "He killed Dutchy and Harkey."

Long she argued it with him, but the argument was one-sided, for he contented himself with repeating again and again, "He killed Dutchy and Harkey." But she could not escape from her childhood training nor from the blood that was in her. The heritage of law was hers, and right conduct, to her, was the fulfilment of the law. She could see no other righteous course to pursue. Hans's taking the law in his own hands was no more justifiable than

Dennin's deed. Two wrongs did not make a right, she contended, and there was only one way to punish Dennin, and that was the legal way arranged by society. At last Hans gave in to her.

"All right," he said. "Have it your own way. And to-morrow or next day look to see him kill you and me."

She shook her head and held out her hand for the shot-gun. He started to hand it to her, then hesitated.

"Better let me shoot him," he pleaded.

Again she shook her head, and again he started to pass her the gun, when the door opened, and an Indian, without knocking, came in. A blast of wind and flurry of snow came in with him. They turned and faced him, Hans still holding the shot-gun. The intruder took in the scene without a quiver. His eyes embraced the dead and wounded in a sweeping glance. No surprise showed in his face, not even curiosity. Harkey lay at his feet, but he took no notice of him. So far as he was concerned, Harkey's body did not exist.

"Much wind," the Indian remarked by way of salutation. "All well? Very well?"

Hans, still grasping the gun, felt sure that the Indian attributed to him the mangled corpses. He glanced appealingly at his wife.

"Good morning, Negook," she said, her voice betraying her effort. "No, not very well. Much trouble."

"Good-by, I go now, much hurry," the Indian said, and without semblance of haste, with great deliberation stepping clear of a red pool on the floor, he opened the door and went out.

The man and woman looked at each other.

"He thinks we did it," Hans gasped, "that I did it."

Edith was silent for a space. Then she said, briefly, in a businesslike way:

"Never mind what he thinks. That will come after. At present we have two graves to dig. But first of all, we've got to tie up Dennin so he can't escape."

Hans refused to touch Dennin, but Edith lashed him securely, hand and foot. Then she and Hans went out into the snow. The ground was frozen. It was impervious to a blow of the pick. They first gathered wood, then scraped the snow away and on the frozen surface built a fire. When the fire had burned for an hour, several inches of dirt had thawed. This they shovelled out, and then built a fresh fire. Their descent into the earth progressed at the rate of two or three inches an hour.

It was hard and bitter work. The flurrying snow did not permit the fire to burn any too well, while the wind cut through their clothes and chilled their bodies. They held but little conversation. The wind interfered with speech. Beyond wondering at what could have been Dennin's motive, they remained silent, oppressed by the horror of the tragedy. At one o'clock, looking toward the cabin, Hans announced that he was hungry.

"No, not now, Hans," Edith answered. "I couldn't go back alone into that cabin the way it is, and cook a meal."

At two o'clock Hans volunteered to go with her; but she held him to his work, and four o'clock found the two graves completed. They were shallow, not more than two feet deep, but they would serve the purpose. Night had fallen. Hans got the sled, and the two dead men were dragged through the darkness and storm to their frozen sepulchre. The funeral procession was anything but a pageant. The sled sank deep into the drifted snow and pulled hard. The man and the woman had eaten nothing since the previous day, and were weak from hunger and exhaustion. They had not the strength to resist the wind, and at times its buffets hurled them off their feet. On several occasions the sled was overturned, and they were compelled to reload it with its sombre freight. The last hundred feet to the graves was up a steep slope, and this they took on all fours, like sled-dogs, making legs of their arms and thrusting their hands into the snow. Even so, they were twice dragged backward by the weight of the sled, and slid and fell down the hill, the living and the dead, the haul-ropes and the sled, in ghastly entanglement.

"To-morrow I will put up head-boards with their names," Hans said, when the graves were filled in.

Edith was sobbing. A few broken sentences had been all she was capable of in the way of a funeral service, and now her husband was compelled to half-carry her back to the cabin.

Dennin was conscious. He had rolled over and over on the floor in vain efforts to free himself. He watched Hans and Edith with glittering eyes, but made no attempt to speak. Hans still refused to touch the murderer, and sullenly watched Edith drag him across the floor to the men's bunk-room. But try as she would, she could not lift him from the floor into his bunk.

"Better let me shoot him, and we'll have no more trouble," Hans said in final appeal.

Edith shook her head and bent again to her task. To her surprise the body rose easily, and she knew Hans had relented and was helping her. Then came the cleansing of the kitchen. But the floor still shrieked the tragedy, until Hans planed the surface of the stained wood away and with the shavings made a fire in the stove.

The days came and went. There was much of darkness and silence, broken only by the storms and the thunder on the beach of the freezing surf. Hans was obedient to Edith's slightest order. All his splendid initiative had vanished. She had elected to deal with Dennin in her way, and so he left the whole matter in her hands.

The murderer was a constant menace. At all times there was the chance that he might free himself from his bonds, and they were compelled to guard him day and night. The man or the woman sat always beside him, holding the loaded shot-gun. At first, Edith tried eight-hour watches, but the continuous strain was too great, and afterwards she and Hans relieved each other every four hours. As they had to sleep, and as the watches extended through the night, their whole waking time was expended in guarding Dennin. They had barely time left over for the preparation of meals and the getting of firewood.

Since Negook's inopportune visit, the Indians had avoided the cabin. Edith sent Hans to their cabins to get them to take Dennin down the coast in a canoe to the nearest white settlement or trading post, but the errand was fruitless. Then Edith went herself and interviewed Negook. He was head man of the little village, keenly aware of his responsibility, and he elucidated his policy thoroughly in few words.

"It is white man's trouble," he said, "not Siwash trouble. My people help you, then will it be Siwash trouble too. When white man's trouble and Siwash trouble come together and make a trouble, it is a great trouble, beyond understanding and without end. Trouble no good. My people do no wrong. What for they help you and have trouble?"

So Edith Nelson went back to the terrible cabin with its endless alternating four-hour watches. Sometimes, when it was her turn and she sat by the prisoner, the loaded shot-gun in her lap, her eyes would close and she would doze. Always she aroused with a start, snatching up the gun and swiftly looking at him. These were distinct nervous shocks, and their effect was not good on her. Such was her fear of the man, that even though she were wide awake, if he moved under the bedclothes she could not repress the start and the quick reach for the gun.

She was preparing herself for a nervous break-down, and she knew it. First came a fluttering of the eyeballs, so that she was compelled to close her eyes for relief. A little later the eyelids were afflicted by a nervous twitching that she could not control. To add to the strain, she could not forget the tragedy. She remained as close to the horror as on the first morning when the unexpected stalked into the cabin and took possession. In her daily ministrations upon the prisoner she was forced to grit her teeth and steel herself, body and spirit.

Hans was affected differently. He became obsessed by the idea that it was his duty to kill Dennin; and whenever he waited upon the bound man or watched by him, Edith was troubled by the fear that Hans would add another red entry to the cabin's record. Always he cursed Dennin savagely and handled him roughly. Hans tried to conceal his homicidal mania, and he would say to his wife: "By and by you will want me to kill him, and then I will not kill him. It would make me sick." But more than once, stealing into the room, when it was her watch off, she would catch the two men glaring ferociously at each other, wild animals the pair of them, in Hans's face the lust to kill, in Dennin's the fierceness and savagery of the cornered rat. "Hans!" she would cry, "wake up!" and he would come to a recollection of himself, startled and shamefaced and unrepentant.

So Hans became another factor in the problem the unexpected had given Edith Nelson to solve. At first it had been merely a question of right conduct in dealing with Dennin, and right conduct, as she conceived it, lay in keeping him a prisoner until he could be turned over for trial before a proper tribunal. But now entered Hans, and she saw that his sanity and his salvation were involved. Nor was she long in discovering that her own strength and endurance had become part of the problem. She was breaking down under the strain. Her left arm had developed involuntary jerkings and twitchings. She spilled her food from her spoon, and could place no reliance in her afflicted arm. She judged it to be a form of St. Vitus's dance, and she feared the extent to which its ravages might go. What if she broke down? And the vision she had of the possible future, when the cabin might contain only Dennin and Hans, was an added horror.

After the third day, Dennin had begun to talk. His first question had been, "What are you going to do with me?" And this question he repeated daily and many times a day. And always Edith replied that he would assuredly be dealt with according to law. In turn, she put a daily question to him,— "Why did you do it?" To this he never replied. Also, he received the question with out-bursts of anger, raging and straining at the rawhide that bound him and threatening her with what he would do when he got loose, which he said he was sure to do sooner or later. At such times she cocked both triggers of the gun, prepared to meet him with leaden death if he should burst loose, herself trembling and palpitating and dizzy from the tension and shock.

But in time Dennin grew more tractable. It seemed to her that he was growing weary of his unchanging recumbent position. He began to beg and plead to be released. He made wild promises. He would do them no harm.

He would himself go down the coast and give himself up to the officers of the law. He would give them his share of the gold. He would go away into the heart of the wilderness, and never again appear in civilization. He would take his own life if she would only free him. His pleadings usually culminated in involuntary raving, until it seemed to her that he was passing into a fit; but always she shook her head and denied him the freedom for which he worked himself into a passion.

But the weeks went by, and he continued to grow more tractable. And through it all the weariness was asserting itself more and more. "I am so tired, so tired," he would murmur, rolling his head back and forth on the pillow like a peevish child. At a little later period he began to make impassioned pleas for death, to beg her to kill him, to beg Hans to put him our of his misery so that he might at least rest comfortably.

The situation was fast becoming impossible. Edith's nervousness was increasing, and she knew her break-down might come any time. She could not even get her proper rest, for she was haunted by the fear that Hans would yield to his mania and kill Dennin while she slept. Though January had already come, months would have to elapse before any trading schooner was even likely to put into the bay. Also, they had not expected to winter in the cabin, and the food was running low; nor could Hans add to the supply by hunting. They were chained to the cabin by the necessity of guarding their prisoner.

Something must be done, and she knew it. She forced herself to go back into a reconsideration of the problem. She could not shake off the legacy of her race, the law that was of her blood and that had been trained into her. She knew that whatever she did she must do according to the law, and in the long hours of watching, the shot-gun on her knees, the murderer restless beside her and the storms thundering without, she made original sociological researches and worked out for herself the evolution of the law. It came to her that the law was nothing more than the judgment and the will of any group of people. It mattered not how large was the group of people. There were little groups, she reasoned, like Switzerland, and there were big groups like the United States. Also, she reasoned, it did not matter how small was the group of people. There might be only ten thousand people in a country, yet their collective judgment and will would be the law of that country. Why, then, could not one thousand people constitute such a group? she asked herself. And if one thousand, why not one hundred? Why not fifty? Why not five? Why not—two?

She was frightened at her own conclusion, and she talked it over with Hans. At first he could not comprehend, and then, when he did, he added convincing evidence. He spoke of miners' meetings, where all the men of a locality came together and made the law and executed the law. There might be only ten or fifteen men altogether, he said, but the will of the majority became the law for the whole ten or fifteen, and whoever violated that will was punished.

Edith saw her way clear at last. Dennin must hang. Hans agreed with her. Between them they constituted the majority of this particular group. It was the group-will that Dennin should be hanged. In the execution of this will Edith strove earnestly to observe the customary forms, but the group was so small that Hans and she had to serve as witnesses, as jury, and as judges—also as executioners. She formally charged Michael Dennin with the murder of Dutchy and Harkey, and the prisoner lay in his bunk and listened to the testimony, first of Hans, and then of Edith. He refused to plead guilty or not guilty, and remained silent when she asked him if he had anything to say in his own defence. She and Hans, without leaving their seats, brought in the jury's verdict of guilty. Then, as judge, she imposed the sentence. Her voice shook, her eyelids twitched, her left arm jerked, but she carried it out.

"Michael Dennin, in three days' time you are to be hanged by the neck until you are dead."

Such was the sentence. The man breathed an unconscious sigh of relief, then laughed defiantly, and said, "Thin I'm thinkin' the damn bunk won't be achin' me back anny more, an' that's a consolation."

With the passing of the sentence a feeling of relief seemed to communicate itself to all of them. Especially was it noticeable in Dennin. All sullenness and defiance disappeared, and he talked sociably with his captors, and even with flashes of his old-time wit. Also, he found great satisfaction in Edith's reading to him from the Bible. She read from the New Testament, and he took keen interest in the prodigal son and the thief on the cross.

On the day preceding that set for the execution, when Edith asked her usual question, "Why did you do it?" Dennin answered, "'Tis very simple. I was thinkin'—"

But she hushed him abruptly, asked him to wait, and hurried to Hans's bedside. It was his watch off, and he came out of his sleep, rubbing his eyes and grumbling.

"Go," she told him, "and bring up Negook and one other Indian. Michael's going to confess. Make them come. Take the rifle along and bring them up at the point of it if you have to."

Half an hour later Negook and his uncle, Hadikwan, were ushered into the death chamber. They came unwillingly, Hans with his rifle herding them along.

"Negook," Edith said, "there is to be no trouble for you and your people. Only is it for you to sit and do nothing but listen and understand."

Thus did Michael Dennin, under sentence of death, make public confession of his crime. As he talked, Edith wrote his story down, while the Indians listened, and Hans guarded the door for fear the witnesses might bolt.

He had not been home to the old country for fifteen years, Dennin explained, and it had always been his intention to return with plenty of money and make his old mother comfortable for the rest of her days.

"An' how was I to be doin' it on sixteen hundred?" he demanded. "What I was after wantin' was all the goold, the whole eight thousan'. Thin I cud go back in style. What ud be aisier, thinks I to myself, than to kill all iv yez, report it at Skaguay for an Indian-killin', an' thin pull out for Ireland? An' so I started in to kill all iv yez, but, as Harkey was fond of sayin', I cut out too large a chunk an' fell down on the swallowin' iv it. An' that's me confession. I did me duty to the devil, an' now, God willin', I'll do me duty to God."

"Negook and Hadikwan, you have heard the white man's words," Edith said to the Indians. "His words are here on this paper, and it is for you to make a sign, thus, on the paper, so that white men to come after will know that you have heard."

The two Siwashes put crosses opposite their signatures, received a summons to appear on the morrow with all their tribe for a further witnessing of things, and were allowed to go.

Dennin's hands were released long enough for him to sign the document. Then a silence fell in the room. Hans was restless, and Edith felt uncomfortable. Dennin lay on his back, staring straight up at the moss-chinked roof.

"An' now I'll do me duty to God," he murmured. He turned his head toward Edith. "Read to me," he said, "from the book;" then added, with a glint of playfulness, "Mayhap 'twill help me to forget the bunk."

The day of the execution broke clear and cold. The thermometer was down to twenty-five below zero, and a chill wind was blowing which drove the frost through clothes and flesh to the bones. For the first time in many weeks Dennin stood upon his feet. His muscles had remained inactive so long, and he was so out of practice in maintaining an erect position, that he could scarcely stand.

He reeled back and forth, staggered, and clutched hold of Edith with his bound hands for support.

"Sure, an' it's dizzy I am," he laughed weakly.

A moment later he said, "An' it's glad I am that it's over with. That damn bunk would iv been the death iv me, I know."

When Edith put his fur cap on his head and proceeded to pull the flaps down over his ears, he laughed and said:

"What are you doin' that for?"

"It's freezing cold outside," she answered.

"An' in tin minutes' time what'll matter a frozen ear or so to poor Michael Dennin?" he asked.

She had nerved herself for the last culminating ordeal, and his remark was like a blow to her self-possession. So far, everything had seemed phantom-like, as in a dream, but the brutal truth of what he had said shocked her eyes wide open to the reality of what was taking place. Nor was her distress unnoticed by the Irishman.

"I'm sorry to be troublin' you with me foolish spache," he said regretfully. "I mint nothin' by it. 'Tis a great day for Michael Dennin, an' he's as gay as a lark."

He broke out in a merry whistle, which quickly became lugubrious and ceased.

"I'm wishin' there was a priest," he said wistfully; then added swiftly, "But Michael Dennin's too old a campaigner to miss the luxuries when he hits the trail."

He was so very weak and unused to walking that when the door opened and he passed outside, the wind nearly carried him off his feet. Edith and Hans walked on either side of him and supported him, the while he cracked jokes and tried to keep them cheerful, breaking off, once, long enough to arrange the forwarding of his share of the gold to his mother in Ireland.

They climbed a slight hill and came out into an open space among the trees. Here, circled solemnly about a barrel that stood on end in the snow, were Negook and Hadikwan, and all the Siwashes down to the babies and the dogs, come to see the way of the white man's law. Near by was an open grave which Hans had burned into the frozen earth.

Dennin cast a practical eye over the preparations, noting the grave, the barrel, the thickness of the rope, and the diameter of the limb over which the rope was passed.

"Sure, an' I couldn't iv done better meself, Hans, if it'd been for you."

He laughed loudly at his own sally, but Hans's face was frozen into a sullen ghastliness that nothing less than the trump of doom could have broken. Also, Hans was feeling very sick. He had not realized the enormousness of the task of putting a fellow-man out of the world. Edith, on the other hand, had realized; but the realization did not make the task any easier. She was filled with doubt as to whether she could hold herself together long enough to finish it. She felt incessant impulses to scream, to shriek, to collapse into the snow, to put her hands over her eyes and turn and run blindly away, into the forest, anywhere, away. It was only by a supreme effort of soul that she was able to keep upright and go on and do what she had to do. And in the midst of it all she was grateful to Dennin for the way he helped her.

"Lind me a hand," he said to Hans, with whose assistance he managed to mount the barrel.

He bent over so that Edith could adjust the rope about his neck. Then he stood upright while Hans drew the rope taut across the overhead branch.

"Michael Dennin, have you anything to say?" Edith asked in a clear voice that shook in spite of her.

Dennin shuffled his feet on the barrel, looked down bashfully like a man making his maiden speech, and cleared his throat.

"I'm glad it's over with," he said. "You've treated me like a Christian, an' I'm thankin' you hearty for your kindness."

"Then may God receive you, a repentant sinner," she said.

"Ay," he answered, his deep voice as a response to her thin one, "may God receive me, a repentant sinner."

"Good-by, Michael," she cried, and her voice sounded desperate.

She threw her weight against the barrel, but it did not overturn.

"Hans! Quick! Help me!" she cried faintly.

She could feel her last strength going, and the barrel resisted her. Hans hurried to her, and the barrel went out from under Michael Dennin.

She turned her back, thrusting her fingers into her ears. Then she began to laugh, harshly, sharply, metallically; and Hans was shocked as he had not been shocked through the whole tragedy. Edith Nelson's break-down had come. Even in her hysteria she knew it, and she was glad that she had been able to hold up under the strain until everything had been accomplished. She reeled toward Hans.

"Take me to the cabin, Hans," she managed to articulate.

"And let me rest," she added. "Just let me rest, and rest, and rest."

With Hans's arm around her, supporting her weight and directing her helpless steps, she went off across the snow. But the Indians remained solemnly to watch the working of the white man's law that compelled a man to dance upon the air.

BROWN WOLF

She had delayed, because of the dew-wet grass, in order to put on her overshoes, and when she emerged from the house found her waiting husband absorbed in the wonder of a bursting almond-bud. She sent a questing glance across the tall grass and in and out among the orchard trees.

"Where's Wolf?" she asked.

"He was here a moment ago." Walt Irvine drew himself away with a jerk from the metaphysics and poetry of the organic miracle of blossom, and surveyed the landscape. "He was running a rabbit the last I saw of him."

"Wolf! Wolf! Here Wolf!" she called, as they left the clearing and took the trail that led down through the waxen-belled manzanita jungle to the county road.

Irvine thrust between his lips the little finger of each hand and lent to her efforts a shrill whistling.

She covered her ears hastily and made a wry grimace.

"My! for a poet, delicately attuned and all the rest of it, you can make unlovely noises. My ear-drums are pierced. You outwhistle—"

"Orpheus."

"I was about to say a street-arab," she concluded severely.

"Poesy does not prevent one from being practical—at least it doesn't prevent *me*. Mine is no futility of genius that can't sell gems to the magazines."

He assumed a mock extravagance, and went on:

"I am no attic singer, no ballroom warbler. And why? Because I am practical. Mine is no squalor of song that cannot transmute itself, with proper exchange value, into a flower-crowned cottage, a sweet mountain-meadow, a grove of redwoods, an orchard of thirty-seven trees, one long row of blackberries and two short rows of strawberries, to say nothing of a quarter of a mile of gurgling brook. I am a beauty-merchant, a trader in song, and I pursue utility, dear Madge. I sing a song, and thanks to the magazine editors I transmute my song into a waft of the west wind sighing through our redwoods, into a murmur of waters over mossy stones that sings back to me another song than the one I sang and yet the same song wonderfully—er—transmuted."

"O that all your song-transmutations were as successful!" she laughed.

"Name one that wasn't."

"Those two beautiful sonnets that you transmuted into the cow that was accounted the worst milker in the township."

"She *was* beautiful—" he began,

"But she didn't give milk," Madge interrupted.

"But she was beautiful, now, wasn't she?" he insisted.

"And here's where beauty and utility fall out," was her reply. "And there's the Wolf!"

From the thicket-covered hillside came a crashing of underbrush, and then, forty feet above them, on the edge of the sheer wall of rock, appeared a wolf's head and shoulders. His braced fore paws dislodged a pebble, and with sharp-pricked ears and peering eyes he watched the fall of the pebble till it struck at their feet. Then he transferred his gaze and with open mouth laughed down at them.

"You Wolf, you!" and "You blessed Wolf!" the man and woman called out to him.

The ears flattened back and down at the sound, and the head seemed to snuggle under the caress of an invisible hand.

They watched him scramble backward into the thicket, then proceeded on their way. Several minutes later, rounding a turn in the trail where the descent was less precipitous, he joined them in the midst of a miniature avalanche of pebbles and loose soil. He was not demonstrative. A pat and a rub around the ears from the man, and a more prolonged caressing from the woman, and he was away down the trail in front of them, gliding effortlessly over the ground in true wolf fashion.

In build and coat and brush he was a huge timber-wolf; but the lie was given to his wolfhood by his color and marking. There the dog unmistakably advertised itself. No wolf was ever colored like him. He was brown, deep brown, red-brown, an orgy of browns. Back and shoulders were a warm brown that paled on the sides and underneath to a yellow that was dingy because of the brown that lingered in it. The white of the throat and paws and the spots over the eyes was dirty because of the persistent and ineradicable brown, while the eyes themselves were twin topazes, golden and brown.

The man and woman loved the dog very much; perhaps this was because it had been such a task to win his love. It had been no easy matter when he first drifted in mysteriously out of nowhere to their little mountain cottage. Footsore and famished, he had killed a rabbit under their very noses and under their very windows, and then crawled away and slept by the spring at the foot of the blackberry bushes. When Walt Irvine went down to inspect the intruder, he was snarled at for his pains, and Madge likewise was snarled at when she went down to present, as a peace-offering, a large pan of bread and milk.

A most unsociable dog he proved to be, resenting all their advances, refusing to let them lay hands on him, menacing them with bared fangs and bristling hair. Nevertheless he remained, sleeping and resting by the spring, and eating the food they gave him after they set it down at a safe distance and retreated. His wretched physical condition explained why he lingered; and when he had recuperated, after several days' sojourn, he disappeared.

And this would have been the end of him, so far as Irvine and his wife were concerned, had not Irvine at that particular time been called away into the northern part of the state. Riding along on the train, near to the line between California and Oregon, he chanced to look out of the window and saw his unsociable guest sliding along the wagon road, brown and wolfish, tired yet tireless, dust-covered and soiled with two hundred miles of travel.

Now Irvine was a man of impulse, a poet. He got off the train at the next station, bought a piece of meat at a butcher shop, and captured the vagrant on the outskirts of the town. The return trip was made in the baggage car, and so Wolf came a second time to the mountain cottage. Here he was tied up for a week and made love to by the man and woman. But it was very circumspect love-making. Remote and alien as a traveller from another planet, he snarled down their soft-spoken love-words. He never barked. In all the time they had him he was never known to bark.

To win him became a problem. Irvine liked problems. He had a metal plate made, on which was stamped: Return to Walt Irvine, Glen Ellen, Sonoma County, California. This was riveted to a collar and strapped about the dog's neck. Then he was turned loose, and promptly he disappeared. A day later came a telegram from Mendocino County. In twenty hours he had made over a hundred miles to the north, and was still going when captured.

He came back by Wells Fargo Express, was tied up three days, and was loosed on the fourth and lost. This time he gained southern Oregon before he was caught and returned. Always, as soon as he received his liberty, he fled away, and always he fled north. He was possessed of an obsession that drove him north. The homing instinct, Irvine called it, after he had expended the selling price of a sonnet in getting the animal back from northern Oregon.

Another time the brown wanderer succeeded in traversing half the length of California, all of Oregon, and most of Washington, before he was picked up and returned "Collect." A remarkable thing was the speed with which he travelled. Fed up and rested, as soon as he was loosed he devoted all his energy to getting over the ground. On the first day's run he was known to cover as high as a hundred and fifty miles, and after that he would average a hundred miles a day until caught. He always arrived back lean and hungry and savage, and always departed fresh and vigorous, cleaving his way northward in response to some prompting of his being that no one could understand.

But at last, after a futile year of flight, he accepted the inevitable and elected to remain at the cottage where first he had killed the rabbit and slept by the spring. Even after that, a long time elapsed before the man and woman succeeded in patting him. It was a great victory, for they alone were allowed to put hands on him. He was fastidiously exclusive, and no guest at the cottage ever succeeded in making up to him. A low growl greeted such approach; if any one had the hardihood to come nearer, the lips lifted, the naked fangs appeared, and the growl became a snarl—a snarl so terrible and malignant that it awed the stoutest of them, as it likewise awed the farmers' dogs that knew ordinary dog-snarling, but had never seen wolf-snarling before.

He was without antecedents. His history began with Walt and Madge. He had come up from the south, but never a clew did they get of the owner from whom he had evidently fled. Mrs. Johnson, their nearest neighbor and the one who supplied them with milk, proclaimed him a Klondike dog. Her brother was burrowing for frozen pay-streaks in that far country, and so she constituted herself an authority on the subject.

But they did not dispute her. There were the tips of Wolf's ears, obviously so severely frozen at some time that they would never quite heal again. Besides, he looked like the photographs of the Alaskan dogs they saw published in magazines and newspapers. They often speculated over his past, and tried to conjure up (from what they had read and heard) what his northland life had been. That the northland still drew him, they knew; for at night they sometimes heard him crying softly; and when the north wind blew and the bite of frost was in the air, a great restlessness would come upon him and he would lift a mournful lament which they knew to be the long wolf-howl. Yet he never barked. No provocation was great enough to draw from him that canine cry.

Long discussion they had, during the time of winning him, as to whose dog he was. Each claimed him, and each proclaimed loudly any expression of affection made by him. But the man had the better of it at first, chiefly because he was a man. It was patent that Wolf had had no experience with women. He did not understand women. Madge's skirts were something he never quite accepted. The swish of them was enough to set him a-bristle with suspicion, and on a windy day she could not approach him at all.

On the other hand, it was Madge who fed him; also it was she who ruled the kitchen, and it was by her favor, and her favor alone, that he was permitted to come within that sacred precinct. It was because of these things that she bade fair to overcome the handicap of her garments. Then it was that Walt put forth special effort, making it a practice to have Wolf lie at his feet while he wrote, and, between petting and talking, losing much time from his work. Walt won in the end, and his victory was most probably due to the fact that he was a man, though Madge averred that they would have had another quarter of a mile of gurgling brook, and at least two west winds sighing through their redwoods, had Wait properly devoted his energies to song-transmutation and left Wolf alone to exercise a natural taste and an unbiassed judgment.

"It's about time I heard from those triolets," Walt said, after a silence of five minutes, during which they had swung steadily down the trail. "There'll be a check at the post-office, I know, and we'll transmute it into beautiful buckwheat flour, a gallon of maple syrup, and a new pair of overshoes for you."

"And into beautiful milk from Mrs. Johnson's beautiful cow," Madge added. "To-morrow's the first of the month, you know."

Walt scowled unconsciously; then his face brightened, and he clapped his hand to his breast pocket.

"Never mind. I have here a nice beautiful new cow, the best milker in California."

"When did you write it?" she demanded eagerly. Then, reproachfully, "And you never showed it to me."

"I saved it to read to you on the way to the post-office, in a spot remarkably like this one," he answered, indicating, with a wave of his hand, a dry log on which to sit.

A tiny stream flowed out of a dense fern-brake, slipped down a mossy-lipped stone, and ran across the path at their feet. From the valley arose the mellow song of meadow-larks, while about them, in and out, through sunshine and shadow, fluttered great yellow butterflies.

Up from below came another sound that broke in upon Walt reading softly from his manuscript. It was a crunching of heavy feet, punctuated now and again by the clattering of a displaced stone. As Walt finished and looked to his wife for approval, a man came into view around the turn of the trail. He was bare-headed and sweaty. With a handkerchief in one hand he mopped his face, while in the other hand he carried a new hat and a wilted starched collar which he had removed from his neck. He was a well-built man, and his muscles seemed on the point of bursting out of the painfully new and ready-made black clothes he wore.

"Warm day," Walt greeted him. Walt believed in country democracy, and never missed an opportunity to practise it.

The man paused and nodded.

"I guess I ain't used much to the warm," he vouchsafed half apologetically. "I'm more accustomed to zero weather."

"You don't find any of that in this country," Walt laughed.

"Should say not," the man answered. "An' I ain't here a-lookin' for it neither. I'm tryin' to find my sister. Mebbe you know where she lives. Her name's Johnson, Mrs. William Johnson."

"You're not her Klondike brother!" Madge cried, her eyes bright with interest, "about whom we've heard so much?"

"Yes'm, that's me," he answered modestly. "My name's Miller, Skiff Miller. I just thought I'd s'prise her."

"You are on the right track then. Only you've come by the foot-path." Madge stood up to direct him, pointing up the canyon a quarter of a mile. "You see that blasted redwood? Take the little trail turning off to the right. It's the short cut to her house. You can't miss it."

"Yes'm, thank you, ma'am," he said. He made tentative efforts to go, but seemed awkwardly rooted to the spot. He was gazing at her with an open admiration of which he was quite unconscious, and which was drowning, along with him, in the rising sea of embarrassment in which he floundered.

"We'd like to hear you tell about the Klondike," Madge said. "Mayn't we come over some day while you are at your sister's? Or, better yet, won't you come over and have dinner with us?"

"Yes'm, thank you, ma'am," he mumbled mechanically. Then he caught himself up and added: "I ain't stoppin' long. I got to be pullin' north again. I go out on to-night's train. You see, I've got a mail contract with the government."

When Madge had said that it was too bad, he made another futile effort to go. But he could not take his eyes from her face. He forgot his embarrassment in his admiration, and it was her turn to flush and feel uncomfortable.

It was at this juncture, when Walt had just decided it was time for him to be saying something to relieve the strain, that Wolf, who had been away nosing through the brush, trotted wolf-like into view.

Skiff Miller's abstraction disappeared. The pretty woman before him passed out of his field of vision. He had eyes only for the dog, and a great wonder came into his face.

"Well, I'll be damned!" he enunciated slowly and solemnly.

He sat down ponderingly on the log, leaving Madge standing. At the sound of his voice, Wolf's ears had flattened down, then his mouth had opened in a laugh. He trotted slowly up to the stranger and first smelled his hands, then licked them with his tongue.

Skiff Miller patted the dog's head, and slowly and solemnly repeated, "Well, I'll be damned!"

"Excuse me, ma'am," he said the next moment "I was just s'prised some, that was all."

"We're surprised, too," she answered lightly. "We never saw Wolf make up to a stranger before."

"Is that what you call him—Wolf?" the man asked.

Madge nodded. "But I can't understand his friendliness toward you—unless it's because you're from the Klondike. He's a Klondike dog, you know."

"Yes'm," Miller said absently. He lifted one of Wolf's fore legs and examined the foot-pads, pressing them and denting them with his thumb. "Kind of soft," he remarked. "He ain't been on trail for a long time."

"I say," Walt broke in, "it is remarkable the way he lets you handle him."

Skiff Miller arose, no longer awkward with admiration of Madge, and in a sharp, businesslike manner asked, "How long have you had him?"

But just then the dog, squirming and rubbing against the newcomer's legs, opened his mouth and barked. It was an explosive bark, brief and joyous, but a bark.

"That's a new one on me," Skiff Miller remarked.

Walt and Madge stared at each other. The miracle had happened. Wolf had barked.

"It's the first time he ever barked," Madge said.

"First time I ever heard him, too," Miller volunteered.

Madge smiled at him. The man was evidently a humorist.

"Of course," she said, "since you have only seen him for five minutes."

Skiff Miller looked at her sharply, seeking in her face the guile her words had led him to suspect.

"I thought you understood," he said slowly. "I thought you'd tumbled to it from his makin' up to me. He's my dog. His name ain't Wolf. It's Brown."

"Oh, Walt!" was Madge's instinctive cry to her husband.

Walt was on the defensive at once.

"How do you know he's your dog?" he demanded.

"Because he is," was the reply.

"Mere assertion," Walt said sharply.

In his slow and pondering way, Skiff Miller looked at him, then asked, with a nod of his head toward Madge:

"How d'you know she's your wife? You just say, 'Because she is,' and I'll say it's mere assertion. The dog's mine. I bred 'm an' raised 'm, an' I guess I ought to know. Look here. I'll prove it to you."

Skiff Miller turned to the dog. "Brown!" His voice rang out sharply, and at the sound the dog's ears flattened down as to a caress. "Gee!" The dog made a swinging turn to the right. "Now mush-on!" And the dog ceased his swing abruptly and started straight ahead, halting obediently at command.

"I can do it with whistles," Skiff Miller said proudly. "He was my lead dog."

"But you are not going to take him away with you?" Madge asked tremulously.

The man nodded.

"Back into that awful Klondike world of suffering?"

He nodded and added: "Oh, it ain't so bad as all that. Look at me. Pretty healthy specimen, ain't I?"

"But the dogs! The terrible hardship, the heart-breaking toil, the starvation, the frost! Oh, I've read about it and I know."

"I nearly ate him once, over on Little Fish River," Miller volunteered grimly. "If I hadn't got a moose that day was all that saved 'm."

"I'd have died first!" Madge cried.

"Things is different down here," Miller explained. "You don't have to eat dogs. You think different just about the time you're all in. You've never ben all in, so you don't know anything about it."

"That's the very point," she argued warmly. "Dogs are not eaten in California. Why not leave him here? He is happy. He'll never want for food—you know that. He'll never suffer from cold and hardship. Here all is softness and gentleness. Neither the human nor nature is savage. He will never know a whip-lash again. And as for the weather—why, it never snows here."

"But it's all-fired hot in summer, beggin' your pardon," Skiff Miller laughed.

"But you do not answer," Madge continued passionately. "What have you to offer him in that northland life?"

"Grub, when I've got it, and that's most of the time," came the answer.

"And the rest of the time?"

"No grub."

"And the work?"

"Yes, plenty of work," Miller blurted out impatiently. "Work without end, an' famine, an' frost, an all the rest of the miseries—that's what he'll get when he comes with me. But he likes it. He is used to it. He knows that life. He was born to it an' brought up to it. An' you don't know anything about it. You don't know what you're talking about. That's where the dog belongs, and that's where he'll be happiest."

"The dog doesn't go," Walt announced in a determined voice. "So there is no need of further discussion."

"What's that?" Skiff Miller demanded, his brows lowering and an obstinate flush of blood reddening his forehead.

"I said the dog doesn't go, and that settles it. I don't believe he's your dog. You may have seen him sometime. You may even sometime have driven him for his owner. But his obeying the ordinary driving commands of the Alaskan trail is no demonstration that he is yours. Any dog in Alaska would obey you as he obeyed. Besides, he is undoubtedly a valuable dog, as dogs go in Alaska, and that is sufficient explanation of your desire to get possession of him. Anyway, you've got to prove property."

Skiff Miller, cool and collected, the obstinate flush a trifle deeper on his forehead, his huge muscles bulging under the black cloth of his coat, carefully looked the poet up and down as though measuring the strength of his slenderness.

The Klondiker's face took on a contemptuous expression as he said finally, "I reckon there's nothin' in sight to prevent me takin' the dog right here an' now."

Walt's face reddened, and the striking-muscles of his arms and shoulders seemed to stiffen and grow tense. His wife fluttered apprehensively into the breach.

"Maybe Mr. Miller is right," she said. "I am afraid that he is. Wolf does seem to know him, and certainly he answers to the name of 'Brown.' He made friends with him instantly, and you know that's something he never did with anybody before. Besides, look at the way he barked. He was just bursting with joy. Joy over what? Without doubt at finding Mr. Miller."

Walt's striking-muscles relaxed, and his shoulders seemed to droop with hopelessness.

"I guess you're right, Madge," he said. "Wolf isn't Wolf, but Brown, and he must belong to Mr. Miller."

"Perhaps Mr. Miller will sell him," she suggested. "We can buy him."

Skiff Miller shook his head, no longer belligerent, but kindly, quick to be generous in response to generousness.

"I had five dogs," he said, casting about for the easiest way to temper his refusal. "He was the leader. They was the crack team of Alaska. Nothin' could touch 'em. In 1898 I refused five thousand dollars for the bunch. Dogs was high, then, anyway; but that wasn't what made the fancy price. It was the team itself. Brown was the best in the team. That winter I refused twelve hundred for 'm. I didn't sell 'm then, an' I ain't a-sellin' 'm now. Besides, I think a mighty lot of that dog. I've ben lookin' for 'm for three years. It made me fair sick when I found he'd ben stole—not the value of him, but the—well, I liked 'm like hell, that's all, beggin' your pardon. I couldn't believe my eyes when I seen 'm just now. I thought I was dreamin'. It was too good to be true. Why, I was his wet-nurse. I put 'm to bed, snug every night. His mother died, and I brought 'm up on condensed milk at two dollars a can when I couldn't afford it in my own coffee. He never knew any mother but me. He used to suck my finger regular, the darn little cuss—that finger right there!"

And Skiff Miller, too overwrought for speech, held up a fore finger for them to see.

"That very finger," he managed to articulate, as though it somehow clinched the proof of ownership and the bond of affection.

He was still gazing at his extended finger when Madge began to speak.

"But the dog," she said. "You haven't considered the dog."

Skiff Miller looked puzzled.

"Have you thought about him?" she asked.

"Don't know what you're drivin' at," was the response.

"Maybe the dog has some choice in the matter," Madge went on. "Maybe he has his likes and desires. You have not considered him. You give him no choice. It has never entered your mind that possibly he might prefer California to Alaska. You consider only what you like. You do with him as you would with a sack of potatoes or a bale of hay."

This was a new way of looking at it, and Miller was visibly impressed as he debated it in his mind. Madge took advantage of his indecision.

"If you really love him, what would be happiness to him would be your happiness also," she urged.

Skiff Miller continued to debate with himself, and Madge stole a glance of exultation to her husband, who looked back warm approval.

"What do you think?" the Klondiker suddenly demanded.

It was her turn to be puzzled. "What do you mean?" she asked.

"D'ye think he'd sooner stay in California?"

She nodded her head with positiveness. "I am sure of it."

Skiff Miller again debated with himself, though this time aloud, at the same time running his gaze in a judicial way over the mooted animal.

"He was a good worker. He's done a heap of work for me. He never loafed on me, an' he was a joe-dandy at hammerin' a raw team into shape. He's got a head on him. He can do everything but talk. He knows what you say to him. Look at 'm now. He knows we're talkin' about him."

The dog was lying at Skiff Miller's feet, head close down on paws, ears erect and listening, and eyes that were quick and eager to follow the sound of speech as it fell from the lips of first one and then the other.

"An' there's a lot of work in 'm yet. He's good for years to come. An' I do like him. I like him like hell."

Once or twice after that Skiff Miller opened his mouth and closed it again without speaking. Finally he said:

"I'll tell you what I'll do. Your remarks, ma'am, has some weight in them. The dog's worked hard, and maybe he's earned a soft berth an' has got a right to choose. Anyway, we'll leave it up to him. Whatever he says, goes. You people stay right here settin' down. I'll say good-by and walk off casual-like. If he wants to stay, he can stay. If he wants to come with me, let 'm come. I won't call 'm to come an' don't you call 'm to come back."

He looked with sudden suspicion at Madge, and added, "Only you must play fair. No persuadin' after my back is turned."

"We'll play fair," Madge began, but Skiff Miller broke in on her assurances.

"I know the ways of women," he announced. "Their hearts is soft. When their hearts is touched they're likely to stack the cards, look at the bottom of the deck, an' lie like the devil—beggin' your pardon, ma'am. I'm only discoursin' about women in general."

"I don't know how to thank you," Madge quavered.

"I don't see as you've got any call to thank me," he replied. "Brown ain't decided yet. Now you won't mind if I go away slow? It's no more'n fair, seein' I'll be out of sight inside a hundred yards."—Madge agreed, and added, "And I promise you faithfully that we won't do anything to influence him."

"Well, then, I might as well be gettin' along," Skiff Miller said in the ordinary tones of one departing.

At this change in his voice, Wolf lifted his head quickly, and still more quickly got to his feet when the man and woman shook hands. He sprang up on his hind legs, resting his fore paws on her hip and at the same time licking Skiff Miller's hand. When the latter shook hands with Walt, Wolf repeated his act, resting his weight on Walt and licking both men's hands.

"It ain't no picnic, I can tell you that," were the Klondiker's last words, as he turned and went slowly up the trail.

For the distance of twenty feet Wolf watched him go, himself all eagerness and expectancy, as though waiting for the man to turn and retrace his steps. Then, with a quick low whine, Wolf sprang after him, overtook him, caught his hand between his teeth with reluctant tenderness, and strove gently to make him pause.

Failing in this, Wolf raced back to where Walt Irvine sat, catching his coat-sleeve in his teeth and trying vainly to drag him after the retreating man.

Wolf's perturbation began to wax. He desired ubiquity. He wanted to be in two places at the same time, with the old master and the new, and steadily the distance between them was increasing. He sprang about excitedly, making short nervous leaps and twists, now toward one, now toward the other, in painful indecision, not knowing his own mind, desiring both and unable to choose, uttering quick sharp whines and beginning to pant.

He sat down abruptly on his haunches, thrusting his nose upward, the mouth opening and closing with jerking movements, each time opening wider. These jerking movements were in unison with the recurrent spasms that attacked the throat, each spasm severer and more intense than the preceding one. And in accord with jerks and spasms the larynx began to vibrate, at first silently, accompanied by the rush of air expelled from the lungs, then sounding a low, deep note, the lowest in the register of the human ear. All this was the nervous and muscular preliminary to howling.

But just as the howl was on the verge of bursting from the full throat, the wide-opened mouth was closed, the paroxysms ceased, and he looked long and steadily at the retreating man. Suddenly Wolf turned his head, and over his shoulder just as steadily regarded Walt. The appeal was unanswered. Not a word nor a sign did the dog receive, no suggestion and no clew as to what his conduct should be.

A glance ahead to where the old master was nearing the curve of the trail excited him again. He sprang to his feet with a whine, and then, struck by a new idea, turned his attention to Madge. Hitherto he had ignored her, but now, both masters failing him, she alone was left. He went over to her and snuggled his head in her lap, nudging her arm with his nose—an old trick of his when begging for favors. He backed away from her and began writhing and twisting playfully, curvetting and prancing, half rearing and striking his fore paws to the earth, struggling with all his body, from the wheedling eyes and flattening ears to the wagging tail, to express the thought that was in him and that was denied him utterance.

This, too, he soon abandoned. He was depressed by the coldness of these humans who had never been cold before. No response could he draw from them, no help could he get. They did not consider him. They were as dead.

He turned and silently gazed after the old master. Skiff Miller was rounding the curve. In a moment he would be gone from view. Yet he never turned his head, plodding straight onward, slowly and methodically, as though possessed of no interest in what was occurring behind his back.

And in this fashion he went out of view. Wolf waited for him to reappear. He waited a long minute, silently, quietly, without movement, as though turned to stone—withal stone quick with eagerness and desire. He barked once, and waited. Then he turned and trotted back to Walt Irvine. He sniffed his hand and dropped down heavily at his feet, watching the trail where it curved emptily from view.

The tiny stream slipping down the mossy-lipped stone seemed suddenly to increase the volume of its gurgling noise. Save for the meadow-larks, there was no other sound. The great yellow butterflies drifted silently through the sunshine and lost themselves in the drowsy shadows. Madge gazed triumphantly at her husband.

A few minutes later Wolf got upon his feet. Decision and deliberation marked his movements. He did not glance at the man and woman. His eyes were fixed up the trail. He had made up his mind. They knew it. And they knew, so far as they were concerned, that the ordeal had just begun.

He broke into a trot, and Madge's lips pursed, forming an avenue for the caressing sound that it was the will of her to send forth. But the caressing sound was not made. She was impelled to look at her husband, and she saw the sternness with which he watched her. The pursed lips relaxed, and she sighed inaudibly.

Wolf's trot broke into a run. Wider and wider were the leaps he made. Not once did he turn his head, his wolf's brush standing out straight behind him. He cut sharply across the curve of the trail and was gone.

THE SUN-DOG TRAIL

Sitka Charley smoked his pipe and gazed thoughtfully at the *Police Gazette* illustration on the wall. For half an hour he had been steadily regarding it, and for half an hour I had been slyly watching him. Something was going on in that mind of his, and, whatever it was, I knew it was well worth knowing. He had lived life, and seen things, and performed that prodigy of prodigies, namely, the turning of his back upon his own people, and, in so far as it was possible for an Indian, becoming a white man even in his mental processes. As he phrased it himself, he had come into the warm, sat among us, by our fires, and become one of us. He had never learned to read nor write, but his vocabulary was remarkable, and more remarkable still was the completeness with which he had assumed the white man's point of view, the white man's attitude toward things.

We had struck this deserted cabin after a hard day on trail. The dogs had been fed, the supper dishes washed, the beds made, and we were now enjoying that most delicious hour that comes each day, and but once each day, on the Alaskan trail, the hour when nothing intervenes between the tired body and bed save the smoking of the evening pipe. Some former denizen of the cabin had decorated its walls with illustrations torn from magazines and newspapers, and it was these illustrations that had held Sitka Charley's attention from the moment of our arrival two hours before. He had studied them intently, ranging from one to another and back again, and I could see that there was uncertainty in his mind, and bepuzzlement.

"Well?" I finally broke the silence.

He took the pipe from his mouth and said simply, "I do not understand."

He smoked on again, and again removed the pipe, using it to point at the *Police Gazette* illustration.

"That picture—what does it mean? I do not understand."

I looked at the picture. A man, with a preposterously wicked face, his right hand pressed dramatically to his heart, was falling backward to the floor. Confronting him, with a face that was a composite of destroying angel and Adonis, was a man holding a smoking revolver.

"One man is killing the other man," I said, aware of a distinct bepuzzlement of my own and of failure to explain.

"Why?" asked Sitka Charley.

"I do not know," I confessed.

"That picture is all end," he said. "It has no beginning."

"It is life," I said.

"Life has beginning," he objected.

I was silenced for the moment, while his eyes wandered on to an adjoining decoration, a photographic reproduction of somebody's "Leda and the Swan."

"That picture," he said, "has no beginning. It has no end. I do not understand pictures."

"Look at that picture," I commanded, pointing to a third decoration. "It means something. Tell me what it means to you."

He studied it for several minutes.

"The little girl is sick," he said finally. "That is the doctor looking at her. They have been up all night—see, the oil is low in the lamp, the first morning light is coming in at the window. It is a great sickness; maybe she will die, that is why the doctor looks so hard. That is the mother. It is a great sickness, because the mother's head is on the table and she is crying."

"How do you know she is crying?" I interrupted. "You cannot see her face. Perhaps she is asleep."

Sitka Charley looked at me in swift surprise, then back at the picture. It was evident that he had not reasoned the impression.

"Perhaps she is asleep," he repeated. He studied it closely. "No, she is not asleep. The shoulders show that she is not asleep. I have seen the shoulders of a woman who cried. The mother is crying. It is a very great sickness."

"And now you understand the picture," I cried.

He shook his head, and asked, "The little girl—does it die?"

It was my turn for silence.

"Does it die?" he reiterated. "You are a painter-man. Maybe you know."

"No, I do not know," I confessed.

"It is not life," he delivered himself dogmatically. "In life little girl die or get well. Something happen in life. In picture nothing happen. No, I do not understand pictures."

His disappointment was patent. It was his desire to understand all things that white men understand, and here, in this matter, he failed. I felt, also, that there was challenge in his attitude. He was bent upon compelling me to show him the wisdom of pictures. Besides, he had remarkable powers of visualization. I had long since learned this. He visualized everything. He saw life in pictures, felt life in pictures, generalized life in pictures; and yet he did not understand pictures when seen through other men's eyes and expressed by those men with color and line upon canvas.

"Pictures are bits of life," I said. "We paint life as we see it. For instance, Charley, you are coming along the trail. It is night. You see a cabin. The window is lighted. You look through the window for one second, or for two seconds, you see something, and you go on your way. You saw maybe a man writing a letter. You saw something without beginning or end. Nothing happened. Yet it was a bit of life you saw. You remember it afterward. It is like a picture in your memory. The window is the frame of the picture."

I could see that he was interested, and I knew that as I spoke he had looked through the window and seen the man writing the letter.

"There is a picture you have painted that I understand," he said. "It is a true picture. It has much meaning. It is in your cabin at Dawson. It is a faro table. There are men playing. It is a large game. The limit is off."

"How do you know the limit is off?" I broke in excitedly, for here was where my work could be tried out on an unbiassed judge who knew life only, and not art, and who was a sheer master of reality. Also, I was very proud of that particular piece of work. I had named it "The Last Turn," and I believed it to be one of the best things I had ever done.

"There are no chips on the table," Sitka Charley explained. "The men are playing with markers. That means the roof is the limit. One man play yellow markers—maybe one yellow marker worth one thousand dollars, maybe two thousand dollars. One man play red markers. Maybe they are worth five hundred dollars, maybe one thousand dollars. It is a very big game. Everybody play very high, up to the roof. How do I know? You make the dealer with blood little bit warm in face." (I was delighted.) "The lookout, you make him lean forward in his chair. Why he lean forward? Why his face very much quiet? Why his eyes very much bright? Why dealer warm with blood a little bit in the face? Why all men very quiet?—the man with yellow markers? the man with white markers? the man with red markers? Why nobody talk? Because very much money. Because last turn."

"How do you know it is the last turn?" I asked.

"The king is coppered, the seven is played open," he answered. "Nobody bet on other cards. Other cards all gone. Everybody one mind. Everybody play king to lose, seven to win. Maybe bank lose twenty thousand dollars, maybe bank win. Yes, that picture I understand."

"Yet you do not know the end!" I cried triumphantly. "It is the last turn, but the cards are not yet turned. In the picture they will never be turned. Nobody will ever know who wins nor who loses."

"And the men will sit there and never talk," he said, wonder and awe growing in his face. "And the lookout will lean forward, and the blood will be warm in the face of the dealer. It is a strange thing. Always will they sit there, always; and the cards will never be turned."

"It is a picture," I said. "It is life. You have seen things like it yourself."

He looked at me and pondered, then said, very slowly: "No, as you say, there is no end to it. Nobody will ever know the end. Yet is it a true thing. I have seen it. It is life."

For a long time he smoked on in silence, weighing the pictorial wisdom of the white man and verifying it by the facts of life. He nodded his head several times, and grunted once or twice. Then he knocked the ashes from his pipe, carefully refilled it, and after a thoughtful pause, lighted it again.

"Then have I, too, seen many pictures of life," he began; "pictures not painted, but seen with the eyes. I have looked at them like through the window at the man writing the letter. I have seen many pieces of life, without beginning, without end, without understanding."

With a sudden change of position he turned his eyes full upon me and regarded me thoughtfully.

"Look you," he said; "you are a painter-man. How would you paint this which I saw, a picture without beginning, the ending of which I do not understand, a piece of life with the northern lights for a candle and Alaska for a frame."

"It is a large canvas," I murmured.

But he ignored me, for the picture he had in mind was before his eyes and he was seeing it.

"There are many names for this picture," he said. "But in the picture there are many sun-dogs, and it comes into my mind to call it 'The Sun-Dog Trail.' It was a long time ago, seven years ago, the fall of '97, when I saw the woman first time. At Lake Linderman I had one canoe, very good Peterborough canoe. I came over Chilcoot Pass with two thousand letters for Dawson. I was letter carrier. Everybody rush to Klondike at that time. Many people on trail. Many people chop down trees and make boats. Last water, snow in the air, snow on the ground, ice on the lake, on the river ice in the eddies. Every day more snow, more ice. Maybe one day, maybe three days, maybe six days, any day maybe freeze-up come, then no more water, all ice, everybody walk, Dawson six hundred miles, long time walk. Boat go very quick. Everybody want to go boat. Everybody say, 'Charley, two hundred dollars you take me in canoe,' 'Charley, three hundred dollars,' 'Charley, four hundred dollars.' I say no, all the time I say no. I am letter carrier.

"In morning I get to Lake Linderman. I walk all night and am much tired. I cook breakfast, I eat, then I sleep on the beach three hours. I wake up. It is ten o'clock. Snow is falling. There is wind, much wind that blows fair. Also, there is a woman who sits in the snow alongside. She is white woman, she is young, very pretty, maybe she is twenty years old, maybe twenty-five years old. She look at me. I look at her. She is very tired. She is no dance-woman. I see that right away. She is good woman, and she is very tired.

"'You are Sitka Charley,' she says. I get up quick and roll blankets so snow does not get inside. 'I go to Dawson,' she says. 'I go in your canoe—how much?'

"I do not want anybody in my canoe. I do not like to say no. So I say, 'One thousand dollars.' Just for fun I say it, so woman cannot come with me, much better than say no. She look at me very hard, then she says, 'When you start?' I say right away. Then she says all right, she will give me one thousand dollars.

"What can I say? I do not want the woman, yet have I given my word that for one thousand dollars she can come. I am surprised. Maybe she make fun, too, so I say, 'Let me see thousand dollars.' And that woman, that young woman, all alone on the trail, there in the snow, she take out one thousand dollars, in greenbacks, and she put them in my hand. I look at money, I look at her. What can I say? I say, 'No, my canoe very small. There is no room for outfit.' She laugh. She says, 'I am great traveller. This is my outfit.' She kick one small pack in the snow. It is two fur robes, canvas outside, some woman's clothes inside. I pick it up. Maybe thirty-five pounds. I am surprised. She take it away from me. She says, 'Come, let us start.' She carries pack into canoe. What can I say? I put my blankets into canoe. We start.

"And that is the way I saw the woman first time. The wind was fair. I put up small sail. The canoe went very fast, it flew like a bird over the high waves. The woman was much afraid. 'What for you come Klondike much afraid?' I ask. She laugh at me, a hard laugh, but she is still much afraid. Also is she very tired. I run canoe through rapids to Lake Bennett. Water very bad, and woman cry out because she is afraid. We go down Lake Bennett, snow, ice, wind like a gale, but woman is very tired and go to sleep.

"That night we make camp at Windy Arm. Woman sit by fire and eat supper. I look at her. She is pretty. She fix hair. There is much hair, and it is brown, also sometimes it is like gold in the firelight, when she turn her head, so, and flashes come from it like golden fire. The eyes are large and brown, sometimes warm like a candle behind a curtain, sometimes very hard and bright like broken ice when sun shines upon it. When she smile—how can I say?—when she smile I know white man like to kiss her, just like that, when she smile. She never do hard work. Her hands are soft, like baby's hand. She is soft all over, like baby. She is not thin, but round like baby; her arm, her leg, her muscles, all soft and round like baby. Her waist is small, and when she stand up, when she walk, or move her head or arm, it is—I do not know the word—but it is nice to look at, like—maybe I say she is built on lines like the lines of a good canoe, just like that, and when she move she is like the movement of the good canoe sliding through still water or leaping through water when it is white and fast and angry. It is very good to see.

"Why does she come into Klondike, all alone, with plenty of money? I do not know. Next day I ask her. She laugh and says: 'Sitka Charley, that is none of your business. I give you one thousand dollars take me to Dawson. That only is your business.' Next day after that I ask her what is her name. She laugh, then she says, 'Mary Jones, that is my name.' I do not know her name, but I know all the time that Mary Jones is not her name.

"It is very cold in canoe, and because of cold sometimes she not feel good. Sometimes she feel good and she sing. Her voice is like a silver bell, and I feel good all over like when I go into church at Holy Cross Mission, and when she sing I feel strong and paddle like hell. Then she laugh and says, 'You think we get to Dawson before freeze-up, Charley?' Sometimes she sit in canoe and is thinking far away, her eyes like that, all empty. She does not see Sitka Charley, nor the ice, nor the snow. She is far away. Very often she is like that, thinking far away. Sometimes, when she is thinking far away, her face is not good to see. It looks like a face that is angry, like the face of one man when he want to kill another man.

"Last day to Dawson very bad. Shore-ice in all the eddies, mush-ice in the stream. I cannot paddle. The canoe freeze to ice. I cannot get to shore. There is much danger. All the time we go down Yukon in the ice. That night there is much noise of ice. Then ice stop, canoe stop, everything stop. 'Let us go to shore,' the woman says. I say no, better wait. By and by, everything start down-stream again. There is much snow. I cannot see. At eleven o'clock at night, everything stop. At one o'clock everything start again. At three o'clock everything stop. Canoe is smashed like eggshell, but is on top of ice and cannot sink. I hear dogs howling. We wait. We sleep. By and by morning come. There is no more snow. It is the freeze-up, and there is Dawson. Canoe smash and stop right at Dawson. Sitka Charley has come in with two thousand letters on very last water.

"The woman rent a cabin on the hill, and for one week I see her no more. Then, one day, she come to me. 'Charley,' she says, 'how do you like to work for me? You drive dogs, make camp, travel with me.' I say that I make too much money carrying letters. She says, 'Charley, I will pay you more money.' I tell her that pick-and-shovel man get fifteen dollars a day in the mines. She says, 'That is four hundred and fifty dollars a month.' And I say, 'Sitka Charley is no pick-and-shovel man.' Then she says, 'I understand, Charley. I will give you seven hundred and fifty dollars each month.' It is a good price, and I go to work for her. I buy for her dogs and sled. We travel up Klondike, up Bonanza and Eldorado, over to Indian River, to Sulphur Creek, to Dominion, back across divide to Gold Bottom and to Too Much Gold, and back to Dawson. All the time she look for something, I do not know what. I am puzzled. 'What thing you look for?' I ask. She laugh. 'You look for gold?' I ask. She laugh. Then she says, 'That is none of your business, Charley.' And after that I never ask any more.

"She has a small revolver which she carries in her belt. Sometimes, on trail, she makes practice with revolver. I laugh. 'What for you laugh, Charley?' she ask. 'What for you play with that?' I say. 'It is no good. It is too small. It is for a child, a little plaything.' When we get back to Dawson she ask me to buy good revolver for her. I buy a Colt's 44. It is very heavy, but she carry it in her belt all the time.

"At Dawson comes the man. Which way he come I do not know. Only do I know he is *checha-quo*—what you call tenderfoot. His hands are soft, just like hers. He never do hard work. He is soft all over. At first I think maybe he is her husband. But he is too young. Also, they make two beds at night. He is maybe twenty years old. His eyes blue, his hair yellow, he has a little mustache which is yellow. His name is John Jones. Maybe he is her brother. I do not know. I ask questions no more. Only I think his name not John Jones. Other people call him Mr. Girvan. I do not think that is his name. I do not think her name is Miss Girvan, which other people call her. I think nobody know their names.

"One night I am asleep at Dawson. He wake me up. He says, 'Get the dogs ready; we start.' No more do I ask questions, so I get the dogs ready and we start. We go down the Yukon. It is night-time, it is November, and it is very cold—sixty-five below. She is soft. He is soft. The cold bites. They get tired. They cry under their breaths to themselves. By and by I say better we stop and make camp. But they say that they will go on. Three times I say better to make camp and rest, but each time they say they will go on. After that I say nothing. All the time, day after day, is it that way. They are very soft. They get stiff and sore. They do not understand moccasins, and their feet hurt very much. They limp, they stagger like drunken people, they cry under their breaths; and all the time they say, 'On! on! We will go on!'

"They are like crazy people. All the time do they go on, and on. Why do they go on? I do not know. Only do they go on. What are they after? I do not know. They are not after gold. There is no stampede. Besides, they spend plenty of money. But I ask questions no more. I, too, go on and on, because I am strong on the trail and because I am greatly paid.

"We make Circle City. That for which they look is not there. I think now that we will rest, and rest the dogs. But we do not rest, not for one day do we rest. 'Come,' says the woman to the man, 'let us go on.' And we go on. We leave the Yukon. We cross the divide to the west and swing down into the Tanana Country. There are new diggings there. But that for which they look is not there, and we take the back trail to Circle City.

"It is a hard journey. December is most gone. The days are short. It is very cold. One morning it is seventy below zero. 'Better that we don't travel to-day,' I say, 'else will the frost be unwarmed in the breathing and bite all the edges of our lungs. After that we will have bad cough, and maybe next spring will come pneumonia.' But they are *checha-quo*. They do not understand the trail. They are like dead people they are so tired, but they say, 'Let us go on.' We go on. The frost bites their lungs, and they get the dry cough. They cough till the tears run down their cheeks. When bacon is frying they must run away from the fire and cough half an hour in the snow. They freeze their cheeks a little bit, so that the skin turns black and is very sore. Also, the man freezes his thumb till the end is like to come off, and he must wear a large thumb on his mitten to keep it warm. And sometimes, when the frost bites hard and the thumb is very cold, he must take off the mitten and put the hand between his legs next to the skin, so that the thumb may get warm again.

"We limp into Circle City, and even I, Sitka Charley, am tired. It is Christmas Eve. I dance, drink, make a good time, for to-morrow is Christmas Day and we will rest. But no. It is five o'clock in the morning—Christmas morning. I am two hours asleep. The man stand by my bed. 'Come, Charley,' he says, 'harness the dogs. We start.'

"Have I not said that I ask questions no more? They pay me seven hundred and fifty dollars each month. They are my masters. I am their man. If they say, 'Charley, come, let us start for hell,' I will harness the dogs, and snap the whip, and start for hell. So I harness the dogs, and we start down the Yukon. Where do we go? They do not say. Only do they say, 'On! on! We will go on!'

"They are very weary. They have travelled many hundreds of miles, and they do not understand the way of the trail. Besides, their cough is very bad—the dry cough that makes strong men swear and weak men cry. But they go on. Every day they go on. Never do they rest the dogs. Always do they buy new dogs. At every camp, at every post, at every Indian village, do they cut out the tired dogs and put in fresh dogs. They have much money, money without end, and like water they spend it. They are crazy? Sometimes I think so, for there is a devil in them that drives them on and on, always on. What is it that they try to find? It is not gold. Never do they dig in the ground. I think a long time. Then I think it is a man they try to find. But what man? Never do we see the man. Yet are they like wolves on the trail of the kill. But they are funny wolves, soft wolves, baby wolves who do not understand the way of the trail. They cry aloud in their sleep at night. In their sleep they moan and groan with the pain of their weariness. And in the day, as they stagger along the trail, they cry under their breaths. They are funny wolves.

"We pass Fort Yukon. We pass Fort Hamilton. We pass Minook. January has come and nearly gone. The days are very short. At nine o'clock comes daylight. At three o'clock comes night. And it is cold. And even I, Sitka Charley, am tired. Will we go on forever this way without end? I do not know. But always do I look along the trail for that which they try to find. There are few people on the trail. Sometimes we travel one hundred miles and never see a sign of life. It is very quiet. There is no sound. Sometimes it snows, and we are like wandering ghosts. Sometimes it is clear, and at midday the sun looks at us for a moment over the hills to the south. The northern lights flame in the sky, and the sun-dogs dance, and the air is filled with frost-dust.

"I am Sitka Charley, a strong man. I was born on the trail, and all my days have I lived on the trail. And yet have these two baby wolves made me very tired. I am lean, like a starved cat, and I am glad of my bed at night, and in the morning am I greatly weary. Yet ever are we hitting the trail in the dark before daylight, and still on the trail does the dark after nightfall find us. These two baby wolves! If I am lean like a starved cat, they are lean like cats that have never eaten and have died. Their eyes are sunk deep in their heads, bright sometimes as with fever, dim and cloudy sometimes like the eyes of the dead. Their cheeks are hollow like caves in a cliff. Also are their cheeks black and raw from many freezings. Sometimes it is the woman in the morning who says, 'I cannot get up. I cannot move. Let me die.' And it is the man who stands beside her and says, 'Come, let us go on.' And they go on. And sometimes it is the man who cannot get up, and the woman says, 'Come, let us go on.' But the one thing they do, and always do, is to go on. Always do they go on.

"Sometimes, at the trading posts, the man and woman get letters. I do not know what is in the letters. But it is the scent that they follow, these letters themselves are the scent. One time an Indian gives them a letter. I talk with him privately. He says it is a man with one eye who gives him the letter, a man who travels fast down the Yukon. That is all. But I know that the baby wolves are after the man with the one eye.

"It is February, and we have travelled fifteen hundred miles. We are getting near Bering Sea, and there are storms and blizzards. The going is hard. We come to Anvig. I do not know, but I think sure they get a letter at Anvig, for they are much excited, and they say, 'Come, hurry, let us go on.' But I say we must buy grub, and they say we must travel light and fast. Also, they say that we can get grub at Charley McKeon's cabin. Then do I know that they take the big cut-off, for it is there that Charley McKeon lives where the Black Rock stands by the trail.

"Before we start, I talk maybe two minutes with the priest at Anvig. Yes, there is a man with one eye who has gone by and who travels fast. And I know that for which they look is the man with the one eye. We leave Anvig with little grub, and travel light and fast. There are three fresh dogs bought in Anvig, and we travel very fast. The man and woman are like mad. We start earlier in the morning, we travel later at night. I look sometimes to see them die, these two baby wolves, but they will not die. They go on and on. When the dry cough take hold of them hard, they hold their hands against their stomach and double up in the snow, and cough, and cough, and cough. They cannot walk, they cannot talk. Maybe for ten minutes they cough, maybe for half an hour, and then they straighten up, the tears from the coughing frozen on their faces, and the words they say are, 'Come, let us go on.'

"Even I, Sitka Charley, am greatly weary, and I think seven hundred and fifty dollars is a cheap price for the labor I do. We take the big cut-off, and the trail is fresh. The baby wolves have their noses down to the trail, and they say, 'Hurry!' All the time do they say, 'Hurry! Faster! Faster!' It is hard on the dogs. We have not much food and we cannot give them enough to eat, and they grow weak. Also, they must work hard. The woman has true sorrow for them, and often, because of them, the tears are in her eyes. But the devil in her that drives her on will not let her stop and rest the dogs.

"And then we come upon the man with the one eye. He is in the snow by the trail, and his leg is broken. Because of the leg he has made a poor camp, and has been lying on his blankets for three days and keeping a fire going. When we find him he is swearing. He swears like hell. Never have I heard a man swear like that man. I am glad. Now that they have found that for which they look, we will have rest. But the woman says, 'Let us start. Hurry!'

"I am surprised. But the man with the one eye says, 'Never mind me. Give me your grub. You will get more grub at McKeon's cabin to-morrow. Send McKeon back for me. But do you go on.' Here is another wolf, an old wolf, and he, too, thinks but the one thought, to go on. So we give him our grub, which is not much, and we chop wood for his fire, and we take his strongest dogs and go on. We left the man with one eye there in the snow, and he died there in the snow, for McKeon never went back for him. And who that man was, and why he came to be there, I do not know. But I think he was greatly paid by the man and the woman, like me, to do their work for them.

"That day and that night we had nothing to eat, and all next day we travelled fast, and we were weak with hunger. Then we came to the Black Rock, which rose five hundred feet above the trail. It was at the end of the day. Darkness was coming, and we could not find the cabin of McKeon. We slept hungry, and in the morning looked for the cabin. It was not there, which was a strange thing, for everybody knew that McKeon lived in a cabin at Black Rock. We were near to the coast, where the wind blows hard and there is much snow. Everywhere there were small hills of snow where the wind had piled it up. I have a thought, and I dig in one and another of the hills of snow. Soon I find the walls of the cabin, and I dig down to the door. I go inside. McKeon is dead. Maybe two or three weeks he is dead. A sickness had come upon him so that he could not leave the cabin. The wind and the snow had covered the cabin. He had eaten his grub and died. I looked for his cache, but there was no grub in it.

"'Let us go on,' said the woman. Her eyes were hungry, and her hand was upon her heart, as with the hurt of something inside. She bent back and forth like a tree in the wind as she stood there. 'Yes, let us go on,' said the man. His voice was hollow, like the *klonk* of an old raven, and he was hunger-mad. His eyes were like live coals of fire, and as his body rocked to and fro, so rocked his soul inside. And I, too, said, 'Let us go on.' For that one thought, laid upon me like a lash for every mile of fifteen hundred miles, had burned itself into my soul, and I think that I, too, was mad. Besides, we could only go on, for there was no grub. And we went on, giving no thought to the man with the one eye in the snow.

"There is little travel on the big cut-off. Sometimes two or three months and nobody goes by. The snow had covered the trail, and there was no sign that men had ever come or gone that way. All day the wind blew and the snow fell, and all day we travelled, while our stomachs gnawed their desire and our bodies grew weaker with every step they took. Then the woman began to fall. Then the man. I did not fall, but my feet were heavy and I caught my toes and stumbled many times.

"That night is the end of February. I kill three ptarmigan with the woman's revolver, and we are made somewhat strong again. But the dogs have nothing to eat. They try to eat their harness, which is of leather and walrus-hide, and I must fight them off with a club and hang all the harness in a tree. And all night they howl and fight around that tree. But we do not mind. We sleep like dead people, and in the morning get up like dead people out of their graves and go on along the trail.

"That morning is the 1st of March, and on that morning I see the first sign of that after which the baby wolves are in search. It is clear weather, and cold. The sun stay longer in the sky, and there are sun-dogs flashing on either side, and the air is bright with frost-dust. The snow falls no more upon the trail, and I see the fresh sign of dogs and sled. There is one man with that outfit, and I see in the snow that he is not strong. He, too, has not enough to eat. The young wolves see the fresh sign, too, and they are much excited. 'Hurry!' they say. All the time they say, 'Hurry! Faster, Charley, faster!'

"We make hurry very slow. All the time the man and the woman fall down. When they try to ride on sled the dogs are too weak, and the dogs fall down. Besides, it is so cold that if they ride on the sled they will freeze. It is very easy for a hungry man to freeze. When the woman fall down, the man help her up. Sometimes the woman help the man up. By and by both fall down and cannot get up, and I must help them up all the time, else they will not get up and will die there in the snow. This is very hard work, for I am greatly weary, and as well I must drive the dogs, and the man and woman are very heavy with no strength in their bodies. So, by and by, I, too, fall down in the snow, and there is no one to help me up. I must get up by myself. And always do I get up by myself, and help them up, and make the dogs go on.

"That night I get one ptarmigan, and we are very hungry. And that night the man says to me, 'What time start to-morrow, Charley?' It is like the voice of a ghost. I say, 'All the time you make start at five o'clock.' 'To-morrow,' he says, 'we will start at three o'clock.' I laugh in great bitterness, and I say, 'You are dead man.' And he says, 'To-morrow we will start at three o'clock.'

"And we start at three o'clock, for I am their man, and that which they say is to be done, I do. It is clear and cold, and there is no wind. When daylight comes we can see a long way off. And it is very quiet. We can hear no sound but the beat of our hearts, and in the silence that is a very loud sound. We are like sleep-walkers, and we walk in dreams until we fall down; and then we know we must get up, and we see the trail once more and bear the beating of our hearts. Sometimes, when I am walking in dreams this way, I have strange thoughts. Why does Sitka Charley live? I ask myself. Why does Sitka Charley work hard, and go hungry, and have all this pain? For seven hundred and fifty dollars a month, I make the answer, and I know it is a foolish answer. Also is it a true answer. And after that never again do I care for money. For that day a large wisdom came to me. There was a great light, and I saw clear, and I knew that it was not for money that a man must live, but for a happiness that no man can give, or buy, or sell, and that is beyond all value of all money in the world.

"In the morning we come upon the last-night camp of the man who is before us. It is a poor camp, the kind a man makes who is hungry and without strength. On the snow there are pieces of blanket and of canvas, and I know what has happened. His dogs have eaten their harness, and he has made new harness out of his blankets. The man and woman stare hard at what is to be seen, and as I look at them my back feels the chill as of a cold wind against the skin. Their eyes are toil-mad and hunger-mad, and burn like fire deep in their heads. Their faces are like the faces of people who have died of hunger, and their cheeks are black with the dead flesh of many freezings. 'Let us go on,' says the man. But the woman coughs and falls in the snow. It is the dry cough where the frost has bitten the lungs. For a long time she coughs, then like a woman crawling out of her grave she crawls to her feet. The tears are ice upon her cheeks, and her breath makes a noise as it comes and goes, and she says, 'Let us go on.'

"We go on. And we walk in dreams through the silence. And every time we walk is a dream and we are without pain; and every time we fall down is an awakening, and we see the snow and the mountains and the fresh trail of the man who is before us, and we know all our pain again. We come to where we can see a long way over the snow, and that for which they look is before them. A mile away there are black spots upon the snow. The black spots move. My eyes are dim, and I must stiffen my soul to see. And I see one man with dogs and a sled. The baby wolves see, too. They can no longer talk, but they whisper, 'On, on. Let us hurry!'

"And they fall down, but they go on. The man who is before us, his blanket harness breaks often, and he must stop and mend it. Our harness is good, for I have hung it in trees each night. At eleven o'clock the man is half a mile away. At one o'clock he is a quarter of a mile away. He is very weak. We see him fall down many times in the snow. One of his dogs can no longer travel, and he cuts it out of the harness. But he does not kill it. I kill it with the axe as I go by, as I kill one of my dogs which loses its legs and can travel no more.

"Now we are three hundred yards away. We go very slow. Maybe in two, three hours we go one mile. We do not walk. All the time we fall down. We stand up and stagger two steps, maybe three steps, then we fall down again. And all the time I must help up the man and woman. Sometimes they rise to their knees and fall forward, maybe four or five times before they can get to their feet again and stagger two or three steps and fall. But always do they fall forward. Standing or kneeling, always do they fall forward, gaining on the trail each time by the length of their bodies.

"Sometimes they crawl on hands and knees like animals that live in the forest. We go like snails, like snails that are dying we go so slow. And yet we go faster than the man who is before us. For he, too, falls all the time, and there is no Sitka Charley to lift him up. Now he is two hundred yards away. After a long time he is one hundred yards away.

"It is a funny sight. I want to laugh out loud, Ha! ha! just like that, it is so funny. It is a race of dead men and dead dogs. It is like in a dream when you have a nightmare and run away very fast for your life and go very slow. The man who is with me is mad. The woman is mad. I am mad. All the world is mad, and I want to laugh, it is so funny.

"The stranger-man who is before us leaves his dogs behind and goes on alone across the snow. After a long time we come to the dogs. They lie helpless in the snow, their harness of blanket and canvas on them, the sled behind them, and as we pass them they whine to us and cry like babies that are hungry.

"Then we, too, leave our dogs and go on alone across the snow. The man and the woman are nearly gone, and they moan and groan and sob, but they go on. I, too, go on. I have but one thought. It is to come up to the stranger-man. Then it is that I shall rest, and not until then shall I rest, and it seems that I must lie down and sleep for a thousand years, I am so tired.

"The stranger-man is fifty yards away, all alone in the white snow. He falls and crawls, staggers, and falls and crawls again. He is like an animal that is sore wounded and trying to run from the hunter. By and by he crawls on hands and knees. He no longer stands up. And the man and woman no longer stand up. They, too, crawl after him on hands and knees. But I stand up. Sometimes I fall, but always do I stand up again.

"It is a strange thing to see. All about is the snow and the silence, and through it crawl the man and the woman, and the stranger-man who goes before. On either side the sun are sun-dogs, so that there are three suns in the sky. The frost-dust is like the dust of diamonds, and all the air is filled with it. Now the woman coughs, and lies still in the snow until the fit has passed, when she crawls on again. Now the man looks ahead, and he is blear-eyed as with old age and must rub his eyes so that he can see the stranger-man. And now the stranger-man looks back over his shoulder. And Sitka Charley, standing upright, maybe falls down and stands upright again.

"After a long time the stranger-man crawls no more. He stands slowly upon his feet and rocks back and forth. Also does he take off one mitten and wait with revolver in his hand, rocking back and forth as he waits. His face is skin and bones and frozen black. It is a hungry face. The eyes are deep-sunk in his head, and the lips are snarling. The man and woman, too, get upon their feet and they go toward him very slowly. And all about is the snow and the silence. And in the sky are three suns, and all the air is flashing with the dust of diamonds.

"And thus it was that I, Sitka Charley, saw the baby wolves make their kill. No word is spoken. Only does the stranger-man snarl with his hungry face. Also does he rock to and fro, his shoulders drooping, his knees bent, and his legs wide apart so that he does not fall down. The man and the woman stop maybe fifty feet away. Their legs, too, are wide apart so that they do not fall down, and their bodies rock to and fro. The stranger-man is very weak. His arm shakes, so that when he shoots at the man his bullet strikes in the snow. The man cannot take off his mitten. The stranger-man shoots at him again, and this time the bullet goes by in the air. Then the man takes the mitten in his teeth and pulls it off. But his hand is frozen and he cannot hold the revolver, and it falls in the snow. I look at the woman. Her mitten is off, and the big Colt's revolver is in her hand. Three times she shoot, quick, just like that. The hungry face of the stranger-man is still snarling as he falls forward into the snow.

"They do not look at the dead man. 'Let us go on,' they say. And we go on. But now that they have found that for which they look, they are like dead. The last strength has gone out of them. They can stand no more upon their feet. They will not crawl, but desire only to close their eyes and sleep. I see not far away a place for camp. I kick them. I have my dog-whip, and I give them the lash of it. They cry aloud, but they must crawl. And they do crawl to the place for camp. I build fire so that they will not freeze. Then I go back for sled. Also, I kill the dogs of the stranger-man so that we may have food and not die. I put the man and woman in blankets and they sleep. Sometimes I wake them and give them little bit of food. They are not awake, but they take the food. The woman sleep one day and a half. Then she wake up and go to sleep again. The man sleep two days and wake up and go to sleep again. After that we go down to the coast at St. Michaels. And when the ice goes out of Bering Sea, the man and woman go away on a steamship. But first they pay me my seven hundred and fifty dollars a month. Also, they make me a present of one thousand dollars. And that was the year that Sitka Charley gave much money to the Mission at Holy Cross."

"But why did they kill the man?" I asked.

Sitka Charley delayed reply until he had lighted his pipe. He glanced at the *Police Gazette* illustration and nodded his head at it familiarly. Then he said, speaking slowly and ponderingly:

"I have thought much. I do not know. It is something that happened. It is a picture I remember. It is like looking in at the window and seeing the man writing a letter. They came into my life and they went out of my life, and the picture is as I have said, without beginning, the end without understanding."

"You have painted many pictures in the telling," I said.

"Ay," he nodded his head. "But they were without beginning and without end."

"The last picture of all had an end," I said.

"Ay," he answered. "But what end?"

"It was a piece of life," I said.

"Ay," he answered. "It was a piece of life."

NEGORE, THE COWARD

He had followed the trail of his fleeing people for eleven days, and his pursuit had been in itself a flight; for behind him he knew full well were the dreaded Russians, toiling through the swampy lowlands and over the steep divides, bent on no less than the extermination of all his people. He was travelling light. A rabbit-skin sleeping-robe, a muzzle-loading rifle, and a few pounds of sun-dried salmon constituted his outfit. He would have marvelled that a whole people—women and children and aged—could travel so swiftly, had he not known the terror that drove them on.

It was in the old days of the Russian occupancy of Alaska, when the nineteenth century had run but half its course, that Negore fled after his fleeing tribe and came upon it this summer night by the head waters of the Pee-lat. Though near the midnight hour, it was bright day as he passed through the weary camp. Many saw him, all knew him, but few and cold were the greetings he received.

"Negore, the Coward," he heard Illiha, a young woman, laugh, and Sunne, his sister's daughter, laughed with her.

Black anger ate at his heart; but he gave no sign, threading his way among the camp-fires until he came to one where sat an old man. A young woman was kneading with skilful fingers the tired muscles of his legs. He raised a sightless face and listened intently as Negore's foot crackled a dead twig.

"Who comes?" he queried in a thin, tremulous voice.

"Negore," said the young woman, scarcely looking up from her task.

Negore's face was expressionless. For many minutes he stood and waited. The old man's head had sunk back upon his chest. The young woman pressed and prodded the wasted muscles, resting her body on her knees, her bowed head hidden as in a cloud by her black wealth of hair. Negore watched the supple body, bending at the hips as a lynx's body might bend, pliant as a young willow stalk, and, withal, strong as only youth is strong. He looked, and was aware of a great yearning, akin in sensation to physical hunger. At last he spoke, saying:

"Is there no greeting for Negore, who has been long gone and has but now come back?"

She looked up at him with cold eyes. The old man chuckled to himself after the manner of the old.

"Thou art my woman, Oona," Negore said, his tones dominant and conveying a hint of menace.

She arose with catlike ease and suddenness to her full height, her eyes flashing, her nostrils quivering like a deer's.

"I was thy woman to be, Negore, but thou art a coward; the daughter of Old Kinoos mates not with a coward!"

She silenced him with an imperious gesture as he strove to speak.

"Old Kinoos and I came among you from a strange land. Thy people took us in by their fires and made us warm, nor asked whence or why we wandered. It was their thought that Old Kinoos had lost the sight of his eyes from age; nor did Old Kinoos say otherwise, nor did I, his daughter. Old Kinoos is a brave man, but Old Kinoos was never a boaster. And now, when I tell thee of how his blindness came to be, thou wilt know, beyond question, that the daughter of Kinoos cannot mother the children of a coward such as thou art, Negore."

Again she silenced the speech that rushed up to his tongue.

"Know, Negore, if journey be added unto journey of all thy journeyings through this land, thou wouldst not come to the unknown Sitka on the Great Salt Sea. In that place there be many Russian folk, and their rule is harsh. And from Sitka, Old Kinoos, who was Young Kinoos in those days, fled away with me, a babe in his arms, along the islands in the midst of the sea. My mother dead tells the tale of his wrong; a Russian, dead with a spear through breast and back, tells the tale of the vengeance of Kinoos.

"But wherever we fled, and however far we fled, always did we find the hated Russian folk. Kinoos was unafraid, but the sight of them was a hurt to his eyes; so we fled on and on, through the seas and years, till we came to the Great Fog Sea, Negore, of which thou hast heard, but which thou hast never seen. We lived among many peoples, and I grew to be a woman; but Kinoos, growing old, took to him no other woman, nor did I take a man.

"At last we came to Pastolik, which is where the Yukon drowns itself in the Great Fog Sea. Here we lived long, on the rim of the sea, among a people by whom the Russians were well hated. But sometimes they came, these Russians, in great ships, and made the people of Pastolik show them the way through the islands uncountable of the many-mouthed Yukon. And sometimes the men they took to show them the way never came back, till the people became angry and planned a great plan.

"So, when there came a ship, Old Kinoos stepped forward and said he would show the way. He was an old man then, and his hair was white; but he was unafraid. And he was cunning, for he took the ship to where the sea sucks in to the land and the waves beat white on the mountain called Romanoff. The sea sucked the ship in to where the waves beat white, and it ground upon the rocks and broke open its sides. Then came all the people of Pastolik, (for this was the plan), with their war-spears, and arrows, and some few guns. But first the Russians put out the eyes of Old Kinoos that he might never show the way again, and then they fought, where the waves beat white, with the people of Pastolik.

"Now the head-man of these Russians was Ivan. He it was, with his two thumbs, who drove out the eyes of Kinoos. He it was who fought his way through the white water, with two men left of all his men, and went away along the rim of the Great Fog Sea into the north. Kinoos was wise. He could see no more and was helpless as a child. So he fled away from the sea, up the great, strange Yukon, even to Nulato, and I fled with him.

"This was the deed my father did, Kinoos, an old man. But how did the young man, Negore?"

Once again she silenced him.

"With my own eyes I saw, at Nulato, before the gates of the great fort, and but few days gone. I saw the Russian, Ivan, who thrust out my father's eyes, lay the lash of his dog-whip upon thee and beat thee like a dog. This I saw, and knew thee for a coward. But I saw thee not, that night, when all thy people—yea, even the boys not yet hunters—fell upon the Russians and slew them all."

"Not Ivan," said Negore, quietly. "Even now is he on our heels, and with him many Russians fresh up from the sea."

Oona made no effort to hide her surprise and chagrin that Ivan was not dead, but went on:

"In the day I saw thee a coward; in the night, when all men fought, even the boys not yet hunters, I saw thee not and knew thee doubly a coward."

"Thou art done? All done?" Negore asked.

She nodded her head and looked at him askance, as though astonished that he should have aught to say.

"Know then that Negore is no coward," he said; and his speech was very low and quiet. "Know that when I was yet a boy I journeyed alone down to the place where the Yukon drowns itself in the Great Fog Sea. Even to Pastolik I journeyed, and even beyond, into the north, along the rim of the sea. This I did when I was a boy, and I was no coward. Nor was I coward when I journeyed, a young man and alone, up the Yukon farther than man had ever been, so far that I came to another folk, with white faces, who live in a great fort and talk speech other than that the Russians talk. Also have I killed the great bear of the Tanana country, where no one of my people hath ever been. And I have fought with the Nuklukyets, and the Kaltags, and the Sticks in far regions, even I, and alone. These deeds, whereof no man knows, I speak for myself. Let my people speak for me of things I have done which they know. They will not say Negore is a coward."

He finished proudly, and proudly waited.

"These be things which happened before I came into the land," she said, "and I know not of them. Only do I know what I know, and I know I saw thee lashed like a dog in the day; and in the night, when the great fort flamed red and the men killed and were killed, I saw thee not. Also, thy people do call thee Negore, the Coward. It is thy name now, Negore, the Coward."

"It is not a good name," Old Kinoos chuckled.

"Thou dost not understand, Kinoos," Negore said gently. "But I shall make thee understand. Know that I was away on the hunt of the bear, with Kamo-tah, my mother's son. And Kamo-tah fought with a great bear. We had no meat for three days, and Kamo-tah was not strong of arm nor swift of foot. And the great bear crushed him, so, till his bones cracked like dry sticks. Thus I found him, very sick and groaning upon the ground. And there was no meat, nor could I kill aught that the sick man might eat.

"So I said, 'I will go to Nulato and bring thee food, also strong men to carry thee to camp.' And Kamo-tah said, 'Go thou to Nulato and get food, but say no word of what has befallen me. And when I have eaten, and am grown well and strong, I will kill this bear. Then will I return in honor to Nulato, and no man may laugh and say Kamo-tah was undone by a bear.'

"So I gave heed to my brother's words; and when I was come to Nulato, and the Russian, Ivan, laid the lash of his dog-whip upon me, I knew I must not fight. For no man knew of Kamo-tah, sick and groaning and hungry; and did I fight with Ivan, and die, then would my brother die, too. So it was, Oona, that thou sawest me beaten like a dog.

"Then I heard the talk of the shamans and chiefs that the Russians had brought strange sicknesses upon the people, and killed our men, and stolen our women, and that the land must be made clean. As I say, I heard the talk, and I knew it for good talk, and I knew that in the night the Russians were to be killed. But there was my brother, Kamo-tah, sick and groaning and with no meat; so I could not stay and fight with the men and the boys not yet hunters.

"And I took with me meat and fish, and the lash-marks of Ivan, and I found Kamo-tah no longer groaning, but dead. Then I went back to Nulato, and, behold, there was no Nulato—only ashes where the great fort had stood, and the bodies of many men. And I saw the Russians come up the Yukon in boats, fresh from the sea, many Russians; and I saw Ivan creep forth from where he lay hid and make talk with them. And the next day I saw Ivan lead them upon the trail of the tribe. Even now are they upon the trail, and I am here, Negore, but no coward."

"This is a tale I hear," said Oona, though her voice was gentler than before. "Kamo-tah is dead and cannot speak for thee, and I know only what I know, and I must know thee of my own eyes for no coward."

Negore made an impatient gesture.

"There be ways and ways," she added. "Art thou willing to do no less than what Old Kinoos hath done?"

He nodded his head, and waited.

"As thou hast said, they seek for us even now, these Russians. Show them the way, Negore, even as Old Kinoos showed them the way, so that they come, unprepared, to where we wait for them, in a passage up the rocks. Thou knowest the place, where the wall is broken and high. Then will we destroy them, even Ivan. When they cling like flies to the wall, and top is no less near than bottom, our men shall fall upon them from above and either side, with spears, and arrows, and guns. And the women and children, from above, shall loosen the great rocks and hurl them down upon them. It will be a great day, for the Russians will be killed, the land will be made clean, and Ivan, even Ivan who thrust out my father's eyes and laid the lash of his dog-whip upon thee, will be killed. Like a dog gone mad will he die, his breath crushed out of him beneath the rocks. And when the fighting begins, it is for thee, Negore, to crawl secretly away so that thou be not slain."

"Even so," he answered. "Negore will show them the way. And then?"

"And then I shall be thy woman, Negore's woman, the brave man's woman. And thou shalt hunt meat for me and Old Kinoos, and I shall cook thy food, and sew thee warm parkas and strong, and make thee moccasins after the way of my people, which is a better way than thy people's way. And as I say, I shall be thy woman, Negore, always thy woman. And I shall make thy life glad for thee, so that all thy days will be a song and laughter, and thou wilt know the woman Oona as unlike all other women, for she has journeyed far, and lived in strange places, and is wise in the ways of men and in the ways they may be made glad. And in thine old age will she still make thee glad, and thy memory of her in the days of thy strength will be sweet, for thou wilt know always that she was ease to thee, and peace, and rest, and that beyond all women to other men has she been woman to thee."

"Even so," said Negore, and the hunger for her ate at his heart, and his arms went out for her as a hungry man's arms might go out for food.

"When thou hast shown the way, Negore," she chided him; but her eyes were soft, and warm, and he knew she looked upon him as woman had never looked before.

"It is well," he said, turning resolutely on his heel. "I go now to make talk with the chiefs, so that they may know I am gone to show the Russians the way."

"Oh, Negore, my man! my man!" she said to herself, as she watched him go, but she said it so softly that even Old Kinoos did not hear, and his ears were over keen, what of his blindness.

* * * * *

Three days later, having with craft ill-concealed his hiding-place, Negore was dragged forth like a rat and brought before Ivan—"Ivan the Terrible" he was known by the men who marched at his back. Negore was armed with a miserable bone-barbed spear, and he kept his rabbit-skin robe wrapped closely about him, and though the day was warm he shivered as with an ague. He shook his head that he did not understand the speech Ivan put at him, and made that he was very weary and sick, and wished only to sit down and rest, pointing the while to his stomach in sign of his sickness, and shivering fiercely. But Ivan had with him a man from Pastolik who talked the speech of Negore, and many and vain were the questions they asked him concerning his tribe, till the man from Pastolik, who was called Karduk, said:

"It is the word of Ivan that thou shalt be lashed till thou diest if thou dost not speak. And know, strange brother, when I tell thee the word of Ivan is the law, that I am thy friend and no friend of Ivan. For I come not willingly from my country by the sea, and I desire greatly to live; wherefore I obey the will of my master—as thou wilt obey, strange brother, if thou art wise, and wouldst live."

"Nay, strange brother," Negore answered, "I know not the way my people are gone, for I was sick, and they fled so fast my legs gave out from under me, and I fell behind."

Negore waited while Karduk talked with Ivan. Then Negore saw the Russian's face go dark, and he saw the men step to either side of him, snapping the lashes of their whips. Whereupon he betrayed a great fright, and cried aloud that he was a sick man and knew nothing, but would tell what he knew. And to such purpose did he tell, that Ivan gave the word to his men to march, and on either side of Negore marched the men with the whips, that he might not run away. And when he made that he was weak of his sickness, and stumbled and walked not so fast as they walked, they laid their lashes upon him till he screamed with pain and discovered new strength. And when Karduk told him all would he well with him when they had overtaken his tribe, he asked, "And then may I rest and move not?"

Continually he asked, "And then may I rest and move not?"

And while he appeared very sick and looked about him with dull eyes, he noted the fighting strength of Ivan's men, and noted with satisfaction that Ivan did not recognize him as the man he had beaten before the gates of the fort. It was a strange following his dull eyes saw. There were Slavonian hunters, fair-skinned and mighty-muscled; short, squat Finns, with flat noses and round faces; Siberian half-breeds, whose noses were more like eagle-beaks; and lean, slant-eyed men, who bore in their veins the Mongol and Tartar blood as well as the blood of the Slav. Wild adventurers they were, forayers and destroyers from the far lands beyond the Sea of Bering, who blasted the new and unknown world with fire and sword and clutched greedily for its wealth of fur and hide. Negore looked upon them with satisfaction, and in his mind's eye he saw them crushed and lifeless at the passage up the rocks. And ever he saw, waiting for him at the passage up the rocks, the face and the form of Oona, and ever he heard her voice in his ears and felt the soft, warm glow of her eyes. But never did he forget to shiver, nor to stumble where the footing was rough, nor to cry aloud at the bite of the lash. Also, he was afraid of Karduk, for he knew him for no true man. His was a false eye, and an easy tongue—a tongue too easy, he judged, for the awkwardness of honest speech.

All that day they marched. And on the next, when Karduk asked him at command of Ivan, he said he doubted they would meet with his tribe till the morrow. But Ivan, who had once been shown the way by Old Kinoos, and had found that way to lead through the white water and a deadly fight, believed no more in anything. So when they came to a passage up the rocks, he halted his forty men, and through Karduk demanded if the way were clear.

Negore looked at it shortly and carelessly. It was a vast slide that broke the straight wall of a cliff, and was overrun with brush and creeping plants, where a score of tribes could have lain well hidden.

He shook his head. "Nay, there be nothing there," he said. "The way is clear."

Again Ivan spoke to Karduk, and Karduk said:

"Know, strange brother, if thy talk be not straight, and if thy people block the way and fall upon Ivan and his men, that thou shalt die, and at once."

"My talk is straight," Negore said. "The way is clear."

Still Ivan doubted, and ordered two of his Slavonian hunters to go up alone. Two other men he ordered to the side of Negore. They placed their guns against his breast and waited. All waited. And Negore knew, should one arrow fly, or one spear be flung, that his death would come upon him. The two Slavonian hunters toiled upward till they grew small and smaller, and when they reached the top and waved their hats that all was well, they were like black specks against the sky.

The guns were lowered from Negore's breast and Ivan gave the order for his men to go forward. Ivan was silent, lost in thought. For an hour he marched, as though puzzled, and then, through Karduk's mouth, he said to Negore:

"How didst thou know the way was clear when thou didst look so briefly upon it?"

Negore thought of the little birds he had seen perched among the rocks and upon the bushes, and smiled, it was so simple; but he shrugged his shoulders and made no answer. For he was thinking, likewise, of another passage up the rocks, to which they would soon come, and where the little birds would all be gone. And he was glad that Karduk came from the Great Fog Sea, where there were no trees or bushes, and where men learned water-craft instead of land-craft and wood-craft.

Three hours later, when the sun rode overhead, they came to another passage up the rocks, and Karduk said:

"Look with all thine eyes, strange brother, and see if the way be clear, for Ivan is not minded this time to wait while men go up before."

Negore looked, and he looked with two men by his side, their guns resting against his breast. He saw that the little birds were all gone, and once he saw the glint of sunlight on a rifle-barrel. And he thought of Oona, and of her words: "And when the fighting begins, it is for thee, Negore, to crawl secretly away so that thou be not slain."

He felt the two guns pressing on his breast. This was not the way she had planned. There would be no crawling secretly away. He would be the first to die when the fighting began. But he said, and his voice was steady, and he still feigned to see with dull eyes and to shiver from his sickness:

"The way is clear."

And they started up, Ivan and his forty men from the far lands beyond the Sea of Bering. And there was Karduk, the man from Pastolik, and Negore, with the two guns always upon him. It was a long climb, and they could not go fast; but very fast to Negore they seemed to approach the midway point where top was no less near than bottom.

A gun cracked among the rocks to the right, and Negore heard the war-yell of all his tribe, and for an instant saw the rocks and bushes bristle alive with his kinfolk. Then he felt torn asunder by a burst of flame hot through his being, and as he fell he knew the sharp pangs of life as it wrenches at the flesh to be free.

But he gripped his life with a miser's clutch and would not let it go. He still breathed the air, which bit his lungs with a painful sweetness; and dimly he saw and heard, with passing spells of blindness and deafness, the flashes of sight and sound again wherein he saw the hunters of Ivan falling to their deaths, and his own brothers fringing the carnage and filling the air with the tumult of their cries and weapons, and, far above, the women and children loosing the great rocks that leaped like things alive and thundered down.

The sun danced above him in the sky, the huge walls reeled and swung, and still he heard and saw dimly. And when the great Ivan fell across his legs, hurled there lifeless and crushed by a down-rushing rock, he remembered the blind eyes of Old Kinoos and was glad.

Then the sounds died down, and the rocks no longer thundered past, and he saw his tribespeople creeping close and closer, spearing the wounded as they came. And near to him he heard the scuffle of a mighty Slavonian hunter, loath to die, and, half uprisen, borne back and down by the thirsty spears.

Then he saw above him the face of Oona, and felt about him the arms of Oona; and for a moment the sun steadied and stood still, and the great walls were upright and moved not.

"Thou art a brave man, Negore," he heard her say in his ear; "thou art my man, Negore."

And in that moment he lived all the life of gladness of which she had told him, and the laughter and the song, and as the sun went out of the sky above him, as in his old age, he knew the memory of her was sweet. And as even the memories dimmed and died in the darkness that fell upon him, he knew in her arms the fulfilment of all the ease and rest she had promised him. And as black night wrapped around him, his head upon her breast, he felt a great peace steal about him, and he was aware of the hush of many twilights and the mystery of silence.

About Author

John Griffith London (born **John Griffith Chaney**; January 12, 1876 – November 22, 1916) was an American novelist, journalist, and social activist. A pioneer in the world of commercial magazine fiction, he was one of the first writers to become a worldwide celebrity and earn a large fortune from writing. He was also an innovator in the genre that would later become known as science fiction.

His most famous works include The Call of the Wild and White Fang, both set in the Klondike Gold Rush, as well as the short stories "To Build a Fire", "An Odyssey of the North", and "Love of Life". He also wrote about the South Pacific in stories such as "The Pearls of Parlay", and "The Heathen".

London was part of the radical literary group "The Crowd" in San Francisco and a passionate advocate of unionization, workers' rights, socialism, and eugenics. He wrote several works dealing with these topics, such as his dystopian novel The Iron Heel, his non-fiction exposé The People of the Abyss, The War of the Classes, and Before Adam.

Family

Jack London's mother, Flora Wellman, was the fifth and youngest child of Pennsylvania Canal builder Marshall Wellman and his first wife, Eleanor Garrett Jones. Marshall Wellman was descended from Thomas Wellman, an early Puritan settler in the Massachusetts Bay Colony. Flora left Ohio and moved to the Pacific coast when her father remarried after her mother died. In San Francisco, Flora worked as a music teacher and spiritualist, claiming to channel the spirit of a Sauk chief, Black Hawk.

Biographer Clarice Stasz and others believe London's father was astrologer William Chaney. Flora Wellman was living with Chaney in San Francisco when she became pregnant. Whether Wellman and Chaney were legally married is unknown. Stasz notes that in his memoirs, Chaney refers to London's mother Flora Wellman as having been his "wife"; he also cites an advertisement in which Flora called herself "Florence Wellman Chaney".

According to Flora Wellman's account, as recorded in the San Francisco Chronicle of June 4, 1875, Chaney demanded that she have an abortion. When she refused, he disclaimed responsibility for the child. In desperation, she shot herself. She was not seriously wounded, but she was temporarily deranged. After giving birth, Flora turned the baby over for care to Virginia Prentiss, an African-American woman and former slave. She was a major maternal figure throughout London's life. Late in 1876, Flora Wellman married John London, a partially disabled Civil War veteran, and brought her baby John, later known as Jack, to live with the newly married couple. The family moved around the San Francisco Bay Area before settling in Oakland, where London completed public grade school.

In 1897, when he was 21 and a student at the University of California, Berkeley, London searched for and read the newspaper accounts of his mother's suicide attempt and the name of his biological father. He wrote to William Chaney, then living in Chicago. Chaney responded that he could not be London's father because he was impotent; he casually asserted that London's mother had relations with other men and averred that she had slandered him when she said he insisted on an abortion. Chaney concluded by saying that he was more to be pitied than London. London was devastated by his father's letter; in the months following, he quit school at Berkeley and went to the Klondike during the gold rush boom.

Early life

London was born near Third and Brannan Streets in San Francisco. The house burned down in the fire after the 1906 San Francisco earthquake; the California Historical Society placed a plaque at the site in 1953. Although the family was working class, it was not as impoverished as London's later accounts claimed. London was largely self-educated.

In 1885, London found and read Ouida's long Victorian novel Signa. He credited this as the seed of his literary success. In 1886, he went to the Oakland Public Library and found a sympathetic librarian, Ina Coolbrith, who encouraged his learning. (She later became California's first poet laureate and an important figure in the San Francisco literary community).

In 1889, London began working 12 to 18 hours a day at Hickmott's Cannery. Seeking a way out, he borrowed money from his foster mother Virginia Prentiss, bought the sloop Razzle-Dazzle from an oyster pirate named French Frank, and became an oyster pirate himself. In his memoir, John Barleycorn, he claims also to have stolen French Frank's mistress Mamie. After a few months, his sloop became damaged beyond repair. London hired on as a member of the California Fish Patrol.

In 1893, he signed on to the sealing schooner Sophie Sutherland, bound for the coast of Japan. When he returned, the country was in the grip of the panic of '93 and Oakland was swept by labor unrest. After grueling jobs in a jute mill and a street-railway power plant, London joined Coxey's Army and began his career as a tramp. In 1894, he spent 30 days for vagrancy in the Erie County Penitentiary at Buffalo, New York. In The Road, he wrote:

> Man-handling was merely one of the very minor unprintable horrors of the Erie County Pen. I say 'unprintable'; and in justice I must also say undescribable. They were unthinkable to me until I saw them, and I was no spring chicken in the ways of the world and the awful abysses of human degradation. It would take a deep plummet to reach bottom in the Erie County Pen, and I do but skim lightly and facetiously the surface of things as I there saw them.
>
> —Jack London, The Road

After many experiences as a hobo and a sailor, he returned to Oakland and attended Oakland High School. He contributed a number of articles to the high school's magazine, The Aegis. His first published work was "Typhoon off the Coast of Japan", an account of his sailing experiences.

As a schoolboy, London often studied at Heinold's First and Last Chance Saloon, a port-side bar in Oakland. At 17, he confessed to the bar's owner, John Heinold, his desire to attend university and pursue a career as a writer. Heinold lent London tuition money to attend college.

London desperately wanted to attend the University of California, located in Berkeley. In 1896, after a summer of intense studying to pass certification exams, he was admitted. Financial circumstances forced him to leave in 1897 and he never graduated. No evidence has surfaced that he ever wrote for student publications while studying at Berkeley.

While at Berkeley, London continued to study and spend time at Heinold's saloon, where he was introduced to the sailors and adventurers who would influence his writing. In his autobiographical novel, John Barleycorn, London mentioned the pub's likeness seventeen times. Heinold's was the place where London met Alexander McLean, a captain known for his cruelty at sea. London based his protagonist Wolf Larsen, in the novel The Sea-Wolf, on McLean.

Heinold's First and Last Chance Saloon is now unofficially named Jack London's Rendezvous in his honor.

Gold rush and first success

On July 12, 1897, London (age 21) and his sister's husband Captain Shepard sailed to join the Klondike Gold Rush. This was the setting for some of his first successful stories. London's time in the harsh Klondike, however, was detrimental to his health. Like so many other men who were malnourished in the goldfields, London developed scurvy. His gums became swollen, leading to the loss of his four front teeth. A constant gnawing pain affected his hip and leg muscles, and his face was stricken with marks that always reminded him of the struggles he faced in the Klondike. Father William Judge, "The Saint of Dawson", had a facility in Dawson that provided shelter, food and any available medicine to London and others. His struggles there inspired London's short story, "To Build a Fire" (1902, revised in 1908), which many critics assess as his best.

His landlords in Dawson were mining engineers Marshall Latham Bond and Louis Whitford Bond, educated at Yale and Stanford, respectively. The brothers' father, Judge Hiram Bond, was a wealthy mining investor. The Bonds, especially Hiram, were active Republicans. Marshall Bond's diary mentions friendly sparring with London on political issues as a camp pastime.

London left Oakland with a social conscience and socialist leanings; he returned to become an activist for socialism. He concluded that his only hope of escaping the work "trap" was to get an education and "sell his brains". He saw his writing as a business, his ticket out of poverty, and, he hoped, a means of beating the wealthy at their own game. On returning to California in 1898, London began working to get published, a struggle described in his novel, Martin Eden (serialized in 1908, published in 1909). His first published story since high school was "To the Man On Trail", which has frequently been collected in anthologies. When The Overland Monthly offered him only five dollars for it—and was slow paying—London came close to abandoning his writing career. In his words, "literally and literarily I was saved" when The Black Cat accepted his story "A Thousand Deaths", and paid him $40—the "first money I ever received for a story".

London began his writing career just as new printing technologies enabled lower-cost production of magazines. This resulted in a boom in popular magazines aimed at a wide public audience and a strong market for short fiction. In 1900, he made $2,500 in writing, about $77,000 in today's currency. Among the works he sold to magazines was a short story known as either "Diable" (1902) or "Bâtard" (1904), two editions of the same basic story; London received $141.25 for this story on May 27, 1902. In the text, a cruel French Canadian brutalizes his dog, and the dog retaliates and kills the man. London told some of his critics that man's actions are the main cause of the behavior of their animals, and he would show this in another story, The Call of the Wild.

In early 1903, London sold The Call of the Wild to The Saturday Evening Post for $750, and the book rights to Macmillan for $2,000. Macmillan's promotional campaign propelled it to swift success.

While living at his rented villa on Lake Merritt in Oakland, California, London met poet George Sterling; in time they became best friends. In 1902, Sterling helped London find a home closer to his own in nearby Piedmont. In his letters London addressed Sterling as "Greek", owing to Sterling's aquiline nose and classical profile, and he signed them as "Wolf". London was later to depict Sterling as Russ Brissenden in his autobiographical novel Martin Eden (1910) and as Mark Hall in The Valley of the Moon (1913).

In later life London indulged his wide-ranging interests by accumulating a personal library of 15,000 volumes. He referred to his books as "the tools of my trade".

First marriage (1900–04)

London married Elizabeth "Bessie" Maddern on April 7, 1900, the same day The Son of the Wolf was published. Bess had been part of his circle of friends for a number of years. She was related to stage actresses Minnie Maddern Fiske and Emily Stevens. Stasz says, "Both acknowledged publicly that they were not marrying out of love, but from friendship and a belief that they would produce sturdy children." Kingman says, "they were comfortable together... Jack had made it clear to Bessie that he did not love her, but that he liked her enough to make a successful marriage."

London met Bessie through his friend at Oakland High School, Fred Jacobs; she was Fred's fiancée. Bessie, who tutored at Anderson's University Academy in Alameda California, tutored Jack in preparation for his entrance exams for the University of California at Berkeley in 1896. Jacobs was killed aboard the USAT Scandia in 1897, but Jack and Bessie continued their friendship, which included taking photos and developing the film together. This was the beginning of Jack's passion for photography.

During the marriage, London continued his friendship with Anna Strunsky, co-authoring The Kempton-Wace Letters, an epistolary novel contrasting two philosophies of love. Anna, writing "Dane Kempton's" letters, arguing for a romantic view of marriage, while London, writing "Herbert Wace's" letters, argued for a scientific view, based on Darwinism and eugenics. In the novel, his fictional character contrasted two women he had known.

London's pet name for Bess was "Mother-Girl" and Bess's for London was "Daddy-Boy". Their first child, Joan, was born on January 15, 1901, and their second, Bessie (later called Becky), on October 20, 1902. Both children were born in Piedmont, California. Here London wrote one of his most celebrated works, The Call of the Wild.

While London had pride in his children, the marriage was strained. Kingman says that by 1903 the couple were close to separation as they were "extremely incompatible". "Jack was still so kind and gentle with Bessie that when Cloudsley Johns was a house guest in February 1903 he didn't suspect a breakup of their marriage."

London reportedly complained to friends Joseph Noel and George Sterling:

> [Bessie] is devoted to purity. When I tell her morality is only evidence of low blood pressure, she hates me. She'd sell me and the children out for her damned purity. It's terrible. Every time I come back after being away from home for a night she won't let me be in the same room with her if she can help it.

Stasz writes that these were "code words for fear that was consorting with prostitutes and might bring home venereal disease."

On July 24, 1903, London told Bessie he was leaving and moved out. During 1904, London and Bess negotiated the terms of a divorce, and the decree was granted on November 11, 1904.

War correspondent (1904)

London accepted an assignment of the San Francisco Examiner to cover the Russo-Japanese War in early 1904, arriving in Yokohama on January 25, 1904. He was arrested by Japanese authorities in Shimonoseki, but released through the intervention of American ambassador Lloyd Griscom. After travelling to Korea, he was again arrested by Japanese authorities for straying too close to the border with Manchuria without official permission, and was sent back to Seoul. Released again, London was permitted to travel with the Imperial Japanese Army to the border, and to observe the Battle of the Yalu.

London asked William Randolph Hearst, the owner of the San Francisco Examiner, to be allowed to transfer to the Imperial Russian Army, where he felt that restrictions on his reporting and his movements would be less severe. However, before this could be arranged, he was arrested for a third time in four months, this time for assaulting his Japanese assistants, whom he accused of stealing the fodder for his horse. Released through the personal intervention of President Theodore Roosevelt, London departed the front in June 1904.

Bohemian Club

On August 18, 1904, London went with his close friend, the poet George Sterling, to "Summer High Jinks" at the Bohemian Grove. London was elected to honorary membership in the Bohemian Club and took part in many activities. Other noted members of the Bohemian Club during this time included Ambrose Bierce, Gelett Burgess, Allan Dunn, John Muir, Frank Norris, and Herman George Scheffauer.

Beginning in December 1914, London worked on The Acorn Planter, A California Forest Play, to be performed as one of the annual Grove Plays, but it was never selected. It was described as too difficult to set to music. London published The Acorn Planter in 1916.

Second marriage

After divorcing Maddern, London married Charmian Kittredge in 1905. London had been introduced to Kittredge in 1900 by her aunt Netta Eames, who was an editor at Overland Monthly magazine in San Francisco. The two met prior to his first marriage but became lovers years later after Jack and Bessie London visited Wake Robin, Netta Eames' Sonoma County resort, in 1903. London was injured when he fell from a buggy, and Netta arranged for Charmian to care for him. The two developed a friendship, as Charmian, Netta, her husband Roscoe, and London were politically aligned with socialist causes. At some point the relationship became romantic, and Jack divorced his wife to marry Charmian, who was five years his senior.

Biographer Russ Kingman called Charmian "Jack's soul-mate, always at his side, and a perfect match." Their time together included numerous trips, including a 1907 cruise on the yacht Snark to Hawaii and Australia. Many of London's stories are based on his visits to Hawaii, the last one for 10 months beginning in December 1915.

The couple also visited Goldfield, Nevada, in 1907, where they were guests of the Bond brothers, London's Dawson City landlords. The Bond brothers were working in Nevada as mining engineers.

London had contrasted the concepts of the "Mother Girl" and the "Mate Woman" in The Kempton-Wace Letters. His pet name for Bess had been "Mother-Girl;" his pet name for Charmian was "Mate-Woman."Charmian's aunt and foster mother, a disciple of Victoria Woodhull, had raised her without prudishness.Every biographer alludes to Charmian's uninhibited sexuality.

Joseph Noel calls the events from 1903 to 1905 "a domestic drama that would have intrigued the pen of an Ibsen.... London's had comedy relief in it and a sort of easy-going romance." In broad outline, London was restless in his first marriage, sought extramarital sexual affairs, and found, in Charmian Kittredge, not only a sexually active and adventurous partner, but his future life-companion. They attempted to have children; one child died at birth, and another pregnancy ended in a miscarriage.

In 1906, London published in Collier's magazine his eye-witness report of the San Francisco earthquake.

Beauty Ranch (1905–16)

In 1905, London purchased a 1,000 acres (4.0 km2) ranch in Glen Ellen, Sonoma County, California, on the eastern slope of Sonoma Mountain.He wrote: "Next to my wife, the ranch is the dearest thing in the world to me." He desperately wanted the ranch to become a successful business enterprise. Writing, always a commercial enterprise with London, now became even more a means to an end: "I write for no other purpose than to add to the beauty that now belongs to me. I write a book for no other reason than to add three or four hundred acres to my magnificent estate."

Stasz writes that London "had taken fully to heart the vision, expressed in his agrarian fiction, of the land as the closest earthly version of Eden ... he educated himself through the study of agricultural manuals and scientific tomes. He conceived of a system of ranching that today would be praised for its ecological wisdom." He was proud to own the first concrete silo in California, a circular piggery that he designed. He hoped to adapt the wisdom of Asian sustainable agriculture to the United States. He hired both Italian and Chinese stonemasons, whose distinctly different styles are obvious.

The ranch was an economic failure. Sympathetic observers such as Stasz treat his projects as potentially feasible, and ascribe their failure to bad luck or to being ahead of their time. Unsympathetic historians such as Kevin Starr suggest that he was a bad manager, distracted by other concerns and impaired by his alcoholism. Starr notes that London was absent from his ranch about six months a year between 1910 and 1916 and says, "He liked the show of managerial power, but not grinding attention to detail .... London's workers laughed at his efforts to play big-time rancher the operation a rich man's hobby."

London spent $80,000 ($2,280,000 in current value) to build a 15,000-square-foot (1,400 m2) stone mansion called Wolf House on the property. Just as the mansion was nearing completion, two weeks before the Londons planned to move in, it was destroyed by fire.

London's last visit to Hawaii, beginning in December 1915, lasted eight months. He met with Duke Kahanamoku, Prince Jonah Kūhiō Kalaniana'ole, Queen Lili'uokalani and many others, before returning to his ranch in July 1916. He was suffering from kidney failure, but he continued to work.

The ranch (abutting stone remnants of Wolf House) is now a National Historic Landmark and is protected in Jack London State Historic Park.

Animal activism

London witnessed animal cruelty in the training of circus animals, and his subsequent novels Jerry of the Islands and Michael, Brother of Jerry included a foreword entreating the public to become more informed about this practice. In 1918, the Massachusetts Society for the Prevention of Cruelty to Animals and the American Humane Education Society teamed up to create the Jack London Club, which sought to inform the public about cruelty to circus animals and encourage them to protest this establishment. Support from Club members led to a temporary cessation of trained animal acts at Ringling-Barnum and Bailey in 1925.

Death

London died November 22, 1916, in a sleeping porch in a cottage on his ranch. London had been a robust man but had suffered several serious illnesses, including scurvy in the Klondike. Additionally, during travels on the Snark, he and Charmian picked up unspecified tropical infections, and diseases, including yaws. At the time of his death, he suffered from dysentery, late-stage alcoholism, and uremia; he was in extreme pain and taking morphine.

London's ashes were buried on his property not far from the Wolf House. London's funeral took place on November 26, 1916, attended only by close friends, relatives, and workers of the property. In accordance with his wishes, he was cremated and buried next to some pioneer children, under a rock that belonged to the Wolf House. After Charmian's death in 1955, she was also cremated and then buried with her husband in the same spot that her husband chose. The grave is marked by a mossy boulder. The buildings and property were later preserved as Jack London State Historic Park, in Glen Ellen, California.

Suicide debate

Because he was using morphine, many older sources describe London's death as a suicide, and some still do. This conjecture appears to be a rumor, or speculation based on incidents in his fiction writings. His death certificate gives the cause as uremia, following acute renal colic.

The biographer Stasz writes, "Following London's death, for a number of reasons, a biographical myth developed in which he has been portrayed as an alcoholic womanizer who committed suicide. Recent scholarship based upon firsthand documents challenges this caricature." Most biographers, including Russ Kingman, now agree he died of uremia aggravated by an accidental morphine overdose.

London's fiction featured several suicides. In his autobiographical memoir John Barleycorn, he claims, as a youth, to have drunkenly stumbled overboard into the San Francisco Bay, "some maundering fancy of going out with the tide suddenly obsessed me". He said he drifted and nearly succeeded in drowning before sobering up and being rescued by fishermen. In the dénouement of The Little Lady of the Big House, the heroine, confronted by the pain of a mortal gunshot wound, undergoes a physician-assisted suicide by morphine. Also, in Martin Eden, the principal protagonist, who shares certain characteristics with London, drowns himself.

Plagiarism accusations

London was vulnerable to accusations of plagiarism, both because he was such a conspicuous, prolific, and successful writer and because of his methods of working. He wrote in a letter to Elwyn Hoffman, "expression, you see—with me—is far easier than invention." He purchased plots and novels from the young Sinclair Lewis and used incidents from newspaper clippings as writing material.

In July 1901, two pieces of fiction appeared within the same month: London's "Moon-Face", in the San Francisco Argonaut, and Frank Norris' "The Passing of Cock-eye Blacklock", in Century Magazine. Newspapers showed the similarities between the stories, which London said were "quite different in manner of treatment, patently the same in foundation and motive." London explained both writers based their stories on the same newspaper account. A year later, it was discovered that Charles Forrest McLean had published a fictional story also based on the same incident.

Egerton Ryerson Young claimed The Call of the Wild (1903) was taken from Young's book My Dogs in the Northland (1902). London acknowledged using it as a source and claimed to have written a letter to Young thanking him.

In 1906, the New York World published "deadly parallel" columns showing eighteen passages from London's short story "Love of Life" side by side with similar passages from a nonfiction article by Augustus Biddle and J. K. Macdonald, titled "Lost in the Land of the Midnight Sun". London noted the World did not accuse him of "plagiarism", but only of "identity of time and situation", to which he defiantly "pled guilty".

The most serious charge of plagiarism was based on London's "The Bishop's Vision", Chapter 7 of his novel The Iron Heel (1908). The chapter is nearly identical to an ironic essay that Frank Harris published in 1901, titled "The Bishop of London and Public Morality". Harris was incensed and suggested he should receive 1/60th of the royalties from The Iron Heel, the disputed material constituting about that fraction of the whole novel. London insisted he had clipped a reprint of the article, which had appeared in an American newspaper, and believed it to be a genuine speech delivered by the Bishop of London.

Views

Atheism

London was an atheist. He is quoted as saying, "I believe that when I am dead, I am dead. I believe that with my death I am just as much obliterated as the last mosquito you and I squashed."

Socialism

London wrote from a socialist viewpoint, which is evident in his novel The Iron Heel. Neither a theorist nor an intellectual socialist, London's socialism grew out of his life experience. As London explained in his essay, "How I Became a Socialist", his views were influenced by his experience with people at the bottom of the social pit. His optimism and individualism faded, and he vowed never to do more hard physical work than necessary. He wrote that his individualism was hammered out of him, and he was politically reborn. He often closed his letters "Yours for the Revolution."

London joined the Socialist Labor Party in April 1896. In the same year, the San Francisco Chronicle published a story about the twenty-year-old London's giving nightly speeches in Oakland's City Hall Park, an activity he was arrested for a year later. In 1901, he left the Socialist Labor Party and joined the new Socialist Party of America. He ran unsuccessfully as the high-profile Socialist candidate for mayor of Oakland in 1901 (receiving 245 votes) and 1905 (improving to 981 votes), toured the country lecturing on socialism in 1906, and published two collections of essays about socialism: The War of the Classes (1905) and Revolution, and other Essays (1906).

Stasz notes that "London regarded the Wobblies as a welcome addition to the Socialist cause, although he never joined them in going so far as to recommend sabotage." Stasz mentions a personal meeting between London and Big Bill Haywood in 1912.

In his late (1913) book The Cruise of the Snark, London writes about appeals to him for membership of the Snark's crew from office workers and other "toilers" who longed for escape from the cities, and of being cheated by workmen.

In his Glen Ellen ranch years, London felt some ambivalence toward socialism and complained about the "inefficient Italian labourers" in his employ. In 1916, he resigned from the Glen Ellen chapter of the Socialist Party, but stated emphatically he did so "because of its lack of fire and fight, and its loss of emphasis on the class struggle." In an unflattering portrait of London's ranch days, California cultural historian Kevin Starr refers to this period as "post-socialist" and says "... by 1911 ... London was more bored by the class struggle than he cared to admit."

Race

London shared common concerns among many European Americans in California about Asian immigration, described as "the yellow peril"; he used the latter term as the title of a 1904 essay. This theme was also the subject of a story he wrote in 1910 called "The Unparalleled Invasion". Presented as an historical essay set in the future, the story narrates events between 1976 and 1987, in which China, with an ever-increasing population, is taking over and colonizing its neighbors with the intention of taking over the entire Earth. The western nations respond with biological warfare and bombard China with dozens of the most infectious diseases. On his fears about China, he admits, "it must be taken into consideration that the above postulate is itself a product of Western race-egotism, urged by our belief in our own righteousness and fostered by a faith in ourselves which may be as erroneous as are most fond race fancies."

By contrast, many of London's short stories are notable for their empathetic portrayal of Mexican ("The Mexican"), Asian ("The Chinago"), and Hawaiian ("Koolau the Leper") characters. London's war correspondence from the Russo-Japanese War, as well as his unfinished novel Cherry, show he admired much about Japanese customs and capabilities. London's writings have been popular among the Japanese, who believe he portrayed them positively.

In "Koolau the Leper", London describes Koolau, who is a Hawaiian leper—and thus a very different sort of "superman" than Martin Eden—and who fights off an entire cavalry troop to elude capture, as "indomitable spiritually—a ... magnificent rebel". This character is based on Hawaiian leper Kaluaikoolau, who in 1893 revolted and resisted capture from forces of the Provisional Government of Hawaii in the Kalalau Valley.

An amateur boxer and avid boxing fan, London reported on the 1910 Johnson–Jeffries fight, in which the black boxer Jack Johnson vanquished Jim Jeffries, known as the "Great White Hope". In 1908, London had reported on an earlier fight of Johnson's, contrasting the black boxer's coolness and intellectual style, with the apelike appearance and fighting style of his Canadian opponent, Tommy Burns:

> [What won] on Saturday was bigness, coolness, quickness, cleverness, and vast physical superiority ... Because a white man wishes a white man to win, this should not prevent him from giving absolute credit to the best man, even when that best man was black. All hail to Johnson. ... superb. He was impregnable ... as inaccessible as Mont Blanc.

Those who defend London against charges of racism cite the letter he wrote to the Japanese-American Commercial Weekly in 1913:

> In reply to yours of August 16, 1913. First of all, I should say by stopping the stupid newspaper from always fomenting race prejudice. This of course, being impossible, I would say, next, by educating the people of Japan so that they will be too intelligently tolerant to respond to any call to race prejudice. And, finally, by realizing, in industry and

government, of socialism—which last word is merely a word that stands for the actual application of in the affairs of men of the theory of the Brotherhood of Man.

In the meantime the nations and races are only unruly boys who have not yet grown to the stature of men. So we must expect them to do unruly and boisterous things at times. And, just as boys grow up, so the races of mankind will grow up and laugh when they look back upon their childish quarrels.

In 1996, after the City of Whitehorse, Yukon, renamed a street in honor of London, protests over London's alleged racism forced the city to change the name of "Jack London Boulevard"[failed verification] back to "Two-mile Hill".

Eugenics

London supported eugenics, including forced sterilization of criminals or those deemed feeble minded. His novel Before Adam(1906–07) has been described as having pro-eugenic themes.

London wrote to Frederick H. Robinson of the periodical Medical Review of Reviews, stating, "I believe the future belongs to eugenics, and will be determined by the practice of eugenics."

Works

Short stories

Western writer and historian Dale L. Walker writes:

London's true métier was the short story ... London's true genius lay in the short form, 7,500 words and under, where the flood of images in his teeming brain and the innate power of his narrative gift were at once constrained and freed. His stories that run longer than the magic 7,500 generally—but certainly not always—could have benefited from self-editing.

London's "strength of utterance" is at its height in his stories, and they are painstakingly well-constructed. "To Build a Fire" is the best known of all his stories. Set in the harsh Klondike, it recounts the haphazard trek of a new arrival who has ignored an old-timer's warning about the risks of traveling alone. Falling through the ice into a creek in seventy-five-below weather, the unnamed man is keenly aware that survival depends on his untested skills at quickly building a fire to dry his clothes and warm his extremities. After publishing a tame version of this story—with a sunny outcome—in The Youth's Companion in 1902, London offered a second, more severe take on the man's predicament in The Century Magazine in 1908. Reading both provides an illustration of London's growth and maturation as a writer. As Labor (1994) observes: "To compare the two versions is itself an instructive lesson in what distinguished a great work of literary art from a good children's story."

Other stories from the Klondike period include: "All Gold Canyon", about a battle between a gold prospector and a claim jumper; "The Law of Life", about an aging American Indian man abandoned by his tribe and left to die; "Love of Life", about a trek by a prospector across the Canadian tundra; "To the Man on Trail," which tells the story of a prospector fleeing the Mounted Police in a sled race, and raises the question of the contrast between written law and morality; and "An Odyssey of the North," which raises questions of conditional morality, and paints a sympathetic portrait of a man of mixed White and Aleut ancestry.

London was a boxing fan and an avid amateur boxer. "A Piece of Steak" is a tale about a match between older and younger boxers. It contrasts the differing experiences of youth and age but also raises the social question of the treatment of aging workers. "The Mexican" combines boxing with a social theme, as a young Mexican endures an unfair fight and ethnic prejudice to earn money with which to aid the revolution.

Several of London's stories would today be classified as science fiction. "The Unparalleled Invasion" describes germ warfare against China; "Goliath" is about an irresistible energy weapon; "The Shadow and the Flash" is a tale about two brothers who take different routes to achieving invisibility; "A

Relic of the Pliocene" is a tall tale about an encounter of a modern-day man with a mammoth. "The Red One" is a late story from a period when London was intrigued by the theories of the psychiatrist and writer Jung. It tells of an island tribe held in thrall by an extraterrestrial object.

Some nineteen original collections of short stories were published during London's brief life or shortly after his death. There have been several posthumous anthologies drawn from this pool of stories. Many of these stories were located in the Klondike and the Pacific. A collection of Jack London's San Francisco Stories was published in October 2010 by Sydney Samizdat Press.

Novels

London's most famous novels are The Call of the Wild, White Fang, The Sea-Wolf, The Iron Heel, and Martin Eden.

In a letter dated December 27, 1901, London's Macmillan publisher George Platt Brett, Sr., said "he believed Jack's fiction represented 'the very best kind of work' done in America."

Critic Maxwell Geismar called The Call of the Wild "a beautiful prose poem"; editor Franklin Walker said that it "belongs on a shelf with Walden and Huckleberry Finn"; and novelist E.L. Doctorow called it "a mordant parable ... his masterpiece."

The historian Dale L. Walker commented:

> Jack London was an uncomfortable novelist, that form too long for his natural impatience and the quickness of his mind. His novels, even the best of them, are hugely flawed.

Some critics have said that his novels are episodic and resemble linked short stories. Dale L. Walker writes:

> The Star Rover, that magnificent experiment, is actually a series of short stories connected by a unifying device ... Smoke Bellew is a series of stories bound together in a novel-like form by their reappearing

protagonist, Kit Bellew; and John Barleycorn ... is a synoptic series of short episodes.

Ambrose Bierce said of The Sea-Wolf that "the great thing—and it is among the greatest of things—is that tremendous creation, Wolf Larsen ... the hewing out and setting up of such a figure is enough for a man to do in one lifetime. "However, he noted, "The love element, with its absurd suppressions, and impossible proprieties, is awful."

The Iron Heel is an example of a dystopian novel that anticipates and influenced George Orwell's Nineteen Eighty-Four. London's socialist politics are explicitly on display here. The Iron Heel meets the contemporary definition of soft science fiction. The Star Rover (1915) is also science fiction.

Apocrypha

Jack London Credo

London's literary executor, Irving Shepard, quoted a Jack London Credo in an introduction to a 1956 collection of London stories:

> I would rather be ashes than dust!
>
> I would rather that my spark should burn out in a brilliant blaze than it should be stifled by dry-rot.
>
> I would rather be a superb meteor, every atom of me in magnificent glow, than a sleepy and permanent planet.
>
> The function of man is to live, not to exist.
>
> I shall not waste my days in trying to prolong them.
>
> I shall use my time.

The biographer Stasz notes that the passage "has many marks of London's style" but the only line that could be safely attributed to London was the first. The words Shepard quoted were from a story in the San Francisco Bulletin, December 2, 1916, by journalist Ernest J. Hopkins, who visited the ranch just weeks before London's death. Stasz notes, "Even more so than today journalists' quotes were unreliable or even sheer inventions," and says no direct source in London's writings has been found. However, at least one line, according to Stasz, is authentic, being referenced by London and written in his own hand in the autograph book of Australian suffragette Vida Goldstein:

> Dear Miss Goldstein:–
>
> Seven years ago I wrote you that I'd rather be ashes than dust. I still subscribe to that sentiment.
>
> Sincerely yours,
>
> Jack London
>
> Jan. 13, 1909

In his short story "By The Turtles of Tasman", a character, defending her "ne'er-do-well grasshopperish father" to her "antlike uncle", says: "... my father has been a king. He has lived .... Have you lived merely to live? Are you afraid to die? I'd rather sing one wild song and burst my heart with it, than live a thousand years watching my digestion and being afraid of the wet. When you are dust, my father will be ashes."

"The Scab"

A short diatribe on "The Scab" is often quoted within the U.S. labor movement and frequently attributed to London. It opens:

> After God had finished the rattlesnake, the toad, and the vampire, he had some awful substance left with which he made a scab. A scab is a two-legged animal with a corkscrew soul, a water brain, a combination backbone of jelly and glue. Where others have hearts, he carries a tumor of rotten principles. When a scab comes down the street, men turn their backs and Angels weep in Heaven, and the Devil shuts the gates of hell to keep him out....

In 1913 and 1914, a number of newspapers printed the first three sentences with varying terms used instead of "scab", such as "knocker","stool pigeon"or "scandal monger"

This passage as given above was the subject of a 1974 Supreme Court case, Letter Carriers v. Austin, in which Justice Thurgood Marshall referred to it as "a well-known piece of trade union literature, generally attributed to author Jack London". A union newsletter had published a "list of scabs," which was granted to be factual and therefore not libelous, but then went on to quote the passage as the "definition of a scab". The case turned on the question of whether the "definition" was defamatory. The court ruled that "Jack London's... 'definition of a scab' is merely rhetorical hyperbole, a lusty and imaginative expression of the contempt felt by union members towards those who refuse to join", and as such was not libelous and was protected under the First Amendment.

Despite being frequently attributed to London, the passage does not appear at all in the extensive collection of his writings at Sonoma State University's website. However, in his book The War of the Classes he published a 1903 speech entitled "The Scab", which gave a much more balanced view of the topic:

> The laborer who gives more time or strength or skill for the same wage than another, or equal time or strength or skill for a less wage, is a scab. The generousness on his part is hurtful to his fellow-laborers, for it compels them to an equal generousness which is not to their liking, and which gives them less of food and shelter. But a word may be said for the scab. Just as his act makes his rivals compulsorily generous, so do they, by fortune of birth and training, make compulsory his act of generousness.
>
> [...]
>
> Nobody desires to scab, to give most for least. The ambition of every individual is quite the opposite, to give least for most; and, as a result, living in a tooth-and-nail society, battle royal is waged by the ambitious individuals. But in its most salient aspect, that of the struggle over the division of the joint product, it is no longer a battle between individuals, but between groups of individuals. Capital and labor apply

themselves to raw material, make something useful out of it, add to its value, and then proceed to quarrel over the division of the added value. Neither cares to give most for least. Each is intent on giving less than the other and on receiving more.

Legacy and honors

Mount London, also known as Boundary Peak 100, on the Alaska-British Columbia boundary, in the Boundary Ranges of the Coast Mountains of British Columbia, is named for him.

Jack London Square on the waterfront of Oakland, California was named for him.

He was honored by the United States Postal Service with a 25¢ Great Americans series postage stamp released on January 11, 1986.

Jack London Lake (Russian), a mountain lake located in the upper reaches of the Kolyma River in Yagodninsky district of Magadan Oblast.

Fictional portrayals of London include Michael O'Shea in the 1943 film Jack London, Jeff East in the 1980 film Klondike Fever, Aaron Ashmore in the Murdoch Mysteries episode "Murdoch of the Klondike" from 2012, and Johnny Simmons in the 2014 miniseries Klondike. (Source: Wikipedia)

NOTABLE WORKS

NOVELS

The Cruise of the Dazzler (1902)

A Daughter of the Snows (1902)

The Call of the Wild (1903)

The Kempton-Wace Letters (1903) (published anonymously, co-authored with Anna Strunsky)

The Sea-Wolf (1904)

The Game (1905)

White Fang (1906)

Before Adam (1907)

The Iron Heel (1908)

Martin Eden (1909)

Burning Daylight (1910)

Adventure (1911)

The Scarlet Plague (1912)

A Son of the Sun (1912)

The Abysmal Brute (1913)

The Valley of the Moon (1913)

The Mutiny of the Elsinore (1914)

The Star Rover (1915) (published in England as The Jacket)

The Little Lady of the Big House (1916)

Jerry of the Islands (1917)

Michael, Brother of Jerry (1917)

Hearts of Three (1920) (novelization of a script by Charles Goddard)

The Assassination Bureau, Ltd (1963) (left half-finished, completed by Robert L. Fish)

SHORT STORIES

"An Old Soldier's Story" (1894)

"Who Believes in Ghosts!" (1895)

"And 'FRISCO Kid Came Back" (1895)

"Night's Swim In Yeddo Bay" (1895)

"One More Unfortunate" (1895)

"Sakaicho, Hona Asi And Hakadaki" (1895)

"A Klondike Christmas" (1897)

"Mahatma's Little Joke" (1897)

"O Haru" (1897)

"Plague Ship" (1897)

"The Strange Experience Of A Misogynist" (1897)

"Two Gold Bricks" (1897)

"The Devil's Dice Box" (1898)

"A Dream Image" (1898)

"The Test: A Clondyke Wooing" (1898)

"To the Man on Trail" (1898)

"In a Far Country" (1899)

"The King of Mazy May" (1899)

"The End Of The Chapter" (1899)

"The Grilling Of Loren Ellery" (1899)

"The Handsome Cabin Boy" (1899)

"In The Time Of Prince Charley" (1899)

"Old Baldy" (1899)

"The Men of Forty Mile" (1899)

"Pluck and Pertinacity" (1899)

"The Rejuvenation of Major Rathbone" (1899)

"The White Silence" (1899)

"A Thousand Deaths" (1899)

"Wisdom of the Trail" (1899)

"An Odyssey of the North" (1900)

"The Son of the Wolf" (1900)

"Even unto Death" (1900)

"The Man with the Gash" (1900)

"A Lesson in Heraldry" (1900)

"A Northland Miracle" (1900)

"Proper "GIRLIE"" (1900)

"Thanksgiving on Slav Creek" (1900)

"Their Alcove" (1900)

"Housekeeping in the Klondike" (1900)

"Dutch Courage" (1900)

"Where the Trail Forks" (1900)

"Hyperborean Brew" (1901)

"A Relic of the Pliocene" (1901)

"The Lost Poacher" (1901)

"The God of His Fathers" (1901)

""FRISCO Kid's" Story" (1901)

"The Law of Life" (1901)

"The Minions of Midas" (1901)

"In the Forests of the North" (1902)

"The "Fuzziness" of Hoockla-Heen" (1902)

"The Story of Keesh" (1902)

"Keesh, Son of Keesh" (1902)

"Nam-Bok, the Unveracious" (1902)

"Li Wan the Fair" (1902)

"Lost Face"

"Master of Mystery" (1902)

"The Sunlanders" (1902)

"The Death of Ligoun" (1902)

"Moon-Face" (1902)

"Diable—A Dog" (1902), renamed Bâtard in 1904

"To Build a Fire" (1902, revised 1908)

"The League of the Old Men" (1902)

"The Dominant Primordial Beast" (1903)

"The One Thousand Dozen" (1903)

"The Marriage of Lit-lit" (1903)

"The Shadow and the Flash" (1903)

"The Leopard Man's Story" (1903)

"Negore the Coward" (1904)

"All Gold Cañon" (1905)

"Love of Life" (1905)

"The Sun-Dog Trail" (1905)

"The Apostate" (1906)

"Up the Slide" (1906)

"Planchette" (1906)

"Brown Wolf" (1906)

"Make Westing" (1907)

"Chased by the Trail" (1907)

"Trust" (1908)

"A Curious Fragment" (1908)

"Aloha Oe" (1908)

"That Spot" (1908)

"The Enemy of All the World" (1908)

"The House of Mapuhi" (1909)

"Good-by, Jack" (1909)

"Samuel" (1909)

"South of the Slot" (1909)

"The Chinago" (1909)

"The Dream of Debs" (1909)

"The Madness of John Harned" (1909)

"The Seed of McCoy" (1909)

"A Piece of Steak" (1909)

"Mauki" (1909)

"The Whale Tooth" (1909)

"Goliath" (1910)

"The Unparalleled Invasion" (1910)

"Told in the Drooling Ward" (1910)

"When the World was Young" (1910)

"The Terrible Solomons" (1910)

"The Inevitable White Man" (1910)

"The Heathen" (1910)

"Yah! Yah! Yah!" (1910)

"By the Turtles of Tasman" (1911)

"The Mexican" (1911)

"War" (1911)

"The Unmasking of the Cad" (1911)

"The Scarlet Plague" (1912)

"The Captain of the Susan Drew" (1912)

"The Sea-Farmer" (1912)

"The Feathers of the Sun" (1912)

"The Prodigal Father" (1912)

"Samuel" (1913)

"The Sea-Gangsters" (1913)

"The Strength of the Strong" (1914)

"Told in the Drooling Ward" (1914)

"The Hussy" (1916)

"Like Argus of the Ancient Times" (1917)

"Jerry of the Islands" (1917)

"The Red One" (1918)

"Shin-Bones" (1918)

"The Bones of Kahekili" (1919)

SHORT STORY COLLECTIONS

Son of the Wolf (1900)

Chris Farrington, Able Seaman (1901)

The God of His Fathers & Other Stories (1901)

Children of the Frost (1902)

The Faith of Men and Other Stories (1904)

Tales of the Fish Patrol (1906)

Moon-Face and Other Stories (1906)

Love of Life and Other Stories (1907)

Lost Face (1910)

South Sea Tales (1911)

When God Laughs and Other Stories (1911)

The House of Pride & Other Tales of Hawaii (1912)

Smoke Bellew (1912)

A Son of the Sun (1912)

The Night Born (1913)

The Strength of the Strong (1914)

The Turtles of Tasman (1916)

The Human Drift (1917)

The Red One (1918)

On the Makaloa Mat (1919)

Dutch Courage and Other Stories (1922)

AUTOBIOGRAPHICAL MEMOIRS

The Road (1907)

The Cruise of the Snark (1911)

John Barleycorn (1913)

NON-FICTION AND ESSAYS

Through the Rapids on the Way to the Klondike (1899)

From Dawson to the Sea (1899)

What Communities Lose by the Competitive System (1900)

The Impossibility of War (1900)

Phenomena of Literary Evolution (1900)

A Letter to Houghton Mifflin Co. (1900)

Husky, Wolf Dog of the North (1900)

Editorial Crimes — A Protest (1901)

Again the Literary Aspirant (1902)

The People of the Abyss (1903)

How I Became a Socialist (1903)

The War of the Classes (1905)

The Story of an Eyewitness (1906)

A Letter to Woman's Home Companion (1906)

Revolution, and other Essays (1910)

Mexico's Army and Ours (1914)

Lawgivers (1914)

Our Adventures in Tampico (1914)

Stalking the Pestilence (1914)

The Red Game of War (1914)

The Trouble Makers of Mexico (1914)

With Funston's Men (1914)

POETRY

A Heart (1899)

Abalone Song (1913)

And Some Night (1914)

Ballade of the False Lover (1914)

Cupid's Deal (1913)

Daybreak (1901)

Effusion (1901)

George Sterling (1913)

Gold (1915)

He Chortled with Glee (1899)

He Never Tried Again (1912)

His Trip to Hades (1913)

Homeland (1914)

Hors de Saison (1913)

If I Were God (1899)

In a Year (1901)

In and Out (1911)

Je Vis en Espoir (1897)

Memory (1913)

Moods (1913)

My Confession (1912)

My Little Palmist (1914)

Of Man of the Future (1915)

Oh You Everybody's Girl (19)

On the Face of the Earth You are the One (1915)

Rainbows End (1914)

Republican Rallying Song (1916)

Sonnet (1901)

The Gift of God (1905)

The Klondyker's Dream (1914)

The Lover's Liturgy (1913)

The Mammon Worshippers (1911)

The Republican Battle-Hymn (1905)

The Return of Ulysses (1915)

The Sea Sprite and the Shooting Star (1916)

The Socialist's Dream (1912)

The Song of the Flames (1903)

The Way of War (1906)

The Worker and the Tramp (1911)

Tick! Tick! Tick! (1915)

Too Late (1912)

Weasel Thieves (1913)

When All the World Shouted my Name (1905)

Where the Rainbow Fell (1902)

Your Kiss (1914)

PLAYS

Theft (1910)

Daughters of the Rich: A One Act Play (1915)

The Acorn Planter: A California Forest Play (1916)

CPSIA information can be obtained
at www.ICGtesting.com
Printed in the USA
LVHW021810140920
665984LV00002B/205